# The Chapel in the Woods

## Susan Louineau

Published in 2012 by FeedARead.com Publishing – Arts Council funded

Copyright © Susan Louineau 2012.

First Edition

A CIP catalogue record for this title is available from the British Library.

**For Jack and Anaïs**

For Anne,

Merry Christmas + happy
reading!

Susan Lewis.

## *Acknowledgements*

Needless to say, all the characters in this novel are entirely fictitious apart from Léo, the dog. But there are some real people to whom I owe a great debt of gratitude for their time and advice. I would like to thank Judith Smalley for her painstaking checking and rereading of the manuscript and her unerring support and Sarah Hinds for her advice on archaeological conservation. And my largest debt is to my family whose encouragement and patience carried me through to the end.

Susan Louineau
Cornwall
March 2012

# ONE

### Diana

In the heart of every French village, town and city there is a memorial to the fallen. This one was weathered, but nevertheless it stood tall and proud; a totem to the past, a talisman to ward off the eroding power of time. Diana was admiring it as she approached the bend in her battered 4-wheel drive.

On the other side of the road was a café. A single, tin table adorned with a fraying *Pastis 51* parasol stood on the pavement, conspicuous by its solitude. A far cry from the rows of tiny brasserie tables of the Parisian boulevards, seething with cigarette smoke and foaming beer. The sign above the door read, '*La Petite Folie*'.

Diana gasped as a roar and a blur of red filled the road ahead. She jerked the wheel sending the car hurtling towards the side of the road. The blur sped past bleeding crimson in its wake.

Even seconds afterwards she couldn't remember the impact. There was a throbbing pain in her head. The engine was hissing and steam billowed into the sunshine. As it cleared, she could make out a man standing next to the bonnet. In his arms, Ben was sobbing violently. She tried to move but found she couldn't. It was as if her brain no longer controlled her body. She began to panic as she watched her baby son crying in the arms of a stranger and she, his mother, was powerless to save him. The man was yelling something now, but she couldn't hear the words above the hissing of the engine. She watched uselessly as the stranger shuffled Ben onto one hip and leant over the passenger seat. His free arm came towards her and clamped around her waist, pulling her from the car as if she was made of paper.

People were coming out of the café. Someone shouted, '*Au Feu!*' but there weren't any flames. The stranger helped her to the tin table beneath the parasol, though she couldn't feel her feet touching the ground as she went. A woman took the still screaming Ben from the stranger and sat him on Diana's knee. Ben buried his face in her chest and sobbed with relief. As she hugged her baby boy, she could feel her senses recovering.

The woman was stroking her arm and holding a napkin to her head. She was older than Diana and smelt of sweet beer. 'Marcel, get a

Cognac. Oh, and a *sucette* for the *bout'chou*,' she spoke gently. 'What happened? The noise was incredible!'

A red-headed man in his late twenties returned with a brandy and a lollipop. He smiled revealing a dark chasm lined with black crooked teeth.

'There was a car. It came round the corner so fast,' she tried to control her voice which had begun to tremble. 'It was in the middle of the road, I had to swerve.'

Marcel was shaking his head and looking over at the memorial. 'What sort of car was it?'

'I, I don't know. It was red.'

Marcel and the woman exchanged glances, their eyebrows raised. 'A convertible?' said Marcel.

Diana shook her head, shrugging her shoulders.

'Don't worry about that now. Where do you live, *Madame?*' asked the woman softly.

Where did she live? Paris? No. Here. Saint Gabriel. She felt in her jacket pocket for the keys and remembered. 'We're moving house. We're moving in to the *Champ de Foire* in *rue* Montgommery.'

'Aah, The *Champ de Foire!*' She sounded delighted. 'We wondered when you were coming. *Monsieur* Moreau told us it was sold. I think you are English, no?'

She nodded.

'And your husband, he is a fireman?'

'Yes.' She managed a smile, evidently the jungle drums were in perfect working order. Not so different from Little Watcombe.

'I am Jeanette, I own this café. Very pleased to meet you.'

'Marcel. *Enchanté!*' Marcel held out his hand, though thankfully he didn't smile this time.

The man who'd pulled her from the car ambled over, his great frame casting a shadow over the table. She craned her neck back to look at him and regretted it as a pain shot from her shoulder to her scalp.

'*Madame*, your car is damaged. It will need towing.' His tone was urgent and his accent heavy. Not Parisian, nor southern, maybe local. He wiped some oil from his forehead with the sleeve of his blue overalls. 'I can get my tractor, but we must report this to the police.'

'No need,' snapped Jeanette. Her lips were tightly pursed. 'We will deal with this.'

He stood for a moment, his eyes flecked with anger. He opened his mouth to speak and then shut it again. He shoved his hands in his pockets and strode off muttering under his breath.

'Shouldn't we call the police? My car is really old, but I might have damaged the memorial.'

'I don't think the police would do much,' Jeanette was frowning. 'There were no witnesses; they will say it is your fault.'

'What about him?' Diana pointed at the figure in blue marching up the lane, his head bent.

Jeanette shook her head as if the idea was preposterous.

Frustrated, Diana turned to Marcel, 'Do you know someone with a red convertible?'

Jeanette glanced at him severely and he lowered his eyes.

'It could have been anyone; probably Parisians,' he shrugged. 'They start coming down about now. No idea how to drive.'

'That's right, and no one was hurt,' Jeanette added bossily.

Diana looked over at her car. Its front bumper was smashed in. It was wedged onto the stone pedestal with its two front wheels lifted off the ground. Beneath it, a pool of water ran in steaming rivulets on the surface of the dusty road.

Following her eyes Marcel interjected, 'You're not the first to crash into it. Stupid place to put it. Anyhow it's the mayor's responsibility.'

'In more ways than you could possibly imagine!' Jeanette laughed mischievously and then changed her expression abruptly as if checking herself.

'Jeanette!' It was Marcel's turn to chide.

'Anyway, it looks fine to me. It is your car that has taken the bash,' she continued.

Diana heaved Ben on to her hip and pulled herself to her feet gingerly. She went over to the memorial. Just where the bumper was resting, some lettering was damaged. It was the last name in the list. She could just about make out a capital H, but the rest was scraped and scratched by the twisted metal. She ran her fingers along it; she would definitely put this right.

Jeanette followed her. 'Let's get you home. Your head looks alright but you'd better see the doctor. She's in Jaunay. Your husband is on his way?'

'Err, yes.' Serge! She'd almost forgotten. What was he going to say?'

'Right, I will call the garage in Jaunay to come and take away your car. Marcel, you help *Madame* er ...'

'Lescure, Diana Lescure.'

'*Madame* Lescure to the *Champ de Foire.*'

Marcel took her luggage and the pushchair, thankfully undamaged, from the boot and led Diana up a narrow lane flanked by gardens, neatly ruled with rows of vegetables. Ben had fallen asleep, his head resting on her shoulder. A sign in the clouds of cow parsley read *Rue Jacques de Montgommery.* Behind it a church of rough hewn stone cast its cold shadow across the drive of the *Champ de Foire.*

'Thank you, *monsieur.* You have been very kind. I can manage now.'

He hesitated, 'But your luggage?'

'My husband won't be long; if you leave it there, just by the gate.'

He looked at her beseechingly.

'Really, thank you. You've been very kind, both you and Jeanette.'

'It is normal,' and he shrugged his shoulders in disappointment.

It was bad enough that Serge couldn't be here to share this moment, but she had no wish to be accompanied by a stranger into their new home, their new beginning.

Marcel leant the luggage against the rusted five bar gate at the end of the drive. 'If you're sure?' he insisted, looking down at his feet. 'I live just at the end of that lane on the right, the blue door,' he gestured awkwardly.

As his figure finally disappeared round the end of the lane towards the café, she stood for a moment listening to the sounds of the countryside. Birdsong filled the air and she marvelled at the absence of city rumble. No sirens, no traffic, just the even breathing of her beautiful two year old son, calm at last. She painfully swung open the pushchair and laid him in it as gently as she could, so as not to wake him. She pulled the cluster of oversized keys from her jacket and tried each one in turn, in the huge padlock that hung around the gate. The third key turned reluctantly in the lock and released the gate from its shackle.

The courtyard seemed much bigger than before. It sloped down the side of the house and barn to two immense steel hangars, now bereft of the combine harvesters they had once housed. The sun was high in the sky and its warmth was penetrating. A lizard or two scurried between the shepherd's purse that clung in the dry crevices of the garden wall. She wondered at the ingenuity and tenacity of the builders of seventeenth century France to move such cumbersome, heavy boulders without machinery. She ran her fingers over them, laying claim to her very own stone walls and was surprised by their warmth.

She parked Ben in the shade of an ancient yew on the terrace and dragged the rest of the luggage from the drive. Inside, huge shutters shielded the murky darkness of the interior, from the spring heat. The latches were stiff, but at last, she creaked the first one open, drenching the desolate room with warm sunlight. Outside, the trees and hedges were alive with the bustling of countless birds. She leaned out and took in a deep breath of sweet, green country air. The birds stopped but not one of them flew away. It was as if they were saying, 'Who are you? This is our place.'

She moved on to open the rest of the shutters; there were fourteen. Diana had broken into a sweat by the time she had folded the last wooden panel into place, and flung open every window. This was a far cry from their tiny apartment in *Boulevard Raspail.*

She looked at her watch; Serge must have finished his exam by now. She hadn't dared ask him what time he would arrive with the furniture. His face had been set in an inert snarl as he'd left to catch the *Métro* that morning. A peck on the cheek, not so much as a glance, and he was gone. He was nervous, that she knew.

Ben whimpered from the terrace. She gathered him up and held him close. He stretched luxuriously and then struggled to be put down. Holding his hand tightly, she fetched a bag of toys from the luggage by the gate, and tipped them guiltily onto the filthy floor. At least he had got past the stage of putting everything in his mouth. She could get him cleaned up before Serge arrived. Her shoulder was aching and she felt a little sleepy. She went into the kitchen and despaired at the fine coating of dust-filled grease that appeared to coat every surface. She splashed water over her face and shivered as it cooled her aching head.

# TWO

## Edward

'It is by the wrath of the almighty that I must suffer now, on my route to purgatory. That is where I must go to pay for my sins. Cowardice and self-interest have driven me since the day of my birth; the day I took my mother's life from her. By the grace of God I was offered unto Him, and now I have disgraced his name, in shunning Him and following my own selfish needs, just as his Grace paid for his, through my ignorant folly. And now, must I.' Edward's mind rambled as he lay in the freezing darkness. The pain in his head reassured him that he had not yet met his maker.

The cart must be far in the distance now. He could no longer hear its wooden wheels banging against the bumpy track, nor the sound of the horses' hooves, deadened on the beaten earth. He cursed himself for not being more careful. Hadn't Eldric told him a thousand times, that when transporting the port dues, they must be kept well beneath the cloak, so as not to arouse the interest of passing rogues? Though they must have been afraid, for they had carried Edward for two whole nights and days, only making short stops to rest the horses. Only now, in the dead of night, had they dared abandon him amongst these trees. If they had cut his throat they would not have known the service they should have rendered, in ridding the world of this thieving, betraying oblate. Perhaps they would have even become blessed amongst men, instruments of cleansing on this, His good earth. Instead, Edward lay in the night, beneath the creaking, swaying trees, all around him like sentinels of the devil; their icy, silvered branches reaching for him like fingers.

'Touch me. Swallow me. End this miserable servitude. I beg you.' He lay, waiting for a response, but none came.

Then a voice sparkled on the breeze, '*Frère*'

'Has he heard my prayers?'

'*Frère, Frère*. Do you breathe?' The voice was female, childlike.

He remained motionless fearing hallucination. Brother Eldric had spoken of it. Had he truly reached the pinnacle of shame, like the lunatics that came looking for shelter in Canterbury? But this voice was French. Surely the voices of his mind would speak in his own tongue? There, standing over him, he could see her in the moonlight; a waif with a shawl of rough wool, its fibres frosted by the harsh winter night. He closed his eyes disbelieving the realism of this apparition. He must fight this insanity.

'You cannot stay in this place.'

He told himself to keep his eyes shut, lest this vision of the devil's making continue. He began to chant, 'I must exercise strength, demonstrate that I will not give in, to deliver me from evil.'

'*Frère, Frère.*' The voice was louder, nearer.

He opened one eye unable to resist.

The girl jumped back like frightened game.

This was no apparition, if his eyes and ears were to be believed, and believe in them he must. He coughed to clear his throat. 'I will not hurt you, little one.'

The waif was crouching just a little way off, ready to flee.

'What is this place?' He was careful to enunciate, should his Norman diction cause confusion.

'This is the forest of the House of Montgommery.' She approached him once more.

Edward could make out her features; fresh and fine. A child, yes. Her clogs were bound and caked in mud. 'Montgommery?' he asked. 'Montgommery of Shropshire?'

'I do not know this strange name. *Frère*, you must not stay in this place. It is cold, and the dawn will shortly be upon us. Montgommery's men will ride; the forest at night is forbidden.' Her tone became urgent.

'I am here by the will of God. I must await my fate. God will deal with me as he sees fit.'

'*Frère*, please. I have somewhere you may rest a while. Can you walk?'

Edward had not set a foot on the ground for nearly two days. He pulled himself clumsily to a sitting position. His head was clanging as if an anvil had been lodged in his brain, and was swinging its might to and fro within.

'*Frère*, you bleed'

'It is no matter my child. It is my penance, my cross to bear.'

'Hurry, *Frère*! Sun up is nigh. We must not be caught. They will think we are poaching. They always think we are poaching.' And she was gone.

The moon was too low to cast enough light to see. A little way off, he heard the cracking of twigs. He pulled himself to his feet, and fought the dizziness as he lumbered in the direction of the sound. He shuffled awkwardly in the darkness, fearful of catching his feet on a protruding root, but he could not see the girl, nor hear her. He stopped. An owl fluted its call nearby.

'*Frère*, over here! Follow the owl.'

He stumbled blindly in the direction of the hooting when he tripped, but instead of thudding onto the frozen forest floor, he fell further, downward, below the earth. He landed onto softness, but when he opened his eyes to look around him, it was dark. A thicker darkness than that of the woods; it reminded him of his cloister at night. The noise of the forest was silenced and in its place was a scratching, scrabbling noise. Then a glowing yellow light grew in the corner, the shadows of flames danced on the walls of an earthy cavern, their warmth immediately radiating.

Acclimatising his eyes to the brightness, he gasped in horror, for before him stooped over the fire, was the most terrible creature. 'What is this trickery? It can only be an agent of the devil himself.' As he regarded the creature, he flattened himself against the cavern wall. It was as small as a dwarf; it could stand to its full height in the low roofed cavern. Its face was scabbed with weeping sores. Edward's stomach convulsed, as he saw its long hair drip a red liquid. It could only be blood. In its hand it held a club. Edward clutched his crucifix to him and swung himself forwards onto his knees.

'*Pater noster, qui est in caelis, sanctificetur nomen tuum.*'

The creature didn't flinch. Instead it held its fingers to its mouth. From above, a rhythmic beating pulsated through the soil.

Edward chanted his prayer louder.

The creature lifted its club.

Emerald and amber, swirled and danced, then turned to gold. Pain and light vied for attention in a beautiful but threatening display. Eldric, where are you? Eldric? Edward gasped himself awake. What was he thinking? The cathedral, Eldric, that life was gone. He could never go back. Around him were walls of moss. Only dying embers remained of a fire in the corner; over it, hung a small cauldron. A shaft of sunlight fell from a hole in the earthen ceiling warming his face. Through his aching and straining, the memories of the evening before swam back into his muffled brain. What is this place? It had been dark and cold. The creature! He sat up, suddenly frightened.

A bundle of woollen cloth beside him stirred. '*Frère*, stay quiet. Your head is bad. I didn't mean to hit you with such force, but you didn't leave me a choice.'

He jumped as her hand stretched out and stroked his brow.

'Forgive me, but you were convulsing and making a great deal of noise. We would surely have been caught.'

Edward looked at her in consternation. This was no creature. This was the waif, the waif who found him in the woods. She had long golden hair, not the matted locks dripping with blood, of his memory. The fistulas were real enough, though beneath them, she was beautiful. Then her tunic caught his eye. It was bloodstained.

'The blood! Is it mine?'

She shook her head and threw it back in laughter. 'No, *Frère*. It is the blood of a rabbit.' She reached for its skin and drew it over his knees. 'I was out hunting last eventide, when I found you on the road. Here, I have made you some broth.' She laid a wooden bowl, filled with warm liquid, on the rabbit skin. 'It is still warm, though the fire is dying. You must build your strength.'

'Montgommery? This is the *seigneurie* of Montgommery? You said, last night.'

She nodded. 'You have come from far, *Frère*?'

'Further than even I would have imagined.'

'From Paris?' Her eyes lit up with excitement.

'Much further, from beyond the sea.'

'Beyond the sea! You must be a great traveller, *Frère*. Paris is two good days' ride from here. My brother, Firmin told me,' she spoke his name proudly. 'I have never been much further than Beaugency. For what reason do you travel so far?'

'Through cowardice and fear. Now, I must pay for my folly.'

'Folly, *Frère*?'

'It is no matter to you, my child.' He took a great gulp from the bowl. 'It is sweet!'

'We have little here, but we have plenty of honey.' She gestured to beyond the forest. 'Honey is good. It will help bring back your strength.'

'Why are you so kind to me?'

'Not kind,' she said shaking her head. 'It is normal. If Montgommery's men had found you ..,' her voice trailed off.

'What is your name child?'

Her eyes narrowed abruptly and she tilted her head like a young deer listening for danger. 'You tell me your name first.' She looked away from him childishly, her hair hung around her shoulders, illuminated in the dawn sunshine.

It was a long while since Edward had seen such beauty so close.

'You could be one of Montgommery's spies.'

'Hah! If that were so, would I not already know your name?'

'You'll not be clever with me, *Frère*.' She stood up angrily, her golden head skimming the mud ceiling. 'For all the reading and writing you may have done in your monastery, I know things.'

'I'm sure you do.' He couldn't help smiling at her infantile stubbornness.

'You mock me.'

'Forgive me. My name is Edward and I come from England, a long way over the sea.'

'Why have you come here to Saint Gabriel?'

'Saint Gabriel? I have never heard of that place.'

'The village, it's over there on the edge of the forest. I live there.'

'Now, I have told you my name, you must tell me yours.'

She bowed her head and looked up at him through her eyelashes, 'It is Clothilde.'

'A noble name indeed!'

'Thank you, *Frère*. It was given to me by a friend of my father; a very important man.'

'Tell me, these Montgommerys, I believe I have heard that name amongst my superiors in Canterbury. Are they not Normans?'

'Normans? I do not know, *Frère*. They have been here since before I was born.'

Edward raised his hand, 'Please! Call me Edward.'

'Then you must agree to no longer call me 'child'. You know I am nearly old enough to be betrothed?'

'Indeed?' he said, sounding as impressed as he could. A searing pain shot through his head and he winced.

'You are in pain?'

'It will pass.'

'Drink up, *Frère*. Edward,' she said, correcting herself. 'When you have finished I will clean those wounds, you have not been lucky, you have been hit twice in the same place. Then you must try to walk.

16

I can look after you better in my home and my mother is waiting for this rabbit to feed the little ones.'

'Oh no, I cannot come to your house.'

'You cannot?' She lowered her eyes, 'Of course, I understand that our humble abode would not be worthy.'

'It is I who is not worthy. They may be looking for me and I would not want you to take on my strife.'

Her eyes became wide with curiosity, 'Have you done something bad?'

'Yes, very bad. You must leave me for I will bring you bad fortune. I only ask that I may stay here to heal awhile.'

She nodded. 'You may, of course stay here, but you must not leave the cavern during daylight hours for they will catch you. I will bring you food, and wood or you will die with this cold.' She didn't wait for an answer, and gathered her shawl around her, and lithely shinned up the mossy mud wall, hoisted herself through the shaft of sunlight, and was gone.

# THREE

## Hélène

Hélène Godard - born St Malo - twenty four. Profession: Nurse. Training : *Couvent de Sainte Marie, rue d'Alabastre,* Paris XIIIème. Come to work for the doctor in Jaunay. Codename: FRANCINE. She ran it through in her head, just as she had done for the previous six weeks.

As the Lysander's engines whirred into a descent, she braced herself to jump. Below, tiny lights flashed and flickered in a T-formation. She breathed deeply, the reception party was present; they wouldn't abort it now. In the moonlight, she could just make out the edge of the dropping zone, it was rimmed with dense, black forest. She would have to time it right or risk being caught up in the branches.

'Same procedure as Ringway, no difference, but this was the real thing. Map – check. Compass – Check. Torch – Check, Pass - Check. I - I - M - A - I. Information – Intention – Method – Administration – Intercommunication.'

In just twenty seconds Hélène Godard would be born. The dispatcher nodded at her as he pulled open the trap door. Her stomach lurched, and she cursed herself for her nerves. The red warning light came on, and her mind emptied. With his lamp, the dispatcher flashed a code down through the trap. Immediately, the lights on the ground went out and just one flashed in response. The red changed to green. Then the tap on the shoulder, and GO!

The cold of the rushing air swept upwards pulling at her overalls. Just three hundred feet. She pulled the cord as soon as she was clear of the aircraft, and grabbed the straps of the harness around her legs, ready for the jolt of the opening canopy. By the time her speed slowed the Lysander was gone, as were the flashing lights. The moon was still bright enough to outline the clearing, but the silence was unnerving. She floated towards the ground and prepared for landing. A little way off she heard the cracking of branches, a container must have fallen amongst the trees. As soon as her feet touched the ground, she threw herself sideways to break her fall, and to clear the chute.

Almost immediately a man was on her. He was grabbing at the straps of her harness. She'd been warned to secure her parachute; silk could be sold at a premium. Even the resistance was not above black market dealings.

'*Haut les mains!*' she whispered gruffly, drawing the pistol from her belt.

The man took a step back and shot his arms upwards.

She kept him covered while she caught her breath, and looked him up and down. He was stout, his features were obscured by a scarf wrapped around the lower part of his face.

'The apples are ripe?' she enunciated slowly.

'And ready for harvest,' he replied.

She nodded, lowering her pistol. She extricated herself from her harness whilst the man wrapped her chute into a bundle.

'Come!' Together they headed for the trees.

Under cover of the foliage, was a man crouched with a flashlight. 'Rémy take her to the chapel.'

Rémy nodded and briskly signalled to her to follow.

'What about the containers?' she asked the first man.

'They're picking them up now. *Allez, vite!*' And with that, he passed the parachute bundle to Rémy, stepped back into the darkness of the woods, and disappeared.

Rémy took off silently and at speed along the edge of the trees to the far end of the clearing. She followed at a distance should they be ambushed. He stopped by the entrance to a stone chapel, incongruous in the wildness of the forest. On one side was a pond; its surface glittered in the moonlight. A tree leaned precariously over it, swooping long branches into its waters. The door of the chapel was a simple gate of nailed planks that gave little privacy to the interior.

Noticing her reticence, Rémy said, 'The most public places are the best. They do not look here, it is too obvious a hiding place.'

Inside, a smell of moss and clammy damp filled the air. He began to carefully shroud the makeshift door with black sheeting, checking every crevice was covered. Once satisfied, he switched on his lamp and flashed it around the inside. On the earthen floor, just behind a crude stone altar, was a bedding roll and in the corner, Hélène could just make out the shape of a container dropped by the Lizzie.

'This is where we must spend the night. Here, make yourself comfortable.' He gestured to the bedding roll.

She obediently sat down on the straw-filled mattress, and watched him as he took a short handled shovel from his knapsack, and began to dig the earth at the base of one of the walls. He was a young man, with brown hair and dark eyes. His baggy beige trousers were muddy and held up with braces. On his feet, were black army boots that had seen better days.

'Where will you sleep?'

'I don't sleep. I watch,' he said tersely. He cast the shovel aside and lifted a wooden board from beneath, revealing a metal box. He pulled it out and opened the lid. Beneath were two gas burners. 'You must be hungry.'

She shook her head. Her stomach was tight with nerves and she was almost certain that she wouldn't be able to sleep either.

Rémy simply shrugged his shoulders as if to say, 'Please yourself'.

She lay down on the bedding roll, and watched him, as he emptied a jar, of what looked like butter beans in tomato sauce, into a pan and warmed it on the stove.

Light streaming through the chapel window woke her with a start. Rémy had removed the blackout. She stretched and stood up to look out.

'Get down!' he whispered fiercely. 'You cannot take any risks here.'

She ducked, feeling foolish. He bundled up the bedding roll and pushed it into his knapsack with the shovel. She helped him remove every bit of blackout material and stow them in the boarded hole in the ground, on top of the container.

'You must change. We leave in five minutes.' He turned his back on her and lit a cigarette.

She pulled a cotton print dress from her pack and abandoned her jump suit. As soon as she was dressed, he took her jumpsuit from her and added it to the hole in the ground.

'Best you don't get searched carrying this. Now, we will walk together as far as the *Route de Beaugency*. Then you will walk along it alone, until you reach Jaunay. The Paris train arrives in Beaugency at 5 am. You must arrive in Jaunay from the Beaugency direction at around seven,' he fumbled in his jacket pocket and produced some papers. 'Your ticket, your travel pass. They are expecting you.' He put a black beret on his head, perched to one side, and slung a rifle case over his shoulder. As he stepped out of the chapel into the sunlight, he reached up above the door and unhooked a brace of pheasant. 'Poaching is the best cover – you can always silence them with a bribe of game for supper! If we are stopped we will say that you got lost, and I am showing you the way to Jaunay. You don't know my name and I do not know yours.'

She nodded. She didn't know his name; Rémy would be his cover name. The cold morning air swirled around her bare legs and she shivered. For September there was already a serious nip in the air. Her shoes were old and worn but carefully chosen for their French manufacture, at least they were comfortable. She knew that until she was actually walking on the road from Beaugency to Jaunay, she was in grave danger.

They scrambled through the woods avoiding the paths until they reached open fields. At the edge of the trees, she could see the low slate roofs of the village of Saint Gabriel that rose above the fields, almost concealed by the tall sunflowers that had begun to droop their heads. She made a mental note of the steeple that pierced the sky on the western edge, that would be *L'Eglise St Martin*. They skirted the eastern edge of the village until the sunflower cover came to an end, and they were faced with an open, newly ploughed field.

'We must go fast. There are no buildings but the road is not far.'

They followed the hedge at the edge of the field and reached the other side out of breath. They had not covered more than a couple of miles; she supposed that the tension must be what was exhausting her more than the exertion. They sat at the foot of the hedge and caught their breath. Then without speaking, Rémy got to his feet and set off again. At last they reached the *Route de Beaugency*, winding grey between the hedges.

Rémy suddenly pushed her to the ground with a finger to his lips. They waited there, holding their breath. She could hear the rumble of a truck approaching. It rolled past just a metre from them.

When it had gone, Rémy popped his head above the hedge and sat back down next to her. 'Jaunay is to the north,' he gestured to the left. 'Beaugency to the south. There is a farmer ploughing his field on the other side of the road, he is facing us. When he has turned his horse in the opposite direction, I shall leave you. Wait until you can no longer see me then start walking to Jaunay. Go the café, order a coffee and ask for *Docteur* Legris.'

She opened her mouth to thank him, but he shook his head.

'If you need to get in touch, go to the *épicerie* in Jaunay. Ask for Rémy. When they say they do not know me, say, "He is my friend".' He tentatively peeped over the top of the hedge, and then put his rifle over his arm and headed off across the field, the pheasants' feathers iridescent in the sunlight.

As soon as she could see him no more, she checked the road in both directions. She could just see the back of the plough horse in the field opposite. The farmer was plodding laboriously through the furrows. She climbed through the hedge and walked in the direction Rémy had told her. The sun was beginning to warm her legs now. Just a few hundred yards away was the entrance to the village, bordered by an avenue of plane trees. Beyond, the buildings loomed grey in the bright morning sun. There was a church, its steeple marking the centre of the village, rising high above the square. As she walked between the plane trees she could see a group of children no more than nine or ten, crouched on one side. As she got nearer she could see they were playing marbles.

They stopped and looked up as she got closer. They scooped their marbles into their pockets and ran towards her excitedly.

'*Bonjour Madame*,' said a little girl confidently. This was then followed by a cascade of *Bonjour Madame*s from the others.

'*Bonjour, les enfants*,' she replied smiling.

'I am Miriam.'

A small boy next to her piped up, 'And I am Claude.' He drew himself up to his full height and saluted solemnly.

'I know who you are,' said Miriam proudly.

'Really?'

'You're the new nurse. You're going to work with *Docteur* Legris.'

'Well, news travels fast round here.'

'Have you come from Paris?'

'Yes, this morning.' She was going to say on the train, but had to stop herself; there was no need to justify herself to children, she would have to watch that. It was best to say as little as possible.

'You haven't got many bags?'

'No,' Hélène cast her eyes downwards. 'We lost a lot in the bombing.'

The child's eyes widened, 'Did you see the bombing?'

'I heard it. How did you know I was coming?'

'*Papa* told me. He is the teacher.'

'Well then I am very pleased to meet you.' She leant down and kissed the girl on each cheek. 'Now, please could you direct me to the café?'

The girl skipped delightedly, blowing her chest out with importance and said in a military manner, 'Of course, follow me.' Then she turned to her comrades and said haughtily, 'You run along, I have an important job to do.' She half skipped and half ran in front of Hélène, stopping every now and then to check she was still following. More children appeared on either side of the street to stare at the stranger. Some of them called out *'Bonjour'* to Miriam, but she just hoisted her nose into the air and walked on with a look of disdain.

They came to a grocer's. Above the door, was a cast iron bracket carrying a sign *Epicerie Joly.* Inside, it looked dark, with only the windows on the front looking over the street and the sun still high in the east. The café was next door.

*'Voilà Madame!'* and the little girl took a curtsey.

*'Merci,* Miriam.' Hélène pushed open the door and a bell jingled as it closed. She was relieved to find the café empty.

A stern looking woman, chunky in shape, appeared behind the bar. Her ample bosom was crammed into a dress evidently bought in leaner years. Around her waist was a gigantic canvas apron. Her hair was pulled back tightly from her head and piled up behind, giving her ears a curiously large allure.

*'Oui?'* she uttered gruffly, looking Hélène up and down sneeringly.

*'Bonjour Madame,'* she replied as gracefully as she could. *'Un café s'il vous plaît.'*

The woman paused, staring at her as if she was expecting more.

Not wishing to disappoint she added, 'I am looking for *Docteur* Legris.'

'He will not be open before eight o'clock. *Alors, un café;* if you can call it that. We have only chicory these days.' She turned to the coffee machine without another glance.

'Where will I find the doctor?'

Without turning round she replied, 'In the square opposite the town hall, the house with the railings.'

She sat down at a table near the window and watched the comings and goings of this bleak looking village. It appeared to have just one straight road with only the square off to one side. More and more children were emerging from doorways. The boys wore ties and shirts buttoned up to the top and shorts. The girls wore cotton dresses. They all headed in the direction of the village square and the church.

Her thoughts were interrupted by the clatter of a cup and saucer on the bar.

*'Votre café, mademoiselle.'*

As she reached the bar to collect it, the door swung open and in came two German officers.

She stiffened. They were older than she expected, but then she remembered that Hitler had reinforced the Russian front with his youngest troops. In the flesh they didn't match up to their reputation. They immediately came over to her.

'Your papers?'

She pulled them from her bodice.

The soldier looked at them carefully. His face was ravaged with alcohol abuse; his nose was scarlet and carved with a cauliflower texture. His teeth were too big for his mouth and made him dribble. As he looked up from the papers, he caught her eye, and his hand shot up to wipe the saliva from his chin. He passed her papers on to his companion.

He was younger possibly about forty, and blond with blue eyes; an Arian. They were just men; they could have been the milkman at home, or the coalman, but for their uniform, their accents and their power.

'You have just arrived in Jaunay?'

She nodded.

'On what business?' Evidently the village gossip was successfully concealed from their occupiers.

'I am a nurse. I have come to work for the doctor.'

He took a deep breath. Both of them stared at her intently, looking her up and down. 'These are in order, *Fraulein.*' and the older one handed back her papers. Then they turned their attentions to the landlady, '*Zwei, kaffee.*'

The woman made no answer but mechanically turned to the coffee machine. Hélène returned to her table with relief, and drank her coffee very fast. She put on her coat and headed out into the village, before the Germans had finished theirs. The children were gone from the street. Their classes must have started. Her watch said eight o'clock. The surgery would be opening now. The doctor's house looked like the most welcoming building on the square. Its shutters were painted blue, and its façade was covered with a wisteria that was beginning to turn brown with the approach of autumn. She pulled the brass handle in the wall to the side of the front door, which opened almost immediately.

'Aah, *Mademoiselle* Godard I suppose?'

'*Monsieur le Docteur*?'

'Please, call me Julien.' He was not particularly tall, and despite his greying hair his eyebrows had remained dark, giving him a certain youthfulness. 'Come in, come in! You must be exhausted from your journey. I am sorry I was not able to meet with you earlier, but I have had no help for a few months, and my round sometimes takes me until late into the night.' He led her through the hall and showed her into a dining room at the back of the house. There was a sash window looking out onto the back courtyard. A dark wooden table with a high shine stood in the middle of the room. Against the wall, was a sideboard loaded with yellowing medical journals. 'Please, take a seat.'

She sat down at the table.

'So, *Mademoiselle* Godard. You were trained in Paris and you are qualified with the Red Cross?'

'That's right.'

'Then you will be more than versed in the care of TB patients?'

'Yes.'

'You are not scared of TB?' But he didn't give her a chance to reply. 'Of course you are not, or you would not have been working with the Red Cross. With this war I feel that fear has disappeared. The worst has already happened. We can only thank God that we have lasted this long.' He threw his head back and laughed in a devil may care manner, 'How rude of me! No, I cannot talk you straight into work; you must first see where you will sleep.' He stood up. 'Follow me.'

He led her up the stairs to the very top of the house to what would have been the maid's quarters. 'I am sorry it is small, but I hope you will be quite comfortable.'

The room was indeed tiny. It was right under the roof. It was furnished simply with a single bed covered with a candlewick bedspread. Above it, hung a crucifix with a figurine of Christ on the cross. There was a chest of drawers with a large china bowl and jug set upon it and a rough worn towel.

'The bathroom is on the ground floor, but we are obliged to be very frugal with the hot water; it's the fuel rationing. It is all we can do to keep clean in these terrible times.' He pulled a door set in the wall, to reveal a cupboard with a single rail and a couple of wooden hangers. 'This is for your clothes. *Madame* Clément, my housekeeper, comes in every morning to make breakfast and do a little cleaning. She is not so good at cleaning but she is a wonderful cook, even with our meagre rations. Her boys are away working in Germany; it is good to distract her.' From the pocket of his tweed suit he produced a gold watch on a chain; he flicked it open then snapped it shut decisively. 'Right, I must not stand here chatting. I expect a young lady like you will need some privacy to arrange your things. I will ask *Madame* Clément to set you a little breakfast in the dining room when she arrives, she will not be long. I must go; I shall have patients at the door any moment now.' He turned to go down the stairs and then stopped. 'Please, feel free to explore the house. My waiting room is next to the dining room and the kitchen opposite. We shall talk about eleven yes?'

'Thank you.'

As soon as she heard his last footfall on the stairs and the door of his consulting room close, she quickly set about finding a hiding place for her radio set. She stepped carefully over the boards in the floor to see if she could find any that might be loose, but all were firmly nailed down. She'd noticed a hatch in the roof, on her way up the stairs, but she couldn't be sure if there was a ladder. *Madame* Clément would arrive any minute and there would be no time. She would have to hide it in her room. She opened the door of the cupboard in the wall. The bottom was also boarded. She tapped them each individually and one wobbled. She worked it loose by jamming a metal comb in the edge. Beneath was the perfect hiding place, though she would need to saw through the other boards to fit her radio set in. She opened the door, glanced down the stairs but could hear no noise from the kitchen. *Madame* Clément had not yet arrived, she would have to be quick. She bolted her door, rolled up some blankets and laid them over the gap at the bottom to insulate the sound. Retrieving the mini saw issued to her in London she set about sawing through the two other planks in the base of the cupboard, whilst singing an Edith Piaf song to cover the racket as best she could. She removed the planks just as she reached the end of all nine verses. Downstairs she heard the front door clatter open. *Madame* Clément must have arrived. She quickly slotted the radio set into the gap, still in its case. She replaced the planks and obscured them with a couple of rough knitted jumpers, making a mental note to tack them in later with short nails. She did not want to draw attention to herself. She didn't know if *Docteur* Legris was aware

26

of her true role here. It was better that he knew as little as possible, for his own safety and for hers. She was the first agent to be sent into occupied territory in such a permanent capacity. She knew that the average length of time for an agent to remain safely in the field was six weeks, and she was determined to stay as long as it took to get the job done.

She put the bedclothes back together and unbolted the door. She sat on the bed; the springs creaked noisily against the iron frame. She looked out of the window onto a narrow garden dug over and planted with vegetables. From here, she could see the back of the café building and other narrow gardens, all of them dug over.

At last she was back in France. How she'd missed it! At the outbreak of war, she had believed like so many others that it would be over by Christmas but as soon as Pétain had signed the armistice she was in the firm belief that neither she, nor her parents would ever be able to return. She could not have sat there any longer in her parents' bolthole in Eastbourne watching all those fathers and sons and men, some so young they should still be in school, being called up, whilst she sat helplessly darning socks. She hadn't wanted to upset her parents either, but she had to do something and joining the FANY's was the only thing she could do. How could she allow her nursing training to go to waste when it was so acutely needed?

# FOUR

## Diana

Diana stood back and admired the sitting room floor. She'd mopped it three times to reveal a shining surface of black slate from beneath the grime. The bedrooms were aired and swept and she'd scrubbed every surface and cupboard in the kitchen. Ben was running round and round the enormous sitting room, darting in and out of the bedrooms, mimicking engine sounds. He was soaking wet and black all over from sliding up and down in the soap suds. She took a blanket and the picnic she'd prepared and coaxed him out to the garden, but instantly, he was gone, into the metre high grass like a rabbit bolting for freedom.

Diana followed the twitching blades that gave away his location. No longer would they have to *Keep off the grass* or hold Ben back, when he approached the spoilt Parisian terriers, dressed in tartan coats, for fear of them biting. Now, they had their very own private park. There were willow and lime, pine and poplar and in the front, the oldest and most magical of all, a great spreading yew.

Serge and the boys should have left Paris by now. He'd roped in some of his colleagues to lend a hand with the move. Excitement swept her, just as it always had as a child with the promise of a treat or an impending family holiday . Serge had booked three weeks leave and she was looking forward to spending time with him, without the inevitable interruption of his Parisian social life. Out here, they really could get away from it all and work on the new chapter in their relationship. He'd promised that things would be different.

A rumble of traffic loomed in on the wind. She scooped up Ben and quickly stripped off his dirty clothes, gave him a swift wipe down and dressed him in clean ones. A collection of vans and cars, some pulling trailers, appeared round the corner, in front of the church.

'*Papa!*' yelled Ben excitedly.

Serge got out of his car and stretched his legs. His face was set solemnly.

Maybe the exam didn't go well.

'What happened? I saw your car?' He was angry.

How could she have forgotten? Of course, he would have passed the memorial on the way. The garage had obviously not yet picked it up. 'I had an accident. Don't worry, I'm …'

'I knew that was a bad idea; you driving down here on your own,' he almost spat the words.

'Serge!'

But he'd turned away to direct the other vehicles into the yard. Diana fought tears, cursing herself for her sensitivity. The romance and hope of the sunshine filled garden and Ben's glee had coloured her vision with a golden crown, which with one blow had been cast down smashing her back to reality.

Christian bounded towards her. He grabbed her playfully by the shoulders and kissed her expansively on both cheeks. 'This isn't a house,' he grinned, 'This is a palace!'

Diana recovered her inner composure; no one could help beaming at Christian. He was right, it *was* a palace and she was the queen.

Within an hour the house was strewn with boxes and ill-matching furniture. She located the box of food and drink on the back seat of Serge's Mini. The men carried in their belongings shouting to Diana for instructions as to where to put them. As soon as the wall papering table appeared out of the debris, she set it up on the back terrace, and laid it with plastic cups, a jug of water, bottles of beer and one large one of pastis. She filled bowls with olives and prawns, and arranged a tray with sliced roast beef and another of dry-cured pork sausage stuffed with hazelnuts. Christian had brought the bundle of baguettes that Diana had ordered from the bakery in *Rue Froidevaux* the day before.

By six o'clock the cars and trailers had been emptied and the men collapsed exhausted on the terrace. Serge was pouring a little pastis into the bottom of each of the cups and watching the yellow liquid turn opaque as he added the cold water from the jug.

Diana joined the men and sat on the edge of the terrace trailing her bare feet into the sumptuous greenery of the overgrown lawn.

Ben was rolling over and over, flattening the tall grasses. He stopped and sat up to check that everyone was watching. Satisfied that they were, he started all over again.

Serge had ignored her right the way through the unpacking, bowing his head when they passed each other, or darting into another room if she was coming down a corridor. Suddenly he let out a yell which made her jump.

'Diana!' he pronounced it D-EE-ANA. 'He's going to get dirty.'

'He's alright, he can have a bath tonight,' she crooned as soothingly as she could.

'Diana!' he repeated more urgently.

The men all looked pointedly somewhere else.

Diana stood up quickly, picked up Ben and without a word brushed the grass from his hair. She could feel her cheeks burning with the humiliation.

'Right, we'll be off then.' Christian stood up to leave. 'We mustn't drink too much, we've got plenty of that to come later on. *Café Oz*? Nine o'clock?'

The men murmured their agreement.

Diana's heart sank. The reason for Serge's hostility was now only too clear. He would be furious that he couldn't join in with them celebrating the end of the exam.

When Christian had gone, the others got to their feet and politely filed past Diana, kissing her on each cheek.

When the last car had driven out of the courtyard and down the lane, Serge and Diana fell exhausted onto the sofa. Ben was rummaging through his Lego on the rug in front of the fireplace. They sat quietly for a minute or two.

Serge sank back into the sofa clasping a bottle of beer in one hand and closed his eyes.

'Serge, about the car ...'

'Not now!' he snapped.

'Look, this car flew round the corner; I had to get out of the way.'

'Face it, Diana, you're just not used to driving. I knew it was a bad idea moving out here to the sticks.' And he closed his eyes again. That conversation would have to wait until tomorrow.

She tried a different tack, 'How was the exam?'

At last he opened one eye and sat up. He launched into the technical details of diving procedure. Diana felt herself glazing over, but managed to nod and exclaim where she felt it appropriate. At least he was talking to her.

'Do you think you've passed?' As soon as she said it she regretted it.

'I can't fail,' he snapped. 'We have a mortgage to pay! Oh and a new car? I mean, how long have you had it? Just one week?' The words came out like bullets.

Diana stared at him speechless. Surely he knew that she understood the gamble they had taken? Christian had told her that Serge was the best diver amongst them. He couldn't fail. She noticed dark bags under his eyes. He would feel differently with a good night's sleep behind him.

'Better get Ben in the bath,' she said quietly.

From the sitting room the sad haunting tones of Jacques Brel playing too loudly, were radiating through the bathroom wall. She could picture Serge drinking glass after glass of pastis, wallowing in the misfortune of missing a party in Paris. She bathed her son, and watched him chuckle at the flying bubbles as he splashed and paddled. Not wishing to return to the sitting room to witness Serge's descent into oblivion, on this, their first night in their new home, she went to bed.

She lay awake listening to *Monsieur* Brel crooning *La Valse à Mille Temps'*. She drifted to her wedding day. Serge was whirling her round and round, her dress of gleaming silk and organza flowing out behind her. Friends and family were gathered round smiling as they watched the happy couple dancing faster and faster as the waltz quickened. She struggled to sleep, unaccustomed to the deafening tranquillity, which was only intermittently relieved by the slam of a car door on the village square, then the buzz of a *mobylette* on a distant country road.

Serge was sprawled over most of the bed. He was breathing putrefied alcohol fumes which hung heavily in the air. She slipped out of bed carefully so as not to disturb him. She wretched internally and held her breath until she was out of range. In Ben's room, she was greeted by a pure, wholesome smile. Outside, there were already butterflies skimming the tall grasses, their wings flashing in the sunlight. The birds were back, bustling in their multitudes, all singing different tunes, rather like an orchestra tuning up before a concert.

She made a cup of tea and put Ben's wellingtons on over his sleep suit and took him outside. In the distance, she could see the dark swathe of the Marchenoir forest, stretching like a sleeping giant. A wire fence ran across the bottom boundary of the garden. In front, three poplars rose tall, their branches splayed like fingers clutching at the sky. Beyond was a meadow, and then a road that ran westwards bordering a field of sunflowers in bud. Just there, inside the fence, in between the bonfire pit and the barn, was where she would put her vegetable garden. She had spent long hours poring over gardening books in Paris, planning what she would grow. She willed Serge to get up and share it with her, but knew there was probably no point.

From the kitchen, Diana heard a knock on the French windows. She glanced at her watch; it said eleven. Two men were standing on the front terrace.

'*Bonjour Madame,*' said one, holding out a hand. 'Couteau, Jérôme. I am from the garage in Jaunay, *Bonnet et Fils*. Jeanette, at the café, she called me.'

'*Oui?*' Came Serge's gruff voice from behind her.

'Ah! *Bonjour, Monsieur.*' Jérôme Couteau shuffled from one foot to the other in a display of nervous humility, which somehow didn't fit his demeanour. 'I think you had an accident? We've just picked up the car.'

Diana blushed at the thought of her car balanced on the memorial for a whole afternoon, evening and night for all to see.

'Aah! It was my wife,' Serge raised his eyes upwards. 'She is not used to our roads. She is English.' He said it as if she were deficient in some way.

The second man stepped forward. He was smaller but broader than the first. He smoothed his hands down his filthy blue overalls and held one out for Serge to shake, his eyes averted. 'Bébert,' he muttered from underneath his bushy auburn moustache and quickly retracted his hand and resumed his position behind his companion.

'We have the tow truck ready,' said Jérôme.

Serge hesitated, 'I haven't had a chance to look at it yet. I wonder if it is worth fixing.'

Jérôme shrugged, 'I have not yet looked at it properly myself. But perhaps we can come to an agreement?' He looked at his watch.

'An aperitif perhaps?' Serge asked hopefully.

Both men nodded a little too eagerly for Diana's liking. Serge opened the drinks cabinet and laid the table with three glasses, a bottle of pastis and a bowl of peanuts. Diana obviously wasn't included.

She raised her eyebrows at Serge who served himself a coffee and a paracetamol alongside his pastis. She took Ben off into his bedroom to get him dressed. Diana had lived in France for nearly four years and had become well used to the role of women here. They looked after the children, kept themselves trim and cooked sumptuous four course meals every day of the week, whilst creating and maintaining the interiors of houses worthy of a magazine shoot. They were not expected to drink to excess, nor should they swear. Amongst her college friends, these roles were non-existent, but the wives and girlfriends of Serge's colleagues at the fire station took on more traditional positions and accepted their fates of being relegated to the kitchen sink and the back seat of the car without question.

Serge had always been the leader, taking charge of the paperwork and the finances, deciding where they would go for dinner and what they would do on the weekends. Diana had never had any reason to intervene; his choices would have been her own. But as she listened to the men from the bedroom, she couldn't help feeling she was taking part in some kind of feudal re-enactment and she could feel anger rising deep inside her. Delphine, Christian's girlfriend had warned her that things would be very different out here in the country.

The men's conversation seemed to have moved on to fishing. She could hear Serge extolling the virtues of pike cooked in a white butter sauce. Something she had heard many times in Paris, though she was yet to see him actually go fishing. She heard their chairs scrape on the slate floor. This was her cue to reappear and bid them farewell. She picked up Ben and was stepping towards the sitting room when she heard Serge's voice again.

'So that's agreed. If you dismantle the hangars you can have them in lieu of payment. When will you take them?'

'After the wheat harvest at the end of July?'

The hangars? What was he doing? She knew they would have to get rid of them as they couldn't afford the insurance. Her heartbeat accelerated. How dare he make such arrangements without consulting her? 'In lieu of payment,' for heavens' sake. They were trying to sell them, not give them away. Surely they were worth more than the cost of taking them down?

Diana didn't trust her expression or her voice and waited until she heard the men go out onto the front terrace. Then she crossed the sitting room with Ben in tow, through the corridor and down the concrete steps to the courtyard, and round the corner. Hiding in the garage like an angry child, her heart was pumping fast, making her breathless. She'd argued with Delphine that she wanted 'different', but she had had no idea that 'different' meant being invisible. She heard the tow truck's engine start up. She waited until it had rumbled away into the village before she rearranged her frown, and returned to the house by the back steps.

'Diana, I was looking for you to say goodbye to them?' He paused. 'Are you alright?'

She flicked her hair coolly. 'Were you? I didn't think you needed me,' she said failing to keep her annoyance from her voice.

'What do you mean?' The pitch of his voice was rising.

Diana didn't reply but just stared at him, her eyes narrowed.

He didn't rise to the bait. 'It's great news isn't it? They'll take the hangars away and we won't have to pay a penny,' he said in an attempt to dodge the conflict.

'What if they're worth something?'

'They are, but not more than it would cost to take them away.'

'You should've asked me,' her voice was wobbling now and a tear escaped down her cheek.

'Oh, Diana! I'm sorry. I didn't think you were interested by a boring thing like that.' His eyes softened, his voice plaintive, 'I've always dealt with the maintenance stuff haven't I?'

'This is different,' she sobbed, feeling ashamed at her lack of emotional control 'This is my house too.'

Serge put his arms around her and held her close. 'You're right. I hadn't thought of it like that.' He kissed her tears away.

# FIVE

## Edward

The weather had turned even colder and snow blanketed the paths and fallen branches on the forest floor. The foxes had been out all night looking for food in the harsh temperatures. He had woken at each of the vixens' cries, and now he felt worse. His head was healing, but as the flesh on his scalp knitted together, it stung and ripped. He longed to rub it, but the water in the jar that Clothilde had brought him, was frozen, and he dared not touch the wound with his dirty hands. He was cold to the core. The wood in the cavern had run out and Clothilde would not be back until well after sun up, when her chores would be done.

He rubbed his hands together and rocked backwards and forwards on his knees to warm his muscles, as he recited Matins. Without the bells of the priory he could only guess at the time, and he dared not venture his head above to the forest, to see the position of the moon lest he be spied. He did not know what treatment he would receive should he be discovered. A foreign monk, a stowaway and a Judas; the penalty would surely be severe. When he had been thrown from the cart he had felt brave, ready to face his maker. But now, cold, tired and in pain beneath the ground in a Hades that had become his sanctuary, he was ashamed of his fear of death.

He imagined Eldric and the others filing silently along the cloister from Matins to the refectory. Wooden bowls of steaming pottage and hunks of barley bread waiting for them. He remembered groaning at the cold in the priory in the winter, but it was nothing compared to this. What a fool he had been to imagine that his life had been hard. He had forsaken Eldric, who had guided him and taught him to dispense medicine, to clean wounds and to obey the Lord God Almighty. It was they who had taken him in, when his poor dear mother had been unable to cling to life at his birth. It was the Lord God who had fed him and nurtured him all his life, and how had he repaid Him? By betraying Him, and his Grace, the Archbishop, and all the brothers in that place, through cowardice.

The cold interrupted his thoughts, and he huddled himself in as tight a ball as possible, with his habit gathered around him. He closed his eyes and tried to remember as many of the names of the herbs

Eldric had taught him, to take his mind off his plight. He must have fallen asleep for he was awoken by Clothilde.

'Edward I have brought some fresh water and some wood, it is a little damp with the snow but it will have to do.'

Edward watched her as she cleared the ash from the fire and laid her gathered twigs in their place.

'I must gather more wood for you to keep the fire going tonight.'

'Will they not see the smoke?'

'Only if they look above the tree tops. Look!' She gestured to the roof of the fireplace. 'The smoke goes up the centre of this ancient oak, they will only find it if they notice this is the only trunk to which no snow has clung. But they are too stupid, they will venture into the forest to look for the fire and when they do not find it immediately they will turn back, and think they dreamed it. Montgommery's men are tough and violent but they are not intelligent.' She took a striker and a flint from her cloak and struck them together.

Edward marvelled at the sparks and small flames that sprung from her palm.

'You have never made fire?'

Edward shook his head. 'The fires in the priory were lit in the autumn and kept alight until the spring, but it was not one of my tasks.'

Clothilde tore a tiny piece of cloth from the base of her tunic and held it on the flint, as she struck the edge of it with the steel. The cloth caught the spark and glowed amber in the dark morning light. Edward watched her lips as she carefully blew on the tiny flame. Such beauty! When the cloth was burning in earnest, she set it beneath the carefully arranged twigs, which hissed and crackled, as the heat met their humidity. 'What was your job in the priory?'

Edward sat up straight and said with pride, 'I worked in the infirmary.'

'What is that?'

'The place where the sick are looked after.'

'You know how to heal the sick?'

He nodded, blushing slightly at the exaggeration. In truth, he had only aided Eldric. He would tell him what to do and he did it. It was true that he had come to know the preparations for some of the simpler remedies, and the symptoms of a great many ailments, but he would not have dared take the responsibility of healing someone alone without direction.

'Here, we only have the wise woman of Saint Léonard to help us. But she is a frightening woman, and expects a lot in payment for her services.' She prodded the fire and the flames leapt obediently in response. 'If you healed the sick, then you must know a remedy to heal your head?'

Edward thought for a moment. There was the peasant who had fallen from the harvest cart and gashed his head. What did Eldric do? He made a compress of … 'Alkanet.'

'What do you say?'

'Alkanet. Do you have any in these woods?'

She looked at him blankly.

'It has a blue flower and a red root.'

Clothilde furrowed her brow.

'It is good for dyeing wool and healing wounds.'

'Bugloss you mean? It does grow here though you have forgotten that this is winter, and nothing but ivy thrives in this weather.'

'Eldric used to have me gather its roots in the autumn and dry it for use in winter. Dried, it is not as good as fresh but it will work.'

Clothilde shook her head. 'We do not have any. But what if I go to see the wise woman? She will surely have some stored,' Then her face fell. 'But she will want paying and she is not a good woman to owe a debt to.'

'It is no matter. She will ask why you want it and then you will be in danger for helping me.'

'Let me look at your head and you tell me what it should look like if it is healing.'

Edward bowed his head for her to inspect. 'Its colour should be pink or red; there should be no green or yellow liquid.'

Clothilde carefully parted the hair on the edge of his tonsure.

Edward flinched at her touch.

'I have hurt you?'

'No, no. Your hands are a little cold,' and he blushed.

'There is no liquid at all, though some of the skin is blue and black and raised into a bump.'

'It will be bruised and swollen for a little while yet. As long as the lesion remains a healthy hue, it will heal in good time.'

Clothilde sat back down in front of the fire.

The heat had begun to radiate the cavern and Edward could feel his muscles relaxing.

'Your life in the priory was good?'

'Yes. I think so, though it is the only life I know.'

'If all was done for you it must have been very comfortable.'

'I think I did not know what it would be like outside its walls.'

She looked at him long and hard. 'Edward, what happened? What made you leave and travel so far?'

'Careful! The fire is going out!'

Clothilde turned towards the fire, ready to blow on it, only to find it crackling gaily. 'You really know nothing of practicalities do you!' she laughed. 'It is well underway, Now, I must go and gather some wood, and set it in front of the flames to dry, or it will not burn properly. I will pass the wood down through the opening, be ready to take it from me.' She nimbly stood on an upturned log and shinned out of the opening and disappeared.

While she was gone, Edward thought of his work in the infirmary and tried to remember all the remedies he had prepared for Eldric. If he could write them down, he was sure he would remember more. It wasn't long before Clothilde returned. Edward heard twigs cracking from above just as the end of a branch appeared through the opening. He pulled it through and laid it on one side of the cavern.

'Stack the wood in front of the fire,' she called down to him. In no time there was a healthy stack of wood that should keep the fire going for at least a couple of days. 'Now, your first lesson is that you cannot burn wet wood, it will be difficult to light and it will give little heat. Everything up there is frozen, and covered with snow, so we must stack it by the fire to dry, before burning it.'

Edward nodded.

'The cock will be crowing and my mother will worry. Keep out of sight and I will return at dusk.'

'Clothilde, can you find me some parchment or vellum?'

She shook her head, 'We do not have such things. We are lowly peasants. I cannot read or write, though my brother Firmin, he has been learning with *Père* Barthélemy. My brother is very clever.' She beamed with pride.

'You must think me very ignorant.

'Oh no! You can read and write, and heal people. How could I think you were ignorant!' She flushed in consternation.

'I meant, I was ignorant to imagine that writing equipment would be so easy to come by.'

38

'I will see what I can do. You must continue to put logs on the fire or it will go out and you will get cold again. Choose the driest logs, and don't forget.' She waved a finger at him.

'Now go, or you will be missed.'

'I almost forgot.' She rummaged beneath her cloak and brought out a hunk of barley bread and a heel of hard cheese. 'This is all I have, it will need to last you until tomorrow. If I take too much, Mother will notice.'

# SIX

**Diana**

It was Monday morning and Serge was up early. The exam results would be pinned up on the notice board in the barracks at St Eustache. Diana had harboured a vague hope that he would get Christian to phone him, with his, but when she had suggested it, he had looked at her in complete surprise. 'I have worked hard for this. I want to be with the boys when I find out.'

She put on a brave face and waved him off with Ben in her arms, suppressing her wariness of being left alone in this enormous property. His words were still echoing in her head as the Mini disappeared round the corner. He wanted to be with the boys. Had it not occurred to him that this news would affect both their lives? He had promised to be home on the five o'clock train, he'd only be away for the day. Then, she brightened at the thought of a little time alone to get things straight.

She threw herself into emptying boxes and rearranging the furniture, to have it looking really homely on his return and then they could celebrate, or commiserate together. She polished the old Louis XIV sideboard that Serge's mother had given them as a wedding present. She absorbed herself in the fiddly task of wiping round every curl of the intricate carved inlay, using her nails to obliterate the thick dust that had got encrusted there during their time in Paris. She unpacked the boxes of curtains and hung them over the washing line to air. When she was tired of unpacking, she piled up the flattened, empty cardboard boxes into an old rusty wheelbarrow, that had been left behind by the previous owners, and wheeled them down to the bonfire pit.

Ben trailed behind with a collection of cars and plastic prams full of plastic dolls, some with their heads or a limb missing.

The phone didn't ring until noon.

'Serge?'

'It's good.'

'You mean you passed?'

'Hey! Of course I passed *ma chérie*! You didn't think I'd fail did you?' His voice was jaunty, 'We're going to be fine.'

'Oh Serge! Well...' Before she could finish, he interrupted her.

'We're going to the café to celebrate, I have to go.' He hung up.

She was left holding the disconnected receiver. At least they were high and dry. They could pay the mortgage and start their new life. She looked out of the kitchen window at the forest. So much to explore! A thrill of excitement went through her. If Serge was catching the five o'clock train from Austerlitz, he would be back in Beaugency at about six thirty and home by seven. That gave her plenty of time to organise a tumultuous homecoming. She unpacked their clothes and hung them in the wardrobe. She polished the wooden floor in the bedroom until it shone.

Ben helped her retrieve his toys and clothes. He was enjoying passing them to her, one by one, while she neatly piled them into his cupboards. She hung his mosquito net and fixed his mobile of brightly-coloured balsa wood aeroplanes inside it, above his cot. She tacked his number frieze to the wall, and was just standing back to check it was level, when Ben promptly swung open the cupboard doors and began to fling garments over his shoulder in glee, like a mad professor.

Then he turned with a cheeky twinkle in his eye, and rushed out of the room, willing Diana to chase him.

'Come on Mr Rummage, you'll have to put all these things back again now.' She caught up with him. Grabbing him under the arms, she gently pinned him to the carpet. She tickled him until his face went crimson, and he could hardly breathe from the excitement.

Once again, he passed the things to her, one by one, until the floor was clear again. As she turned to leave the room, Ben made another mischievous dive for the cupboard.

'Oh, no you don't!' She caught him up and kissed his tummy. 'It's time for a snooze, little man.' She plugged in the intercom and closed the door quietly.

She stepped out into the garden and picked a large bundle of wild flowers. She arranged them in a vase on the dining table. She swept out the fireplace and wiped grey ash from the fire irons, restoring them to their rich blackness. She could hear Ben kicking the aeroplanes above his bed and talking to himself, so she went to release him from his boredom.

Her watch said a quarter to six; Serge would be home in just over an hour. Settling Ben in his high chair in the kitchen, she rinsed and spun some endives and tossed them with tomatoes. She sautéed lardons, and drizzled over, a Dijon mustard and tarragon dressing. The steaks and cheese were losing their chill from the fridge on the side while she threw a couple of baking potatoes into the oven to cook slowly. She dug out a bottle of champagne she had been saving for the occasion, and put it in the fridge. She put on some make-up, and pulled on a slightly translucent blouse and her favourite jeans, that had a miraculous effect of taming her unruly stomach muscles. She let her hair loose from the scrunchy that had been restraining it. He wouldn't be long now.

Seven o'clock came, and all was ready. Ben was bathed and dressed in his best pyjamas. Not a toy could be seen, and every corner of the house was scrubbed and tidy. She'd managed to pile the remaining unpacked boxes into a spare bedroom out of sight. She stood at the French windows with Ben, looking out for Serge. At eight o'clock she turned on the radio, perhaps there was a train strike, but the traffic news announced that all roads were flowing and that the trains were running on time. She heard a car rumbling towards the village. She took Ben by the hand, and stood just inside the iron gate. Peering into the lane, she could hear the car engine slowing, as it reached the sharp bend in front of *La Petite Folie*.

'*Papa*?' asked Ben.

Then it speeded up again and headed off towards the forest.

'*Papa*?' asked Ben again.

'*Papa*, will be home soon.' Her voice was struggling to conceal her disappointment. They waited there for another ten minutes but the only sounds of traffic were that of tractors and a *mobylette* heading out towards Fontenay. She went back inside to check the answering machine, perhaps he had tried to call her, but the light next to the handset lay dormant.

In Paris, Serge had often been late, but she'd hoped they'd turned a corner now that he had agreed to a fresh start in the countryside. Besides, with a train to catch, he couldn't miss it. Could he?

Ben was rubbing his eyes with exhaustion. After a supper of bread and cheese, she put him down to sleep. He must have sensed her unease, as he found it difficult to settle. Diana knelt on the floor next to his cot, motionless, until at last, his eyelids lowered and he drifted off to sleep. She crawled out of his bedroom slowly on all fours so as not to disturb him.

Serge was now two hours late. Perhaps she could phone the barracks? She didn't like to. She had heard how the firemen closed ranks on wives and girlfriends that pestered them at work. She could call Delphine; she would know where they were. She picked up the phone and dialled the number.

Delphine's voice came echoing over on her answering machine. Diana replaced the receiver. Of course, she would be out celebrating with them. She felt a twinge of jealousy. Before Ben was born, she would have been there too. Serge would have been proudly parading her in the bars and cafés, like some sort of trophy. Now, she was not even worth calling to let her know he was late.

She turned on the television to catch the ten o'clock news. Jacques Chirac, hands in pockets, was extolling the virtues of nuclear testing in the Pacific Ocean. His speech, slow and theatrical, gave him the stance of a member of The Royal Shakespeare Company rather than the *Président de la République*. She sat through the proposals for the reduction in rates, and the corruption of a minister, who had acquired a villa in the South of France, through dubious means. There was no mention of any great disaster that would require the assistance of all members of the fire brigade, nor any strikes or riots that may prevent Serge from returning home. She stared at the weather report blankly, unable to absorb the information.

The sun had gone down leaving the sky a bright indigo. What could have happened? She couldn't bear to sit in the huge stone room alone, with the darkness of the garden pressing in on her, with only her anxiety for company. The *Brasserie de L'Eglise* at St Eustache didn't close until midnight. She forced herself to picture him at the bar, the life and soul of the party, oblivious to the hurt he was distributing. Feeling cold, despite the muggy weather, she got into bed without undressing. She held Serge's pillow to her face, smelling the scent of his perfume. She had giggled the first time she had heard him call it that. Englishmen would never affect such an effeminate term, but technically his *was* perfume and not after-shave. She lay listening to the sounds of the night, praying that his Mini would turn the corner from the village. Eventually, she fell asleep, aware of the empty space next to her.

She woke early to an impressive volume of birdsong punctuated by the crowing of cockerels. In the distance, she could hear geese cackling for their breakfast. There had been no telephone call. If there was bad news she would have received it by now she thought. He must have got carried away with the drink and stayed at the barracks.

'Please let him be safe!' she whispered aloud. She got up feeling more tired than she had when she'd gone to bed. Her head ached and her limbs felt empty and dead. She switched on the kettle, and glanced at the answering machine; the light was still lifeless. It was seven o'clock. She resisted the temptation to dial Delphine's number. She would not take kindly to being rung up so early.

Suddenly the phone let out a long trill.

Diana pounced on the handset. '*Allô!*' she said urgently.

'Darling, is everything OK?'

Not now, she thought. It was her mother's voice that came over the airways, shrill and domineering. 'Hello, Mother. Yes, I'm fine.'

'Are you *sure* you're alright? You sound ill.'

'No, I'm not ill. It's just.., a little early.'

Her mother was always up at the crack of dawn to walk the dogs and had never had any consideration for other people's timetables.

'But you're an hour ahead, it must be at least seven over there,' her tone was indignant.

'Yes, it is. Not to worry, I was awake anyway. Look, can I ring you back? I think I can hear Ben,' she lied.

'Where's Serge? Can't he see to him?' Clarissa Hunter, having survived a traditionalist marriage that had ended in a sticky divorce, was now a firm advocate of the 'modern man.'

'He's at work.' Diana didn't like lying to her mother, but she had made it clear on more than one occasion, that she did not approve, of either Serge's station, nor his macho beliefs.

There was a pause on the end of the line, 'How's the new house?'

'It's great. Listen, Mummy I really must go – I'll call you.' She felt bad for cutting her short.

She lingered for a moment over the telephone, but it remained silent. She took a cup of tea out to the garden to soak up the early morning rays, in an attempt to lift her spirits. Through the bars of the iron gate, she glimpsed the roof of a red vehicle parked in front of the church. Abandoning her tea on the terrace, she ran towards it. It was Serge's Mini. She pulled open the gate and rushed over. She stopped, the windows were steamed up. She peered through the fug. Serge was slumped over the steering wheel. She gasped, but when reason came to her, she realised that it was his breath that was steaming up the windows. She rapped sharply on the windscreen. His head jolted up and lolled back on to the headrest, his eyes flickered and then fell motionless once more. He wasn't dead, just stone drunk.

She pulled open the door, but he didn't stir. He was snoring loudly, his lips vibrating with every exhalation. His shirt was unbuttoned, his hair dishevelled and he stank. She couldn't believe that this grotesque man, in this alcohol laced car, and her beloved husband, were one and the same. Her relief began to turn to revulsion, and then anger. What if their new neighbours had made the same discovery as her? It was early and she hoped there was no reason for anyone to wander down this lane at such an hour. She had no idea how long he'd been there. Not wanting to touch him, she rapped once again on the windscreen, wincing as her knuckles hit the glass with force.

His eyes flashed open with a start. He struggled to focus. 'Diana!' He wiped a string of dribble from his pale grey chin. 'You locked me out.'

'The back door was open!' Anger and indignity were welling to the surface.

'I banged on the windows but you didn't come.' His voice was higher now, desperate, childlike.

She took his hand and heaved him to his feet. 'I was expecting you around seven,' she spat out the last word.

'I'm sorry, but the others kept buying me drinks, and it would have been rude to leave.' He was looking up at her with doe eyes, and an attempt at boyish innocence which only exacerbated her irritation.

'Get yourself cleaned up!' she ordered with contempt, and marched back into the house, aware of him ambling slowly behind, like an injured animal. She closed the French windows behind her, forcing him to walk all the way round to the back terrace door. She went straight into the kitchen where she was fairly certain he wouldn't follow. She could feel herself shaking and she didn't trust her voice, she wanted to be alone. The bedroom door creaked, he must have gone straight to bed. At least he knew what was good for him this time.

# SEVEN

## Hélène

At eleven o'clock, dressed in her uniform, her hands scrubbed and her long dark hair carefully scraped back into a bun, she went downstairs and into the hall. A door next to the doctor's consulting room was marked *Salle d'Attente*, and from within she could hear the buzz of chatter. She pushed open the door opposite and found, as the doctor had said, that it was the kitchen.

At the sink, stood a woman in a floral apron, her arms up to the elbows in suds, 'Aah, *Mademoiselle* Godard, you did not come down for your breakfast?' Her voice was high-pitched and fussing. 'I would have brought it up, but I did not want to disturb you.' She smiled broadly as she swept the suds from her arms and dried her hands on her apron. 'I shall warm the coffee for you. Please, sit down.'

'Thank you. Err, you must be *Madame* Clément?'

'Oh, oh – *Madame, Madame*! *Non, non*, everyone in this house calls me Cécile.'

'Then you must call me Hélène.'

'Oh, no I could not!' She stared at her in horror.

'I'm sorry, I did not mean to offend.'

Her face didn't change for a moment, then it softened, and returned to its former smile. 'I expect the ways are different in Paris, but here in the country, we are old fashioned. I shall call you *Mademoiselle,* and you shall call me Cécile.' She looked at her expectantly.

'Of course, if that is what you would like.'

'*Bon!* So, please sit down and eat up.'

She sat down obediently. In front of her on a plate, was a croissant. She had not seen one for so long she had to hold herself back whilst Cécile was hovering.

'I bet you didn't see any of those in Paris?' she beamed proudly.

'No, no. It has been a while,' she replied truthfully but uncertain if this would have been normal or not.

'The *Docteur* is very lucky; he is often paid in food. This week, the baker's wife has been very poorly.'

The door was pushed open and the *Docteur* put his head round it. 'Aah, excellent! I see you have met *Madame* Clément.'

46

'Oh, you! Cécile! I have told *Mademoiselle* that everyone calls me Cécile! Now she will not believe me. I will go and lay the fireplace in the dining room and leave you to your talking, talking, talking…' Her voice trailed away as she disappeared through the door.

'*Madame* Clément, she is a good sort. She keeps our spirits up. Lord knows how she stays so positive, her situation is worse than most. Now we must get down to business. This afternoon I will take you to the Meffret farm in Saint Gabriel. Old *Monsieur* Meffret has tuberculosis he does not have very long. I have been visiting him every day, as I have had no nurse to assist me. It will be one of your tasks to deliver his medication and make him comfortable. There is also a new baby to be weighed and checked and *Madame* Camaret needs a dressing changed daily; she was bitten by a dog and it has got infected. Normally, these visits will be done in the morning. In the afternoon, I would like you to hold the fort here, as I have an appointment. I am afraid you will be very busy to begin with – people are curious and would like to see the new nurse that has come amongst them.'

The farm was just at the entrance to Saint Gabriel. So this was the village she had avoided, on her walk with Rémy, to reach the *Route de Beaugency*. The forest must be on the other side of it. The weather had turned for the worse and rain and wind lashed at the dark brown fields, the lolling, shrivelled heads of the sunflowers stood dripping in the fields.

The doctor pulled up a bumpy, muddy drive to a collection of dank, grey farm buildings. Chickens cowered, huddled together under the shelter of the guttering, their heads set back into their bodies. The doctor let himself into the farmhouse calling out as he went, 'Monsieur Meffret. It is *Docteur* Legris.'

They stepped into the kitchen. The floor was of terracotta tiles. A large table stood in the middle of the room, and in the corner, next to a range, was a bed piled high with knitted blankets. Just visible at the other end of it, was the face of a wizened old man, his head motionless on a bolster and his eyes closed.

The doctor approached the bed and sat on a chair next to it. He lowered his voice and said softly, '*Monsieur* Meffret?'

The old man's eyes opened and he immediately convulsed into a painful cough.

The doctor held a bowl to his chin to catch the blood stained sputum that issued forth. 'This is Hélène Godard. She is my new nurse.'

The old man's eyes flickered towards her and his face brightened a little. '*Mademoiselle*,' he whispered hoarsely.

She approached the bed and took his hand from beneath the covers and rubbed it gently. '*Enchanté monsieur*. I will be looking after you now.'

'Where is Antoine, *Monsieur* Meffret?' the doctor asked as he opened his case and took out a syringe and a bulb of morphine.

The old man gestured his head painfully towards the window. Through the rain drenched pane, Hélène looked out on a large expanse of ploughed field.

The doctor drew up the morphine into the syringe. 'He won't be ploughing in this weather.'

The old man looked at the doctor. 'It is raining?' he whispered.

'It's been coming down since lunchtime. Hasn't it Hélène?'

'Oh, yes, but you're safely wrapped up in here *Monsieur*.'

The doctor pulled back the bedclothes and slid the sleeve of the old man's night-gown up and injected his arm with the morphine. The man barely flinched.

She was reminded of the patients in their final days in Saint Malo. It was as if they'd given up. They barely spoke nor moved. The old man's legs beneath the bedclothes were as thin as bamboo canes but she could see he was a tall man. The weight loss seemed to be what finished them off in the end, with no strength to fight the disease.

Just as the doctor was packing his bag, a young man with *Monsieur* Meffret's eyes stepped into the kitchen in stockinged feet.

'Aah, *Docteur* Legris.' The young man stepped forward holding out his hand to shake the doctor's. 'I saw you arrive. Oh and *Mademoiselle*. You must be the new nurse everyone is talking about.'

'Hélène Godard.'

He shook her hand; the calluses were like rough stone against her skin. The young man turned to his father, '*Papa*, I am back!'

The old man's eyes only flickered in recognition. The morphine was sending him into blissful oblivion.

'*Docteur*, can we talk a moment?' He stepped out to the hall gesturing for them to follow. 'He is worse, much, much worse. It is no good for him spending so long on his own here; I want to look after him but with the farm… the onion sets need to go in as soon as this wet weather has stopped … and…'

'Antoine, of course. He would be much better off in a sanatorium. I will look into it but I can't promise anything. Hélène will let you know.'

The young man nodded. 'Thank you *Docteur.*'

'Now, as soon as the rain stops, open the window, he needs as much fresh air as possible. We must get on; we have little Marc to visit next. *Mademoiselle* Godard will visit tomorrow.'

'*Au revoir, Mademoiselle.*'

Dr Legris swung the car out of the courtyard.

'Antoine has not been sent to work in Germany like the others?'

'No, with his father ill and the farm to run he has special dispensation. He is one of the lucky ones, though he doesn't know it.'

'Surely he doesn't want to work for the Germans?'

'No, but he would like to join the cause.' He looked over at her. 'Perhaps with your help, he could ...'

She said nothing. Did he know what her role was? She couldn't risk such a slip up. She pretended she hadn't heard and looked out of the window.

'Here we are.' Dr. Legris pulled up outside a long low farmhouse, that was sat right on the edge of the road leading into the village of Saint Gabriel. '*Madame* Camaret has just had a baby boy; little Marc. He was born just a week ago. All very straight forward but she was bitten by a dog a few weeks before and it has not healed well. Her dressing will need changing every day. She really needs to keep off it but this is her third and her husband Georges is a very busy farmer.'

The doctor knocked on the wooden door and pushed it open. 'Agnès, *c'est le docteur*!'

They stepped into a warm kitchen. A large pine table stood in the centre. A small boy and a toddler were sat on a blanket playing with wooden blocks. To one side, was a range cooker piled high with folded laundry.

*Madame* Camaret appeared through the back door, a baby slung across her in a scarf. She was a pretty woman with curly blonde hair neatly coiffed. She wore a gingham dress that showed a handsome figure for someone who had recently given birth. She looked about the same age as Hélène. 'Ah! *Docteur,* I didn't hear you.' She stopped and smiled warmly at Hélène.

'This is *Mademoiselle* Godard, our new nurse.'

'Please, call me Hélène.'

'And you must call me Agnès.' She beamed at her.

'Now let's look at this leg.'

'This silly leg. It will heal in time.'

'Only if you keep off it.' The doctor waved his finger at her.

She carefully supported the baby while she untied the scarf and settled him in the crook of her arm. She sat down and raised her leg on to a kitchen chair.

'*Mademoiselle,* I shall let you take over.'

# EIGHT

**Diana**

Diana's anger had subsided. Serge emerged from the bedroom, his face had returned to its healthier bronzed hue. He'd pulled on a pair of faded jeans and flung a tee shirt over his shoulder. She wondered if he had done it on purpose. She'd always found his torso irresistible, his training at work meant that he was always in tip top condition. He was the only man she had ever known who could look this good in scruffy old clothes.

'I'm sorry, *chérie*. I got carried away last night. I could have stayed at the barracks, but I wanted to be home with you so I caught the last train. Then, when I got back all the doors were locked and I couldn't even find an open window. I must have been tired and didn't think of the back door.'

'Huh! Tired! Did you not think that the police may stop you? Driving in that state is just downright irresponsible.'

'They're never around on a Monday night. Besides it's always in the paper when there's a road-block planned.'

She raised her eyebrows in despair; drink-driving was still part of everyday life out here in the sticks.

'I promise, Diana. It won't happen again. You must believe me. Things will be different from now on.' He pulled her over to him and held her close.

She remained unreceptive for as long as she could, only giving in when she could no longer resist. 'I was so worried about you.' She could hear herself whining.

'I know. I'm sorry. I really am.'

Outside there was a clunk. Through the window Diana could see a truck. A man was struggling with the latch on the gate.

'They're early,' grinned Serge.

'Who's early?'

'My surprise! Come on little one.' He scooped Ben up on to his bare shoulders and headed out the front to undo the gate.

'Tractor, Tractor!' yelled Ben.

'No that's a truck,' Diana corrected him.

'Tractor! Tractor!' Ben insisted.

The man had driven the truck into the courtyard and was opening up the back to reveal a shiny, red ride-on mower.

'Serge, when did you order this?'

'Yesterday, as soon as I knew I'd passed. We're not going to be able to manage a property this size without one.' He was beaming with pleasure.

The man guided it carefully down the ramp.

Serge lifted Ben into the driving seat and he immediately began to make raspberry engine noises and jiggle the wheel.

'*Monsieur* Plessis.' The man held out his hand.

Diana shook it. '*Monsieur*,'

'It's got a full tank of petrol so you can get straight to work.' With a chuckle he got back into the truck and turned it around and was gone.

Ben's face was alight with sheer excitement as he sat on his father's lap, while Serge steered the mower round the trees and bushes in neat swathes. It took most of the day to mow the long meadow grasses to a smooth undulating green. The *Champ de Foire* was transformed from a forgotten nature reserve, to a stone villa amidst sweeping lawns. Evening was falling and the sweet smell of freshly cut grass intoxicated Diana's senses, her annoyance seemed a thing of a far away land. Their new beginning had started at last, she felt sure this time.

Serge had lifted the blades and was swerving round the trees, ducking and diving to avoid the lower branches, and playfully flashing the mower headlights at Diana. He was laughing. Ben was holding on to his father as if his life depended on it, his features frozen into a tight grin some way between amusement and fear.

The bonfire was piled high with cardboard. Serge put a match to it, and stood holding his son as the flames licked up into the sky, barely visible against the bright sunshine. As the fire burnt lower, the sun sank with it, disappearing behind the barn. Beyond, the forest stood motionless, dark green, almost black in the failing light.

Serge and Diana pulled each other close, breathing in the delicious country smell of bonfire smoke, heavily falling dew and newly mown grass.

'*Maman*! *Papa*! Look at me!' Ben was rolling down the sloping lawn - it could be called that now. They watched his little body roll down the slope, his blond curls picking up the long grass cuttings, giving him the appearance of a small green elf.

Diana held her breath, waiting for Serge to remonstrate. But when no chiding came she let it out again gratefully.

The good weather continued unbroken for Serge's entire three weeks of leave. He became more relaxed than she had ever seen him. The restlessness he used to feel, cooped up in the tiny Parisian apartment, appeared to have been banished for good. They worked side by side on the house and garden.

Diana dug her long dreamed of vegetable patch and put in her first seeds. They bought a slide and a paddling pool for Ben, which kept him entertained all the time he wasn't sleeping, or digging or attempting unsuccessfully to climb trees. Serge found an old table in the barn which he sanded down and set up on the back terrace to catch the evening sun. They breakfasted in the garden, lunched in the garden, and dined in the garden. The sun shone day after day, turning their skin to burnt sienna and their hair flaxen. They dug and weeded, unpacked the last of the boxes, painted, swept and scrubbed.

Serge had managed to exploit the locals' curiosity into unlimited help for lopping branches and felling trees. Their most frequent visitors were Marcel, who had helped Diana that first day in the village, and his elder brother, Pierrot. They lived with their mother and sister in one of the little cottages with the geometric vegetable gardens on the lane approaching the *Champ de Foire*. Marcel, was in his late twenties; a gentle man who paused thoughtfully before he spoke. His head was covered in auburn corkscrew curls which hung rebelliously around his acne scarred face.

Pierrot, must have been at least ten years his senior and spoke slowly, and unlike his brother, with a strong local accent; rolling his 'r's like an Italian. He rummaged nervously in the pockets of his moss-stained parka when his audience's attention was detained elsewhere. They had both lived in the village all their lives. As they were the sole breadwinners for their mother and sister, not even the normally obligatory military service had whisked them away to new horizons. They had instead, been issued with Certificates of Exemption, and had been left to follow their sleepy rural existences unexposed to the changes of modern life. They both worked in a vegetable packaging factory on the *Route d'Orléans*. They were not work-shy and every year they bought a square of trees in the forest which they would fell and saw up into firewood to sell to the villagers for their winter heating.

Serge secured a delivery of ten cubic metres of oak logs at a knock down price, from them. They helped Serge and Diana to pile the logs into a high even pile against the inside wall of the barn.

Diana showed Ben how to count the rings on the log ends to find out the age of the tree they had come from. He ran his tiny fingers along the grains. 'One, two …, sixteen,' he counted so solemnly, Diana couldn't help giggling.

As was the custom, any help must be rewarded, and Serge set some glasses on the table on the sun-drenched terrace and opened a new bottle of pastis.

Marcel took a swig of the jade nectar and let out a satisfied sigh. 'This weather's going to be a problem. There'll be a hosepipe ban before long.'

The men nodded.

'You'll be alright though; you've got your own well.'

'A well! Have we Serge?'

Serge shrugged his shoulders. 'I didn't know we had.'

'Yes, it's right underneath the house. There used to be lots of problems years ago with it, flooding onto the yard.'

Pierrot nodded. 'Ooh yes, I remember, it was often flooded particularly towards the bottom. That's the lowest point in the village you see. Did you not know? Come on we'll show you where it is.'

Marcel and Pierrot led them out into the courtyard and opened the door to the boiler room. Inside, he opened another door to a windowless room where Diana had been storing the packing cases. They pulled them out the way and at the end of the cool, dark passageway was an opening above a low wall, like an alcove.

'It's in there,' Marcel gestured theatrically, clearly pleased with this revelation.

Serge shone a torch and lit up a shaft of water that shone fluorescent blue and green like a grotto.

'You see, you'll have water for nothing.' Marcel was enjoying himself.

'You want to get a pump set up in here,' said Pierrot.

Serge ducked out of the passageway and reappeared with a bucket and a length of rope. He tied it to the handle and threw it to the bottom of the shaft. There was quite a delay before they heard it hit the water. As he pulled it up, it scraped the wall. 'I think I've scraped up a load of mud with it.'

Pierrot nodded. 'Yes, that's what happens when they're not used, they get silted up. You'll need to clean it out.'

Serge heaved the bucket to the top and sure enough it was half full of mud.

'You want to try it again in the morning before the farmers have emptied the water table.' Pierrot took the bucket from him and went to tip it in the courtyard. '*Mon dieu*, this is heavy.'

Serge switched off his torch and they stepped back outside into the sunlight.

Pierrot upended the bucket and the sludge slid onto the courtyard. A curved, solid shape slid with it. Pierrot caught it before it hit the concrete. 'What's this?' He wiped the mud from it.

'It's a pot!' said Diana excitedly.

'It is! It's an old pot!' exclaimed Marcel. 'Is there anything in it?'

'It looks full of mud to me.' Pierrot was peering into it.

'Don't empty it! I was watching one of those archaeology programmes the other day, it's best to leave it to the professionals,' said Serge.

'Do you think this is old enough for that?' asked Diana.

'Could be,' said Pierrot solemnly. 'They say this well was here long before the house was built and that it is at least two hundred years old. It could be really, really old.'

'Where should we take it to get it checked?'

'I'll take it over to old Raymond. He wrote the local history of Saint Gabriel, you know.' Marcel was clearly impressed with this. 'And I will try and sort you out a pump.'

The two men almost scampered out through the gate in their eagerness to tell the rest of the village.

It wasn't long before Marcel and Pierrot brought news that old Raymond was taking the pot to the museum in Blois for dating and they would have to wait a little for any results.

And so, the summer continued with feasting and prolonged aperitifs. Diana was in her element making pastry, preparing salads, whisking up sauces and dressings to be tried and tested on the ever eager taste buds of their new friends and neighbours. The kitchen, although entirely inadequate, was remarkably larger than the one in *Boulevard Raspail* and she managed to churn out an impressive array of dishes that she gleaned from her copy of *Larousse de la Cuisine*. The book had been a present from Serge's mother. Diana suspected that she had been worried for her son's nutrition at the hands of a woman, from a country ill renowned for its culinary delights. This assumption that the British ate badly only fuelled her into educating the locals in the delicacies of English cuisine.

Marcel and Pierrot took them to the café where Diana got to know Jeanette a little better. A divorcee, she lived with her teenage children; Frédeau and Séverine. She had only been in Saint Gabriel for two years, and was as such, deemed a newcomer by the villagers.

It became a habit to visit the café for an early evening drink. It was apparent that this was where all-important, and not so important, village business was thrashed out in intricate detail. Every incident, no matter how trivial was mentioned here. From old *Madame* Carignon forgetting to close her shutters to Fabrice Sanchez's son being arrested for shoplifting in Beaugency.

Diana had herself grown up in a small village in Gloucestershire, but as she had been sent away to boarding school, she had never before witnessed such an obsessive interest in other people's affairs. She was downcast to discover that Serge's sleeping in the car incident had not gone unnoticed in the village, but had been put down to a lovers' tiff. According to Jeanette this showed that Diana had a healthy control of her household and was therefore a person to be revered. Unsure of the accuracy of this diagnosis, Diana began to take more care with the way she did things, nervous that any ambiguity may be misconstrued. She even went to the lengths of hanging her more daring items of underwear on the clothes horse in the bathroom rather than hang them on the washing line, in full view of the village.

# NINE

## Edward

Holly and oak, ivy and blackthorn, and it was still only winter. Edward scanned the forest around him, little vegetation was in leaf and every bare twig and trunk glittered with tiny ice crystals in the failing light. There was ivy that climbed the trunks of the great oaks that towered above his head, and alehoof crawled on the forest floor.

He quickly jumped back down into the cavern; since Clothilde had left he had been careful to feed the fire with wood. He would be too ashamed to face her if he let it die down. She would surely be with him in a little. The sun had risen to its winter highest, where it hung just above the treetops it would not be long before it would be sinking fast and Clothilde would return. He felt in his cloak and pulled out the heel of cheese, she had left him. Hunger had become a familiar companion in this frozen faraway land. Maybe she would again lay her hand on him. The thought sent a warm comfortable wave through his body. Would his mother's touch have felt like Clothilde's had she lived? Warm, enveloping, like the familiar feel of an old habit worn to holes just before the moment when it falls to pieces and must be abandoned.

The way of the world can be so desolate, so desperate. Yes, wretched, but all of our doing. Our wretchedness is of our own production. For man, however devout, however pious, will remain man; a mere servant who must dance and parry, though balance and judge to carry out God's work. He scolded himself. If he had been more observant, more alert, he would not have directed those brutes to his Grace. Just one more season, and he would have taken the habit for eternity. Eldric had great plans for him. He talked about them often as they worked in the garden gathering herbs. He said he wanted to teach him everything he knew, so that he in turn could heal the sick and care for the infirm. Instead, Edward had become the infirm. He had mutated from a young apprentice of the habit to take the place of those poor mites who roamed the countryside with little to eat.

A crack of twigs above frightened him into lying down suddenly, instinctively flattening himself against the cavern wall.

'Edward. It is I, Clothilde.'

His body relaxed.

She jumped down into the cavern. 'I have brought you some parchment and a quill. I took them from Firmin's things so as soon as he notices it missing, I must return them.'

Edward took the scroll from her and a well worn quill pen. He ran his finger over the nib. 'I can make him a new quill with a good strong feather. I suppose you have no ink?'

'I found a small pot with his things but I fear it may be dried up. Perhaps if you add some water?'

Edward looked into the powdery sediment that had set at the bottom of the pot. It looked quite thick. He was sure he could eke out enough to cover the scroll she had brought.

'This is perfect.'

'I managed to take some more bread too. I could have brought some vegetables but my brother was tending the store and I would not have been able to take them discreetly.'

'The bread is good, I thank you.' He tore into the rough loaf ravenously.

'I am sorry for the bugloss. Without going to Saint Léonard I don't know how I can get some.'

'It is no matter. The wound is healing properly. I am sorry, I think I am not a good patient, I am asking you many favours.'

She shrugged. 'If you are a patient it means that you are not good. *Père* Barthèlemy always says that bad things happen to us for a reason; though when we are better we will be good again. It means that God has forgiven us.' Her eyes flashed as if remembering something and she ran her fingers over the red fistulas on her face.

'I saw some alehoof in the forest.'

'Alehoof? You use strange words.'

'Ivy, it is the ivy that crawls along the ground.'

'You left the cavern?' she said aghast.

'Not entirely, I only sat on the edge of the entrance.'

'You must be careful, Edward. When you understand the sounds of the forest better, you will be able to leave the cavern but with the snow settled all around and the leaves fallen they will see you easily. Wait until the forest is in leaf again.'

Edward nodded obediently. 'Then will you gather some of the creeping ivy for me and bring it to me?'

She stopped and looked through the opening, and listened to the sounds of the woods. Then she vaulted agilely out into the forest and returned almost instantly with a handful of alehoof. 'It is a little spoilt by the cold I fear.'

'Everything is better when it has been warmed by the spring sunshine but it is all we have.'

'For what do you need it?'

'You will see. You have a church?'

'Of course, we are not heretics! It stands in the centre of the village by the *Champ de Foire.*'

'Are there any green statues within the church?'

She thought for a moment. 'Well, yes. There is a statue of the virgin saint at the foot of the aisle.'

'If you go there, and scrape off some of the green coating and wrap it carefully in a leaf and bring it to me. It is very fragile fine powder so you will need to take great care not to lose it.'

'I will have to choose my moment. *Père* Barthélemy will not take kindly to me if he sees me touching the statues. I will see if I can do it.' She was frowning again.

'Clothilde, you are very good to me.'

She touched his hand and smiled. A shiver coursed up the nape of his neck despite the warmth of the fire.

'Clothilde, tell me about your family. It will pass the time.'

'There are six of us. My mother and Firmin; he is the eldest. Then there's me and my two younger sisters and Séverin my little brother.'

'And your father?'

'He has been gone for all of my life. He left with the *Seigneur* to fight in the holy wars far away. We trust that one day he will be returned to us. Firmin remembers him a little. He says he is strong and brave and kind. But I was born after he left.'

'But your sisters and brother?'

'Ah. They are not of our blood – my mother took them in when they were orphaned.'

Edward sat and listened to her until it was again time for her to return to her village and her home. When she had departed he sat close to the fire and rhythmically stroked the surface of the parchment, enjoying its smooth, thick texture and its comforting odour whilst he mused on the lives of Clothilde's brothers and sisters

At last Edward awoke with no aching in his bones. A crust was forming over the wound on his head and he could feel it thickening.

59

He stretched his legs out and could feel their energy returned. The fire was only smouldering now but he was sure he could renew it to its fervour of the eventide before. He noticed that his fingers were not as chilled as they had been during the past days. He peered through the opening. It must have been well past Matins, Lauds and Prime for the dawn was past and the steely winter grey had given way to blue and sunshine. The trees were dripping, as the snow and ice melted from their bare branches. Tiny bursts of watery stars flashed and died as the sunlight caught the droplets plummeting to the forest floor. There was no sound other than the distant barking of dogs from the village. There were no beating hooves, nor hunting horns reverberating in the distance. Edward hurriedly sank to his knees and began to pray.

When his prayers were done he took up the quill and examined the well worn nib. Firmin must have worked very hard to wear it down so far. Edward took out his knife and carefully began to work at it to restore it to a perfect shape. He moistened the sediment in the pot with a little water and though, not perfect, it made a mark on the parchment and that was all he required. Edward crouched on the floor of the cavern with the sunshine streaming through the opening and began carefully forming the letters of the herbs and their uses.

He must have been engrossed for it seemed like only a short while later that Clothilde leapt down into the cavern making him jump.

'Here, I managed to get some of that coating from the statue. *Père* Barthélemy had gone to see a dying man, so it was easy.' She produced a small wrap of cloth.

Edward took one of the smaller hearthstones and with the handle of his knife he began to pound the alehoof, bruising the leaves until they had turned a dark green and their juice glistened on the surface.

'What are you making?'

'You will see. Pass me that cauldron, for the remedy must be heated.' He emptied the crushed alehoof into the pot and carefully sprinkled the verdigris over the top. He added a little water from the earthenware jug and set the cauldron over the fire to boil.

Clothilde expertly stoked the fire and added more wood. The young monk and the waif sat side by side and watched the flames leap and duck beneath the pan. So intent on their activity were they that neither spoke, nor did they glance at each other, they simply remained in each others' presence, joined in a common task, though one was not confident of its success and the other ignorant of its purpose. At last the mixture began to bubble and spit.

Edward removed the cauldron and set it carefully on the earthen floor. He let it cool a little before adding two spoonfuls of honey. He swirled it with the tip of his knife, until the mixture became smooth and unctuous. 'I will need a jar in which to store this, but first you must take some of the ointment and apply it to the fistulas on your face.'

Clothilde looked at him a little shocked. 'But ivy is poisonous.'

'Only if you drink it. You must be careful to wash your hands and to apply it away from your mouth.'

'You are kind to give so much thought to heal these fistulas but I have had them for many years, no one has been able to rid me of them. Not even *Père* Barthèlemy with his prayers, or the wise woman of Saint Léonard.' Her face became still like a statue as if she were about to weep.

'Clothilde, you have helped me with no understanding of the danger you have put yourself in. If you do not let me repay your kindness I will be more damned than at that moment when I was tipped from the cart into these woods. This ointment will chase the heat that is troubling your skin.'

She looked up at him, her pupils darting left and right as she considered his words.

'Trust me, Clothilde. Let me try. Let me repay you for your care and attention.'

61

# TEN

## Diana

After visiting the café on a handful of occasions, Diana became struck by the lack of female customers. She realised that she was the only woman to grace the establishment with her presence, other than Jeannette of course. Since living in France she had been careful to honour the silent rule for women to drink alcohol in discreet quantities, but here it didn't seem to matter whether she ordered a coffee, a coke or a pint of Drambuie. Just stepping over the doorstep of *La Petite Folie* seemed to be enough to raise the eyebrows of the men at the bar.

When she'd asked Serge about it, he had replied irritably,

'Don't be so paranoid, it's not a problem.' In Paris she had regularly met up with her friends in cafés and bars. When she'd questioned Jeanette about it, she'd shrugged her shoulders and said,

'The women don't approve of the café.'

'Why not?'

'Jealousy.'

Diana didn't understand.

'I'm divorced Diana. I've been running this place single-handedly for two years. When I first arrived, the business nearly went under. Some things round here haven't changed for hundreds of years. A woman on her own with children is hard enough for them to accept; but one who runs the local café is pushing their tolerance one step too far. They do not think it a respectable job for a woman alone. I paid a fair price for the business, but as soon as I opened the doors the figures dipped. The only customers I had were Marcel and Pierrot.'

'Surely they couldn't stop their husbands coming. It's the only one for kilometres.'

'That's *exactly* what they did.'

'So, how did you get everyone to come back?'

'I ran special promotions on beer and pastis, but that didn't work. It was time that did it in the end. The men got fed up with having to drive to Jaunay. They came trickling back one by one and now, their wives just put up with the fact that I run this place and their men drink here.'

'Surely you've made *some* friends here.'

She shook her head. 'The men come here to get away from their wives and to chat with their neighbours. The women are sure I know things about their husbands that they don't. If only they knew what they were missing.' She rolled her eyes. 'I barely listen to their conversations. They talk about who shot a few too many rabbits for their hunting quota, the price of firewood, the weather and of course the great Saint Gabriel pastime – gossip. The men are worse than the women. Believe me!'

'What must they think of me?' Diana's voice dropped.

'Don't worry about it, Diana. You'll get used to it, nothing anyone does in this village goes unnoticed and after a while you stop caring. I'm very pleased you're here. It makes a change to have a proper conversation.'

Diana smiled, glad of her openness.

Adjoining the café was a smaller room with a separate front door onto the street; it was from here that Jeanette ran a little *épicerie* which sold basic groceries and baguettes. The bread was delivered from the baker's in Beaugency, ten kilometres away. The villagers were obliged to swallow their disapproval and rely on her for their daily baguette or *pain de deux*. The only time Diana came into contact with the village women was when she went to collect her bread or visited the post office in Jaunay. They either passed her by without so much as a glance, or if they felt cornered they would eke out a purely courteous nod or a weak, '*Bonjour M'dame.*' In Paris, it had taken her a couple of months to perfect the Parisian knack of *never* catching a stranger's eye, as if it were a fate worse than death to do so, and took any acknowledgement of her presence as a bonus.

The end of Serge's leave was approaching. The *Champ de Foire* no longer resembled a damp collection of farm buildings, but a cosy well-kept country farmhouse. Her pending solitude loomed on her weightily. They had worked together on the house, breaking from their tasks to sip a drink in the sunshine or to admire one another's work of clearing or painting. They had grown a little closer each day. Now, further adaptation was required and Diana felt herself fearing it.

On the last day of his leave, they lay in bed. Sunlight flooded the bedroom. Serge's bronzed chest was laid bare on the white cotton sheets like a statue of Adonis. His eyes were closed but Diana sensed he was only dozing.

'What shall we do today?' she whispered, stroking his neck.

He opened his eyes slowly and then startling her he leapt on top of her, pinning her down. His face was alight with excitement and he was smiling. 'Today…' he began slowly 'We are going on a mystery tour.' He kissed her neck playfully.

She kissed him back.

'Come on, lazy.' He clambered off her and stood naked in front of the window. He threw a bathrobe at her. 'It's a bit of a trek and we mustn't be late.'

'Where are we going?'

'Now, if I was to tell you *that* it wouldn't be a mystery would it?' he teased.

She obediently showered, dressed and breakfasted. She got Ben ready as quickly as she could; the suspense was agonising.

They climbed into the Mini and headed out of the village. The sunshine gave the fields a luminous glow. One field in particular appeared to be shining pink. It stretched from the edge of the village to the Jaunay road. Diana looked more closely; they were poppies. She'd never seen pink ones before. They crossed the arched grey bridge that spanned the river Loire at Beaugency and were soon on the narrow green lanes heading towards La Sologne. They crossed little villages of houses, striped black and white with timbering. Boxes of scarlet geraniums trailed under the windows giving them a Tyrolean feel. The roads plunged into huge forests of American oaks, their trunks parting every now and then to reveal expanses of lily pads suspended motionless on the surface of large green ponds.

Serge took every opportunity to squeeze Diana's hand or brush her leg in between changing gear. She leant back against the headrest and glimpsed the numerous families of coots and moorhens, paddling and diving into the ponds as they sped onward, deeper into the forest. Just past a sign indicating the boundary of Lamotte Beuvron, Serge pulled off the road into a car park surrounded by towering oaks.

'Where are we?'

'Lamotte Beuvron,' he was grinning cheekily. He took Ben, who had fallen asleep, into his arms and held him close until he awoke. A pang of desperate, ecstatic adoration tugged through her body as she watched his tenderness with their baby boy. Serge led her down a path through thickets of flowering brambles, in companionable silence, until they reached a lake with a wooden jetty that stretched half-way across it.

64

Ben yelled to be put down and charged full pelt for the water's edge.

Diana headed him off just before he reached the shore, holding his struggling arms as he tried to paddle his feet in the green water.

'Wait here a minute, I won't be long.' Diana watched Serge go over to the far side of the lake where a wooden lodge stood shrouded in trees. She could see him knocking on the door. The door opened and he disappeared inside. Just a minute later he reappeared on the doorstep and waved, gesturing for her to come over.

'House!' said Ben.

'*Monsieur* Boiset, this is my wife, Diana.'

Inside the doorway, was a man dressed from head to toe in green waterproofs, evidently togged up to go fishing.

Diana took his outstretched hand.

'*Bonjour M'dame.*' He smiled mischievously.

'*Monsieur* Boiset is the forestry warden for these woods.'

Diana nodded still waiting patiently for an explanation. A strange noise came from the depths of the lodge, a sort of whimpering.

Ben let go of her hand and ran into the far corner of the wooden walled room, darkened by the tree-shrouded windows.

'Ben!'

'It's OK, they will not bite him,' said the man.

In the gloom Diana could make out a huge wicker basket full of puppies. Ben was stroking them carefully and squeaking with delight as they climbed all over him, their tiny teeth tugging on his jumper and licking his face.

'Oh Serge! Look! They're lovely!'

'*Madame*, please.' The man gestured for her to go over to them.

She felt their silky smooth fur as they rolled on their backs and jumped around excitedly. Their soft white coats were splodged with tiny patches of grey. 'Are they Dalmatians?'

'They're your compatriots,' the warden laughed. 'English Setters.'

Serge came over next to her. He put his arm round her. 'Choose one, my darling.'

'For us?'

Serge had always been dead against keeping animals. He couldn't bear the thought of dog hair and mess in the house. Even keeping a cat had been out of the question. He grinned and nodded his head.

'I didn't think you wanted a dog!'

'Paris wasn't the right place for a dog, but out here you will need some company when I'm away working. I'd feel better if you had a dog to protect you.'

The decision was easy, one of the puppies wouldn't leave Ben alone and as they took a step back to have a good look at them, it followed him, biting at the hem of his trousers. 'I think he's chosen us, rather than the other way around,' laughed Diana.

Ben picked him up, the puppy fitted perfectly in his tiny arms. 'For me?' he asked carefully.

'For you, and for *Maman*,' said Serge, bending down to give the creature a stroke.

*Monsieur* Boiset gave them a cardboard box with newspaper in the bottom and Ben carried him with exceptional care all the way back down the path to the car. The journey home was spent thinking up names for the new family member.

'Oscar', 'Thibaud', 'Jack', Jasper', 'Charlie', 'Snoopy'. They said aloud every name they could think of.

It was Serge who found the right one.

'Léo!' he uttered triumphantly. 'Yes, Léo, that's the one.'

'Yoyo. Yoyo!' chanted Ben.

# ELEVEN

## Hélène

SET UP BOITE AUX LETTRES STOP FOUCAUD TO CONTACT STOP ADVISE IN TWENTY-FOUR HOURS STOP

When she arrived at the Meffret Farm the plough horse was tied up in the yard by the front door. She leant her bicycle against the wall and went inside. The kitchen was bitterly cold. Antoine was sitting at his father's bedside, his head bent. The old man was sleeping. As Antoine raised his head she could see his features were drawn and his eyes tired slits.

'*Bonjour,*' she said as breezily as she could.

'He is slipping fast,' he said quietly.

Hélène rushed to the bedside. 'Let me have a look.' She pulled back the bedclothes. '*Monsieur* Meffret?'

He stirred.

'*Monsieur* Meffret?'

The old man's eyes flickered open for a minute and then they closed again. She listened to his breathing and frowned. His chest didn't seem to be rattling as much as on her last visit, though there was a rasping noise coming from his mouth.

'It is bad, isn't it?'

'I don't understand; his breathing doesn't seem as laboured as in recent weeks.' She felt his forehead; no temperature. His pulse was a little fast but that was normal given his condition. 'Is he eating?'

'Not much, but I am not a good cook. I made him some soup and I must admit even I thought it was disgusting.' He picked up a bowl that looked virtually untouched. 'I tried to feed him last night but he just kept spitting it out.'

'He seems to be stable; I don't think he is in imminent danger. I think he may just be very tired, and that rasping is snoring. I have a little time to spare today. Leave me with him for an hour or so, you go and do what you have to do.'

He nodded gratefully and retreated to the hall to put on his boots.

She looked round the room, there were dishes congealing in the stone sink and the floor was filthy. The range was lit but was only burning half-heartedly. It was clear that Antoine was struggling. She gave the old man his morphine injection; even that didn't seem to rouse him. She decided to get on with cleaning the place up while he slept, she would call the doctor if he didn't wake after that.

She hummed a tune as she worked and before long the floor, though not exactly gleaming, was free from mud and the dishes were stacked neatly on the side; she hadn't wanted to put them away for fear of intruding. Better to let Antoine do it, she would hate him to think she was interfering.

She looked around for something to cook but there was only the pot of soup on the stove. If there were chickens, she thought to herself, then there must be eggs. She put on a pair of old clogs she found in the hall and waded across the muddy yard to an open barn door. There were some hens picking in the wet ground at the entrance. Inside, on one side, she found a row of nesting boxes. She lifted the lid of one and found a beautiful brown egg sitting proud on top of the straw. Then she lifted another and sure enough there was another one. She found four more. Some looked as if they had been there for days. Poor Antoine, he was really struggling. She found some swede in a sack just inside the barn door and a couple of onions. She gathered it all up in her skirt and took them into the kitchen.

She cooked up some scrambled eggs and a swede and onion soup. Just as she was tipping them onto a plate, *Monsieur* Meffret stirred.

She went over to him. '*Monsieur,* it is Hélène. I have some lunch for you.'

He pursed his lips stubbornly.

'Here.' She held some of the egg on a spoon and held it to his lips.

At first he pulled back, then he sniffed. He looked at her directly for the first time and opened his mouth. One spoonful, then another, until it was nearly finished then he lifted an arm for her to stop.

'There, that's better. You will only mend yourself by eating *Monsieur.*'

She heard Antoine come in the front door and throw his boots to the ground. She stood up as he came in the room. 'Antoine.'

'*Madem…*' But he stopped and looked around the room. 'You did all of this.' He sounded a little angry.

'I'm sorry, I wanted to help.'

He said nothing but just stared at her.

'My father! He has eaten?'

She looked down at the plate with the remains of the egg. 'I hope you don't mind. I found them in the barn. He has got so thin.'

'Oh, please. Don't be sorry, I am delighted that you got him to eat something. Look! Look at him. *Papa!*'

She turned to look at *Monsieur* Meffret. Although in pretty much the same position, his face had a little colour and his eyes even sparkled.

'He ate nearly all of it.' She held the plate up for him to see.

'But this is not your job.'

'My job is to care for my patients. He is my patient and no one will stop me caring for him.' She could feel her pitch getting higher and higher.

'I can see you are doing a very good job *Mademoiselle*.' His face broke into a broad, beaming smile. 'If that is what you can do for my father on just your first visit, I cannot imagine how he will be after a week!'

'It is not my doing. He just needs fresh air and food and possibly a little company.' She took him by the elbow and guided him into the hall out of earshot of the old man.

'Antoine, this is of course great news but both his lungs are affected and he is unlikely to recover. All we can do is make him comfortable.'

'I know.' He nodded solemnly. Then his face brightened. 'I do not like good turns to go unrewarded. There must be something I can do for you in exchange?'

This man was made of strong stuff, she thought. Funny, how happiness transforms someone's face. When Antoine smiled any signs of fatigue seemed to dissipate and chase away the years, revealing a boyish demeanour. She looked up at his open features gazing at her expectantly and had an idea.

'There is something.'

'Speak. If I can, I shall do it for you.'

'I rather like chickens; it sort of reminds me of peace time. Would you let me collect the eggs and look after them?'

'That doesn't sound like much of a reward!' he laughed.

'It would be for me, I promise.'

'Very well – but I shall think up something more fitting.'

'That's settled then. Now, I have been here far too long, I must go.' She gathered up her bag, stroked *Monsieur* Meffret's hand and went out into the courtyard.

On her way, she had a peep into the barn. The smell of the straw and earth intermingled was like perfume after the pollution of London. At the far end of the barn was a tall thin window, opening much like the one in the chapel. She could set it up tomorrow, but the spot was perfect. There were no dogs here to raise the alarm, though she would be putting Antoine and his father in danger. But contact was urgent. She could find somewhere else later.

LETTERBOX ST. GABRIEL FERME MEFFRET CHICKEN BARN STOP NESTING BOX NIGHT DELIVERIES ONLY STOP AWAIT CONTACT STOP

She let herself in, but today *Monsieur* Meffret was sitting up, his head propped against the bolster.

He smiled and whispered, '*Mademoiselle.*'

'*Bonjour, Monsieur*. I can see you are feeling a little better.'

He smiled and nodded. He tried to move.

'Stay there, one step at a time. Now let me see, another plate of scrambled egg? Or some of that soup I made yesterday?'

'Egg,' he whispered.

'Egg it is. But first we must give you your morphine.' She opened her bag and took out the syringe.

'*Non, non.*' He waved his arm vehemently. 'Not today, I am alright.'

She put down her bag. 'Well, that is good news! Is there anything I can get you before I see to the chickens?'

The old man pointed to the table and opened his mouth.

'Try not to speak. You want the newspaper?'

He nodded.

She picked up the paper and handed it to him. She emptied his sputum bowl. No blood this time.

She went out to the chicken barn and lifted the lid of the first nesting box. There was still a hen spread out, plumped and warm on the straw. She quickly shut it and lifted the next one. There on top of the straw was a beautiful fresh egg. She picked it up and felt the smooth warmth in her hand. In the next one was another, laid on top of a screwed up scrap of paper. She picked up the egg and smoothed the paper flat on her apron. There were faint lines written in pencil. She held it up to the light at the barn door. It simply said R.V. 3EME 14 FC. Foucaud had managed to make contact. She scanned it several times to memorise it and popped it in her mouth. She sucked it until it dissolved.

As she collected the rest of the eggs, she set it out in her head: Rendezvous. Third day. Sunday, Monday, Tuesday 2pm. Foucaud. She would be just on her way back to Jaunay at that time. She must indicate a rendezvous point with plenty of cover, and a good view of the approach, to check him out on arrival. She scolded herself, Foucaud could be a woman. She didn't yet know the area well enough, other than her drive round with *Docteur* Legris. She would not yet be able to reply. She quickly fed the chickens, went back to the farmhouse and cooked up some more eggs for *Monsieur* Meffret. This time, the old man ate every last mouthful on his plate. He only coughed a little, and then with a peaceful expression he settled back into his pillows to sleep.

Antoine didn't appear before she had to leave. She couldn't help feeling disappointed. Of all the people she had met he was the closest in age, apart from Rémy. She shook herself. She was not here to socialise. She cycled back to the surgery just in time for lunch.

The doctor was sitting at the head of the table pushing at his *remoulade* unenthusiastically. 'Aah, celery and celery – so much celery, who would have thought a war could produce just celery!'

Hélène tittered politely. 'It is very good though, in Paris we were not even lucky enough to have that.'

'No, no. You are right. Moaning will bring nothing to us.'

'It's very beautiful round here.'

'You think so? I find it all a little desolate. The landscape is so open, apart from the forest of course.' He looked up at her. 'You know the forest of Marchenoir on the other side of Saint Gabriel?'

'No, I haven't been there yet,' she lied.

'Oh you must go for a walk, but not after dark mind – it is *Verboten.*' He laughed feebly.

'I thought I might go for a walk around Jaunay this afternoon. Would that be alright, you don't need me till three?',

'Be my guest, though I don't think you'll find much of interest to look at.'

She helped Cécile clear the plates and stack them on the draining board by the sink. She took her coat from the peg in the hallway and set out walking briskly. She was just stepping out of the front gate when she heard a little voice.

'*Mademoiselle!*'

71

She looked to her left, and sitting on the low wall that held the railings was little Miriam. '*Bonjour* Miriam!'

'*Bonjour Mademoiselle*. Where are you going?'

'For a walk – what about you? Shouldn't you be at school?'

'No, *Papa* was called to do some work for the *Boche*.'

'Miriam you must not use that word you will get into a lot of trouble.'

'That's what *Papa* calls them.'

'Don't tell anyone that either. What work does he do for them?'

'I don't know he's not allowed to say. Can I come for a walk with you?'

'If you like, you can show me round.'

She immediately broke into a smile and hopped and skipped along in front of her. 'Where would you like to go?'

'Well, I don't think the village is very big – I think I'd like to see...hmm let me see. Erm Everything!'

'Everything it is then! First we will go past the school.'

Hélène followed her out onto the *Route de Beaugency*. A little way along it, there was a lane on the right. They crossed the road and walked down to the end of it, where there was an old barn with rickety old windows in it. Around it was a playground of beaten earth. Marble circles and hopscotch squares had been scraped in it by small fingers.

'My school.'

'Oh, it doesn't look much like a school.'

'It's not the real one, the *B..*,' she stopped herself. 'The Germans took over the real one - both bits; the boys and the girls. Come.' She ran ahead and pushed open a makeshift gate that looked as if it had been made from scrap wood. She ran up to one of the rickety windows and said, 'Please will you lift me up?'

Hélène was surprised at how little she weighed. The war had clearly kept people on minimum food rations, even here in the country, except for the landlady at the café of course.

'There, that's where I sit,' Miriam pointed into a sea of small wooden chairs in a classroom. Claude sits behind me. You know, the boy you met on your first day?'

She nodded.

'I like having school with the boys. Their games are much better.' Miriam gestured to be put down, and they carried on up the lane a little way. Just behind it, on the edge of a neighbouring field, there was a shed. The roof was made of tin and the walls of stone. The pointing was missing in places leaving little peepholes between the stone blocks. A large, wide hedge surrounded the field. 'This is the woodshed. We play here sometimes.'

'Who does it belong to?'

She shrugged raising her eyebrows vacantly. 'They keep the wood for the school in here, but apart from that no one comes here. Except us, when it's raining. We are allowed!' she said, raising her voice and her eyes widening in vehemence.

'I'm sure you are.'

'Follow me.' She ran a little way past the field and through a gap in the hedge opposite.

Hélène followed, struggling to keep up over the long tussocks of grass.

'See. This is a path. It would be almost gone if it wasn't for us. No one uses it anymore. They're all too busy worrying about the war. Work, work, work that's all they talk about. You can see everything that goes on in the village from here. See, there are bushes. Here come and sit down.' Miriam immediately crossed her legs and sank to the ground. 'Claude and me, we sit here and watch everyone. They can't see us. They don't think to look. I don't ever want to be a grown up. They moan all the time, and fight, and worry. Do you?'

'I try not to. So, do you often have no school?'

She shrugged again. 'Sometimes. Only in the afternoon though. We always have to go in the mornings.'

She would have to change the rendezvous to the morning, or she would risk the children getting in the way.

# TWELVE

## Diana

June was coming to a close. The school had broken up and the playground across the square lay empty and silent. There was more traffic than usual in the quiet country lanes. The annual summer exodus from the capital had commenced and Parisians had come to occupy their summer residences. It was most noticeable in the supermarkets, where women in shiny belts with matching high heeled shoes stood elegantly at the checkouts, in contrast to the baggy ageing population of the *Beauce* in their overalls and clogs.

The heat-wave had officially been announced and watering was banned during daylight hours, to minimise evaporation waste. All night long, Diana could hear the clicking and spraying of the watering canons in the fields. The price of lettuce and tomatoes had shot up with the temperature. Serge called every night to tell Diana of his day. He told her of the corpses and the carcasses of horses that they had fished out of the Seine, before they contaminated the capital's drinking water. In Paris, a state of emergency had been declared, with thousands of pensioners succumbing to the soaring temperatures. The hospitals were overflowing and Serge was kept exceptionally busy. He'd been away for nearly a fortnight; the barracks had asked him to stay on as the heat-wave continued unerringly to seize the country. During the day, the searing heat drove Diana and Ben indoors behind the protection of the shutters, tilted against the sun.

Not being able to go outside, made Serge's long absence even harder. Even in the shade of the barn the heat was stifling. Nothing stirred and the air hung thick and heavy. Ben could only go in the paddling pool when the sun had at last dropped behind the barn. Eventually, a complete hosepipe ban was imposed, and Diana began to save their bath and washing-up water. Every evening she carried it down to the vegetable patch in buckets to save her crops from frazzling in the heat. The tomato plants were flowering, and with the treat of their evening soaking they still managed to flourish.

Diana unpacked the boxes of books that had been stowed away in the cellar at *Boulevard Raspail*, to make way for Ben's cot before he was born. In the garage, she found some old planks of wood, which she cleaned up as best she could and rubbed them over with sandpaper.

She piled them up in the study with the squarest logs from the log pile supporting each one, to form a makeshift bookshelf.

Whilst Ben slept through the hottest part of the day, she lay dripping with sweat on her own bed, stripped of duvets, and read. The wooden shutters remained closed and tilted, day after day, in the hope that a vagrant breeze would slip underneath to cool the air. Léo lay on the floor beside her, panting desperately. She hadn't told Serge that she allowed him to sleep in the bedroom. He'd laughed at her when she'd insisted that his basket be put in the back hall by the door to the garage.

'Hunting dogs should live outside,' he'd said jeering.

At home with her parents, hunting dogs were pets. This was something Serge had thought was soft. But even her father, a seasoned hunter, allowed his pair of Springer Spaniels to follow him everywhere, even to the lavatory. Diana had been horrified at the wire runs she had seen in several gardens in Saint Gabriel. The dogs incarcerated inside them barked furiously and hurled themselves against the metal, gnashing their teeth at passersby.

Every morning, Diana and Ben rose early to take Léo for a walk, before the sun took on its full strength and drove them indoors again. That particular morning her walk took her into the village past *La Petite Folie*, its doors still closed, and out onto the road to Jaunay. She walked past one or two stone houses with their shutters firmly fastened against the impending heat. Then, they passed in front of a row of houses, identical in design, with neat front gardens. Their immaculate appearance stood out amongst the higgledy, rambling buildings of the rest of the village.

'Look *Maman*, horsey!' Ben clicked his tongue to imitate the clopping sound of horses' hooves. A little further on, past the tidy gardens, two shire horses were leaning their heads over the rail of a fence. Diana took Ben to get a closer look at them. She stroked the nearest horse's nose. It leant down to nuzzle her pockets for food. Ben gasped, thinking he was going to bite her.

Diana laughed and showed him how to pick clumps of grass and feed them to the horses, holding his hand flat so they wouldn't nip him. The smell of the animals, and the aroma of the hay, that hung from the net at the fence, reached Diana's nostrils and she felt an instant pang of homesickness. She had ridden horses since she was old enough to hold on. Since leaving home for university she had only ridden on the rare occasions she had visited her father, who still kept a couple of ageing hunters. Serge wasn't interested in horses. When she'd taken him home to meet her father, he'd refused point blank to get on one.

'*Madame*'.

Diana looked up startled. A man in blue overalls was pushing a wheelbarrow full of hay down a track that ran up alongside the field. The horses lollopped expectantly towards him.

'*Bonjour.*' Diana recognised him from the day of the crash. 'Thank you for your help that day, with my car,' she hesitated, 'I, err don't know your name.' She could feel herself reddening.

'My name is Michaud, and for the accident, I did what anybody would have done. It is normal.' He gestured matter-of-factly.

'*Cheval*!' yelled Ben, pointing.

'You like horses?' asked the man. His accent definitely wasn't local, she could tell now.

'Yes. Are they yours?'

His dark blue eyes stood out against his swarthy sun-beaten face. 'Only that grey over there. These others I look after for people. They're cart horses.' He hoisted some hay from the barrow and stuffed it in the net hanging on the fence. He was older than Diana. She estimated him to be at least forty.

'Would your little boy like to sit on one?'

Diana looked worriedly at the size of these plough giants.

Noticing her alarm he added, 'Old Marrakech is a friendly giant, he's perfectly safe.' He pushed a lock of coal-black hair out of his eyes, looking at her, waiting for a response. He was handsome in a firmly Gallic manner. He wasn't as tall as Serge, but was definitely broader.

She suddenly felt ashamed to be comparing him to her husband. 'No, no I don't think so,' she said glancing away and then remembered her manners. 'I'm sorry, I mean thank you. Maybe, another time.' She smiled weakly.

She saw disappointment flicker across his face.

'We'd better get back,' she continued awkwardly. She turned to leave but in her haste she hadn't noticed that Léo had tangled his lead in the wheel of the pushchair.

The man climbed through the fence and knelt down to free him. When he stood up again, a clean smell of soap wafted over to her. 'I check the horses about this time every morning.' He paused. 'If you pass this way again…' He left the sentence unfinished.

Diana smiled and turned the pushchair round with difficulty, Léo was chewing a wheel.

'*A bientôt!*' he called after her.

As she walked back along the road, she felt churlish not allowing Ben to sit on Marrakech. He would have loved it. She hoped that he would love horses as much as she did. There was something about the man that unsettled her. What had come over her? What had made her flee? He'd looked at her, as if it mattered what she thought. Serge never did that. She shook herself, the heat and Serge's absence was simply getting to her. The quicker he came home the better.

The café's doors were open now, and a queue of women stretched out onto the pavement. She looped Léo's lead around the drainpipe and joined the back of the queue. A couple of the women turned their heads to see who had arrived. On seeing Diana, they quickly looked away; their blank facial expressions switching to stern and haughty.

At last Diana reached the counter and Jeanette greeted her warmly, handing over her baguette. 'Come and take a coffee with me. The rush is over; I won't have any more customers for hours.' She pushed open the side door and ushered them through in to the darkness of the shuttered café. She flung open the front door, throwing a shaft of sunlight over the floor.

'*Cheval!*' shrieked Ben to Jeanette, repeating his now well rehearsed clippy-cloppy sounds.

'Horses? Where have you seen horses, my little man?'

'We've just been for a walk up the road towards Jaunay. We met that chap; the one who pulled me from my car. He was feeding his horses.'

'Aah! Yes.' Jeanette's expression became serious.

'Now, my little man, would you like a lollipop?' She lifted down a round plastic display stand, stuck with lollipops, wrapped in every hue of paper.

'He seems like a nice chap,' insisted Diana. 'He offered Ben a ride.'

Jeanette frowned. She glanced round the deserted café as if checking for eavesdroppers. 'You keep well away. He's not quite right that chap. Don't go down there, my dear.'

'Why ever not?'

'Never you mind. Just take my advice and don't go asking questions.' She set about pouring the thick, black steaming liquid into a pair of tiny coffee cups on the counter.

As they wandered back up the garden path to the house, Diana could hear the trill of the telephone. She unclipped the dog and released Ben from his pushchair and sprinted to catch it in time.

It was Serge. '*Chérie*, I'm coming home tomorrow. The *Capitaine* has allowed me four days' leave.'

Diana was overjoyed; the past two weeks alone without him had felt like a year. She felt a spurt of energy, and despite the heat, she took Ben into the garden, donning broad-brimmed hats to protect their heads from the powerful rays of the sun. Ben helped her sow some pumpkin seeds. She watched as each seed went into the earth, the excitement of creating new life touching her senses. She remembered growing pumpkins as a child and watching with fascination as the tiny green baubles that appeared on the rambling stems, grew into oversized orange footballs. The sun's force became quickly unbearable, driving them once more into the confines of the stone farmhouse.

When the temperature had at last subsided, they returned to the garden to burn off some energy. They played hide and seek amongst the trees. Only Ben always hid, and Diana always counted. She opened her eyes and spotted him instantly. Having tried to make himself as thin as possible, he was standing behind a tree trunk the size of a post.

'I wonder where Ben is,' she exclaimed theatrically.

At which point, Ben could no longer cope with the suspense and erupted into fervent laughter. By the end he'd even abandoned hiding behind anything and just covered up his eyes, with the reasoning that if he couldn't see his mother, she couldn't possibly see him. When he tired of that he went on to his old faithful game of 'What's that?' He walked around the garden pointing at things and Diana told him what they were; once in English and once in French. He never repeated the words, he just nodded, satisfied with the response. He pointed at every tree trunk in the garden and Diana told him the names of each species.

As they wandered round, she began tugging on the ivy that had woven itself tightly around all the trunks. She pulled bits off, here and there. Then Ben began to copy, trying to pull the thicker bits off lower down. Before long, both mother and son were ensconced in stripping the tree trunks of their parasitic growth. In no time at all they'd created

78

two four foot high piles of ivy in the middle of the lawn. She was pleased to have achieved something to show Serge when he came back. She dragged the ivy down to the bonfire pit and realised that Ben's help really was help, not a hindrance. Her baby was growing up. He set to the task like a miniature navvy on a mission. With the trunks clear of ivy the view of the garden was quite different, lighter somehow.

That Sunday Diana and Serge woke with a start. The sound of church bells came pealing across the garden. The estate agent had told them that the church hosted just two masses each year; obviously this was one of them. The clock said ten o'clock. She peered through the shutters, amazed at how late they had slept and was surprised at the pleasure of seeing grey clouds shrouding the sun's venomous heat. She lay back on her pillows and basked in the bewitching carillon that swept through the windows. She could hear Léo whimpering from his basket by the back door.

Serge was still dozing.

Ben called out. '*Maman! Papa!* Ding dong! Ding dong!'

Diana reluctantly pulled herself from the bedclothes and went to retrieve him. There were a lot of cars outside the church, and Diana noticed with irritation that some of them had parked right across their gateway. She swallowed the annoyance, they were the newcomers here and she mustn't make a fuss. Anyway, she couldn't exactly haul the owners out to move them in the middle of the service. It *was* only twice a year after all.

Despite the clouds, it was still very warm, stormy evening. They ate their breakfast slowly on the front terrace, while Ben pottered around the garden. The haunting tones of the first hymn came drifting through the yew hedge like honey. Diana, although not religious, loved church music. As a schoolgirl she had sung hymns in Latin. She still remembered them by heart and often sang Schubert's *Agnus Dei* to herself while she washed up or dug the garden. When Serge had asked her to marry him, he had assumed they would marry civilly, given Diana's lack of religious conviction, but she couldn't bear the thought of standing in a modern unimaginative office block making those important promises that would be the mainstay of her life. Such an important event had to take place in a beautiful building. They had married in the Catholic Church in Little Watcombe. The priest was also a keen horseman and often rode with her father. He'd agreed to marry them on the strength of Serge's baptism, and Diana suspected, on the quality of her father's hunters.

Serge poured himself another coffee. 'I think it's time we thought about getting Ben baptised.'

Diana looked at him in alarm, as much for his statement, as for his apparent knack for hearing her thoughts. 'Baptised?'

'He's already two, we really shouldn't leave it any longer.'

'I had no idea you intended to have him baptised.'

Serge looked at her as if she had lost her senses. 'Of course he'll be baptised. Everyone is baptised.'

Diana looked at him hard, thinking how to reply. 'I'm not!'

'No, well, your parents are different. Anyway you're English. You have that funny Church of England religion.'

'There's nothing funny about the Church of England,' Diana replied huffily. She immediately felt ridiculous defending beliefs which had never even been her own. They both fell silent as the second hymn struck up inside the church.

'If you feel so strongly about Ben being baptised, well, I shall support you. But don't expect me to go all religious.'

'You don't have to go 'all religious' to be baptised,' he said indignantly. 'You just *have* to be baptised.'

Diana could see that for Serge to not baptise his children would be like not having Christmas. He wasn't really interested in why he wanted it done, except that it had to *be* done. Serge had been baptised for the self-same reason. His parents were not church goers but it was what was expected.

'Alright, but you'll have to arrange it. You're the Catholic.'

'We shall go over and see the priest as soon as the service is over.'

'We?' she said alarmed.

'You have to come with me. It'll look strange if you don't.'

Diana looked through the bars of the gate to the arched church door. From her literature studies at the University of Paris, she had read of the fire and brimstone methods of French Catholicism and felt more than just a little nervous. She remembered one title in particular, *Le Recteur de l'Ile de Sein,* with its grim local priest that ruled the island with threats of eternal damnation. She shook herself, the Loire Valley was, of course, a far cry from the hostile sea-swept islands of seventeenth century Brittany.

The door of the church creaked open. A white-haired man wearing a long white cassock appeared stooping in the doorway. As he stepped outside he drew himself up until he appeared to be almost as tall as the pillars adorning the doorframe behind him.

'Let's go.' Serge stood up, smoothed his hair back and fussily brushed at his jeans.

Diana quickly wiped the chocolate spread from Ben's face and they set off down the path with Ben gaily singing,

'Ding! Dong! Ding dong!'

The congregation began to spill from the doorway. Each person stopped to reverently shake the priest's hand. Diana was startled by the apparel of the church-goers, not a nylon housecoat or a pair of clogs amongst them. They really *were* in their Sunday best. The last of the worshippers left the church.

Serge stepped forward purposefully. He held out a hand towards the columnar clergyman. '*Mon Père*. My name is Serge Lescure.'

The gentleman took his hand and shook it majestically.

'My wife, Diana,'

Diana fought a strong urge to curtsey.

'And my son Benjamin.'

The priest didn't smile he just stared at the trio expectantly.

'We would like to baptise our son,' announced Serge importantly.

The Priest raised his eyebrows. 'He has not already been baptised?' His expression was polite but leaning to the incredulous.

'No, we have only recently moved to this parish from Paris. We particularly wanted him to be baptised in the country.'

It was Diana's turn to raise her eyebrows in the face of this brazen lie.

'We would need to have a few meetings,' he paused and looked Diana up and down, 'With both you and your wife.'

Her heart sank. She was regretting having agreed to this already.

'Please come inside, I shall introduce you to our lay preachers.'

They followed him into the grey damp interior of the church. A man and a woman were collecting up the hymn books from the pews and piling them into an ornate wooden cupboard.

'Pierre and Chantal will book you into my diary.'

The couple turned to them smiling rather over enthusiastically.

'This is *Monsieur* and *Madame* Lescure. They wish to baptise their son, Benjamin.'

The smiley couple glanced down at Ben who was evidently over awed by this huge man in the strange gown, and was momentarily speechless. They continued to smile but Diana caught a trace of the same consternation that the priest had failed to conceal.

'Now, let me see,' Pierre was thumbing through a large diary emblazoned with a gilded cross. 'Yes, *Père* Auguste is holding a baptism meeting tomorrow at our house. Our farm is over on the Fontenay road just past the chateau. *La Ferme de la Cavée.* Do you know it?'

'We'll find it,' replied Serge in a syrupy voice.

'Six o'clock? Would that be alright?'

'Yes, thank you,' replied Serge smiling inanely. It was obviously catching.

'Until tomorrow then. God be with you!'

'And with you.' Returned Serge.

Diana was beginning to wonder if she really knew her husband at all.

# THIRTEEN

## Edward

Clothilde had become busier with the growing season approaching and she had not been able to visit so often in the daytime. He spent his days painstakingly writing out all the remedies he could remember. When his memory failed him, or his body became stiff from crouching over the scroll, he ventured out of the cavern to gather the dried out skeletons of oak apples that he could find amongst the twigs on the forest floor. He crushed and soaked them to make a fresh supply of ink. It was not as good as the ink he was used to using at the priory, but he would have to wait until the trees were again awoken by the spring sunshine before he could lay his hands on fresh oak apples.

It was rare that he heard Montgommery's men in the woods, but when he did the terror that swept him was overwhelming. He huddled in the bottom of the cavern in a tiny ball with his forehead resting on the earthen floor and prayed. Clothilde had told him that this end of the forest was not the best hunting ground for them but that he must take no risks. Now he was accustomed to the natural sounds of the forest and could distinguish them from the sounds of the village beyond. He would sit a while on the edge of the opening, his legs dangling into the cavern, feeling the sunshine on his skin, but he was careful to wrap his cloak tightly around him, to keep out the nip that still hung in the air. His head was healed and he knew he must think about moving on, and leaving Clothilde to live her life safely. Every time he thought about it he pushed the idea from his mind and instead watched for the position of the sun, to guess when she would next appear.

He longed to visit her home, to meet her brother and her mother of whom she spoke so dearly. How blessed she is to have a mother who loves her so openly. He yearned to look upon the smiling face of the woman who gave life to such a beautiful creature as Clothilde, she must indeed be beautiful also.

He was beginning to tire of the tight perimeter of the cavern, for he had not yet wandered out of sight of the giant oak that served as his chimney. Even the quill and parchment she had so kindly slipped from *Père* Barthélemy's vestry could no longer keep him entertained. He yearned to tour the forest and to begin cataloguing the plants that were only now beginning to burgeon and shoot. He listened hard to the forest sounds. There were blackbirds and some tiny birds, that he had not seen in England, that chattered to each other from the shooting branches of a bush that he could now recognise as blackthorn. In the distance he could hear the dogs barking in the village.

He took his gourd from beneath his cloak and tipped the last few drops of water into his mouth. The rest of his water he had poured on the oak apples that morning. He decided he must find the spring from whence Clothilde fetched his water. She would most likely not visit him until sundown and she would be glad of a task less to do. Besides, if he were to move on he must begin to look after himself. Satisfied that he could justify his disobedience he set off in the direction that he had seen Clothilde take after each visit; towards the sound of the barking dogs.

He stepped carefully trying only to tread on soft leaves lest there be a hunter close by. He cut a small cross in the base of each tree trunk as he went, fearful of losing his way and finding himself stranded and alone in the myriad of uniform trees.

The smell of wood smoke reached his nostrils accompanied by laughing children. He paused, leaning against an old oak to listen to the children calling and whistling to each other. The sound of human activity so close was too much for him to bear. He had to get closer to actually see them. As he stepped nearer he saw smoke rising through the trees and five or six small children, dark and swarthy were running to and fro, diving and dodging in and out of the shelter of their simple houses; little more than huts.

A little way off from the children, appeared a young man. He was carrying a bundle of faggots. His hood was pulled up over his face against the chill spring morning. One of the children ran towards him playfully calling 'Firmin, Firmin.'

This must be Clothilde's brother. A good man, certainly, caring for his family with his father gone is a big responsibility for a boy so young. He could not imagine taking such a responsibility himself.

The child ran up to Firmin and jumped pulling his hood down. Firmin chided him and made a swoop at him smiling, but the child dodged out of his reach. Firmin turned to continue his path and Edward could see his face. He was as dark as the children that ran around him. His nose was a good strong shape but he did not resemble Clothilde in any way. Then he was gone around the side of the houses bearing his bundle of firewood. Were these children the orphans of whom she had spoken? Clothilde's hair so bleached and golden, was a striking contrast to these swarthy mites.

Through the veil of smoke that drifted from the huts into the blue sky he could see a steeple, he had not realised the church was so close. The chateau could not be too far beyond.

The children had begun to throw what looked like a pig's bladder to each other. The smallest child threw it inexpertly and it veered from its intended path and landed not far from Edward's tree trunk. He scuttled off reluctantly, he longed to reveal his existence, to laugh and chat with them. They have nothing but they are happy and in that they have everything. As he trudged through the woods, all thoughts of stealth were replaced by visions of rosy, smiling faces. At his feet, the premise of spring brought new clean, green shoots that would soon carpet the forest floor. Inside him he felt the anticipation of their growth flip his stomach. Never before had he lived so closely to the seasons and all that they brought.

He stopped a moment and listened to the trees. He could just make out the sound of a distant trickle of water. He walked towards it and came upon a clearing. He hesitated. The clearing was about the size of the courtyard at the priory and provided no cover. The grass was sumptuous and a rich green that shone in the sunlight, almost magical. A pond nestled at the edge, its banks bordered by brown shrubs, burnt by the winter frosts. A tree grew close by its branches held sprinklings of pink tinged buds just waiting to burst open.

He skirted the edge of the clearing and approached the pond. Its waters were still, apart from a thin finger that slipped and splashed over gleaming rocks. Across the surface there were one or two fresh green lily pads, nosing for space amongst the dead brown rotting debris of the season before. He lent down to set his gourd beneath the running water. As he did so, he caught sight of a reflection in the water. He jumped, he must have been followed. He turned expecting the worst. But there was no one there. He turned back to the surface of the water and there was the reflection again and he realised his foolishness. This was his own reflection. Before him, on the surface of the green water, was the image of a man that he did not recognise. His hair had grown long and whiskers had appeared on his chin. This monk was not the youth that had left Canterbury in the dead of night with the port dues secreted beneath his cloak, his red frightened face twitching with an equal measure of fear of what he was about to do, and disgust at what he had just done. He could not be sure how long ago he had left the priory, but he knew his journey could not be measured in time for he had left a boy and arrived a man. He took a long draught of the icy cold liquid and then topped up his gourd again.

The sun was reaching its zenith, he hadn't intended on being so far from the cavern for so long. He turned and retraced his steps, carefully following the marked trunks until he reached the safety of Clothilde's cavern, beneath the branches and roots of the magnificent oak, and waited for her visit at sundown.

Edward had stoked up the fire, he was proud of his new found skills and he was eager to show off to Clothilde. When she at last leapt down through the opening, he was hard at work on his parchment, making a list of all the emerging plants that he had managed to identify from their young shoots.

Clothilde watched with fascination. 'You are so clever, Edward. Your writing is beautiful, though I cannot read it.'

'It is not as beautiful as the works they produced at the priory, but it takes years to perfect the skills of a scribe.'

'Would you do something for me?'

'Gladly, I will. Just mention it and it will be done.'

'Oh Edward, such an offer is too amusing. For you do not know what I am to request of you. What I ask for may be impossible!'

He liked it when she played with him like this. 'I consider you to be an intelligent person and if you were to request the impossible, you would know beforehand that your request could not be granted. Under those circumstances you would not make that request.'

She laughed at his pomposity. 'Aren't you going to ask me?'

'Of course, what is that you would like me to do?'

'You might say no.' She was peeping at him naughtily through her hair which had fallen across her face.

'I cannot say yes until you have told me what your request is.'

'I want to learn to read and write. I want to be able to read your writings about the plants in this forest. I know a little. Firmin has taught me some that he learned from *Père* Barthélemy but I want to do it properly.'

'But of course! I would take enormous pleasure in teaching you how, but it will take time and great patience.'

'Then that is settled.'

They sat together by the fire. Edward did not tell her of his trip into the woods. She would be angry and he did not want to spoil the moment. He showed her how to hold the quill and found some scraps of parchment that he had discarded, for her to form her first letters.

He came to look forward to his evenings, sitting by the glow of the fire, listening to her stories of the Montgommerys and the villagers, while she painstakingly practised her alphabet.

She told him how her father, a loyal servant to the Lord of the manor, had been chosen to accompany him on his important voyage to the holy lands. 'My mother says that before *Seigneur* Montgommery left, the village was well looked after. The *Seigneur* was fair and there was an abundance of food. Now, with his younger brother in charge of the *seigneuriale* we must hide our food to survive the winter. He sends his men to check our stores and take our grain, and sometimes even the pork that we have carefully smoked and cured. He takes hefty tithes, much larger proportions than the true *Seigneur*.

'I built this cavern to hide the rabbits that I catch. Before I was born, the villagers were allowed to hunt rabbits for their own meals but now even that is punishable. Sometimes I hide the food reserves here too. I have kept the position of the cavern secret even from my family. If it was ever to be discovered I would take the blame. I could not bear to see my mother suffer at the hands of that evil man. He is greedy and fat and has little kindness or thought for the well-being of his subjects. He is so lazy he does not even hunt or hawk himself.

'Firmin often talks of the day when our father and the true *Seigneur* will return to Saint Gabriel. He thinks that when he sees how his brother has treated his peasants, he will banish him from these lands. Mother gets very angry with him for such talk. She is scared that he will be overheard and Firmin will be taken away from us. Montgommery the younger has his spies everywhere. We are sure that even some of our neighbours keep him informed of the goings on in the village.'

'Then I am putting you in graver danger than I imagined.'

'We must look after each other. If we bow down to this tyranny we will be no better than the tyrant himself.' She spoke with conviction, her features solemn and forthright.

In the light of the fire, Edward studied her face while he thought of Firmin. There really was no resemblance to her brother at all. Perhaps she resembled her mother. Looking closely at her complexion he started, 'Clothilde, your face!'

Her hand shot up to her cheek and stroked the smooth skin. 'I know, that is one of the reasons I was coming to see you. You were right. You are very clever Edward.'

'Not me, it is Eldric who has taught me all I know.'

'People are getting suspicious of my daily walks into the woods. They have asked me how I have rid myself of the fistulas.'

'Tell them, they just went on their own.'

'That is what I have done, but it has made them of a mind to watch me more closely. It is difficult for me to get away unnoticed. *Père* Barthélemy has begun to look at me strangely too. I fear that your presence will soon be discovered.'

'Then you must not come here for a while.' Saying these words hurt him.

'But what will you do for food and water?'

'I know where the spring is now and I can forage in the woods for food. There is chickweed and enough millet in the sack you brought me to last a fair few days. Besides I can hunt rabbit too. Leave me your bow and some arrows and I shall be fine. I still have a handsome bundle of parchment and I can continue to make ink from the oak trees. You must go back to your family. I do not want to bring you misfortune.'

'Edward, surely it is time to end this solitude and step back into the world,' her tone was pleading. 'You could arrive in the village from the Jaunay road asking for alms. Then you would be safe. If you are discovered doing what is expected of your station there will be few questions asked. But if they happen upon you hiding in a cavern beneath the forest, deep in the *Seigneuriale* of Montgommery, I cannot be sure of the consequences.'

Edward bowed his head and remained silent.

'I do not know what happened to you to make you travel so far from your home. But surely that is your protection, for they will not know it either. There is an abbey at Pontigny, it is a few days' walk from here. They would surely take you in.'

Edward shook his head. He was not yet ready to face the world. 'You go back to your family and stay safe. I am a good deal older than you and I can look after myself.'

She stood up and then hesitated looking at him earnestly, as if she were a mother leaving her child, for a moment, in an emergency.

# FOURTEEN

## Diana

Six o'clock loomed on her all the following day. She couldn't quite settle to anything. Why was she so nervous? She thought of Father James, in Little Watcombe, with his welcoming smile and jodhpur boots peeping out from under his cassock, all set to dash off to the stables as soon as his round of weddings and funerals was over. Somehow, she knew this was to be an altogether different experience.

The clouds of the day before had hung ominously over the plain, and the heat had increased. The night had been uncomfortable and sticky. Diana and Serge pulled away from *La Petite Folie* where they'd left Ben with Jeanette and the giant display of lollipops. The weather was beginning to break. Lightning flashed on the horizon over the sunflower fields and thunder had begun to beat its distant drum roll. By the time they pulled up outside Chantal and Pierre's farm in Fontenay, warm rain was sheeting onto the dusty lanes. There were already a couple of cars parked outside precariously, on the narrow country road, obviously not daring to drive in through the farm gates and park in the expanse of yard.

Serge followed suit and pulled up behind them. She couldn't help noticing that one of the cars had a crucifix hanging from the rear view mirror. She sighed, resigned to her fate.

Pierre and Chantal were already in the doorway armed with their plastic smiles. 'Come in, come in!' they chirruped in unison, like a couple of harpies luring unsuspecting victims into their lair. They led them into a dining room where three other couples were sitting around a large square table. The priest presided regally at one end taking up a whole side of the table, whilst the couples were obliged to shuffle closer together to make room for Diana and Serge.

'We could go into the main dining hall but this is much cosier don't you think?' said Chantal through her relentless grin.

The couples murmured their agreement in polite simpers. Two of the couples were dark-haired with olive skins. Diana thought they must be of southern Mediterranean origin. They spoke with slight accents. She felt bolstered that she would not be the only foreigner.

*Père* Auguste cleared his throat. 'We are gathered here today to talk about the reasons for baptism.'

89

The Mediterranean couples looked puzzled.

'*Monsieur* and *Madame* Sanchez, why are you baptising your child?'

The couple looked up at the priest fearfully. Eventually the husband managed to utter in a croaky voice, 'Because we would like to bring our children up in the Catholic faith.'

The priest grunted, not giving away whether this was the right answer or not. His eyes looked to the next couple, 'And *Monsieur* and *Madame* Pilar?'

The couples' eyes both looked downwards in perfect synchronization either through nerves or extreme reverence for this mountainous man of God. 'Yes, it is the same for us.' The woman spluttered in a strong accent.

Diana swallowed hard, they were next in line.

'*Madame* Lescure!' the priest almost boomed.

Hang on, thought Diana. What about *Monsieur* Lescure? He's the reason we're here.

'I understand you are not of our faith?' *Père* Auguste had done his homework.

Diana darted a glare at Serge, as if to say 'You got me into this, you can get me out.' Serge averted his eyes and Diana felt that she was freefalling.

Everyone's eyes were on her. Even Pierre and Chantal had erased their permanent grins. Word must have got round.

'No, I am not a baptised Catholic,' she replied with as much dignity as she could muster.

'So, *why* is it that you would like your son Benjamin to be welcomed into the Catholic faith?'

Diana paused for a moment in the vague hope that Serge would come to her rescue, but he had obviously abandoned ship and remained silent. 'My husband is a baptised Catholic and feels very strongly that he would like his children to be Catholic also. We married in a Catholic church in England, and to uphold the promises I made there, I am supporting his wish.' Diana winced internally at the triteness of her reply.

The priest breathed in sharply. 'I see,' he said slowly.

Diana held her breath.

'If you are not Catholic, what is your faith?'

Here we go, she thought. In for a penny, in for a pound. 'I was educated at a Church of England school where I studied the Bible, and

90

the life of Jesus. However my parents chose not to christen me due to their own conflicting views.' At this revelation the gathering began to shuffle their feet.

The colour drained from *Père* Auguste's face. 'I must assume from that, that you are of no particular faith?' he said it so slowly it was as if she had just announced she was the member of a terrorist group.

The couple next to her leaned away from her as if she was unclean.

'No,' she replied simply, if not a little glumly. No wonder the Catholic Church was in decline in France, it was harder to get into than the freemasonry.

At last the priest turned his attentions away from the foreign heathen seated so brazenly before him. '*Monsieur* Lescure. Can you tell me why terrible things happen in the world and God does nothing to stop them?'

Diana was now beginning to think that she had got off lightly.

'Because he is not the *Gendarme* of the World. Although God created us and put us here, we must make our own mistakes and learn from them, *Mon Père*.'

Diana was dumbfounded. They had been together for three years and had never discussed religion once. Not even when they were getting married. How could she have missed his obviously deep-seated beliefs? She tried to catch his eye for some confirmation that he was still the Serge that she knew, but he was staring straight ahead.

'That's right.' *Père* Auguste smiled for the first time. 'I couldn't have put it better myself.' The priest talked on for another twenty minutes about the importance of unwavering belief.

Diana switched off and gazed out of the window at the gushing rain that smashed the panes with huge drops.

*Père* Auguste finished his monotone oratorio. They were free to go. The Mediterranean couples backed out of the door, virtually bowing and tugging their forelocks like serfs of the manor.

The baptism date was fixed for Sunday tenth July at the church in Jaunay, just six days away. There wouldn't be another mass in St Gabriel for six months. Serge was due back at work the following day. Now that it was raining again, the pressure of the drought on the emergency services would at least ease off. Normally five or six meetings with the Priest were required before baptising a child or getting married, but either because of the proximity of the baptism date, or the priest had been so impressed with Serge that he felt him eminently equipped to save his poor, fallen wife from the depths of heathenism.

Diana threw herself into a frenzy of organization. She called their friends in Paris and Diana's mother booked a last minute flight. Her father had declined the invitation as Diana knew he would, given his disapproval of organised religion, together with the added deterrent that her mother had accepted. They had been apart for five years yet Clarissa Hunter still felt it necessary to confront her ex-husband at public gatherings. Serge and Diana's wedding had been overshadowed by a skilfully orchestrated operation to keep her mother as busy as possible whilst Harry Hunter was allowed to hold his office of Father of the Bride, free of antagonism.

Serge's parents had been called urgently to the bedside of an ageing Aunt in Brittany and were thankfully unable to come. Although Bernadette Lescure's support of Diana's plan to move to the country, had certainly improved their relations, her initial disapproval of her foreign daughter-in-law still hung threateningly above them; neither woman quite trusting the other. Diana hadn't relished the prospect of mediating between them and her mother, who, on grounds of propriety, would refuse to communicate in French.

Diana made two huge Quiche Lorraines, a lentil and raisin salad with a hint of curry and for Delphine, an avid advocate of British desserts, an apple crumble and a lemon meringue pie. She ordered the baguettes from Jeanette and the cold meats from the *charcuterie* in Beaugency. Delphine had agreed to be godmother and Christian, the godfather. They would bring the traditional parcels of sugared almonds.

Serge returned early on Friday morning having done the late shift at the barracks the night before. He mowed the lawns and picked up the drinks order from the wine cellar in Beaugency. Clarissa Hunter would be arriving on the 7.15pm train from Paris. Diana scrubbed every floor, door frame and light switch. She cleaned the twenty-five windows and prayed ironically, that the once again scorching temperatures, would not break into another storm and splatter them with mud and dust before Sunday. Everyone would be staying the night, except for Jeanette, Pierrot and Marcel who had accepted the invitation to the church but had cried off the party afterwards. Diana suspected they were a little shy of their Parisian friends.

92

She blew up airbeds, set up camp beds and moved Ben's cot into their room to liberate another bedroom for guests. Jeanette had lent her two zed beds. They'd bought a second hand bed for her mother, from the furniture depot in Blois, and installed it in the spare room with the least alarming wallpaper. Diana was looking forward to seeing her mother, despite the risk of her disapproval of the rusty shutters and cobwebbed outbuildings. With Chelsea Flower Show, Wimbledon and Henley Regatta out the way, she had acquiesced to visiting her daughter's new home.

The iron gate in the yew hedge creaked and Ben began bouncing up and down on the sofa shouting, 'Grammaa! Grammaa! Grammaa!'

Her mother was beaming. 'Oh darling, it's absolutely gorgeous!'

The palatial size fitted perfectly with her standards, thought Diana scathingly but was still touched by her pride. She knew it wasn't quite Watcombe House, but then her mother didn't live there anymore either.

She was laden with bags which, once inside, divulged gifts of toys and clothes for Ben.

He loved his grandmother particularly as her visits equated unlimited affection and attention not to mention the Hamleyesque quantity of toys she always brought with her.

But with her mother came another problem. Her disapproval of Serge was ill-concealed. She would never actually speak outright but through a display of facial expressions of distaste and insinuations at his lack of education, she would spark Serge's fiery temper, creating an uncomfortable atmosphere.

If Diana kept Serge busy, well out of her mother's way, then perhaps this visit could take place harmoniously. Her mother had grown up in a world where men wore gardenias and women sat on the lawn sipping martinis. She had always regarded money as tedious, but then up until her acrimonious divorce, she had not only been provided with an unlimited supply of it, but had had little to do with generating it.

Diana sighed as she pulled a crumpled tablecloth from the blanket box and dreamt of such a world existing for *her*.


'*Monsieur* Jeanneau. The godfather of this infant,' *Père* Auguste's voice boomed around the stone statues and carvings of Jaunay's village church. 'Who in the bible said "He that believeth and is baptized shall be saved; but he that believeth not shall be damned"?'

The congregation raised their heads expectantly as the baptism party hesitated and shifted nervously, looking hopefully at Christian.

He swallowed and uttered in a clean confident tone. 'Jesus Christ, *Mon Père'*.

There was a murmur of satisfaction and the baptism party exhaled in relief.

Ben was standing between Serge and Diana trying to paddle his hands in the font. Diana had no idea how *Père* Auguste would douse him in the holy water, but at this rate there would be no need, he'd be soaked to the skin before he got started.

Clarissa Hunter was standing in the front row, bolt upright with her nose in the air, evidently very proud of this public display in honour of her family. She looked neither left nor right, but straight ahead with the confident assurance of royalty. The congregation eyed her as they might an alien landing in their midst. This English Lady dressed in Bond-Street-best stood out amidst the sea of crimplene.

Diana scanned the pews, running through her guest list to see if everyone was there; Jean-François and Gaëlle, the boys from *Finnegan's Wake*; Cameron, Shane and Colm. It was easy to spot them in the front row. She could just make out Jeanette's bowed head at the back. There were very few men in attendance, the harvest was underway and the majority of them would be working in the fields, even on a Sunday.

Serge was standing next to Christian. He had donned a cherubic expression of the blessed. He nodded reverently at *Père* Auguste at every opportunity.

Delphine, stood next to Christian, with her habitual constancy and poise, yet simultaneously disowning any responsibility for any situation she may find herself in, unlike Diana who had always felt entirely responsible for everything and everybody in her vicinity.

'Let us pray,' thundered *Père* Auguste.

The congregation sunk to their knees as if they had been shot down. The baptism party bowed their heads. Diana followed suit, keeping an eye on Serge who had closed his eyes and was moving his lips in time to the Lord's Prayer. Was he really praying? If he was, was he praying for a cleaner house, a more beautiful wife or unlimited free beer in the café?

The main door of the church banged. Diana glanced up as inconspicuously as she could manage. A young woman appeared inside the doorway. The congregation shuffled and fell silent.

*Père* Auguste glared at the woman, who bowed her blonde head and slipped into the nearest pew.

A few moments later, Ben was officially pronounced a member of God's tribe and the baptism party was freed. Ben ran down the aisle first. He was singing 'Ding, Dong! Ding, Dong!' as if he had been released from Alcatraz, closely pursued by Delphine.

The friends gathered outside the church laughing and clicking their cameras, relishing their reunion. Surrounded by her friends, Diana felt keenly the isolation she had been feeling since their exodus from the capital. She looked around for Serge but couldn't see him; he must still be inside the church, probably talking to old high-and-mighty again. Best leave him to it, she thought.

He eventually appeared engaged in animated conversation with the blonde latecomer. Diana prickled. She was not a naturally jealous person but this was hardly the time or the place to chat up a woman. The latecomer turned her head slightly and Diana gasped. She hadn't recognised her with her hair swept back all tight and shiny, like a brass door-knob. What on earth was Liesel doing here? She nudged Delphine throwing her an accusing look, but her eyes were as round as her own. If Delphine hadn't invited her who else could have? Surely not Serge? He knew how she felt about Liesel. When would he have seen her to invite her? She had to find out.

'Liesel, what a surprise!' said Diana aware that Serge may spot the over laboured joyfulness in her tone. 'What *are* you doing here?'

'I'll leave you two girls to chat.' Sensing the barbs in the air, Serge went to find Christian.

'It's lovely to see you. What a beautiful little boy!' syruped Liesel. 'I hope you don't mind me coming, it's just I moved down here just a couple of weeks ago. I read the announcement in the paper.'

'Gosh, what a small world!' So, she *was* gate-crashing Diana thought with relief.

'I just couldn't resist giving you all a surprise.'

No, I bet you couldn't, thought Diana.

'I'm working in Mer and I've managed to find an adorable little pad in Beaugency.'

'How nice!'

'When I saw the name Lescure in the paper I thought I'd take my chances and see if it was you.'

Diana stared at her a little too long for Liesel's comfort, searching her face for any traces of insincerity.

Liesel began to fidget from one foot to the other. 'And since we're all out here on a limb, so to speak, I figured I should get in touch; birds of a feather and all that.'

'Diana, darling. Don't you think we'd better be getting home? It's getting on a bit and poor Ben is terribly hungry.' Diana had wondered how long it would be before her mother took over.

'You must be Mrs Hunter,' said Liesel with a sudden plum in her voice.

Diana was a little taken aback that Liesel even knew her maiden name.

'Liesel O'Ryan.' She held out her hand.

Clarissa Hunter shook it politely, looking to Diana for background information.

Getting none, Liesel acquiesced. 'We were friends in Paris.'

Diana winced at the description.

'Did you enjoy the service?'

'Oh yes, it was lovely,'her mother replied quickly. 'Tell me do you have a car?'

'Err yes.'

'Excellent! Come on then, you can take Ben and I back, then at least the poor little mite can have something to eat. You see, Diana didn't think to bring him something to nibble on.'

Diana glared at her.

With that, Clarissa Hunter took Liesel by the arm and whisked her off in the direction of the car park, with little Ben trotting alongside. Not only had her mother managed to make a public dig at Diana's maternal capabilities but she had also managed to take a gatecrasher back to join in the festivities at home.

'What the hell is she doing here?' Delphine was at Diana's elbow.

'Lord only knows.'

'You didn't invite her then?'

'No I didn't. I thought you must have done,' she replied indignantly. 'Apparently she's living in Beaugency.'

'Oh no! You'll never shake her off.'

Back at the house, Diana noticed immediately that all the dishes on the buffet table had been rearranged. Although, she knew her mother wasn't trying to get at her, but that she genuinely thought it would be better her way round, she couldn't help feeling irritated.

96

Serge and Christian were already tucking into a bottle of pastis with the priest. Diana was more than a little surprised to see him but realised it was simply good manners to invite him.

Liesel was nowhere to be seen. Diana hoped that she'd realised coming back to the house uninvited was going just too far, until she stepped into the kitchen to find her packing sugar coated almonds into pale blue voile pouches with Delphine.

'I don't want to sit around being a spare part. Just let me know what else I can do.' Diana ignored her and stalked back into the garden.

Cameron had struck up on the guitar and was playing *Danny Boy* while Colm sang in his deep gentle Irish brogue. Shane was beating his bodhrán, his head tilted to one side, immersed in the spiritual tones of his homeland. The boys could eat for Ireland while the French politely nibbled, but mainly drank. Christian had instigated a game of football on the side lawn. Jean-François was giving Ben wheelbarrow rides up and down the courtyard, making him laugh until his sides split. Gaëlle was running alongside with her arms out ready to catch Ben should he fall. When he eventually tired of the game, Clarissa spotted his waning energy and took him off to tuck him up in bed.

The food had been satisfyingly demolished. Christian and Delphine helped Diana clear away and distributed the sugar almonds, while all the time she tried to ignore the level of attention Serge had been affording Liesel.

The next morning, Clarissa Hunter was prodding her hair fussily as she looked in the mirror. 'What a nice girl that Liesel is?'

'Mmm.'

'She grew up in Maison Lafitte she tells me. Very nice area, that. What a lovely figure too! Apparently, she's half Irish, how extraordinary, she doesn't have the slightest bit of an accent. How nice for you to have her so near.'

'Right, you'd better get your skates on. Your train leaves in half an hour. Your luggage is already in the car and Serge is waiting outside for you.'

'Good party!' said Diana when Serge had returned from the station. 'It was hard work cooking for that many people. At least I won't have to do it for a bit.'

'Oh, that reminds me, I've invited Liesel round for dinner on Wednesday evening. I'll be home by six. It's just a short shift this time.' Serge looked back at the newspaper he was reading on the sofa.

'What on earth did you do that for?'

'Don't be mean, Diana. She's all on her own and we're the only people she knows round here. Anyway, it was nice of her to come yesterday. *And* she brought Ben a present.'

Diana looked at the enormous shiny fire engine gleaming on the table. It was big enough for Ben to sit on and push himself around, clanging its bell. He hadn't been off it since he'd set eyes on it. Diana now felt duly heartless.

# FIFTEEN

## Hélène

3EME 11 CONF JAUNAY DERRIERE L'ECOLE CABANE QU: OU EST JAUNAY MP: 5KM - FR

She carefully screwed it up and put it into the third nesting box along where she'd found the first one.

'Ten eggs today,' she called out as she carried them into the kitchen.

*Monsieur* Meffret was sitting up in bed listening to the radio. '*Charabi, charabia* – what a load of hot air. I shall wait and listen to the BBC later when Antoine can tell me what they're saying.'

'Antoine speaks English?'

'A little, he was very good at school. He is wasted on the farm but at least it is the farm that has saved him from the war.'

'*Dis-donc*, that smells good!' Antoine appeared in the doorway, looking excitedly over at the range where a pan was bubbling with pumpkin soup.

'I found the pumpkins in the barn – do you mind?'

'I would never argue with a woman who cooks as well as you do*! Papa*, I won't be able to listen to the radio with you tonight I have to go out.'

'Aah, they will catch you one day.'

'Oh *Papa*, they never come down here to Saint Gabriel, except to steal our food. Anyway I have to meet Céline. She wants to talk about the wedding.'

Hélène's heart leapt.

'That girl! She's only marrying you for the farm,' *Monsieur* Meffret harrumphed.

'You're obviously feeling better. You mustn't be so bad tempered; it's not good for your health! I know she's not a country girl, but she'll learn. Anyway, I am sure that some will say I am marrying her for her money.'

Hélène composed herself. How stupid could she be? She was the nurse here; she could not afford to fall in love in her situation. If London got wind of it she would be recalled immediately. 'You are getting married?' she asked as evenly as she could.

99

'Yes, as soon as we can get permission from *La Mairie*.'

'Does she live nearby?'

'In Jaunay. Her father, you may have met him? He is the manager of the *Crédit Solognot*.'

She shook her head. 'I have not yet had the pleasure.'

'She'll be no good to you. Mark my words. She's never seen a hard day's work in her life, that one.'

'*Papa*!' Antoine raised his voice.

'Well I must be on my way.' She bid her goodbyes and continued on her rounds.

After afternoon surgery was over Hélène sank into a chair at the kitchen table. Cécile was preparing the evening meal.

'*Docteur* Legris has a guest this evening. He has asked if you would mind having your meal in the kitchen, as they have some private matters to discuss.'

'Not at all,' she was quite relieved to have an easy supper alone and retire to her room.

'Who is coming?'

'The bank manager – things are not good I think.'

At half past six the doorbell rang, as Hélène was going down the stairs. *Docteur* Legris opened it. A short stocky man, very elegantly dressed greeted the doctor jovially.

'Julien.' They shook hands smiling.

'Philippe, it has been a little while. Please, this is Hélène Godard our new nurse. Hélène, Philippe Cottereau, manager of the *Crédit Solognot* here, in Jaunay.'

'*Mademoiselle*, I am delighted to meet you at last.' The bank manager shook her hand; a cygnet ring on his finger pinched her palm. He took a small bow. 'I hear you have been working hard, the villagers are very pleased with their new nurse.'

'Thank you, *monsieur*. I am pleased to be away from Paris and the bombing.' There was something about his eyes that Hélène recognized but she couldn't place.

The doctor showed *Monsieur* Cottereau into the dining room and Hélène retreated to the kitchen.

CONF RV 11 HOM BLO PIP - FC

She popped the note in her mouth and swallowed hard. She screwed up her own scrap and put it in the box. She set off on her bicycle towards Saint Gabriel. As she cycled through Jaunay, she eyed the path Miriam had shown her. It was strange how invisible it was. The high grass on either side of it obscured it making the area look like continual pasture. Even someone walking along would be relatively hidden by the tall cow parsley and the blackthorn bushes that grew along it. She cycled past the café where little Miriam was leaning against the wall with the little boy, Claude.

'*Salut*!' she called.

Hélène waved back. Past the plane trees at the exit to the village and down the road between the fields to Saint Gabriel she cycled. First she called on little Marc and Agnès Camaret. She liked to visit Agnès, her leg was well on its way to healing now. She was made of strong stuff and Hélène liked her no nonsense approach to life, though she was sure it was that same approach that had caused her leg to get infected in the first place.

She changed her dressing. She could see that she could change it now just once every two days, possibly for another week and then the dressings could be left off to allow it heal and dry in the fresh air. She weighed little Marc and checked him over and then settled down at the table with a cup of chicory coffee and a piece of honey pumpkin cake.

'How is *Monsieur* Meffret getting on?'

'He is very poorly but he has made some recent improvement.'

'TB is an evil disease. My father died of it you know, just after surviving Spanish flu. It seems that there is always something to try us; war or pestilence.' She sipped her coffee and sighed. 'Well, at least old *Monsieur* Meffret has Antoine. Such a good man! He is very close to my husband you know.'

'He is a good man, though I do not know him well.'

'He is quite a catch that one.'

'It appears that he has already been caught.'

'Ah you will be talking about Céline Cottereau. If there was ever a mismatch on this earth, it was that one. I don't like to speak ill of people, Lord knows we have enough gossip in Saint Gabriel, but that woman was born bad. With all her airs and graces and what is she really? Just an ordinary girl from the countryside, whose father happens to have slightly more money than the rest of us. She behaves as if she is the *Chatelaine*. If there was a bachelor to be had, in line to inherit the chateau, you can be sure that Antoine wouldn't stand a chance with her. She has no idea how lucky she is. Well, I suppose he will have to find out for himself.'

Hélène changed Marc's nappy to allow Agnès to rest a little longer and then packed up her bag and cycled almost to the Meffret Farm. She'd started earlier that morning so they wouldn't be expecting her for another hour and a half. She glanced around her, and when she was certain Antoine was not about, she wheeled her bicycle down the side of the chicken barn and set off on foot to the other end of Miriam's path. It only took about twenty minutes to reach the blackthorn bushes that overlooked the village. but then she had been going at a bit of a trot.

Foucaud would have to come down the lane to the school and he would be expecting her to do the same. She looked at her ; ten thirty. She crouched beneath one of the blackthorns. The village looked as quiet as could be; there was only the noise of the children playing in the school yard. They would be back inside the classroom in fifteen minutes. If Foucaud came through the village from the Saint Gabriel road she would see him from here, but if he were to approach from Beaugency, she would be better off hiding in the hedge surrounding the woodshed's field. She plumped for the latter, he would be more likely to arrive from the larger town.

As she got settled, she heard Miriam's father ringing the hand bell to call the children back to class. The door of the school slammed and a young man appeared in the lane. He was blond and about the same age as her. He passed the school with his head bowed, though she could see he was scanning the buildings on each side. He reached the opening in the field, and out of his pocket, he pulled a pipe. He looked about him for a moment and then headed for the woodshed.

Hélène looked up the lane behind him; there was no one. She glanced back along the path she had come on and again no one. As soon as her watch said eleven o'clock exactly she slipped out of her hiding place and walked towards the woodshed.

'*Excusez-moi, monsieur.* Please can you tell me the way to Jaunay?'

'*Il est à cinq kilomètres.* ' His response was mechanical.

They shook hands. His accent betrayed an American twang. Not the best cut-out she thought.

'I will be brief; The Orléans network is in trouble, they need money to continue their work. If they abandon, all the work we have done with them will be lost. For those of them who are hiding out they desperately need money to send to their families. We need a drop as soon as possible.'

'But there was a drop when I arrived!'

'I thought as much but we have seen nothing.'

'So I must find out who is responsible and organise another.'

'I suggest you set up a completely new cell beforehand or we risk losing the new drop too. There is a traitor or thief in our midst.'

'But that will take time and we cannot have families going hungry. Can your cell leader help?'

He shook his head, 'He was called back. He was making mistakes.'

Hélène looked at her watch. They had to be away by half past if she was to be back at the Meffret Farm on time so as not to arouse suspicion.

'What is most needed?'

'Food, soap, blankets, clothing and money.'

'Come back to the *Boîte aux Lettres* in one week from today.'

He nodded, shook her hand and ducked out of the woodshed. Instead of walking back up the lane he went to the far end of the field and disappeared through the hedge.

She checked that the coast was clear and crossed the lane back onto the path to Saint Gabriel and set off at a hearty pace. What had happened to the money? She needed to find out who the big man was in the reception committee, the one who had met her off the plane. He said he would deal with the containers. She would need to return to the chapel but now she must go and see to *Monsieur* Meffret.

At the Meffret Farm everything was as usual.

'*Mademoiselle!*' Old *Monsieur* Meffret was sitting up in bed smiling.

She was taken aback at the resemblance to Antoine, which had been previously veiled in illness. '*Bonjour Monsieur*, how is your chest?'

'Oh, it is not so bad. This old body of mine, it has served me well up until now. When it's time, it's time – none of us can change that.'

'I suppose not. Still, that's enough of the morbid talk. Since you're feeling better, I think we should give you a nice bath,' and she put a huge vat of water on the range to warm. Antoine had not yet come in for his soup; she would need to wait for him to get the old man into the tub. There was a little pumpkin left but she would have to bulk it up with potatoes, at least there were plenty of those. With the nights drawing in the hens were laying less and the nesting boxes were emptier than usual. They would have to rely more and more on ration coupons. While the soup bubbled and the bathwater warmed she read a little of the newspaper to the old man.

'Poppycock, all of it. What do they think we are? Imbeciles?' he snorted. 'With the *Maréchal* at our helm they'd be right.'

'*Monsieur*, you must be careful what you say.'

'Huh, the *Boche* – they don't come here. Scared of tuberculosis they are.'

Hélène hadn't thought of that, her letterbox was safer than she'd imagined. 'Right, that's enough of this paper. We can't have you getting upset.' She folded it up and put it back on the table.

'Aah, *Mademoiselle*, I thought I saw your bicycle leaning outside.' Antoine was standing in the doorway – his head just skimmed the lintel.

'Please, call me Hélène.'

The edges of his mouth twitched slightly. 'Hélène,' he said quietly, eyeing her shyly.

'Aah, Hélène, *la belle* Hélène,' sang *Monsieur* Meffret senior.

Antoine caught her eye and laughed.

In the bath, the evidence of Albert Meffret's disease was only too clear. He was as tall as his son but there was little flesh hanging from his huge frame. His skin was wizened and it wrinkled very quickly in the heat of the water. Together, they hoisted him out of the tub. While he leant against Antoine, Hélène wrapped him in a rough towel. They helped him back over to the bed and after drying him off carefully she pulled a clean nightgown over his head and laid him back onto his pillows. She served up the soup and left the men to eat while she emptied the tub and swept the floor.

Antoine finished his soup and stood up. 'Right, I must get back to work. The onions are nearly in; I'd like to get it finished today.' He strode out of the kitchen and pulled on his boots in the hall and went outside.

Hélène finished clearing up and she too said her goodbyes and went on her way. As she stepped out into the courtyard, she could see the blue of Antoine's jacket through the doorjamb of the barn. She peeped a little closer, and she could see he was reading something. Her heart raced. She boldly walked into the barn. 'So, Antoine, I will be off.'

As soon as she spoke Antoine jumped and stuffed what looked like a sheet of newspaper beneath a bale of straw. Hélène relaxed it was not one of her messages.

'See you tomorrow,' he replied awkwardly.

As she cycled towards the forest she wondered what it could have been that Antoine had not wanted her to see. She took the route between the drying sunflowers where their height would shield her presence from prying eyes. Once she got to the edge of the forest she hid her bicycle and covered it with branches and brush until it was completely obscured.

The sun on the chapel gave it quite a different allure to the chilly darkness of her arrival. The tree, with its branches dipped into the pond, had begun to lose its leaves and they floated on the surface of the green water. From the shiny striations on its trunk she could tell it was a cherry. Amongst the oak and chestnut it seemed a little incongruous. The makeshift door on the front of the chapel hung open and was creaking in the autumn breeze. She looked around her but there was not a soul. She peeped inside and everything seemed to be just as she and Rémy had left it a few weeks before. She went inside and closed the door behind her.

She scraped away at the earth just by the altar; it was hard work without Rémy's shovel. The board was still there beneath. Below it the hole was empty. No container, nor black out sheeting. They had obviously been back and cleared everything out. Had they abandoned this place or were they just being thorough? She needed to find Rémy.

# SIXTEEN

## Diana

Diana pulled a chair up under the buddleia bush and watched the butterflies while Ben splashed in the paddling pool. She thought back to Paris, when Ben had just mastered the art of walking. Diana had read a book which preached the belief that children should experience as many activities as possible. For want of a garden, she had covered the bathroom floor in newspaper and poured different coloured paints into dinner plates. She'd stripped Ben down to his underwear and let him put his hands and feet in the paint and then print them on pieces of paper. He'd loved it. By the end of it Ben was covered from head to toe in every colour of the rainbow, as was Diana. Serge had come home unexpectedly early from work.

'Look how clever your little boy is,' she had said proudly, holding up the paper sheets of hand and footprints.

In a millisecond Serge's expression had veered to rage. 'What on earth do you think you are doing? That child is absolutely filthy. Do you have absolutely no sense of responsibility?'

Diana was speechless.

'Get that lot cleaned up, immediately.' And he stormed into the bedroom and slammed the door.

Ben had started to cry. Since then Diana had always carefully orchestrated Ben's messy activities to coincide with Serge's absence, which as their marriage progressed had become more and more common. She watched Ben's soft tanned body as he lay on his tummy in the blue paddling pool, his arms mimicking breast stroke. He looked so much like his father. Would he grow up to be obsessive about cleanliness like him, she wondered. Would he expect the world from his wife? She felt suddenly sad that this gorgeous child would grow up into a man with habits, possibly a bad temper and selfishness.

'*Maman?*' Ben was looking at her quizzically, noticing her change in mood.

'Yes, my darling.' No, not *my* baby, she thought. She picked up his soaking body and dried him off with a towel. 'Let's go for a walk.'

She loaded Ben into the push chair and battled with Léo to get his lead on without it getting wrapped around his legs, and set off down the lane past Marcel and Pierrot's cottage.

Just as she passed their gate, a large elderly lady appeared on the doorstep. She threw her arms in the air and in a high-pitched siren whined, 'Aah, the little Englishman. Hello, my little man.' She bent down and tweaked Ben's cheek with a plump finger and thumb. She stood up again and beamed at Diana. '*Bonjour Madame*. I am Claudette, Marcel and Pierrot's *Maman*. But you must call me Mémère. Mémère Claudette, that's what everyone round here calls me. Come in, Come in.' With one hand she tugged at the wig which was in danger of slipping off her head sideways, with the other she ushered Diana and Ben into a small kitchen, kicking an overweight, greasy black Labrador that was sprawled across the doorstep on her way.

At a Formica-topped table on one side, was a young woman. She was a similar age to Diana. This must be Marcel and Pierrot's younger sister. She looked up from the magazine she was reading.

'This is my daughter Marie-Pierre,' Mémère announced. The volume of the siren was thankfully significantly reduced. Marie-Pierre stood up and leaned forwards for Diana to kiss her. She was dressed in leggings and a baggy ill-fitting white tee-shirt. Her hair obviously hadn't yet been brushed and there was evidence of stubble on her chin.

Diana obediently lunged forward and brushed cheeks trying to dodge her whiskers. '*Bonjour, Madame*'

'*Aah Non*!' she laughed in a similar squeal to that of her mother's. 'I never married.' She shook a finger expansively. 'Marie-Pierre will do.'

Mémère obviously thrilled with her unexpected visitors seemed to be rummaging vigorously in the pockets of her blue check nylon house coat, as if it was an outlet for her excruciating pleasure, a trait Pierrot had a tendency to. 'Now let me see. I think you English drink tea.' And she turned to peer into the depths of a huge wooden larder.

'I was just taking the dog for a walk,' Diana attempted. She could hear Léo whimpering outside, still attached to the pushchair.

'Oh, you've got all day to do that,' she trilled. She came out of the cupboard like a hippo coming up for air. She was waving a dog-eared teabag above her head like a trophy exclaiming, 'I knew we had some somewhere.'

At least it was only tea she would be obliged to drink. When they visited Serge's family the Muscadet was uncorked at impressively early times of the morning and it would of course be nothing less than ungrateful if it were refused.

'Now I think I can find a little something for you, little man.' Her hand shot into the front pocket of her housecoat once more and produced a boiled sweet stuck with dirt and dust. Diana grimaced but managed to turn it to a smile when Mémère suggested running it under the tap. Mémère poured herself and Marie-Pierre tiny cups of thick black coffee and launched into a long discourse, which seemed to cover just about any subject that came into her head; Marcel's dental history, Pierrot's bankruptcy, the death of her husband, at which Diana made appropriate commiserating noises. But Mémère waved away her condolences explaining that his expiration was a blessing. 'You don't know how lucky you are to have contraception you know. In our day it was a baby a year if you were fertile. Nowadays, you can pick and choose when you have them. You can even check if it's a boy or a girl to make planning the wallpaper easier.' Her eyes became wider with the incredulity, as she considered the breadth of the advances of modern medicine.

Whilst Mémère talked and Marie-Pierre's grunts and nods of confirmation punctuated her flow, the floor became swamped with a comprehensive range of toys, all uniformly coated in a grimy film of dust-ingrained grease. Diana drained her tea, bar the bottom centimetre, for fear of revealing anything that could have been missed by the stained tea towel she'd noticed hung out to dry over the sink. On the right-hand side was a large iron urn with a dial on the lid. It was sitting on a tripod over a gas flame.

'Beans,' exclaimed Mémère following her gaze.

'Beans?' Diana replied.

'Beans. Green beans. My Marcel and Pierrot; they are good boys. They grow them for me in our vegetable garden out the back.' Mémère stood up and with a filthy tea-towel wrapped around her plump arm she removed the dialled lid from the urn. Inside, were a collection of Kilner jars filled with French beans. They bobbed around clunking the sides. 'I seal them in the jars and then boil them in the steriliser. We can eat them all year round. Come and see.' She took Diana's hand and led her back outside into the little courtyard. A ramshackle shed was balanced precariously against the outside wall of her cottage. She pulled the doors open.

Diana narrowed her eyes as she watched the frame shudder as if it was ready to give way and collapse there and then on the concreted ground. Inside, were shelves of rows and rows of jars with orange rubber seals. They were filled with green beans, yellow beans and butter beans. Diana pointed to some other jars full of something red.

'Tomatoes, and those down there are pâté; wild boar, hare and pheasant. My boys shot them all. They are good hunters.'

At last she was waved off down the road like some long-lost relative. They got as far as *La Petite Folie* when Ben began to chant 'Horsey, horsey, horsey'.

She hesitated, thinking of what Jeanette had said. It was the afternoon, Michaud wouldn't be there. He said he checked the horses in the mornings. She chided herself for taking any notice of village gossip. She was only going to show Ben the horses. They pushed on, past the replica suburban houses, towards the track where she could see Marrakech trotting towards the fence ready to greet them.

'Horsey, horsey, horsey!' Ben chanted even louder.

The horse leaned over the rail and nuzzled Diana's top pocket. 'Look, he's hungry.'

'Hungry,' Ben squealed delightedly and began tearing at the long grass that was out of reach of the great creature. As soon as Marrakech nuzzled his nose into Ben's outstretched hand, the other horses came lolloping over in the hope of a morsel.

Worried that the horses all cantering over to them would draw attention and bring Michaud out of his farmhouse, she called to Ben and they carried on up the lane to a field full of poppy heads turned to seed, their pods stood upright towards the sky. These must have been the pink poppies she'd seen the day they'd gone to fetch Léo. Along the edge of the field was a long low greenhouse. She peered through the misted windows and saw great sheaves of green leaves hanging upside down. She couldn't think what they were. Beside it, was a sign indicating a footpath. The path was a wide track rutted by tractors and patched with rubble in places. It was hard going with the pushchair and Léo darting around hungrily, smelling every inch of ground and tugging at the buggy. They reached the far end where the track ran through an opening in a fir hedge. On the other side was a large enclosure with chickens milling about scratching at the ground.

Ben rushed up to them and they flapped and squawked a little way off. He started to count them. She watched him dance up and down the fence pointing at each chicken in turn.

'One, two, fourteen, twenty-five,' he counted. 'Lotsa Tickens *Maman*!'

'Yes, lots of chickens my boy!'

A large black cloud appeared from nowhere and was floating menacingly above them. It was threateningly dark. She sensed it would be prudent to turn back should the heavens decide to open. Ben was running up the track ahead of her, followed in close pursuit by Léo who was dragging Diana and the pushchair so hard that he was almost choking on his collar. The pushchair lurched violently against an unruly lump of rubble, pulling the wheel out of its flimsy socket. Ben tripped over and lay silent for a second. Then he let out a great squeal, tears flooding his face. Diana abandoned the pushchair with the dog attached and scooped her son up to console him. He buried his face in her chest and sobbed.

At that moment the heavens opened. It didn't come down in drops but in strings of solid water. The dips and ruts in the track filled up in seconds and what had been a bumpy dry track just a few seconds before, had turned into a gushing muddy stream. With Ben on one hip, sobbing rhythmically in time with his breathing, she pulled the now three-wheeled pushchair with Léo attached, the wheel-less corner dragging in the mud, back towards the greenhouse and the lane. The rain stopped as quickly as it had started.

She put Ben down to untangle the lead and wondered how to get her son, the unruly puppy and the broken pushchair home. She didn't relish the thought of carrying Ben all the way, at the same time as dragging the broken buggy with the dog attached, pulling it in every other direction. All three of them were soaked to the skin. Her arms ached with Ben's weight. Her desperation got the better of her and she could feel tears welling up.

'Clip! Clop! Clip! Clop!' squealed Ben suddenly, his accident forgotten.

Round the bend, appeared a large shire horse pulling a cart. Michaud was sitting on the coachbox, a long whip in his hand and water running down his face from the shower.

She bowed her head in an attempt to feign ignorance at his presence, but quickly realised the ridiculousness of this as the sound of the horse's hooves echoed round the village. Instead she bent down to fiddle with the tangled lead. The cart pulled to a halt just in front of them.

'Let me help you get that pushchair home.' And he began to climb down from the cart.

'No, no. Thank you. Honestly we're fine,' she said in a forceful,l in charge sort of voice.

'Don't be silly, you're soaked to the skin.'

Silly? Who did he think he was speaking to? If she didn't want his help she was quite within her rights to refuse it. She hesitated to think of an answer by which time he'd picked Ben up and sat him on the coachbox next to his seat. He stood with his hand out to help her into the cart.

'Thank you.'

Michaud loaded the damaged pushchair and Léo into the back, carefully tying his lead to the cart. With Ben sitting between them he pulled a tarpaulin from the back over their heads to protect them from the rain which had begun to fall again. 'I'll get you home.'

They drove up the lane in silence with just the horse's steps echoing through the wet village. He handled the horse and cart deftly, turning the sharp corner in front of the church. She watched his huge brown hands flicking and steering the reins with practice. He pulled the horse up outside the iron gate and lifted Ben down.

'Thank you,' she said again. 'I am so sorry to trouble you.'

'It's no trouble,' he replied. He undid the dog's lead from the pushchair and lifted him down, pushing him inside the gate. 'Leave me the pushchair I'll see if I can mend it.'

She was going to object but he'd already climbed back into the cart and was turning the horse round. The next moment he was gone taking the pushchair with him.

# SEVENTEEN

### Edward

The forest was alive with flowers of every shade, size and form; an apothecary's dream. Not quite as abundant as the priory garden but these had grown up naturally, even without monks to tend and weed the ground. How Eldric would love to see this! The sun was at its highest. He was glad of the task of fetching water now that Clothilde could not visit until the evening. He picked specimens of each of the different plants that grew wild by the pond in the clearing. He relished writing them all down and sketching them on parchment. He cursed himself for leaving it behind in the cavern, he could have sat in the sunshine, hidden amongst the bushes of course.

He thought of Clothilde and how she would sit and watch him for hours in the evenings, as he scratched out the uses of an infinite number of plants onto the stolen parchment. Then she would sit and read them back to him for practice. He stored samples of each of the plants in the earthen pots that she brought him. He feared she would be caught. Should he move on and leave this poor waif to a life without danger? The villagers nor the *seigneurie* would be lenient were they to discover how she had secreted him, a stranger, here in these woods, little more than a criminal in hiding. His will incited dishonest actions and he realised he was unwilling to renounce them. How could he leave such a stock of plants, that could relieve almost any ill, unrecorded? Where would he go? Clothilde had talked of an abbey at Pontigny. If he were to find himself there he could claim memory loss; an untruth to be sure but not to God, just the abbey. He could return to the life he lived before, though he would have to abandon Clothilde. His heart swooped at the suggestion. He scolded himself. He must deviate from such self-indulgence. A man of the cloth is a servant of the Lord and no other.

'Edward!'

He was so taken by surprise that he lost his footing and almost fell into the green depths of the pond.

'You will be caught. I have told you before, you must not be found in these woods. I don't know what they would do were they to find you here.'

He struck out his arm and grabbed the protruding branch of a willow to keep himself from slipping down the muddy bank. His feet continued to slide and he sat down hard to break his glide. Only then did he breathe again.

'No, I am sure I don't know what they would do to me, but perhaps it would be too late as you could be the cause of my drowning!'

Clothilde started to laugh, 'Your drowning? Do you not know how to swim?'

Edward shook his head.

'Aha, at last I have found something I can do, that you do not know how.' She beamed with satisfaction. 'I could teach you. Do you want to learn?'

Edward nodded sheepishly. 'Yes, I would like to learn. When I was travelling across the sea from Sandwich, I dreamt that the ship had sunk and that I drowned just a short distance from shore.'

'You have so many dreams. It is no matter. I will teach you to swim.' She held out her arm securing herself to a large rowan and pulled him away from the water's edge. She stopped and stared at him for a moment.

'What is the matter?'

'You are quite tall!' She was laughing again. 'How funny to talk to someone that I feel I know so well, but have never seen standing up in daylight!'

'What are you doing here?'

'The well in the village is running low so I came to fetch some fresher water from the spring. When the weather is warm like this you must be careful, for villagers come here also to fetch water. Now we must both go.' She held a water carrier beneath the spring until it was filled and disappeared into the undergrowth with a wave.


The nights had turned warm and Edward was glad of his underground home; it was cooler beneath the roots of the trees. The full moon was up and it cast an eerie twilight across the forest. He gathered up the rough cloth that Clothilde had left him and set off in the semi-darkness towards the pond. The forest at night was silent save for the screaming of the vixens and the hoot of an owl. He reached the edge of the clearing and scanned the edges of the pond shining in the moonlight. He couldn't see Clothilde. Close by, he heard the call of an owl, now he realised it was not the same as the resident owls of the forest. It was

113

the same sound he had heard on his first night in these woods. He stopped, waiting for it to come again. This time it came from behind the spring and he could just make out the shape of a person huddled low on the ground.

'Clothilde,' he whispered, stepping towards the shape.

'I am here.'

As he got closer he could see that she was leaning against the boulder that guided the spring's torrent into the pond. Her legs were bare and bent up towards her. Edward was glad of the semi-darkness for he could pretend he hadn't seen.

'You are not ready!'

'I have brought my spare clothing, here.' He held up the bundle he was carrying.

Clothilde stood up and Edward closed his eyes. 'Look, you must hitch your tunic up like this.'

Edward opened one eye and he could feel himself blushing.

Clothilde was wearing some sort of undertunic. It was pale in colour and she had folded up the skirt under a girdle of rope to keep it in place. Her legs were strong and athletic, they glowed with a pearly sheen in the moonlight. At the neck, the garment hung loose around her pale shoulders, the hint of a curve of her young bosom was illuminated against the dark forest.

He breathed in closing his eyes once more.

'You are afeared?'

'No, just a little out of breath,' he lied, though it was not the swimming that filled him with apprehension.

'I will not let anything happen to you.'

'Let's get on with it then!'

'You go in those bushes and arrange your tunic.'

Edward dutifully disappeared. When he had removed his habit and pulled his undertunic up around his legs just like Clothilde's and fastened it in place with a belt, he tugged on it to check it would not release itself in the water. He stepped shyly from the shadows fearing Clothilde's jesting, but as he got to the water's edge she was already in the pond.

'Here, sit on this stone and dangle your feet in the water.'

He did as he was told, the sooner he got into the pond the less of him she would be able to see. The water was refreshingly cool in contrast to the heavy night heat that hung beneath the branches.

114

'Now, lift a leg and put it back in the water, and then the other. Now, faster, as if you are running. Have you ever seen a dog swim?'

'Yes.' He laughed as he remembered seeing a dog swim in the river near the priory. His head had been high out of the water and his paws paddling furiously beneath it.

'That is what you must do. Like this.' Clothilde splashed her hands down into the pond in almost the same way as he had paddled his legs, though she didn't seem to travel very far. 'Help me with this branch.' She pointed to a long thick branch lying on the bank. 'Roll it into the water towards me.'

Edward pushed it, it was very heavy, as it hit the water it disappeared for a second and then bounced back up to the surface.

Clothilde held one end of it. 'Now, slip yourself slowly into the water and hold on to the other end.'

As Edward slid his body into the cool waters a shiver travelled up his neck. The feeling of every surface of his skin being enveloped in the water was so exalting that he felt he must be committing a sin. It was as if the pond was holding him in a loving embrace. He dipped his shoulders beneath the surface and stretched his toes to touch the bottom, but he felt nothing. In his panic his head plunged beneath the surface, he held tightly to the log and pulled himself back above the water gasping and spluttering. His ears were filled with it and he spat the musty water from his mouth. This water was not the same as that which he drank from his gourd.

Clothilde was laughing. 'That is the best encouragement to learn to swim! You must paddle or you will sink. Watch me.' She stretched herself long in the water and kicked her feet behind her. As she did so the log moved pushing Edward towards the bank. 'Now it's your turn.'

Edward clutched the log with all his might and stretched his body out behind him. He kicked his legs clumsily and with such strength, that he pushed the log beneath the water and almost took another mouthful of pond. 'Clothilde, I cannot do it.'

She was laughing again, 'Of course you can, you must move your legs without moving your body, dangle them just like you did from the stone.'

He tried again, this time loosening his hips. His splashing was not as elegant as Clothilde's but the log moved forwards pushing her back a little way.

'Yes, yes, yes!' called Clothilde in delight. 'Now rest and I will push you.' They hung onto the log and splashed like that pushing each other round and round the pond until Edward could no more. He realised that his weeks huddled in the cavern had taken its toll on his body and he was no longer fit. Clothilde kicked and splashed until he was again by the stone from which he had entered the water. He scrambled out and sat catching his breath in the moonlight.

Clothilde scrambled up the bank next to him. Her tunic clung to her body like a second skin. He couldn't take his eyes from her bosom which pointed outwards and was tipped with two tiny buds. Her hair was dark with the water and clung to her head and shoulders as if she was a sculpture.

He took her hand and kissed it. 'You are truly beautiful.'

'Only in the dark!' she joked.

'No, no. You are truly beautiful; both inside and outside, in daylight and in darkness.'

She pulled her hand away. 'I think you are missing company, hiding away in the cavern for so long. The moon will be good again tomorrow so we will meet here again. You will be swimming in no time. If only reading and writing came so quick. Come, we must go.' She kissed him on the cheek and disappeared into the undergrowth.

Edward shivering with excitement returned to his clothing on the edge of the clearing and put on his habit and wrung out his under tunic. He would hang it from the opening of the cavern to dry in the heat.

# EIGHTEEN

## Diana

When she was sure the last of the villagers would have collected their bread and Jeanette would be free to chat, Diana, with Ben on her hip, set off to *La Petite Folie.*

Jeanette was sweeping away the crumbs from the floor. When she saw Diana she put her broom to one side. 'Diana, be careful. People talk in a small village.'

'What on earth do you mean?'

'You were seen yesterday.'

'I was seen?'

'On Michaud's cart.'

'He only gave me a lift because the pushchair broke and it was pouring with rain.' She couldn't stop the whine entering her voice.

'Nevertheless.'

'Jeanette, *please* tell me what is wrong with this man.'

'Just keep away; I've warned you, I'm only doing it as your friend, remember that.' She was almost spitting the words. She turned her back on Diana and began to wipe crumbs from the rack.

Diana stood dumbfounded. Was all this animosity really necessary in the name of village decency? Jeanette didn't interrupt her task to turn round again, so Diana muttered a goodbye and turned to leave.

Jeanette dropped her cloth and threw her hands in the air. 'Diana, I'm sorry! Come. My chores are nearly done. Let's have a coffee next door.' She opened the door that connected to the café and gestured her through. The shutters in the café were still closed and the chairs and tables were shrouded in darkness. Jeanette unbolted the front door letting in a shaft of light that lit up the table football, and a man. Both women jumped.

'*Mesdames,*' said the man. He was smiling but no warmth radiated from him.

'*Monsieur,* you are early. I was not expecting you so soon.' Jeanette's face was flushed.

'I can see that. Business must be booming since you are opening so late.' He slid up his sleeve to look at his watch revealing a tattooed insignia on the back of his wrist. A cygnet ring glinted in the shaft of light from the front door.

Jeanette glanced at the clock on the wall. 'It is only five minutes and as you can see I have no queue at the door.' She looked at Diana warningly, gesturing with her head that she should go.

'Well, I shall not keep you any longer. I have plenty to get on with. *Au revoir,* Jeanette. *Monsieur.*'

The man nodded at her solemnly.

When she returned home Ben's pushchair was standing on the front terrace. The wheel was mended and the mud had been cleaned off it. She searched for a note but there was none. She was glad to have it back; she had been wondering how she would explain its absence to Serge. A pang of guilt hit her like a cold shower. Why was she planning on being secretive with Serge? I've done nothing wrong, she thought. This was all Jeanette's fault. If she hadn't made such a thing out of her cadging a lift back in the cart she wouldn't be feeling like this. She cursed herself for accepting the tar brush Jeanette had menaced her with and vowed not to get caught up in village gossip.

Serge would be back the following afternoon. The meal with Liesel! How could she have forgotten that? She toyed with the idea of ringing her and cancelling it. She could feign illness. No, that would only upset Serge. Besides she didn't have her number. She would just have to think of something that would make it more bearable. In Paris she would have invited some other guests to dilute her. Correction! Liesel would not have been coming round to dinner in Paris. Liesel had always had a million other people to spend time with and had always had a knack for taking the best offer. It struck Diana as a little peculiar. If she had so many friends and contacts why on earth had she moved out here where she knew no one? Although she realised good jobs were not easy to come by for newly qualified graduates, but with all Liesel's connections surely she could have found something. There was no point churning that one over, she was coming and that was that.

She couldn't remember exactly how they'd met Liesel. They used to frequent the same student bar in *Rue* Mouffetard, and Liesel had always just sort of been there. She would sometimes turn up at the parties they went to after the bar shut, but Diana couldn't be sure if she had been invited or whether she had just strung along. The thing about Liesel, that Diana disliked, was her fickleness. She would be in one crowd one week and with another the next. She was shallow and self-centred. With Diana she had always donned an air of indigenous superiority. She assumed it was because they shared the same mother tongue except Liesel had lived in Paris all her life giving her some kind of monopoly on experience.

There was a knock on the French doors. Marcel stood on the doorstep holding a carrier bag. At least no one would speculate why Marcel was visiting. No one could possibly imagine that anything untoward was going on between her and Marcel. He was smiling, revealing his black teeth with pride. He held the bag out to her.

'From my mother.'

Inside was an industrial quantity of French beans. 'Marcel, thank you.'

'My mother said that if you'd like to bottle them, she'll show you how.'

'That's terribly kind of you, but I think it might be simpler to freeze them.' Noticing his reluctance to leave she offered him a coffee.

'I don't want to disturb you,' he mumbled.

'You're not. Please, come in.'

He wiped his shoes on the back of his trouser legs and stepped inside. When Diana reappeared from the kitchen with a steaming coffee pot, Marcel had installed himself at the table, topping and tailing the beans with the knife that hung permanently from his belt.

Diana fetched a knife for herself and sat down opposite him. She had an idea. 'I wonder. Would you be free to come for dinner tomorrow evening and taste them with us?'

'I don't know,' he hesitated shyly.

'Please. Serge will be back from work around six, he would insist,' she added.

'Well in that case, yes. I'll look forward to it.'

'About seven o'clock then?'

Diana hated being unkind or rude and struggled with people who were perfectly comfortable with it. At times like this she knew she had no option, she couldn't bear the idea of Liesel coming to dinner so she must plan it carefully. Perhaps if she made something really complicated she could be busy in the kitchen for most of the meal and then she wouldn't have to talk to her too much. Serge could entertain her. Her heart swung at the thought of it. She was jealous. She scolded herself. Now she was just being silly. At least with Marcel coming Serge would be obliged to entertain Liesel *and* Marcel, putting paid to Serge's whole attentions being concentrated on Queen Bee. Satisfied and even a little impressed with herself, she selected a starter of French beans in vinaigrette, sprinkled with shallots; followed by Serge's favourite dish, *Galettes au blé noir* with a filling of Bayonne Ham and ewe's milk cheese. She would normally avoid making *crêpes* or *galettes* for guests as it was so time consuming but this time it fitted the bill perfectly. She would have to prepare the pancake mixture in advance but the rest of the preparations she would save for the moment Liesel crossed the threshold.

The toys were tidied away and the mixture for the *galettes* stood ready on the side in the kitchen. She made a fresh pot of coffee and set it on the dining table with a mug and a bowl of sugar lumps. If he was late, she could reheat it in the microwave. She heard the courtyard gate clang. She picked up Ben and carried him to the back door and waited at the top of the steps to welcome him. Serge got out of the Mini and climbed the steps. His eyes rested on her for a second, and then as if he hadn't quite registered her presence he pushed past her into the house.

A barely audible '*Ca va?*' seemed to come from his lips but Diana couldn't be sure.

Ben was calling, '*Papa, papa*!' dismayed at his father's lack of response.

Serge glanced at the coffee pot steaming and ready for him on the table and ignoring it too he sloped off to the bedroom.

Diana stood in the middle of the sitting room, feeling snubbed. Was it unreasonable to crave some attention after his absence? To preserve her pride she went into the kitchen away from his mood and began tidying an imaginary mess, a tear escaping down her cheek. He had often behaved like this in Paris, but there had always been something to spark it off. She searched her mind for something she could have done to upset him, but found none. She hadn't yet told him that Marcel would be joining them for dinner. Now, she regretted having invited him. She heard the shower fizz into life. Only half an hour to go before their guests would arrive.

'*Papa?*' asked Ben plaintively.

'*Papa's* washing, darling.'

'Shshshsh?'

'Yes, he's in the shower.' She felt shaky. Would things ever go smoothly? She laid the table with glasses and bowls of tiny gherkins and olives.

Liesel arrived first. 'How lovely! Is it just us three?' She was looking around the room hopefully. Seeing no one, she continued, 'I am so looking forward to catching up on old times.'

Old times? Diana sneered to herself. They'd only left Paris a couple of months before and she'd never taken much interest in Diana then. 'Actually, I've invited one of our neighbours. You know, to make up numbers.'

'I hope he's good looking!' she laughed tossing her head back like a pony, her silky hair flying out provocatively behind her.

'Who's good looking?' Serge appeared from the bedroom, his wet hair neatly combed back.

'I've invited Marcel tonight.' She glanced at Serge nervously, feeling foolish.

'Serge, darling!' Liesel threw her arms around him as if she hadn't seen him in years.

Diana eyed her great long legs clad in skin tight paisley leggings and a little bolero that clung to the curve of her breasts. She looked fabulous.

'You look tired out,' said Liesel, rubbing Serge's shoulder affectionately.

'I've just finished work. It was a busy shift.'

Diana noticed the shadows under his eyes. Perhaps she'd judged him a little harshly earlier on. He was just dead beat.

'You look great, Liesel,' she said as a decoy and regretted it immediately.

'Oh, this little number? I picked it up in Milan.'

Diana looked down at her tired Lycra pencil skirt which she saved for smarter occasions and saw in horror that there was a bit of egg on the hem.

'Where is that gorgeous little boy?'

Ben hearing her voice and recognizing it as fire engine lady's, came trundling in proudly on his new vehicle.

Liesel picked him up and gave him a warm hug. 'I've got something for you.'

'Oh Liesel you mustn't, really. You've already spoilt him enough.'

'I saw this little outfit in that charming little designer shop in Beaugency, you know the one just behind the castle.'

Diana *did* know the one. The one with the ominously absent price tags. She often looked wistfully in the window on market day.

'Well, I couldn't resist it, so I bought it for my favourite little boy,' she uttered in a contrived squeaky baby voice. She held up the most gorgeous sailor suit.

The iron gate clunked at the end of the front path, Marcel had arrived, wearing obviously new jeans. As he turned round Diana caught a glimpse of a label he had forgotten to remove. A pungent smell of *eau de toilette* followed him in, making Diana cough. She'd never seen his hair brushed before, though the curls around his ears remained untamed.

Liesel tore herself away from Serge and did little to hide her disappointment when she set eyes on Marcel. She held out a hand gingerly, as if he was not worthy of her touch.

For a moment Diana thought Marcel was going to bow. He took her hand fleetingly casting his eyes humbly downwards. His head and neck seemed to go into a spasm of uncontrollable nodding. He held out a bottle to Serge. '*Poire William,*' he stuttered. 'A friend of mine makes it.'

'Excellent! *Poire William.* I've not had a taste of this for years.' Serge cradled the label-less bottle like a baby. 'We shall save this for our digestive.' His hand stroked the smooth curved neck of the bottle. Serge's fatigue seemed to slip away as he sipped his pastis.

Diana managed to busy herself in the kitchen, skipping the majority of the aperitif, whilst keeping an ear on the conversation in the sitting room. Every time she felt Liesel was monopolising Serge's attention she would nip in and interrupt.

'Marcel, do tell Liesel about your logging,' or 'Marcel, has a fabulous vegetable garden. Don't you Marcel?' successfully heading off any possible flirting.

She served the beans in vinaigrette and managed to bolt hers in record time and dart back to the kitchen to fill the *galettes*. Liesel ummed and aahed expansively about the food while Marcel ate hungrily, saying very little. By the time the chocolate soufflés were served it was getting pretty late and Diana hoped that Liesel would be heading off home at a reasonable hour. After all, it was a Wednesday, she must have to be at work early in the morning.

'Those beans were delicious, Marcel. Thank you for bringing them,' said Diana as she cleared away the plates.

Liesel, seized a pile of dirty dishes and joined her in the kitchen, throwing her plan of avoiding her into serious jeopardy.

'What a funny chap that is. Where did you dig him up?'

'We *dug him up* in the village. He's helped us a lot with the garden and getting settled. He's a very kind man.'

'I'm sure he is,' said Liesel standing corrected. 'But he's not really your sort is he?'

'I don't know what you think my sort is Liesel.'

'Well, you know. His appearance he's so, so..,' she hesitated, 'Primitive.' Her lip curled with distaste.

'He's grown up in this village and as far as I can tell he's never lived anywhere else. I guess you *would* have a limited outlook in those circumstances.' Not wanting this conversation to go any further Diana continued on another avenue. 'Tell me about your work Liesel. You're a psychology graduate aren't you?'

'I graduated last year, like you.' She stopped, her pupils flashed backwards and forwards in her sockets for a moment. 'Oh, no, you didn't graduate did you? You gave up.' She coughed, 'Silly of me. Well, anyway. I graduated and began to look for a job. The only posts available for someone of my limited experience were in hospitals. I really didn't fancy wearing a white coat and talking to 'real' lunatics,' she laughed horsily.

Diana cringed.

'So I began to look elsewhere. I found this practice in Mer. I work for a psychotherapist. She's got four children and needed someone for a job share. It's just right for me really. I escape the serious violence and drug problems of the inner city and to boot she sends me away to all the conferences, and pays for my training sessions, as she finds it difficult to leave her brood. I've got it made really. What about you?'

'Me, what do you mean?'

'Well, you're obviously not going to be a housewife forever *are* you?'

'I, I don't know. I hadn't really thought about it. At the moment, Ben needs me and with Serge working away we don't really have a routine. I can't very well go and get a job.'

The women returned to the sitting room where Serge had lined up a row of liqueur thimbles. He produced the unlabelled bottle and tilted it, pouring the clear honey coloured liquid into each tiny glass. Serge's face was aglow with excitement.

'Not for me, thank you,' said Liesel.

Serge's face fell. 'Oh come on, Liesel. You would never have turned down a *Poire William* in Paris.'

'Aah! Yes, but that was when I didn't have to drive home.'

'Well, you don't have to drive home tonight either. Does she, Diana?'

Diana couldn't believe her ears. 'But the bed's not made!'

'No, really I must be getting home, I don't want to intrude,' minced Liesel.

'You wouldn't be intruding. Would she Diana?'

'No, no, of course not,' her voice sounding like a ventriloquist's.

'Well, if you're sure. I'd love to!' Liesel was looking straight at Diana, beaming. Either she was terrible at picking up hints or she was hell bent on staying the night. 'I wouldn't want to impose.'

Yes, you would, thought Diana.

'Of course you wouldn't be imposing,' she replied obediently. She picked up a thimble of *Poire* and knocked it back. The fiery liquid slipped down her throat making her splutter. She left the others to theirs while she went to make up a bed for Liesel.

Marcel was bidding his goodbyes as she reappeared. She yawned as he disappeared into the shadows of the yew hedge. She felt exhausted, her head began to spin. That morning seemed like a year ago. 'Well, I must go to bed.' She stood up and waited for Liesel to reciprocate.

'Oh don't go to bed yet Diana. Let's have another drink!' pleaded Liesel.

'I'm sorry but I really am so tired.'

'She's always tired.' Serge rolled his eyes. 'I can't think why. She doesn't go out to work.'

Diana glared at him.

'Right, well. *We* can have another. *She* can go to bed.' And he reached for the bottle. Liesel promptly held out her glass.

Diana had already melted into the background as far as they were concerned. She took herself off to bed, too tired to care about her failed plan, and fell straight to sleep.

When Diana awoke it was obviously quite late. The sun was already high in the sky and she could feel the heat of the day beginning to seep under the shutters. The bed was empty next to her. She rushed into Ben's room; it was empty. She went into the sitting room, all was quiet. On the table were two cups with dregs of coffee in the bottom and Ben's plastic dalmatian plate with traces of boiled egg. The clock in the kitchen said ten a.m. Surely she hadn't slept that long? She must have been tired. She knocked on the spare room door. There was no reply, so she turned the handle and went in. The bed had been made and Liesel's make up bag was on the dressing table. She looked out of the window onto the front lawn. The lane beyond was empty as usual. Then something caught her eye. Next to Liesel's make-up bag was a toothbrush. It didn't strike her at first. She hadn't thought to offer her a toothbrush. Was it normal to carry a toothbrush around with you? Surely, only if you were in the habit of sleeping away from home. She could feel her face heating up with the awful thought that Liesel had been planning this.

Serge's car was missing from the garage, as was the pushchair from the hall. Why hadn't they woken her? She went into the kitchen. All the dishes had been washed and cleared away. It must have been Liesel, Serge would never have done that. Resentment welled up in her. The thought of Liesel playing happy families with her husband and baby boy made her feel sick. She felt like a ghost in her own home. Could Liesel have orchestrated the whole thing? Or was she being paranoid? She shook herself, not wanting to believe it and got in the shower to ease her aching head. *Poire William* obviously didn't agree with her.

As she emerged from the bathroom feeling revitalised, Liesel bustled in with Ben in her arms. It was all she could do not to snatch him away from her.

'Diana you're awake. I hope you had a lovely long sleep.'

'*Maman!*' He held out his arms. He was wearing the sailor suit that Liesel had brought him. Ben clasped his little arms around Diana's neck and squeezed tight. She nuzzled into his hair drinking in his baby smell of shampoo and lotion.

'We went for a walk in the woods. Didn't we Benno?' Serge appeared from the back steps to the garage.

'Why didn't you wake me?'

'Liesel wouldn't let me. She insisted that you needed a rest and I'm sorry for what I said last night, I didn't realise how tired you were.' He kissed her warmly.

Diana eyed Liesel suspiciously. 'I'm sorry Liesel, I should have thought, I've got a spare toothbrush in the bathroom I'll just get it for you.'

'No need, I've got into the habit of keeping one in my handbag.'

Diana raised her eyebrows.

'I'm away such a lot at conferences that I've rather got into the habit of living out of a suitcase.'

Diana reddened, embarrassment replacing rancour. Perhaps she really did mean well. 'Well, thank you, Liesel. I haven't slept so well in a long time. I feel really fresh.'

Liesel beamed.

'And thank you for clearing up the kitchen,' she added.

'All in a day's work my dear. Well, I must love you and leave you. Thank you for the lovely dinner. I've written my number on your kitchen blackboard. Give me a ring, we'll have coffee in town or something.'

# NINETEEN

## Hélène

MONEY MISSING STOP HOLD DROPS STOP

She was careful never to transmit too long, she hadn't yet seen a German radio detector van but she had no intention of being caught by one. Downstairs all seemed to be quiet. The doctor was out on his rounds and *Madame* Clément was in the village on an errand. She went out of the front door and headed for the *Épicerie*.

As she pulled the door open the bell jangled. The shelves inside were nearly all empty. A man appeared behind the counter. He was slight and bookish with small wire-rimmed round glasses perching on the end of his nose.

*'Mademoiselle.'* His smile appeared more like a reticent grimace.

Hélène glanced round the shop. They were alone. *'Bonjour Monsieur.* I am looking for Rémy.'

He bristled. 'I do not know him.'

'I am a friend,' said Hélène checking behind her that the shop was still empty.

The shopkeeper nodded and nervously grabbed a brown paper bag, into which he stuffed a bruised apple.

'Nothing for me, thank you.'

'Here, take it!' he almost barked. She took it from him. The shopkeeper tilted his head, gesturing to the door. Hélène did as she was told and as she emerged onto the pavement, he called after her in a suddenly jolly voice. *'Bonne journée, Mademoiselle.'*

DEFENSE de la FRANCE was the paper. The hens were clucking round her feet excitedly. On the front there were photos of naked, emaciated children. They were so thin their ages could not even be guessed at. A caption below read 'Children in the 'protected' countries.' So Antoine had been hiding a clandestine journal. She'd heard of this one at HQ, it had the widest distribution. If Antoine was hiding this maybe he could be recruited. She heard the engine of a car approach. She quickly replaced the paper. Through the doorjamb she saw *Docteur* Legris' car swing into the courtyard. She gathered up some eggs in her skirt and stepped out to greet him.

'*Docteur*, I didn't know you were planning to visit today.'

'I wasn't but a place has come up for Albert at the sanatorium in Tours.'

'In Tours? But that is a long way away.'

'They've closed down the one in Blois. The Germans have taken it over.'

'Does he really have to go? He seems so much better!'

'Well, it will be Antoine's decision ultimately. Right, let me have a look at him.'

After the check up *Docteur* Legris left Hélène to pass the news on to Antoine when he returned. She said goodbye to *Monsieur* Meffret and went to wait for Antoine in the barn away from the old man's ears.

'Tours! That is too far, too far to even visit once a week!'

'I know.'

'If I turn it down and he gets worse again it could be bad for him, but Tours!' He was shaking his head. 'I don't want him to die surrounded by strangers, after all he has been through.'

She touched his arm. 'Antoine, I will be here to look after him if you decide against it.'

'Hélène. You have been so good to us.'

'Now stop that. It is my job.'

His eyes caught hers and lingered. He took her elbow and leant in close. 'Hélène. *La belle* Hélène. I know why my father calls you that.'

'Antoine,' she chided, 'I must speak to you about something.'

He released her arm and coughed as if to compose himself.

'I found the paper, the newspaper under the straw.'

His eyes flashed angrily. 'What are you talking about?'

'It's alright, I am on your side.'

'I don't know what you mean.'

She disregarded his display of ignorance. 'You know you said you wanted to help me. Well now, you can. You can help France too.'

He stopped and stared at her. Then he ducked out of the barn and skimmed its perimeter. When he came back inside he pulled the door to. 'You are taking great risks talking to me like this.'

'I don't think I am. I know where your heart lies and it is with your country. Am I right?'

He nodded solemnly.

'There is something I need you to help me with…'

A week went by and there had been no news from Rémy, she hadn't been able to send a message to Foucaud, with no information there was no point. But she knew she must arrange a drop or the resistants in Orléans would starve.

CONFIRMING DZ STOP NEXT MOON STOP

Just two weeks until the next moon. The weather had turned for the worse and Hélène was doubtful it would be clear for the Lizzie to come in low enough. There would be just three possible days. She concealed the radio set, removed the crystals and returned them to the crevice behind the skirting board. As she descended the stairs she glanced out of the tall window above the front door.

Across the square, people were gathering outside the church. A couple of German soldiers were leaning up against the wall of the church smoking. Did they have no respect? She recognized the older one from the café. A young woman with long shiny blonde hair came into view. Her clothes were expensive. They were dark and beautifully cut. She yearned to wear clothes like that again. She stopped on the stairs to watch her a little longer. On her head was a black hat worthy of Bette Davis, an ornate arrangement of feathers and sparkling hat pins pierced the air to one side of it. The woman stopped and turned to call to someone, she was holding out her arm. A tall man came into view, his hair was scraped back to his head tightly. In his hand he carried a trilby. He took Bette's hand and as he overtook her to lead the way into church his face turned slightly towards the house. It was Antoine!

Hélène sat down hard on the stair. So that was her; Antoine's fiancée. Suddenly she understood old man Meffret's concerns. She could not imagine someone so glamorous, so well groomed, living at *Ferme* Meffret. What's more she could not imagine Antoine with her or was that just a symptom of jealousy?

That night she struggled to get to sleep. Every time she closed her eyes Antoine's kind features flooded her vision. He was promised to another. She knew she was getting in too deep. This was dangerous and the one thing she had been told categorically not to do. For all the training she had undergone, they hadn't trained them how not to fall in love.

There was a tap on the window. Hélène automatically slid beneath her covers and rolled herself off the bed away from the window, onto the floor and beneath the bed. She peered up from her hiding place and saw a shape at the window. She was two floors up. She stiffened. As her eyes focused on the silhouette she saw that it was Rémy.

He tapped again and whispered, 'Francine.'

Hélène leapt up and slid the window open. Rémy jumped in and landed almost soundlessly. She pulled him to the other side of the bed and made him crouch with her. 'Thank you for coming.'

He nodded, not speaking.

'There is a problem. The supplies from the container drops are going missing. I went to the chapel; the space in the floor is empty. Everything is gone.'

'They are always transferred to another hiding place before distribution.'

'Who transfers them?'

'The *maquisard*.'

'The *maquisard*? The man on my reception committee?'

Rémy nodded. 'I do not know where he takes them, it is better we know as little as possible. We operate on trust.'

'What is his name?'

He shook his head. 'I cannot tell you. The less you know the better. I will look into it.' He was frowning. Without another word he crawled low towards the window. He slid up the sash and was gone.

# TWENTY

## Diana

The day had turned into another hot one. Serge was in the barn hammering bits of old pallets together to make a compost bin. Diana settled herself on the seat of the mower. He'd taken his shirt off and she was admiring the brown flesh of his tightly sculpted muscles undulating as he swung the hammer. Ben was trundling up and down the courtyard on his shiny fire engine. He'd discovered that if he got up a great enough speed down the slightly sloping concrete and then suddenly swerved to a halt, an impressive cloud of dust would fly up into the air above his head.

Serge and Diana didn't speak, but every now and then Serge would look up and smile at her. When she saw him like this his irritability and high expectations seemed a world away. She watched as the structure he was working on took shape. She felt touched that he was making something for her. She'd planned to buy one, but he'd insisted on making it. She had married a handsome, charming and capable man.

It was nearly lunchtime, she disappeared into the kitchen to make a goat's cheese omelette, throwing in some red basil and shallots. She piled the plates onto a tray and carried them out to the courtyard. They ate sitting on the steps in the sun. Serge took a mouthful and chewed slowly.

'Aah, Diana you really are a marvellous cook.' He leant over and kissed her. 'Thank you for making such an effort with Liesel last night.'

Diana pursed her lips and looked away in an attempt to conceal her guilt. Liesel obviously wasn't as shallow and self centred as she'd always imagined. 'That's alright,' she squeaked lamely.

Serge mopped up the traces of omelette with a bit of baguette. 'Right. I shall go and install this composter by your vegetable patch and then I thought we'd get cracking on the sitting room. I know how much you want it done.' He pulled her close and kissed her again.

Diana's heart swung as she realised how much she needed this!

They pulled the brown carpet-textured wallpaper from the walls in whole pieces. The material was so thick no glue was strong enough to make it tear. Ben squealed with delight as the huge sheets fell to the

131

floor. By the evening the walls had been stripped and washed and the sills sanded. The first coat of clean white paint made the room glow in the evening light. Exhaustion had got the better of them and after putting Ben to bed, they retired to the back terrace to sip blackcurrant kirs and watch the butterflies dance between the trunks of the trees, their wings gilded in the fading sunlight. They chatted companionably of their plans for their homestead, each idea becoming more grandiose with each sip.

'The courtyard would be big enough for a tennis court when the hangars were dismantled.' Serge knew how much Diana loved tennis.

There was a row of Scots pine slanting across the garden from the corner of Ben's room. Diana wanted to cut them down leaving just two trunks to make Ben a swing. Serge listened intently and praised her ideas, he didn't yawn or sigh impatiently like he might have done in Paris, but was visibly interested and maybe even a little impressed, she thought.

They talked late into the evening until the sun had gone down over the forest and they could hear the chorus of frogs and grasshoppers drowning out even the sound of cars approaching the village. He took her hand and drew her towards him kissing her hungrily. He led her onto the lawn under the curtain of the willow branches and laid her on the soft green moss at the base of its trunk and made love to her slowly and luxuriously. Diana felt like the most blessed person in the entire universe. If every time Serge was home he was to be like this, she thought, she would be the happiest woman in France.


The rumble of an engine shook the walls of the house, waking them.

'Tractor!' shouted Ben from his cot. Diana looked out. Bébert jumped down from the cab of a huge lorry with a crane attached to the back. The wheat harvest must be over. Serge pulled on a tracksuit and went out to greet him.

Together they began dismantling the largest hangar straight away. Bébert was already unscrewing the huge corrugated metal panels from the sides of the structure. He let them fall with a huge clang on to the concrete courtyard. Serge helped until Diana, in the guise of bringing coffee to the workers, reminded him that the sitting room was still bereft of its second coat of paint.

With the heat of the day, it was dry in a couple of hours and together they heaved the sofas and bookshelves from the garage and

Diana arranged them into their final resting places. Their mish-mash of dark and light wood furniture suited the blank background of white paint and made the unlikely combination somehow blend together into a pleasing rustic medley. They stood back to admire, Serge put his arm around her waist and squeezed.

After Bébert had joined them for a lunch of pâté and baguette washed down with beer, Serge went off to cut down the row of pine trees that shaded Ben's bedroom. Diana busied herself with emptying boxes of books into the newly installed bookshelves. When she had finished only two of the trees remained.

Bébert had worked hard on the hangar all day, removing all the side panels except for the sliding door which covered the entire front end of the building. By six o'clock the once imposing structure resembled a gigantic skeleton which towered above, like an angular Tyrannosaurus Rex. Another car had joined the lorry in the courtyard and Diana peeped out of the window to see Jérôme Couteau standing chatting to Serge. Diana went out to join them.

'*Bonjour, Madame.*' He shuffled, his eyes cast down and then winked at her.

Diana ignored the wink and offered them a drink.

'Actually, *Chérie*, we were thinking of going to *La Petite Folie.*'

'Oh, good idea! I'll go and get Ben ready.' She disappeared back into the house to clean him up. She strapped him into his pushchair and wheeled him out onto the back terrace. As she skirted the house she glimpsed Serge and the others through the iron gate. They were heading off towards the café without her.

'Hey, wait for me!'

They stopped and turned to look at her. Serge was frowning.

She was clearly not invited. Humiliation swept her. If she turned back the pushchair now, her humiliation would be complete. Surely he wasn't going to exclude her. She decided to ignore him and ran to catch up. They got to the door of the café. Bébert held it open wide for her to wheel in the pushchair, the others were already at the bar.

Jeanette was wiping down the bar ready for the Friday night rush. Diana released Ben from the pushchair. She dropped a coin into the slot of the table football and pulled up a chair for Ben to reach. No sooner had she settled herself on a bar stool next to her husband, he had turned to face his companions presenting her his back. Serge ordered a round of drinks though he had not asked Diana what she would like. She assumed that he had chosen for her.

Jeanette served the men, and realised that no drink had been ordered for Diana. She went over to her and expertly covering the faux pas asked her what she would like.

The main door of the café had been hooked open in a futile attempt to catch any breath of a breeze, to relieve the oppressive heat of the day. The evening's customers began to arrive and Jeanette was busy washing glasses and serving drinks leaving Diana alone at the end of the bar. Diana knew most of the customers, either by sight or having been introduced to them at some time or another. Each of them greeted her politely with either a nod or a courteous '*Bonjour*' but then detached themselves awkwardly to join Serge's crowd.

Claude Villard, the retired farmer from the Fontenay road, was gesticulating animatedly on the benefits of communism. Pierrot had arrived and was launching into a story of how he had seen Fabrice Clément shooting yet another pheasant.

'He'll be in trouble with the committee if he shoots anymore,' he exclaimed triumphantly. Pierrot loved a bit of gossip.

Ben was as happy as could be. No sooner had one coin ran out, than another was provided by one of the men. Bébert showed him how to put the money in the slot and press the trigger to set the ball rolling by himself. He was so delighted with it that he became distracted and seemed to have missed the point of putting any money in at all.

Serge continued to ignore Diana. If she were to leave, he may still not take any notice, which would draw even more attention to his behaviour. She cursed herself for being so stubborn. She looked at the men leaning on the bar. All eyes were on Pierrot and his hunting gossip. They probably hadn't even noticed that Serge was shunning her. She was grateful when Marcel crossed the threshold and immediately came to her side, simply nodding his greetings to the men. He leant against the bar next to her and offered her a drink.

'Thank you for dinner the other night. Really delicious!' He put his forefinger and thumb to his lips and made a kissing sound.

She slowly sipped her brandy and coke, while Marcel talked of his firewood sales and the fruit packaging factory. Diana kept an eye on Serge's pastis consumption. She had counted at least six. The sunlight was waning but the air was still close. Ben was tugging at her trouser leg to be picked up. He snuggled into her, rubbing his eyes and moaning. Diana could see he needed to go to bed. She waited for a break in the conversation and tapped Serge on the shoulder. 'Serge, we need to go. Ben is sleepy.'

'I'm in the middle of my pastis!' he snapped incredulously.

'Well, perhaps we could go after that?'

The men fell silent. Diana detected the hint of a smirk on Pierrot's face.

'But Claude owes me one.'

*Chéri*, Ben is little, he needs to go home. It's getting dark now.' She managed to keep the anger that was welling up in her out of her voice. She wasn't about to cause a scene in front of the villagers. Serge stared at her as if it was none of his affair. She thought of the dark unlit lane that led up to the house. She didn't relish the thought of picking her way over the lawn to the back door. There was no moon to light her way tonight.

'I'll take you home,' piped up Marcel as if he could read her thoughts.

Diana thanked him and fired a venomous look at Serge who only glanced at her for a second and then returned to his friends exclaiming, 'Come on Claude you old stinge, it's your turn to get them in.'

She strapped Ben into his pushchair, the humiliation of being publicly abandoned pouring on her shoulders like ice cold water. She went out of the door into the night with Marcel holding a torch to light her way. She pushed Ben past the willow tree, and the same smell of earth and leaves drifted through her senses, as it had done the evening before when they had both lain underneath its branches in ecstatic silence. She tucked Ben up in bed and returned to the sitting room. The clean, white, freshly-painted walls brought her no comfort or excitement now. The room echoed with the ghosts of her mind. A shiver went down her spine. How could a person veer from being golden and special to such a dark heinous character in just twenty-four hours? She curled up in bed in a tight ball feeling cold despite the humidity of the night.

Serge's car drove out through the gates, rounded the corner and was gone. She hadn't asked what time he'd got home. He'd got up solemnly and thrown some stuff in a bag, downed a coffee and left with no hint of the kindness or romance of the days before. Ben was crying as he always did when his father went to work.

'Let's go for a walk,' she suggested brightly to distract him from his misery.

Instead of going into the village as they usually did, she decided to take the road that led west to the forest. She somehow didn't want to go to see Jeanette and remind herself of her foolishness in joining the men. On one side of the road, sunflowers stood tall, their cocoa coloured faces held tilted towards the sun. On the other, a field of maize now grown to its full height, made the road appear shorter than it had when they'd visited the village in the depths of winter. The sky was clear but it was early and the hammering heat had not yet risen to its full potential. As long as they got home by ten they should escape the heat.

Léo was beginning to pull a little less now that he had more practice. It took half an hour to reach the edge of the forest. She looked back towards the village. She could just make out the tip of the slate roof and the stone chimneys peeping up over the sunflowers. The woods were cool and smelt of moss and pine needles. She unclipped Ben's harness and he climbed out of the pushchair. He ran along the paths between the pines, planted in geometric rows.

Some distance ahead of her, she heard breaking twigs. She looked up. The lumbering bulky figure of Marie-Pierre was trudging towards them. She was pushing herself along with a stick. The black labrador was lolloping painfully along, behind.

'*Bonjour Madame!*' she smiled.

'*Bonjour!*' Diana was pleased to have some female company. 'Please, call me Diana.'

Marie-Pierre beamed. 'May I walk with you?'

'Of course.' She couldn't help noticing the odd whisker that had obviously escaped Marie-Pierre's razor that morning and embarrassedly looked away. 'What's your dog's name?'

'Napoléon,' she laughed, 'Pierrot's idea.'

Diana looked at Napoléon and thought that a more ill-fitting name could not have been found for this arthritic pudding shaped animal. Marie-Pierre lumbered alongside her not speaking. Her gait was awkward as if her body didn't really belong to her and she was learning to manoeuvre it for the first time.

'Do you work?' asked Diana breaking the silence.

'I help *Maman* with the children.'

'Children?'

'She's a childminder for a family in the village. There's no work around here. I don't drive so I'm stuck,' she sighed. 'The tobacco starts next week and after that it's the potatoes and the onions. I shall do those too. It pays very well.'

'Tobacco grows here?'

'Yes, down at *Ferme* Meffret.'

'Is that where the greenhouses are on the road to Jaunay?'

'That's right. We pick them and then hang them up in the greenhouses to dry, before they are packed and sent off to the cigarette companies. It's hard-going but you can't turn down work in these parts.

'I saw pink poppies there too.'

'Yes, that's right, opium for medicine.'

Diana suppressed a smile at the thought of opium fields in sleepy Saint Gabriel. The women walked on in silence for a while.

'We're lucky to have these woods so close by,' proffered Diana.

Marie-Pierre shrugged. 'I've known this forest all my life. It's good for *cêpes*; mushrooms, you know?'

Diana looked blank.

'Have you never tasted *cêpes*?'

Diana shook her head.

'There is nothing better than a *cêpe* omelette. They generally come in September with the autumn rain. But after a wet summer we can get them as early as August. They're not easy to find. They're the same colour as the fallen oak leaves, you see. This heatwave is no good though. It needs to be wet for a good mushroom season. I expect they'll be out a bit later this year. When they start growing again I could bring you out and show you where to find them.' She hesitated and blushed, 'If you like?'

'Yes. I should like that. Thank you.'

She smiled. She probably didn't really have any friends. It was a sad existence growing up out here and still living with her mother with not much chance of an exit. There couldn't be many eligible bachelors in the area. If there were they would most likely be put off by the shaving thing. She would have been almost grotesque if her manner was not so kind and easy.

They turned round and headed back towards the village. Ben was beginning to get a little grumpy. It was time for his morning nap. As they neared the edge of the trees a man on horseback was cantering towards the entrance to the path. When he saw the ladies he gathered up his reins and slowed the horse to a walk.

'Horsey!' let out Ben, true to form.

Michaud sat tall in the saddle. As he passed them he lifted his cap and bid them, '*Bonne Journée!*'

'*Bonne journée, monsieur.*' Replied Diana politely.

Marie-Pierre said nothing. Surprised by her silence Diana glanced at her. She had turned her head away from him and was snootily avoiding his stare. Michaud looked embarrassed and kicked the horse into a trot.

When he had disappeared from view, Diana spoke, 'Do you not know Michaud?'

'Everyone knows Michaud.' Her expression was stern.

'He seems nice.'

She didn't answer straight away. 'He is a *bad* man, Diana.' She said it theatrically.

'Why do you say that?' Diana was determined to get to the bottom of this.

'The whole village are against him.'

'What has he done?'

Marie-Pierre shook her head. 'Just keep away from him. You must not accept his help.' Her tone became urgent. So Marie-Pierre knew about him giving her a lift home. 'The whole village are against him,' she repeated. 'Trust me they have good reason.'

They reached the edge of the forest and walked down the now sun-baked tarmac between the sunflowers and maize. It seemed shorter on the way back. It was strange that one could be so hated by an entire community. As for upsetting the village, she felt she'd already done that simply by stepping over the threshold of *La Petite Folie.* She decided that whatever it was he had done, it was most likely as serious as her own misdemeanour of drinking coke in a public bar.

She waved goodbye to Marie-Pierre and popped in to *La Petite Folie* for her baguette. The *épicerie* was closed at this hour but it would be quiet and she was sure Jeanette wouldn't mind fetching her bread for her.

The front door to the café was closed. Diana pulled it open. There was no one inside. She called out but there was no reply. She listened for a noise but there was silence. On the bar was a baguette, with a twist of paper wrapped round its middle with 'Diana' scribbled on it in biro. She picked it up and slotted it into the back of the pushchair, leaving a coin on the counter. She turned the pushchair round when she heard a voice from the kitchen.

'It's just too soon for me.' It was Jeanette.

Diana waited, perhaps she would come into the bar.

'I've told you, I will pay but I simply don't have it yet.'

Diana realised she must be on the phone. Ashamed to be listening in to a private conversation, she quickly slipped out of the front door and went home.

# TWENTY-ONE

## Edward

'Pound the root with water,' Clothilde read slowly, careful to pronounce each letter, 'Add a little honey and warm over the fire.'

'Excellent. You have got the hang of it so quickly!'

'Thank you.' She reddened with delight. 'But your swimming has not improved.' She shook a finger at him playfully. 'To improve you must practise. As soon as the next moon is here we can begin again. If only we could swim in the day.'

'We cannot. You do not want to be caught with me Clothilde.'

'I wish you would tell me what you have done that you are so ashamed of. You are such a good kind person I cannot imagine you doing a dreadful deed.'

'I made a mistake, a big mistake.'

'But it all happened in a land beyond the sea! How can it matter to the good people of France?'

'Do not forget that the Normans are ruling my country. Although we are separated by water, we are of the same nation.'

She looked at him pleadingly.

It was true that he did owe her an explanation.

'Very well, my priory is a very important priory, for the head of the cathedral is... was ..,' he corrected himself, 'A very important man. He was an advisor to the King, and he was the head of all the churches in England. Just after Christmas I saw him man walk into the Cathedral, as I was going about my business. He would often go to the chancel and sit alone. As I walked towards the priory, some men; they were big and strong, and I now know that they were the knights of King Henry. They told me they were looking for his Grace and I told them where he was.' Edward stopped and took a deep breath.

'Well then you did a good deed.'

'Don't say that!'

'Edward!'

'Don't say that! There is nothing good about me. You do not know me, nor the danger you are in for every second you spend with me. Now go! Leave me!'

Clothilde stared at him.

'Go. I beg you. Let me at least save you.' And he lay on the floor and sobbed.

Clothilde did as she was told and climbed out of the opening.

When his sobbing had at last subsided Edward knew he must leave Saint Gabriel and Clothilde. The time had come. He prayed for a long time and then began to plan his departure. He would go to the abbey at Pontigny and face whatever was awaiting him. Hiding was just another form of cowardice. If he was truly to absolve his crimes he must take his punishment with dignity.

Clothilde did not visit him the next day and Edward was glad. He ventured out into the woods and headed in the opposite direction to the village. If he was to travel on foot he must find his route. He must skirt the village to reach Beaugency away from prying eyes.

He arrived at the edge of the trees and the track where he thought he must have been dumped by the cart. He followed it a little way keeping him just inside the tree line. On the opposite side of the road was open pasture punctuated with outcrops of patchwork squares of cultivated land. These were the tenures; some were bare still waiting for their crops to appear above the ground, and others were dotted with the palest green. He kept checking them lest a peasant appear to tend his plot and spy him. The track twisted and turned and swung through the very centre of the village ahead. The towers of the chateau beyond simmered in the midday heat. He could not see how he could leave the forest without being seen. The heat of the sun began to make his head swim. He was not used to such temperatures. He loosened his habit and retraced his steps to the cavern.

He had not long returned when Clothilde leapt down from the opening.

'Clothilde! What are you doing here? I told you to leave me.'

Her face was pale and distressed.

Edward's heart swung at the pain he was causing her.

'It is my mother, she is not well. She is so terribly hot and trembles severely. I am very afraid.'

'I shall come at once.'

'You cannot – it is still daylight. The *Seigneurie* would carry you off in an instant.'

'Sit down and catch your breath, then tell me her symptoms.'

'At times, she is writhing like the devil. As if she is possessed. *Père* Barthélemy has visited and fears she will die. Even the soothsayer has shaken her head and said that she has the look of death

141

about her.' Tears began to roll down her cheeks. 'Her eyes are sunken and she has not slept.'

'Is she yellow?'

'Yellow? No, not yellow, but pale, so terribly pale and she is sweating so much I fear there will be no more moisture in her body.' She peered up at the opening nervously. 'I should go. I have left Firmin tending to her. I said I would fetch some water for the potage. The little ones will be crying and ...'

'Go! But come back just before sun up and I will have something for you.'

Edward spent the night in prayer. He could not bear to imagine that another loved person could be banished from the planet, leaving more hurt and upset around him. This, he believed was a sign; an opportunity to right all the wrongs that his own birth had inflicted.

'Eldric, if only you were here to guide me. You have taught me well though I am not certain of what I do. Fistulas and wounds are child's play but this, I believe is the ague. Tell me Eldric. Tell me.' He knelt down and laid his forehead on the earth as if it would impart the knowledge he required. What if she were to die? What if it were he who killed her through ignorance or negligence? But she is not an old woman and she surely has committed no sins that God could be punishing her for. No, it was down to him. He must succeed where others had failed.

He stayed like that for a short while and then it came to him. There had been that man at the priory. He had been carried from a neighbouring farm, just outside the town. He had been thrashing on a bed of straw, sweat pouring out of his skin and from his mouth were uttered strange unintelligible noises. When he slept his breathing rasped like the creak of the iron gate of the herb garden. It was all a few years hence and Edward struggled to remember the details. He remembered being very afraid. He'd asked Eldric if the man was possessed, but he had said that he was very poorly with the ague. It was warm weather, like now. He remembered because they had been allowed to have their teachings outside in the sunshine. Eldric, what did you do? Of course he could not be sure Clothilde's mother was overcome by the same affliction. Eldric said it was rare but that he had heard of it more often in southern Europe where the weather was eternally warm. From the bad air he'd said. For heat: agrimony or barberry, black bilberries, buck's horn plantain. That, he knew he would not find, for there were no sandy outcrops in these parts. He took some parchment and began to scribble. For convulsions: calamint or eringo. Not eringo – too far from the coast. Now mallows, he thought, they would grow by the spring.

Clothilde returned just as dawn was beginning to reach its long fingers through the darkness. Edward was rearranging his sheets of parchment on which he had written from memory the concoction he believed Eldric had prepared for the ague. He had written it in large letters to help her, although much improved, her reading was not yet confident.

'Here I have what you came for and here are the instructions'.

Her eyes flashed agitatedly.

'What is it?'

'I fear it is too late.' Her voice ended in a painful squeak. 'She no longer sleeps at all, she is writhing permanently.'

'Then I will need the buck's horn plantain. It is a plant that grows in sand. I need to see her Clothilde, after dark tonight. Here, take this to her and spread it across her chest it will bring out the heat. What is that on your back?'

'I almost forgot – I have brought you some eels.'

'You are indeed a blessed person. I have not eaten meat for a good few days. Whilst all the time you worry for your mother, you still think of my needs.'

'Oh Edward, if I were blessed I do not think my mother would have been struck down in this terrible violent way. If she were to die I do not know what would become of us. My father away in the holy land and ...'

'Clothilde, all is not lost. Where did those eels come from?'

'The Loire of course.'

'The Loire?'

'Yes, the big river at Beaugency. It is about two hours walk south from here. We do not go often but as a treat when the weather is fine.'

'Who caught them?'

'My mother and Firmin.'

'Is there boggy ground nearby?'

'Yes, there are marshes across the river on the opposite bank, why?'

'Hmm. Is Firmin quite well?'

'I, I think so.'

'This river must be large for such beautiful eels.'

143

'It is the biggest I have ever seen. Firmin says it crosses the whole of France.'

'There is sand along its banks?'

'Yes, why?'

Edward grabbed a piece of parchment and began to sketch.

'You must send Firmin back there today to find this.' He held up the parchment. 'In England we call it buck's horn plantain.'

'I have never seen it.'

'In that case I can only pray to God that it grows there. He must look on sand. He must go quickly. How long has she been ill like this?'

'Three days and nights now.'

'So we are on the fourth day. There is not time to lose. You must send Firmin – on horseback if possible. Can he take a horse? If we are to save your mother we must make haste.'

'Norbert has a cart horse though he is not a fast creature.'

'Listen carefully. The mixture I have given you must be administered this morning, then when the sun is at its highest at midday and again at night. When she convulses and writhes you must strip her clothes from her and douse her in cool water from the spring until her writhing ceases. As soon as she is calm again let her sleep – but do not leave her side. She has been overcome by the hot ague and the heat must be chased from her body. As soon as Firmin returns with the plant you must bruise the leaves and lay them across her stomach to prevent choler and to chase the heat more rapidly.' Edward paused. 'I shall pray for her. Now go, and God be with you, with all of you.'

She nodded solemnly and scampered off through the dark forest as silently as a rabbit.

As the sun rose it was obvious the day was going to be even hotter. The heat would make it difficult to chase the ague from Clothilde's mother's body. It would surely finish her unless Clothilde followed the instructions to the letter. There was nothing he could do but wait for news.

He turned his attentions to the eels she had brought him. They lay glistening in their weed wrappings. He set about extracting their poisonous blood. As he carefully stowed it in a jar and washed his hands meticulously, he thought to himself, this is my destiny. If I cannot be a monk I can at least fulfil Eldric's plan for me and care for the sick. I know not if I am talented at such work but I have succeeded in curing myself and ridding Clothilde of her fistulas. Though I only ever followed Eldric's instructions and he would never have allowed me to treat so sick a person as Clothilde's mother alone, without guidance. But there is no other choice. She is too sick to travel and the abbey at Pontigny is much too far. This family has no power or influence; who would send a delegation? No, it is down to me. I am their only chance and what a poor chance they have. As soon as the work is done I shall leave them to live their lives in safety. He sank to his knees and rested his forehead on the earth again and prayed.

# TWENTY-TWO

## Diana

There was a knock on the French windows. A tall, elderly gentleman stood on the front terrace.

'*Bonjour Madame.*' He was wearing a pair of old battered jeans, trainers and a tee-shirt with *Vive Johnny Halliday!* emblazoned across his chest. From beneath his long peppered grey beard he uttered, 'I hope I'm not disturbing you. I've come about the little boy.'

'The little boy?'

'Pardon me. My name is *Monsieur* Moreau I am the mayor of Saint Gabriel and headmaster of the school.'

Diana looked him up and down in disbelief. All the headmasters and mayors Diana had known wore suits and certainly didn't call round people's houses so informally.

'There is a place for your son at school next term.'

'Oh, but he's only two.'

'You're right they normally have to be three to attend school, but we do not have many children in our little country school. The government allows us to take them at two and a half if they are potty trained.'

'He's far too young to be going to school. He still needs his morning nap!' She almost wanted to laugh, the idea was preposterous. She feared that she had failed to keep the derision from her voice.

'They have a nap in the afternoon in the *Petite Section*. It will be good for him to have contact with other children, particularly for his language.'

This was not the first time she had been disapproved of for speaking to her son in English.

'I shall leave these forms with you. If you have any queries just pop over to the *Mairie*. We are open every Saturday morning between ten o'clock and midday. I will be happy to answer any questions.' With a stroke of his beard, he strode towards the front gate and was gone.

When Diana had discovered that children started school at three in France she'd been quite shocked but two years old was ludicrous. No, she would definitely not send him until his third birthday. He wasn't even talking properly yet. She gulped down a cup of tea to ease her panic and took the baby intercom out to the garden to dig over a new square of vegetable patch despite the heat. The exercise would calm her. She dug until she heard Ben's whimpers over the speaker. She wiped the sweat from her brow and went to get him out of bed, thankful to be out of the heat.

The phone rang and Ben grabbed the receiver before she could get to it. He had recently become fascinated by the telephone but he just picked it up and listened, breathing heavily. She managed to extricate the receiver from his grasp before the caller confusedly hung up.

'*Allô,*'

'Diana, it's me, Liesel. I wondered what you were doing today.'

'I, I don't know.' She thought for a moment,'Nothing really. Why?'

'Serge's at work isn't he?'

'He left this morning.'

'I'm off today and wondered if you'd like to meet for lunch?'

Diana hesitated, she only had enough money in her purse to pay for the baguette she'd ordered from *La Petite Folie*.

'Go on,' insisted Liesel, 'It's my treat.'

It felt like an age since she had been anywhere that didn't require scruffy old gardening clothes. She felt excited at the prospect of going into town for anything other than shopping. 'Ok. That sounds great!' She paused. 'But what about Ben?'

'What about him?'

'Well, I'll have to bring him with me.'

'Of course you will!' she laughed. 'He'll enjoy it. Say half twelve at the *Pizzeria du Pont.*'

She replaced the receiver and went to rifle through her wardrobe for something to match Liesel's elegance. But none of her Parisian clothes fitted her anymore. She vowed she would do more gardening and lose weight. What on earth was she doing going out with the enemy? Delphine would be appalled. Then she reminded herself sharply that Liesel had done nothing wrong. If anything, it was *she* who had behaved badly. She stared despondently at the contents of her wardrobe, and in the end plumped for her newest pair of jeans which were not that new and certainly dated back to pre-Ben. She squeezed into them and chose an ample blue shirt that would hide the spare tyres poking over the waistband. It was too hot for jeans but given the alternatives she was prepared to suffer. Looking in the mirror, she examined her face, which she was convinced was developing jowls. Her hair was lank and lifeless. This outing was supposed to cheer her up but so far it was only making her realise how much she had let herself go. She couldn't possibly go out into Beaugency with her hair in this state. Beaugency was a different world. There were no clogs or berets, wellies or housecoats there, except on market day of course. The residents were smart and modern, and rushed around purposefully. Out here, just six miles away, it was as if a time zone had been crossed. She quickly washed her hair and blow dried it upside down to ensure that it didn't fall flat against her head within minutes of leaving the house. She rummaged in the bottom of her wash bag and retrieved an eye pencil that had been sharpened so short that she was obliged to cut her nails to be able to grip it. She dressed Ben in the sailor suit Liesel had bought him; the smartest thing in his wardrobe and loaded him into the car.

She parked along the banks of the Loire and held Ben's hand as he toddled along the pavement, pointing at the cormorants fishing in the green waters. The *Pizzeria du Pont* was on the corner, opposite the bridge as its name suggested. The terrace was already buzzing with customers. There were two women sitting right on the edge of the pavement, their hair cut into chic, glossy swathes. Their ringed fingers flashed in the sunlight. Their heads were angled intently towards each other. Diana felt envious, once she could have been one of those women on a pavement in Paris with Delphine. Now she was a wobbly, lonely jellyfish. She looked down at her jeans and wished she'd worn at least one of her old office suits, mind you she wasn't sure she'd fit into those anymore either, and she would have overheated just the same. This is ridiculous, she thought to herself, I'm only meeting Liesel for lunch.

Liesel bounded up to her like a sleek excited puppy. Her hair hung to her shoulders as smooth as melted white chocolate, Diana winced as Liesel picked up Ben and hugged him to her spotless linen blouse.

They sat down and Liesel signalled to the waiter whose attention was already fixed on them, or rather on Liesel.

'*Mesdames*? The *calzone* is very good or the *napolitana*.'

'I'll have the same as you,' said Diana.

'Right. Two *calzones* and a carafe of your house red.'

Diana ordered an *Orangina* and a child's cheese and tomato pizza for Ben. The waiter scribbled it all down and retreated.

'Diana you're shaking! Are you alright?'

'Yes, yes I'm fine. I, err… I don't get out much.'

Liesel stared at her, not understanding.

'What with Ben and everything.' She coughed nervously. 'It just feels weird being out in public. Having a life, so to speak,' she faltered and tried to laugh it off.

'Diana, this isn't you. You were always the centre of things in Paris. It was you who organised the parties and decided where everyone should meet up.'

'Did I?'

'Of course you did. Whenever there was a concert or a big meal planned it was always you who let everybody know.'

Diana thought back to the early days when she and Serge were equals. She remembered ringing round and booking restaurants for everyone to meet up. But somehow she simply couldn't remember ever ringing Liesel. Liesel just always seemed to be there.

'Well, since I got pregnant with Ben things have changed rather. We couldn't really afford to go out, with only one of us working. And after that we were stuck for babysitters. I guess you just get into a different groove.'

'When was the last time you and Serge went out then? Just the two of you I mean?'

'I don't know, not for ages. Come to think of it we've never had a babysitter.'

'Never?' Liesel's mouth fell open. 'You mean to say you haven't been out for an evening without Ben for over two years?'

Diana shook her head.

'Right. At least that's something I can do for you then.' She pulled a cigarette from her packet and tapped the end of it on the table decisively.

Diana frowned. 'Do what?'

'Baby-sit, silly!'

'Oh, Liesel, I don't know about that.'

'You can't go on like that. You used to be bubbly and glamorous.'

'Was I?' Was that how Liesel had always seen her?

'Moving out here to the country won't do you any favours. A girl needs to have a change of scene.'

'Well, it would be nice I suppose.' It had always been Liesel that had had the expensive clothes and the flash cars, bought by Mummy and Daddy, of course. Diana remembered her wardrobe crisis and felt suddenly weary. She couldn't face having to go through all that again. She would have to lose some weight if she were to get into them again. It would be much easier just to stay in her lost little village where the competition was pitifully weak and all she had to do was pull on her wellies. They were the only item of clothing she owned that bore a brand name that could be deemed chic.

'Come on where's your spark? I can see I am going to have to take you in hand.'

The prospect of Liesel 'taking her in hand' filled her with panic. Despite her strongest efforts, a tear escaped from the corner of her eye. She turned abruptly to do up Ben's shoelace which had worked its way free as he kicked the step of the high chair in boredom.

'Diana. What's wrong?' She put a hand on her shoulder.

The human contact sent the tears flowing fast. It was all she could do not to sob audibly.

'Things really aren't good are they? Now dry your eyes and tell me all about it.'

The waiter appeared with a tray and set their drinks on the table with a flourish. Diana hurriedly wiped her face and flashed a glance at him but was relieved to see he was too busy leering at Liesel to notice her tears.

'Is everything OK between you and Serge?'

'Yes, yes of course it is. It's just a little difficult adapting to our new life out here. I mean, I love the house and the area, but I'm finding it hard to feel at home. Serge is so changeable. One minute he's the model loving husband and father and the next minute he's shutting me out.' Diana cursed herself for confiding in Liesel. What if she told Serge? He would be furious that she was discussing their private affairs with somebody else. But who else was she to talk to?

'What does he do that's different here then?'

Diana thought for a minute. She took a deep breath and explained the events of their visit to La *Petite Folie* with as little whining as she could manage. 'Liesel I'm sorry, I didn't come here to have a good old moan, I don't know what's come over me.'

'Don't be daft. You obviously need to get it out of your system. I know he loves you. Yours was the great romance amongst all of us. You guys were meant for each other.'

'Yes, I still feel that sometimes. But as soon as I was stuck at home, tired and pregnant, and then with Ben he seemed to lose interest. You see that's partly why I wanted to move out here. I thought that with some space I could get on and achieve something with a garden, and get involved in the village. I could have something to feel proud of instead of spending day after day cooped up in a tiny flat in Paris, waiting for him to come home. And who knows, maybe with time, Serge would be proud of me too.'

'You know, maybe it's you that changed. One minute you were slim, elegant and full of ambition and optimism. Then when you became pregnant you slipped into this homely comfy person that he hadn't bargained for.'

Diana inhaled sharply and was about to protest, but Liesel gestured for her to listen. 'I'm not suggesting anything is wrong with that. Of course you have to change when you become a mother, but perhaps you changed more than you needed to.' She paused. 'Look, you're lonely, that's obvious.'

'I suppose I am.'

'How about we try and get you back to who you were?'

'I can't do that Liesel, I don't have friends here. Most of the villagers are suspicious of me and are not prepared to give me so much as the time of day.'

'*Mesdames.*' The waiter had returned with their pizzas. '*Bon Appétit!*' He raised an eyebrow provocatively at Liesel.

'*Merci,*' she said sternly and returned her attentions to Diana. 'You can't change your neighbours but if you look good you'll feel good too. First things first, here's my hairdresser's number.' She rummaged in her bag and pulled out an expensive fountain pen and leather-backed notebook. 'Before you think of a thousand reasons why you can't go, I'll babysit Ben. Do it before Serge comes back. I've got to go and see a patient out your way later on, so I'll pop in afterwards to check you've made the appointment.'

Over coffee, Liesel elaborated on her plan to resurrect Diana to her former self. 'When you've done your hair we shall go on a shopping trip and get you some new clothes. We could even leave Ben with Serge for the day and go up to Paris. See an exhibition and have lunch.'

Diana nodded wearily. She knew they could never afford it, but it would be easier to pull out at a later date.

She drove home across the far reaching fields which, just a few weeks ago had been her key to freedom, now bleakly yelled their emptiness, like a huge open prison. She felt foolish having confided in

Liesel and was frightened it would backfire. Maybe Liesel was right. Maybe it was *her* who had changed and Serge just couldn't cope with it.

As she swung the gate open, she noticed the netting she had fixed across the bottom three bars had been chewed away. She called out, 'Léo'. She could hear no tapping of claws on the concrete. She called again, nothing. He must have got out. She grabbed Ben out of the car and ran back down the lane towards the café calling him. There was no sign of him.

Mémère was sitting outside her door topping and tailing French beans. She hadn't seen him. She continued on to *La Petite Folie*, Jeanette was leaning at the bar drinking coffee with that awful man who'd visited her the other day. They hadn't seen Léo either. She ran on down to Marrakech's field. Ben seemed to be getting heavier with every step she took. Diana called and called, 'Léo, Léo.' But he was nowhere to be seen.

Michaud was mending the fence at the side of the field. He looked up. 'You've lost your dog?'

'Yes, he must have chewed through the netting on the gate and got out.' She could feel tears welling in the corners of her eyes. Pull yourself together, she thought; there had been quite enough tears for one day.

'I'm taking one of the horses out for a ride now. You take that baby home. I'll look for him for you.'

'Oh, I don't want to put you to any trouble.'

'You get that little one home and out of the sun. Chances are he'll already be back, they always go home even the young'uns.'

He was probably right; Léo would be sitting on the kitchen steps in the garage feeling sorry for himself. She walked back more slowly this time, desperate to get out of her jeans; the sweat was making them cling uncomfortably to her flesh. The kitchen steps were empty and her heart sank.

She undressed Ben and laid him down for his afternoon sleep. Feeling in her pocket for his dummy, her fingers touched a crumpled piece of paper. She pulled it out. Liesel's thick black curly script danced on the paper, even her handwriting was chic. She put the telephone number carefully by the phone in the kitchen promising herself to do something about it later. Right now, she had to find her dog. She went out into every corner of the garden and called 'Léo' over and over again in the hope that it would reach him wherever he had wandered. But he didn't appear.

She must have been out there for hours as the sun had swung right over to the west, hanging suspended above the barn. The sunflowers all had their backs to the house now, it wouldn't be long before it would sink below the horizon and Léo would still be out there, possibly injured and waiting for help. She listened at Ben's window. He was still sound asleep, his lunchtime outing had exhausted him.

She heard a car engine coming towards the house. Then it fell silent. Maybe someone was bringing him back. She ran out to the front gate. Liesel was getting out of her little hatchback in yet another change of clothes.

'Oh it's you.'

'Sorry to disappoint you,' she said teasing. 'I said I'd pop round.'

'Léo's escaped, I thought you might be someone bringing him back. I can't even go and look for him because Ben's asleep.'

'Well, I'm glad I'm here then. I'll stay here in case he wakes up and you can go and look for him.'

'Léo, Léo.' Diana walked up and down every lane, path and alleyway in the village but there was still no sign of him. She passed a few villagers who had hurried off onto the other side of the road, though Diana was too anxious to be hurt. The light was fading, she'd no idea how long she'd been out. She wasn't going to be able to find him in the dark so she reluctantly headed back to the *Champ de Foire*. She could just hear the faint sound of horses' hooves. Michaud! She'd forgotten about him. She waited outside the front gate to see if he would turn in towards her house. He did. He was holding a creamy coloured bundle of fur that was quite clearly trembling aloft the gigantic horse. Léo! Thank the Lord!

'I found this little chappy chasing pheasants in the forest.' He's lucky we found him tonight, tomorrow's hunting day and they'll be shooting in the woods, he could have been mistaken for game.'

Diana took the thirsty, dusty pup from Michaud's arms and cuddled him tight. 'How can I thank you? There must be something I can do in return.'

'There is something,' he paused. 'You can ride can't you?'

'Yes, but that was all a very long time ago. How did you know?'

'Long ago or not, a love for horses is something that never leaves you and I've never missed it in someone,' he paused again. 'You could give me a hand exercising them.'

Diana hadn't ridden for a very long time, certainly not since she'd left England. But he was right, her love of riding had stayed with her and the prospect cheered her. Then she thought of Ben. 'No, I'm sorry I can't. I don't have a babysitter.'

'Yes you do!' A voice came from behind her. Liesel was standing in front of the gate carrying Ben in his pyjamas. 'I'll look after him. Just let me know when.'

Diana felt awkward as she thought of Jeannette and Marie-Pierre's warnings. But this man had been so kind to her, she couldn't refuse. 'Alright I will,' she said decisively and broke into a smile.

Liesel passed Ben back to his mother. 'Who was that?' she asked, her eyes wide.

'His name is Michaud. I shouldn't have said yes. I don't know anything about him, except that the village won't have anything to do with him.'

'To be honest, I think that's a positive sign,' said Liesel laughing. 'Whoever he is, he's rather tasty.'

'It should be *you* going riding with him then, not me.'

'You're joking I don't know anything about horses.'

'I thought you grew up in Maison Lafitte, horse racing country?'

'I did, but I'm afraid I have more chance of knowing one end of the Jockey Club bar from the other than I do of a horse. I've got a better idea. You make friends with him and then invite us both round for dinner one night.'

'Ooh! I didn't know you could be so scheming.'

'Before I go, I called up my hairdresser and booked an appointment for you for four o'clock on Monday. I'll be here by about half three so that should give you plenty of time to get there.'

'Not so soon Liesel. I've got so much to do.'

'What, like mope around until Serge gets back? Not on your nelly!'

'But I don't know what to have done!'

'You don't, but Lionel will. It's the salon on the market place. I'll see you then.'

She could always cancel it, she thought, as she waved her off. When she got inside she headed straight for the telephone to do just that. The piece of paper with the hairdresser's number was no longer next to the telephone. She cursed Liesel, she obviously knew her better than she thought and had taken the paper away just in case. She racked her brains trying to think of the name of the salon but couldn't. Damn it! She wouldn't even be able to look them up in the directory. Well, there was nothing for it, she would have to ring Liesel when she'd got home and admit that she didn't have enough money to pay him.

'Don't you worry darling. This one's on me.'

'Liesel, No, I won't hear of it.'

'I'm sorry. I can't hear you. The line must be very bad.' And the dial tone returned. Liesel was becoming infuriating. She leant against the work surface exasperated. The microwave was flashing 'PF' *power failure.* There must have been a power cut. Strange, Liesel hadn't mentioned it.

# TWENTY-THREE

## Hélène

The full moon was fast approaching and there had been no contact from Rémy. She would have to go back to the *épicerie*. As she descended the stairs she could see through the window that there was a crowd collecting on the village square in their Sunday best, but it was Friday. They were all wearing black. Then the crowd parted, and a cortège, led by pall bearers carrying a coffin high on their shoulders, turned the corner into the square. Julien hadn't mentioned a death. The cortège was followed by a young woman, dressed in black and not much older than Hélène herself. Next to her stood a little girl holding her hand with an expression of stone. Hélène looked closer and recognised Miriam.

Hélène raced down the stairs and out the front door. Julien was standing in the gateway as the cortège passed. 'Who is it?'

'Jean Legrand, the school teacher.'

'The school teacher? Miriam's father?'

He nodded. 'Such a young man, it is a terrible thing.'

'What happened?'

'He was found shot near the school house, in the log shed.'

'Murder?'

'They cannot say, some think he shot himself but I assisted myself and there is no evidence one way or the other; most likely an accident. Sometimes it is better not to know. At least he can have an official burial that way.'

The cortège had disappeared into the church and the congregation was piling in behind it. Hélène ran back into the house and pulled her black overcoat from the peg. She put it on and buttoned it up to the top to hide her uniform beneath. She followed the last funeral members into the church and took up a pew right at the back. The pall bearers were lowering the coffin onto a trestle in front of the altar. Hélène watched as Miriam hung on to her mother's arm. An elderly lady, possibly Miriam's grandmother, put a framed photograph on top of the coffin.

A couple of women in front of Hélène were whispering to each other. 'They can't open the coffin. A real mess he was.'

'Such a shame! Such a lovely family!'

Hélène sat with her head bent through the whole service. She felt like an intruder. She didn't know this man and she began to feel uncomfortable about being there. She scanned the backs of the heads in front of her. She couldn't see Antoine or Bette Davis. At last the service was over. The family were filing past the coffin and crossing themselves. The pall bearers again hoisted the coffin onto their shoulders and returned down the aisle, with the photograph still perched on the top. The procession was led by a short stocky gentleman; it was Philippe Cottereau, the gentleman who had visited the doctor that evening. As they came past the last row, Hélène looked at the picture. She gasped. There was no mistake. A young man dressed in a smart suit smiled from the frame aloft the coffin. It was Rémy.

Her mind raced. She had called him to investigate the disappearance of the containers and just a short time later he is found dead? Suicide this definitely wasn't. There was no point going to the *épicerie* now. There would surely be an investigation by the police; she would have to tread carefully. She needed to find the man on the reception committee who had greeted her on landing. She looked at her watch. She was due at *Ferme* Meffret any moment. As soon as the cortège had passed she joined the crowds pouring out of the doors and went to fetch her bag. She jumped on her bicycle and pedaled hard all the way to Saint Gabriel. She would have to call in on Agnès Camaret afterwards.

*Monsieur* Meffret was sitting up in bed looking out of the window when she arrived.

'I'm sorry I am late.'

'Oh, it doesn't matter. I didn't think you would be here until much later. Did you not go to the funeral?'

'I did go but I came straight here.'

*Monsieur* Meffret shook his head. 'Such a terrible thing. We are already surrounded by such sadness and difficulty with the war. More killing is too much.'

'It is an awful shock for everyone I think. He was so young,' she hesitated. 'I didn't know him but I knew his little girl, Miriam.'

'Aah yes, very sad for them! His wife lost her father in the first war just before she was born.'

'Do you know them well?'

'A little, Miriam's grandmother used to come and buy eggs from us right up until she died. Then Floriane used to fetch them; that's

Miriam's mother. Aah, I remember when Floriane and Jean met; a fine young man, lucky too to have a profession that kept him out of the camps. Even working for Philippe Cottereau is better than working for the Nazis.'

'Philippe Cottereau? Is he not a banker?'

'Philippe Cottereau seems to be anything he wants to be. He runs the bank, he is the head of the school board, the planning committee and he is mayor of Jaunay. Anything that happens in Jaunay is to do with him.' He raised his eyes to the ceiling and let out a heavy sigh.

'You don't like him?'

'There is nothing to like. He is on the wrong side. He is a *Maréchal* Pétain in our midst. He will be the first to sell us out to the Germans, as long as he can make some money out of it.'

'What do you mean?'

'Have you not noticed how we are all very careful with our fuel rations and use horses and bicycles as much as we can?'

Hélène nodded.

'Well, at least if the Boche haven't commandeered them that is. And there is *Monsieur* ordering dresses from Paris for his beloved daughter and driving her to Tours to see the latest styles in the big shops, while the rest of us scrape together an existence. He is richer than the doctor! I heard the other day that he is having a new bathroom installed in his house; the old monastery at Lusigny.'

'But Antoine is marrying his daughter?'

The old man shrugged his shoulders and sighed again. 'And there is nothing I can do. I have tried to talk to him but he says that he loves her, and that I am old and twisted. He is right on that one, I am old and I am twisted but wrong about that man; I am definitely not.'

Hélène flushed, the thought of Antoine loving Céline Cottereau was too unpleasant. To divert the conversation she got out her bag and prepared *Monsieur* Meffret's injection. 'Now I'm afraid it is eggs again for lunch so I must go and collect them.' She left the old man to drop off with the force of the morphine and went out to the barn.

Glad of a moment to herself to take it all in, she sat down on a bale of straw wrapping her overcoat tightly around her. The weather was damp and cold but the smell of the straw comforted her.

Rémy or rather Jean Legrand was Miriam's father, the school teacher and he was shot in the very same place that she had met with Foucaud. Could Foucaud have had something to do with it? But the log hut was near the school so it wouldn't be unusual for the schoolteacher to pass by that way. There was still the possibility that it was suicide. She barely knew the man and if Philippe Cottereau was as unpleasant as Albert Meffret suggested, there could be another reason for him to end his days. Rémy had said that he would contact the *maquisard* but if the *maquisard* was responsible for stealing the contents of the containers, Rémy would have been in danger. He must have found out what was going on. Hélène knew she had to find out who the *maquisard* was. What if the *maquisard* knew she was on to him? She could be the next target; she would have to be extra alert. With Rémy gone, the only way she would catch the culprit is to catch him in *flagrant délit*. She would have to arrange another drop and trust that it would bring him out of the woodwork.

She checked the laying boxes for messages but there were only eggs and not many at that, with the days getting shorter eggs would become scarce too. She went back into the house and cooked *Monsieur* Meffret's lunch.

It wasn't long before Antoine came in from the fields for his own lunch. When he had finished and put on his boots to return to the farm, she followed him out. She gestured to him to follow her into the barn.

'My contact was Jean Legrand.'

'Jean!' He looked aghast. 'I would never have imagined him doing that.'

'Why not?'

'He was so... well, by the book. He did as he was told.'

'As a teacher?'

'Well, yes. Whatever *Monsieur* Cottereau told him he did without question.'

'*Monsieur* Cottereau is your future father-in-law?'

'Yes, he is the chair of the local education board.'

'Is he a demanding man?'

'I don't wish to speak ill of him but he is used to getting what he wants and woe betide anyone who challenges him.'

'Do you get on with him?'

'He is my fiancée's father.' He shrugged avoiding her stare.

She could sense his resistance and tried another tack. 'Do you think Jean Legrand could have taken his own life?'

Antoine clearly didn't want to talk about it anymore. He just shrugged and said, 'I didn't know him that well.'

'Antoine, I don't mean to put you in a difficult position but I have to know what is going on. Lives are at stake and if I am to organise the next mission I must know where the dangers are.'

He just stared down at his boots. He was clearly not to be moved.

'The mission I spoke of will be in just under a fortnight, we will need an extra man with Jean gone.'

'Leave it to me. I already have four who have agreed.'

# TWENTY-FOUR

## Diana

It had seemed a good idea at the time. She'd got carried away looking through the magazines that Lionel had thrust in front of her so theatrically.

'*Madame* Lescure!' he'd crooned. 'How could you let your hair get into such a terrible state? This is no good for such a beautiful woman.' His effeminate lisp combined with his insistence on speaking a bizarre mix of Franco-American made her feel exotic.

She had to admit that she'd enjoyed herself. Lionel was not unlike Jean-Paul Gaulthier in his baggy striped dungarees disguising his skinny frame and a felt pill box hat on his shaved head. For an hour she'd imagined she was some beautiful model visiting her personal hairdresser. His elf-like figure had danced around her with combs and scissors and sprays and interminable compliments. Her once long straggly hair was now cut into a short stylish bob that swung to and fro with the slightest movement.

She had never had short hair in her life. Her stomach had lurched when she had glanced downwards and seen her long hair lying inert, like a dead animal on the clinical floor tiles. She looked in the rear-view mirror and didn't recognise the person staring back at her. The shy, nervous dowdy woman who had gone into the hairdressers had been captured by Lionel's expert scissors never to return. At least Serge wasn't due back until the following evening she would have time to get used to it before she would have to face him.

As she pulled into the garage she almost drove into the back of Serge's Mini. What was he doing home early? This was a disaster. Something must have happened. She rushed up the steps to the kitchen, forgetting her hair, and called out. Her heart was pumping as she remembered the state she had left the house in. The breakfast and lunch things had been left on the side and Ben's toys were strewn all over the sitting room.

'In here,' came the reply from the sitting room. She glanced through the kitchen doorway as she passed. The surfaces were clear. Thank God! Liesel must have cleared up.

Liesel and Serge were sitting at the dining table. Serge had a glass of pastis, and Liesel a kir. They were both smiling. Obviously there was no harm done. The table was set for supper and there were homely smells coming from the oven. Ben was playing contentedly on the carpet with Lego. There was no sign of the debris she had left when she went out.

'Diana! Wow!' Liesel exclaimed as she went through the door.

Serge looked up in surprise. 'Diana. You look…' Serge just stared open mouthed. 'Your hair!'

Diana could feel herself reddening; she had never enjoyed being the centre of attention, even if it was positively. But Serge hadn't stated whether he actually liked it or not.

'*Maman*?' Even Ben was amazed and ran over to her for reassurance that it was really her.

'You look amazing. I knew Lionel would do a good job.'

'Lionel?' asked Serge.

'My hairdresser. We decided it was time Diana had a change of image.' Liesel was clearly pleased with herself.

'Serge, I didn't know you were coming back so soon!' Diana's voice was high.

'I left a message on the answering machine.'

'A message? What message? When did you leave it?'

'Saturday evening.' She could feel Serge becoming agitated. 'Where were you?'

Saturday, she thought. Léo had escaped she must have been out looking for him. But Liesel was here, she obviously hadn't heard it or she would have said something. 'I, I was in the garden. Oh, I remember there was a power cut it must have erased it.' She glanced at Liesel to see if her memory had been jogged, but she remained quiet whilst tracing lines on the table with a cocktail stick.

'I call and you're out. I come back from work and you're out.'

'Serge, I'm truly sorry. I wasn't expecting you until tomorrow.' She looked to Liesel for back up but none came.

'Well I'd better serve up or it will be spoiled.'

'Oh Liesel, I didn't expect you to cook supper as well, thank you so much.'

'It was nothing, anyway it gave me something to do while you were out.' She bustled off into the kitchen.

Serge glared at Diana. The power of her transformation was evidently insufficient to quell his irritation.

'Right, well. I'd better get Ben ready for bed.'

'Yes, you had. Or were you expecting Liesel to do that too?'

She picked up Ben and stormed off to his bedroom. On her return Liesel was serving supper. She was wearing the apron Serge had given Diana last Christmas. It was a long dark green bistro apron. The strings were tied tightly showing off her tiny waist.

Serge glanced at her curving figure as she leant across him to plunge the serving spoon into the casserole of what looked like *Boeuf Bourguignon.*

She somehow managed to compose her emotions and sat down at the table next to Liesel. It was obvious that Serge was not about to calm down. He averted his eyes from Diana and concentrated over zealously on Liesel and his plate. Diana ignored him and took a mouthful of stew. The beef was so tender it just melted in her mouth. The sauce was a rich, blend of butter and red wine. She often made *Bourguignon* but it had never tasted quite as good as this.

'This is lovely beef. Where did you get it?' She knew there had not been any in the house.

'I saw a butcher's van stop by the green; this was all he had left. I know what Lionel's like. Once he gets talking he can't stop, I knew you wouldn't be back until late.'

'Oh, which butcher's van was that? We only usually get one on Saturday morning.'

'Yes, he said he doesn't normally come on a Monday but he was ill on Saturday.'

She studied both their faces.

Serge was flashing glances of admiration at Liesel whilst supping her nectar hungrily. 'Liesel tells me that Léo ran away.'

Diana scowled at her. 'He chewed through the netting on the gate.'

'Perhaps you didn't fix it properly,' he tutted. 'It's lucky he didn't get run over.'

'Well, he didn't and that's the main thing,' said Liesel at last coming to her rescue. 'That nice man brought him back.'

'What man?' Serge was looking hard at Diana.

'Oh, just a chap from the village. He offered to look for him. I don't know his name.'

'I thought you said his name was Michaud?' said Liesel.

Diana repressed a reflex to kick her hard in the shins. 'Oh Yes, that's right. Michaud. I'd forgotten.'

'How do you know him?' Serge interrogated.

'I don't *know* him as such.' They were both staring at her. 'He lives in one of the farms on the Jaunay road. I got chatting to him on a dog walk.' She could feel herself blushing, bringing up the subject of the car crash would only be adding fuel to the fire. For god's sake, she hadn't done anything wrong.

Serge was frowning.

Diana snapped under the pressure. 'Look, Serge. Léo was lost, and he offered to look for him for me. I was hardly going to refuse was I? And I'm very glad I didn't, he did bring him back, after all.' She was willing Liesel not to mention the offer of riding. Serge could be very jealous and she'd had quite enough for one day. Nor did she want her to expand on her opinion of his appearance.

The next morning Diana was dressing Ben. She opened his cupboard to take out some clothes and was met with a neat multicoloured wall of fabric. Each item of clothing had been folded into a tidy, identically sized package that fitted the exact width of the shelf and then piled up displaying only a fold of fabric. She opened the drawer of the babychanging table and it was the same. The nappies had been lined up in rows and the bottles of cream and talcum powder arranged in order of height. The toy box had been wiped out and rearranged in an orderly fashion. The laundry basket had been emptied and his storybooks were sitting bolt upright on the shelf. In the sitting room, even the logs were lined up geometrically in the raffia basket, the hearth had been swept and wiped and the fire basket emptied of ashes.

Diana's skin crawled. She'd only asked Liesel to baby-sit. Hang on, she hadn't *asked* her to baby-sit. She'd offered. Could Liesel have just been trying to do her a favour? If she had why was she feeling like this? She felt as if her personal space had been invaded. The kitchen was as spotless as everywhere else, even down to the cupboards. It didn't feel like her house.

She was just warming up the coffee pot when Serge slipped his arms around her waist. 'Darling, I forgive you for not being here when I got home. You look fantastic, and the house looks fantastic. You've obviously been working really hard.'

Diana cringed. She couldn't bring herself to reply. Revulsion seeped over her like an oil slick. Her hair was Liesel's doing and so was the house. She pulled away from him. She marched out of the house and down to the vegetable patch leaving Serge standing confused at the kitchen window. She sat on the old poplar stump and stared out towards the forest. Why was she so angry? Hadn't that been what she'd wanted? For him to love her openly, and touch her and want her? But it wasn't *her* that had done all that, it was Liesel. OK he didn't know that, but she knew she could not and would not be Liesel. She had always scorned the archetypal housewife who polished and cleaned from dawn 'til dusk. She loved him with all her heart but she couldn't do that. She heard a noise and looked back nervously towards the house.

Ben was toddling down the garden yelling '*Maman, Maman!*' Her beautiful boy was beaming at her. 'Whassa matter?' he said slowly his head on one side.

Diana wiped away her tears and picked him up. 'Nothing's the matter my bunny. Come on. Let's go and get some breakfast.'

Serge was still in the kitchen where she had left him. 'I'm sorry,' she began. 'I don't know what came over me.' It really wasn't his fault if Liesel had tidied up their house. As long as he never found out, there would be no harm done. She made some coffee and told Serge about the mayor's visit.

'Excellent, with Ben at school you'll get some time to yourself.'

'What do you mean time to myself?' She looked at him in horror. 'Ben's far too little to go to school. He's only two.'

'*I* went to school when I was two.'

'Yes, but your mother was working, I'm lucky enough to be here for him.'

'Every child in the area will be starting school at two, if you keep Ben out he'll be behind when he starts and that's not fair. Anyway, he needs other children; it'll be good for him.'

'I am not sending my son to school in September; he's barely out of nappies!' She was shouting now.

'My son! He's not just your son, he's my son too. And I want him to go to school at the same time as the other kids.'

'Don't shout at me.'

'You're shouting at *me*!' His face was bright red. He stormed out of the back door slamming it behind him.

Ben began to cry and hung onto Diana's trouser leg. She picked him up ashamed at having argued in front of him. She saw Serge cycle through the courtyard gate. She'd never imagined that he would actually want Ben to go to school so young. She had fully expected him to agree with her that he would be better off at home with his mother for as long as possible. She picked up the telephone desperate for someone to talk to.

Delphine was, as she had hoped, missing lectures. 'Oh! *Ma Chère*! Serge is right you know. I went to school at two as well. It will be good for him. He's not a shy child, he'll love it.'

'But Delphine, I don't think I could bear to part with him, not yet.'

'This sounds like this is all about you, not Ben or Serge. You'll have to adapt. You've got plenty to do in that huge house and I'm sure it's not easy trying to get it done with Ben around your feet all the time. He'll have to go to school sooner or later. Besides it would help his language, he's still not talking properly is he?'

'No, but the paediatrician in Paris said that was normal for a bilingual child.'

'Yes, I know that. But it really wouldn't do him any harm, now would it?'

'Oh, I suppose you're right.'

'Perhaps if you go up and see the school and meet the teacher before he starts you'll feel better. Anyhow, term doesn't start for weeks. Tell Serge you'll think about it and just get used to the idea.'

Diana couldn't bring herself to answer.

'Come on Diana. He made a big sacrifice moving to the country to keep you happy. Now it's your turn to respect his wishes. It's not as if Ben won't be *safe* at school.'

'No, of course not. Serge has gone off in a rage. I feel guilty now.'

'It's not your first row and it won't be the last, he'll be back when he's calmed down. Make him a nice lunch and tell him you're sorry.'

Diana was carefully wrapping steaming endives in ham as Serge came up the back steps. She put them in an oven dish and enveloped them in béchamel sauce. She intercepted him in the hall and put her arms round his neck. 'I'm sorry. I shouldn't have lost my temper like that.'

He was about to speak but Diana put her finger to his lips. 'And you're right about Ben and school. It won't do him any harm. Perhaps he could just go for the morning to begin with. I shall talk to *Monsieur* Moreau.'

166

# TWENTY-FIVE

## Edward

There, there is the signal. The owl's screech, just like the one he had heard from Clothilde's lips on that very first night. Edward gathered his habit around him, despite the warmth of the night; it would provide excellent camouflage certainly more than his pale skin in the moonlight. He set off for the village, his bundles of parchment secured neatly beneath his cloak. As he approached he could see the glow of the fire lit outside one of the huts warning of sickness within. There was not a sound, even the dogs were exhausted by the heat of the day and didn't stir. He slipped beneath the animal skin that was slung across the doorway. Once inside,, on the floor by the light of a torch burning faintly in one corner, he could make out small sleeping bodies covered in rough blankets. These must be Clothilde and Firmin's brothers and sisters.

Clothilde was sitting by her mother's bedside frowning. She was anxiously pushing a fine amulet of gold and turquoise up and down her arm. On the opposite side was the young man, as dark as the children, that Edward had seen that day on his travels in the woods.

He stepped towards Edward and shook his hand. 'Can you save her?'

'I shall try. Let me see her.' Edward stretched his arm and placed his hand on the woman's forehead. She was still running a fever and beads of sweat were pouring down the sides of her brow. As his palm came into contact with her skin she gasped and began to rant like a wild animal. High pitched and whining were her moans.

'Mother, sssh! We are here. Calm yourself.'

For a brief moment the woman opened her eyes and looked at Edward, her eyeballs were oversized and staring as if angry. Edward felt an urge to take a step back but he must not. He must be brave. Her hair was as dark as her eldest son's.

Edward looked at Firmin. 'Did you find the plant?'

'Yes but I did not get back until late; I have not yet managed to lay them on her.' Firmin produced a clutch of greenery from a pouch around his waist, the tall beige frond brushes confirmed their species.

'Clothilde, free her midriff from the bedding we must apply this as soon as possible. Firmin, fetch me some cool water and a bowl.'

Clothilde set about undressing her mother and exposing her belly. Edward dipped the leaves carefully into the bowl of water and wrung them out until well bruised. He laid them over the woman's stomach. At their touch she began to writhe more violently and Clothilde had to use all her strength to hold her still.

'It is the cold; the difference in temperature is a shock to someone with a fever. You are doing well. Keep holding her still.'

Edward only just managed to leave the village before the sun let its pink glow engulf the sky. Clothilde's mother was sleeping peacefully now but only time would tell if she were to recover. He left Clothilde and her brother with instructions to repeat the process when she awoke. He returned to the cavern and set about preparing a breakfast of eels and then he prayed for Clothilde's mother's soul and for her full recovery.

At nightfall he waited for news from Clothilde but none came. He ventured through the woods to the edge of the village. The fire was still burning by their door but all was quiet. He could not hear any roaring or hysteria. She cannot have got any worse or he was sure Clothilde would have come to see him.

The next few nights he continued to visit and each time the fire was burning and all was quiet. On the fourth day he was preparing the last of the eels over his fire for breakfast when Clothilde slid herself down into the den. She was beaming.

'Mother is much better. She is still weak but her fever has gone and she even laughed this morning. You are so wonderful.' She leaned towards him and kissed his cheek.

His heart leapt. So he had got it right. Praise be to God! Perhaps it was written. It was God's way. He had sent him here to this place to heal this woman. But why was he made a traitor to get here? God works in mysterious ways and this was indeed His will.

'There is a problem.' Clothilde was frowning. 'Mother can remember you coming to see her and has been talking of a magical monk who cured her. Firmin and I have told her over and over that it was her imagination, but she is convinced of this belief and there is nothing we can say to persuade her otherwise.'

'Do not worry. The villagers know she was very ill?'

'Yes, her howlings could be heard all over the village. Some even thought she was possessed.'

168

'Let them think she was. No one would believe the words of a possessed woman. All we can do is thank God that she continues to recover and is returned to her usual self.'

'But news of her recovery is spreading through the village very quickly and people are asking questions about who cured her. What shall I say?'

'This is a problem I had not thought of.' He paused for a moment, stroking his chin. 'I think you must say that it was you who cured her. Say you only did things that you think you saw the herb wife doing on your visits to her. I suppose they do not know the treatment your mother received?'

'No, they do not, though I am not comfortable with such an untruth.'

'Nor I, Clothilde. I feel sorry for the position I have forced you into. I have thought long and hard and I think that I should leave this place and let you live in peace again.'

'Oh no, Edward you must not leave. And I must continue to study reading and writing. I have grown so attached to our lessons I could not bear to think of an existence without them.'

'Firmin still has lessons with *Père* Barthélemy?'

'Yes, but he is too busy to pass on his teachings, with the animals to tend and the vegetables to grow. Anyway where would you go?'

'There is the abbey at Pontigny you talked of. You said it would take three or four days travelling, but at least I would be amongst my own kind and you would be out of danger.'

'I am saddened by this. You said you would tell me of your trouble over the sea.'

'I must tell my trouble to the abbey at Pontigny. It is there that I can at last be dealt with. I have hidden long enough.'

'Wait! You cannot go yet! I almost forgot; one of the villagers came to me yesterday morning. Her little girl played out in the sun too long in few clothes and her skin has become red and sore. She is hot just like my mother was. I fear for her. I bathed her in the remains of the buck's horn plantain you left us, but today her condition appears to have worsened and her skin is covered in tiny blisters. They all think I am the healer and I do not know what to do. You cannot leave, you must cure this little girl first.'

'You have done the right thing Clothilde. You see, you are a healer. The villagers are not so wrong. The skin turning to blisters is not a worsening of her condition, it is an improvement. The affliction is taking its natural course, only quickened by the treatment. Now you must apply the same mixture as I gave you for your face. There is a little left in this jar, just moisten it with water. It will heal the lesions. In future this child must remember to cover her skin on very hot days. The power of the sun should not be passed over.'

'Of course.' She looked at him solemnly. 'Promise me that you will not leave until my mother is on her feet again.'

'I promise you, but I am sure she will be quite well in just a few days.'

She got up to leave and then stopped. 'The *foire* is coming!' Her face lit up with excitement.

'The *foire*?'

'Yes, every spring there is a fair on the *Champ de Foire*. You know, the one with the well just next to our house.'

Edward nodded.

'There will be many strangers coming to Saint Gabriel!'

'Then I must leave soon.' Edward hung his head.

'No, you don't see. With lots of strangers coming here, you would just be one more. You could pretend you had come to the fair and were looking for work!'

'A monk looking for work is not believable.'

'If you change your clothes and let your hair grow, there is time, they would not know you were a monk!'

'You mean abandon my habit?'

'But, Edward, it would save you. You could come and work the land with us. You could care for us when we are ill and live amongst us as one of us!' She flushed with excitement.

He considered for a moment. 'Clothilde what you are suggesting is very tempting but I am a monk. That is who I am. I have lived in a monastery all of my life. I know nothing else.'

'I can teach you, just as you have taught me.' Her voice was pleading.

'No, I cannot. As much as I would love to live near you and as one of you, my calling is to God. I have many debts to repay him. The day of the fair would be a good day for me to set out to Pontigny, another stranger on the road will not be remarked.'

Her face fell in disappointment. 'As you wish.' She clutched his hand.

# TWENTY-SIX

**Diana**

It was Bastille Day. Blue, white and red bunting was strung between the town hall and the plane trees, it was twisting and flapping in the breeze. Trestle tables had been set up in the shade and swathed in white tablecloths. There were cars parked everywhere. Every driveway was blocked. *La Petite Folie* was already bursting at the seams. There were vans and cars with number plates from all over France; from Paris, the Sarthe and even Bordeaux. Some were unloading bicycles. Men were changing into cycling shorts and brightly coloured jerseys. People crowded the pavements. Families had set up picnic encampments all along the planned route for the race. In fact Serge had already had to turn away a couple of families who had slipped through the privet hedge bordering the *Champ de Foire* to picnic in the garden.

Ben was excitedly waving a paper *Tricolore* as the cyclists lined up and jostled at the start line on the edge of the green. The starting gun was fired and the cyclists were off. They sped out of the village bunched up in a swarm of gleaming wheels and garish jerseys. They headed between the sunflower and maize fields towards the forest. The route would take them to the village of Marchenoir and then loop round through St Léonard and Lusigny and back to Saint Gabriel. As the cyclists streaked through at the end of the first lap, all the picnickers rose to their feet clapping and cheering until they were again out of sight.

Serge, with Ben on his shoulders, and Diana stood just inside the privet hedge. A man was commentating from a PA system by the trestle tables. The cyclists did five laps, each time flaming past in a blur. After the last cyclist had left the village for the fourth time, *Monsieur* Moreau and his deputy held the finish ribbon across the road. The winner cycled through it, his arms held high in true *Tour de France* style. He was presented with a yellow jersey and a bottle of champagne which he immediately shook up and sprayed across the cheering crowd.

The grand prix atmosphere subsided and the families began to pack up their picnics. Bicycles were loaded back into the cars and vans and an hour later only the villagers remained. The streets were littered with competitor numbers and empty drink cans and bottles.

Edouard Moreau was lining up bottles of pastis, wine and cider on the trestles. The villagers, enticed by the offer of a free drink, converged on the green. There was a multitude of elderly people Diana had never seen before, but she was equally surprised by how many villagers were familiar.

Diana and Serge left their viewing haven behind the privet hedge and joined them. Mémère Claudette and Marie-Pierre were at her side in a second; one at each elbow.

'Diana! Your hair! You look wonderful.' Marie-Pierre took Ben's hand and swept Diana off to introduce her to old lady after old lady. After about twenty minutes she was sure that she had shaken hands with every style of nylon housecoat available in the local shops. She glimpsed Serge with his comrades from *La Petite Folie*, and intended to release herself from Marie-Pierre and her mother's clutches to join him, but they had found yet another gaggle of women to introduce her to. Diana smiled at each of them as warmly as she could, aware that she was being examined like some sort of freak at a Victorian travelling fair. She nodded politely although she found it difficult to understand all their deep country accents.

Marcel thrust a glass of cider into her hand. Not wishing to humiliate herself, she nervously glanced round to see what the other women were drinking. To her surprise every woman present was knocking back some sort of alcoholic beverage at quite a pace. So this must be one event where women were permitted to let their hair down; in the name of the revolution!

Someone produced a football, and Serge and Marcel pulled off their shirts and began kicking it around with the teenagers and the younger men of the village.

Ben slipped his hand from Marie-Pierre's and ran towards the football yelling, '*Foot!*' Diana was going to run after him but the men kicked the ball to him gently and he returned it with surprising skill. They let him join in, carefully dodging him when he got in the way.

The cider was beginning to go to her head and she longed to sit down. Drinking cider in full sun had not been a good idea. Marie-Pierre and Mémère were ensconced in conversation with one of the old ladies, so she took the opportunity to sink onto the grass in the shade of a tree and watched her husband kicking the football around, bare-chested like an overgrown teenager. The remaining villagers were sitting on an old fashioned school form set against the school wall. A couple of the older ones were actually slumped and snoring from the effects of their midday festivities.

She had not been sitting down for long when Michaud appeared at her elbow.

'*Madame*,' he murmured softly. 'I hope I am not disturbing your peace.'

'Err, no.' Diana glanced in Serge's direction but he was busy tackling Marcel.

'May I sit down?'

'Of course.' She blushed. What would the village say?

'I, I am surprised to see you here.' As soon as it was out she regretted it.

'And why is that?'

Diana's blush grew deeper.

'You have been listening to gossip.'

'Gossip? No. I don't know anything. I'm sorry I shouldn't have said that.'

'I am accepting the mayor's kind invitation to a drink on Bastille Day. Like you.'

'Yes, of course. I'm sorry, it must be the cider.'

'Oh please don't frown like that. It ruins your beautiful features.'

Diana's muscles tensed and looked away.

'You are embarrassed?'

'No, no. My husband is just over there, playing football,' she said hurriedly.

'I know I can see him. If I was him I would not leave you alone for a second.'

She risked looking back at him. His eyes were on hers piercing as if they could see into her soul.

'*Madame* Lescure?'

Diana looked up rapidly like a startled rabbit. The mayor was standing over them, a tumbler of pastis in his hand. They both scrambled to their feet.

'Michaud.' The mayor acknowledged him with a stern nod and then fell silent.

Michaud retreated diplomatically.

'I wondered if you had given some thought to Ben's school place.'

'Umm, yes. We have discussed it. Would it be possible for him to just go for the morning?'

'Of course!' The mayor was evidently delighted. 'That's what most of the little ones do until they're used to it. Then they can start staying in the afternoon and have a nap there too.'

'Well, I shall come and see you before the holiday's over.'

'I shall look forward to it,' he twinkled.

The sun was now beating down and the trees no longer gave proper shelter from its searing rays so Diana settled herself on one of the now shaded benches against the school wall. To the left of her was an old lady fast asleep, her head lolling. The glass of cider in her hand was tipping dangerously, threatening to empty its contents in her lap. Diana carefully removed it from her grip and set it on the tarmac at her feet. The trestle tables only held empty bottles and glasses and Edouard Moreau was piling them into plastic crates with his deputy. Ben was still tearing around the green after the football. The villagers that hadn't fallen asleep in the sunshine were huddled in groups talking and gesticulating.

Diana looked beyond the green to the privet hedge that ran along the edge of their garden and the slated roof that rose above it. This was exactly what she had hoped for, being in the centre of a community in France's sleepy countryside where nothing mattered but good food, wine and village spirit.

She must have dozed off herself for she was awoken by the engine of a large van parked just feet from her. She sat up with a start. The old lady next to her had left. *Monsieur* Moreau was piling the collapsed trestles into the back of the van. Serge and Marcel were sitting on the grass chatting. Ben was sitting between them his head resting against his father; if he wasn't already asleep he soon would be. She glanced over at the café a white van was pulling off the forecourt, Jeanette must be exhausted after the day's trade. She heaved herself to her feet and went over to Serge.

'I thought I'd pop in on Jeanette, see if she needs any help. Do you mind hanging on to Ben a little longer?'

'This little boy needs his pillows. Marcel is coming for a drink, so I'll put him to bed for a bit. You go ahead.'

Inside the café, Jeanette was nowhere to be seen. She usually appeared when the bell on the door tinkled. She could hear the hum of a radio in the kitchen. She called out but there was no reply. She called out again and peered round the kitchen door. There was a table covered with a plastic cloth depicting flying partridges. On it were three empty glasses with what looked like the dregs of pastis in the bottom. She was about to give up and go home when she heard sobbing. She stepped inside.

Jeanette was huddled on the tiled floor, her shoulders trembling and tears washing over her cheeks. Next to her on the floor a microwave lay smashed and dented.

'Jeanette! What happened?'

She only uttered gasping sobs.

Diana stepped over the broken microwave and leant down putting her arms around her. 'Please, Jeanette. What happened?'

She swallowed her sobs, shaking her head. She wiped at her face. 'I dropped it, that's all.' She scrambled to her feet and prodded at her hair. 'It was stupid of me.' She let out a laugh which didn't fit her facial expression.

'Let me help you clear this up.'

'No, no. It's fine.'

'I will hear no such thing. Now sit down on this chair and I will sort this out.' Diana picked up the pieces of broken turn-plate and heaved the carcass out of the back door and laid it on the concrete in the back yard. 'You'll need a new one I'm afraid.'

Jeanette was calmer now.

'Frédeau is still on the green with Serge and Marcel. Shall I fetch him?'

'No, no. He is young, he is enjoying himself.'

'And you are tired. You need help.'

'I have done everything now. I just got overtired I shouldn't have tried to change things around after such a busy day. Thank you, Diana.' She took her hand. 'You are a good friend. You get off.'

'You must have done well on takings today?'

'Yes, at least that's true.'

'I saw your last customer go just now; I don't think I've ever seen so many people in the village.'

'The cycle race brings so many from all over. It is very good for business.' Then she sighed, 'Alas it is but once a year.'

# TWENTY-SEVEN

## Hélène

She leant her bicycle against the wall of the Camaret's farm. Inside she could hear little Marc crying. She knocked on the door but the child's crying drowned out the noise so she pushed the door to and stepped into the kitchen.

'Aah Hélène! There is no need for you to come to see me. Look my leg is quite well.' She lifted her skirt to reveal a healthy patch of skin which was just a little scarred. 'You look worn out. Come and sit down and I will serve you a coffee.'

'Thank you, a coffee would be lovely.' Hélène picked up little Marc who was still howling from a rug in front of the range. He stopped the instant she held him.

'You will spoil that boy!' said Agnès laughing, then her face became serious. 'Something is troubling you. Tell me.'

'I went to Jean Legrand's funeral this morning.'

'It is so sad, such a young man. They are saying he may have taken his own life.'

'Do you think he did?'

'I did not know him well but I do know Floriane and what I know of him through her, I would say that no, he could not have done it. She always spoke of him as strong and fair. But if he did not take his life then it would be murder!' She frowned. 'If there is a doubt I am sure Gaston will get to the bottom of it.'

'Gaston?'

'He is head of the police. Jean was a good teacher you know.' She was shaking her head. 'So diplomatic. I would not want to work under Philippe Cottereau.'

'Why not?'

'I must watch my tongue.' She stood up and poured coffee into two tiny cups.

'Agnès, please. Anything you say will not go any further, I promise you. I want to help Miriam and her mother, I need to know as much as possible. Please, trust me.'

She sat down again and looked searchingly into Hélène's eyes, as if satisfied that what she saw was convincing. 'Philippe Cottereau is a very powerful man. He is changeable and vain. He uses the power he has to control the village very much to his advantage. He manipulates us, all of us.'

'Really, how?'

'He is threatening. Everyone has something which is dear to them and he seems to find out what that is and think of ways that he could take it away. Then he makes unreasonable requests of people and holds what is valuable to them as ransom.'

'Did he do that to Jean Legrand?'

'Who could say? He is very clever; he is never direct about it. He insinuates that is all.'

'Has he done it to you?'

Agnès shrugged and looked out of the window. 'If I were you I would keep out of village business. As an outsider you would end up in very great trouble. Now, are you going to visit Floriane Legrand?'

'Yes, I expect *Docteur* Legris will ask me to check on her.'

'Please take her some eggs from me. I would like to go over and see her but Georges is too busy at the moment to take me over to Jaunay, and with the little ones I don't think it is what a grieving widow needs. See if you can find out if she has enough to eat, with her husband gone I don't know if she will be provided for. She is a proud woman, Hélène, tread carefully.'

'Of course.' Hélène carefully laid the now sleeping Marc down in his cot by the range while Agnès disappeared to fetch the eggs. She clearly needed to find out what Philippe Cottereau was up to and whether Gaston would be launching a murder investigation.

She climbed on to her bicycle and cycled back up the Jaunay road. The winter daylight was retreating and Cécile Clément would soon be preparing supper. She knew the Legrand family lived at the far end of Jaunay, somewhere not far from where she had met Miriam and little Claude on that first morning. She reached the avenue of plane trees that lined the Beaugency road. Claude was standing by the side of the road with his hands deep in his pockets kicking a stone. Hélène dismounted and went over to him.

'*Bonjour* Claude.'

'*Bonjour Madame.*'

'You are all alone?'

He shrugged.

'Miriam is not with you?'

'No, Miriam is with her mother.' He let out a long sigh.

'Can you show me where she lives?'

His face lit up, clearly delighted to have something to do. 'Yes, follow me.' And he skipped off as only small children can. Hélène was glad of her bicycle to keep up with him. He led her up a rutted track to a collection of low buildings surrounded by open fields. Most of the buildings appeared to be derelict except for one, which had smoke billowing from its chimney. He stopped outside its door.

'This is Miriam's house.'

'Thank you Claude, now you get off home. You must not be out after dark or you will get into trouble.'

'*Au revoir Madame.*' He hung his head and moved off miserably.

'I am sure Miriam will be out to play with you again, very soon.'

He turned and nodded, clearly unconvinced. A day must seem like such a long time to an eight year old and 'soon' must be an unfathomable length of time to consider.

Hélène knocked on the door. No one came immediately. She could hear some scuffling from inside, as if someone was hurriedly tidying up before answering. She waited a little until the scuffling subsided and she knocked again. Miriam answered the door. Although Hélène could see she was pleased to see her, her features were drawn and her cheeks were pale.

'*Bonjour* Miriam.'

'*Bonjour Mademoiselle.*'

'Is your mother home?'

'She is resting.'

'Can I come in a moment?'

Miriam let the door swing open and stepped aside. She was wearing an apron over her clothes which were grubbier than usual and there were patches of wet over her skirt. There was a large stone sink under a window to one side; in front of it was a chair with a puddle of water in its indented seat.

'You have been washing up for your mother?'

'She is very tired; I am trying to help her.'

'You are a good child, Miriam. I am also here to help.'

A voice came from the back of the cottage. 'Miriam? Who is there?'

'*Maman*, it is *Mademoiselle* Godard, the nurse, come to see us.'

'Tell her she is kind but we don't need a nurse.'

'*Madame* Legrand, I have come to offer you help,' called Hélène.

A door at the back of the cottage creaked and a slight woman with a wan, shadowed face stepped into the room. In the light, Hélène could see that Miriam had inherited her eyes, though not her shiny dark hair which must have been very long for it was piled high on her head. 'It is very kind of you, but as you can see Miriam and I have all we need.'

'Please, *Madame*. I did not know your husband but what has happened is truly terrible and I am here to offer you comfort.'

Floriane Legrand gestured for her to sit down. 'Please.'

Hélène obeyed and sat in a large wing-backed armchair covered in a knitted blanket. Floriane sat down opposite her on a stool by the wood burner, sitting upright.

'Miriam, fetch *Mademoiselle* Godard a drink. I think we have some *épine* left.' Miriam jumped up and went through to the back of the house. 'I do not know what sort of help you are offering us.'

'*Madame*, I wanted to ask you about the circumstances of your husband's death.'

The woman frowned, narrowing her eyes suspiciously. 'So you are here to satisfy village gossip?' Her voice was indignant. Hélène could see where Miriam got her fieriness from.

'No, nothing you say to me will go any further. I have heard that people believe he may have taken his own life.'

She blew her lips out dismissively.

'If that were true, they would not have allowed him to be buried in the churchyard.'

'So, if that is not possible, did your husband have any enemies?'

'My husband is the strongest man I have ever known. Aside from my father of course, God rest his soul. He worked hard and he loved hard. Even when things got difficult my husband could always find room in his heart for others, for me and for Miriam. As for enemies…' She shook her head. 'I cannot say that everyone loved him. He kept himself to himself, but no one hated him. He never gave any cause for it. My husband was a good teacher, a good husband and a good father. But he was not a practical man. He was not good with a gun, it was an accident. A very sad accident, that is all.'

Hélène thought about the pheasant that had hung from Rémy's shoulder as they had walked from the forest to Jaunay that morning. The pheasant could have been shot by someone else but the way she had seen him handle the shotgun, carefully checking the safety catch every time he picked it up, she was certain it could not be an accident.

'How did he get on with Philippe Cottereau?'

Her face became alarmed. '*Mademoiselle*, I cannot see what business that is of yours? You said you were here to help. All you are doing is digging up a great deal of trouble.'

'I am sorry; I should not have come so close to your husband's death. I am insensitive. I *am* here to help and you have just to ask.'

Miriam came back into the room carrying a large decanter of a deep russet liquid. 'Here it is *Maman!* I couldn't find it under ...' She frowned. 'I couldn't find it.'

'I almost forgot! Agnès Camaret has sent you some eggs and has asked if she can send you anything else. She wanted to come herself but Georges is too busy to bring her with the farm being so busy at the moment. Miriam, would you go to my bicycle outside and fetch the basket from it?'

Floriane Legrand poured a little of the red liquid into two thimble sized glasses on a low table. 'Here, this was made by my husband two springs ago. It should be perfect now.'

Hélène took a sip. It tasted like a perfect mixture of sherry and port. 'This is delicious.'

'It is made from the first shoots of blackthorn when they appear in the forest. It is particular to this district.' She took a sip. 'I have not been friendly to you. I apologise. Miriam has spoken of you a lot and I am sure that your intentions are good. My husband has had a terrible accident and we have been left alone to fend for ourselves. It is a great sadness but we must bear it with dignity.'

Hélène knocked back the rest of her *épine* and stood up. '*Madame* Legrand, I would like to ask permission to visit you again. I only ask that you think a little about who may have wanted to harm him. If you cannot I promise I will never mention it to you again.'

Miriam came through the front door clutching the basket of eggs. '*Maman* we can have an omelette for supper!'

'That is a wonderful idea, *ma chérie*. Please thank Agnès for me, I will go over and visit her in person when I am feeling a little better. Thank you for coming and I am sure Miriam would be delighted if you were to call again.'

'Oh yes! You could come again tomorrow?'

'I am sure *Mademoiselle* has plenty of work, Miriam, she will come when she is able.'

# TWENTY-EIGHT

## Diana

August was ridden with storms and sultry evenings. The leaves of the great lime tree were turning auburn and had begun to float to the earth beneath. The lawn was growing again and had lost its parched countenance and a smell of autumn tinged the morning air.

Serge had said no more about Ben going to school; Diana was thankful that he was leaving her to accept it in her own time. Ben was becoming restless with his limited life at home and when he came across other children in the supermarket he would throw himself on the ground and then look at them egging them on to laugh at him. Sometimes they would do the same and burst into fits of giggles, delighted with the attention from one another; it would do him good to be with other children. Even Diana's mother had pointed out that Diana had attended nursery from two years old. Besides he would only be going for the morning and since there was no school on Wednesdays it would only be four mornings a week. She swallowed her misgivings and strode over to the *Mairie.*

'Aah, *Madame* Lescure, *bonjour.*'

'*Bonjour Monsieur.* I've come about registering Ben in school.'

'Good. I was worried you were going to leave it too late.' He balanced a pair of pince-nez glasses on his wizened nose, a cygnet ring on his finger sent a flash of sunlight across the room. He scanned a huge bookshelf stuffed with cascading paperwork and pamphlets which lined the wall behind his head. A bundle of papers jutted precariously from a shelf. He pulled on it and the entire pile fell to the floor. Unperturbed he leant down and rifled through the sea of papers.

'*Voilà.* These are the ones we need. Let me fill them out for you then all you have to do is sign. The school term starts on Thursday. Corinne Roméo teaches the little ones. Are you familiar with the French schooling system?' He looked up over his glasses reminding Diana of Merlin giving a mission to a young knight of the round table.

'No, not really.'

He took a piece of paper and carefully listed the names of each year up to middle school. 'After that they go on to Ouzouer-le-Marché. But there is plenty of time before we need to worry about that. Here is a list of things he will need, and a form for his insurance.'

'Insurance?'

'Aah, yes. I suppose this is not necessary in the United Kingdom. In France each child must be insured in case they are injured or they damage any school property; just more of the interminable paperwork so typical of *La belle France!*' he chortled. 'The school is as you probably know split between two sites and the *maternelle* is in the main building in Talcy. The bus leaves Saint Gabriel at eight in the morning from the village green and will return at five.'

Diana frowned. 'Isn't he a little young to be catching the bus?'

He stroked his beard thoughtfully. 'You English, you like to keep your children at home for a long time, *non*? In France we like to give them the confidence to be independent earlier. We find they learn better.' Noticing Diana's consternation he raised an eyebrow. 'Of course if you wish to drive him to Talcy everyday that is your choice. But I'm sure that he will want to catch the bus with his friends. There is a lady who is specially employed to look after the little ones on the bus. You really mustn't worry he will be in good hands.'

Diana looked down at Ben whose attention was firmly fixed on a huge jar of lollipops on the mayor's desk. The mayor tipped the jar forwards and offered him one. Ben beamed at him and plunged his hand into the jar.

She hadn't bargained for the surprise of the school bus. She had seen the children getting on it the term before but assumed it was only for the older ones. She shrugged it off, the mayor had said that she could drive him there if she wanted, so that is what she would do.

A thick mist had settled over the fields of cowering, decaying sunflowers, reflecting Diana's mood. Serge had caught an early train to Paris leaving Diana to take Ben for his first day at school alone.

Talcy was a pretty village with a chateau and a duck pond. The school in contrast to the rest of the village was a modern building, though tastefully designed to blend in with the grey stone of the castle which towered above it. Plane trees edged a gritted playground; the damp air had soaked into their trunks of peeling bark giving them a shiny mottled façade. Diana parked the car and unstrapped Ben from his seat.

Clarissa Hunter had sent a backpack in the shape of a teddy bear to her grandson for his first day. He carried it proudly on his back. There were a few parents standing in groups chatting and laughing, but none of them looked up as she walked round them to get to the front door. Diana wished Serge hadn't had to go to work, today of all days.

Corinne Roméo was waiting on the steps. She was in her mid-forties, with brown-auburn hair that hung below her shoulders. She wore a wide black velvet Alice band to hold it from her face.

'*Bonjour Madame.*' She crouched down to Ben's level. '*Bonjour* Ben. My name is Corinne. You come with me and I shall show you where you will sit.'

Ben smiled at her charmingly and allowed her to take his hand and lead him inside.

'We're going to have a lot of fun today.'

Ben nodded and smiled again. The chemistry was instant. She led them into a big room with a ceiling so high that the low tables and tiny chairs gave the impression of a giant's room arranged for dwarves. The walls were covered with children's paintings of every colour. Ben immediately ran over to the corner of the room where there was a playhouse with plastic pots and pans and a wooden play cooker painted a shiny silver. Corinne found him a plastic apron and showed Diana a notebook with his name on.

'I will put this book in his bag before he goes home every day. In it, I will send messages about the things going on at school and any items he might need. If you would be so kind as to sign each note, so that I can be sure you have read it?'

Diana nodded, impressed at her organisation.

'With them coming on the bus, we don't see the parents often and we find this works.'

'Oh, no! I will be driving him to school and picking him up before lunch.'

She looked surprised.

'*Monsieur* Moreau said that wouldn't be a problem.' She did her best to keep the panic she was feeling out of her voice.

'No, no that's quite alright. But you know it is good for them to stay here all day, that way they don't miss anything.' Seeing her anxiety, she added, 'But it is fine to bring him just for the mornings, to begin with. We break for lunch at twelve o'clock so that would be the best time.'

Diana went to find Ben in the playhouse. He was far too busy to interrupt his play to say goodbye. He just glanced up briefly at her and carried on what he was doing. Diana's throat tightened as she slipped off.

The group of women outside in the playground again ignored her as she skirted them. She was glad no one spoke to her, she was certain she wouldn't have been able to reply. She drove out of the village past the duck pond, her eyes straining with tears. She slowed the car through Briou and then accelerated again as she reached the road that would take her across the open fields back to Saint Gabriel. The mist was still fairly thick in places and a tractor parked on the side of the road suddenly loomed out of the gloom. She managed to swerve round it. As she pulled towards the other side of the road a red convertible headed straight for her from the opposite direction. She managed to pull the car in and skidded to a halt in front of the tractor. The red car's brakes screamed and stopped alongside. She sat stock still as her heart pumped. A woman was getting out of the convertible and came up to the window. Diana wound the pane down ready to launch a tirade of anger, but the driver beat her to it.

'What do you think you're doing?' she shrieked in Diana's face. 'That was my right of way. Didn't you see the tractor?' She paused for a moment. 'You are... Yes, you are the English lady from the *Champ de Foire*. I've heard about you. Are you drunk?'

Diana stared back at her incredulously. A smell of expensive cologne swept through the window.

'Well?' she demanded aggressively. Her hands planted firmly on her hips.

Diana was speechless in the face of this grown woman having a tantrum.

The woman's arms began to wave exasperatedly in the air. Her fingers flashed with gold like a human firework in the fog.

A figure emerged from beneath the tractor and appeared behind the angry medusa. The firework swung round to face Michaud.

'And as for you... What on earth do you think you're doing leaving a tractor in such a place?' She marched over to her car and flung open the door. Rummaging in the glove compartment she pulled out a sheet of printed paper.

'There's no need to fill out an accident report form. There's nothing wrong with your vehicle,' said Michaud taking charge.

'Aah but the law says...'

'The law says that an accident report form should be filled out if there is an accident. But as nobody hit anything, there has been no accident.' He wasn't shouting but the authority in his voice made him menacing. His habitually soft blue eyes had become large and angry.

'Even if you had, you would have needed a witness and from where I was I would say that you were driving at a highly dangerous speed for this stretch of road. Not something that the mayor's wife would want broadcasted around the village.'

She looked at Michaud aghast. She hurriedly put the paper away mumbling that foreigners shouldn't be let loose on French roads and sped off, a cloud of exhaust smoke hung suspended above the tarmac, staining the fog.

'She's a bully that woman. It's not the first time she's thrown her weight around in this village. Are you alright?'

Diana nodded. 'That woman! It was her car that made me crash into the memorial, I am sure of it.'

'I am sure of it too. She drives everywhere like a maniac.'

'Has no one ever reported her?'

'Who knows, but Céline Moreau is the mayor's wife; they have connections in high places, I am not sure it would do any good at all. I'm sorry about leaving the tractor there, but it's broken down.'

'It's not your fault; I should have been paying more attention to the road in this fog. What's wrong with it? Can I give you a lift?'

'Oh no, It's my own fault. I should have changed the plugs ages ago but I've been putting it off. This damp was the last straw for them. I'd just stopped to check out some rattling at the back and I couldn't get her going again. I've got the new ones in the cab. I'll have it on the road in a jiffy.' He jangled the change in his overall pockets obviously wanting to get on.

'Thank you for dealing with that horrible woman. Poor *Monsieur* Moreau, being married to her!'

'Poor is something he isn't.'

Diana thought of the tatty bearded man who had knocked on her door wearing a tee-shirt and faded jeans. He certainly didn't look rich. 'Well, I'd better get back.' She turned the key in the ignition.

Michaud was still leaning on the car. 'I haven't seen you for a long time. I've been keeping an eye out for you in the mornings. What about that ride?'

'Oh! Yes, yes I have been so busy. I shall let you know.'

He smiled, evidently not realising he was being fobbed off. His eyes were shining despite the dull backdrop of the fog and Diana felt guilty for her deception. They waved awkwardly at each other and Diana slowly drove away. She looked in her mirror and watched his broad frame as he returned to the tractor and again slid himself underneath.

Her spirits sank as she pushed open the door from the back terrace. It didn't matter how positive she tried to be, things just seemed to be getting worse. She'd never imagined there could be such appalling behaviour in such a sleepy village as Saint Gabriel. Why had Céline Moreau accused her of being drunk? Had she heard that the English lady in the *Champ de Foire* was an alcoholic? She thought of Michaud and the powerful way he had dealt with her. Why couldn't she be more like that? Serge would probably have exploded; creating an embarrassing public scene. Not Michaud, he had calmly trampled that woman with a few quiet words.

The house echoed Ben's absence mournfully. She looked around the sitting room, his building blocks were strewn across the rug in front of the fireplace, and a trace of hot chocolate remained on the table. It was hours until she would drive back to pick him up. The thought of going through this every weekday and then for longer when he began to go to school full-time just didn't bear thinking about.

The ironing basket was full to overflowing. Living with Serge and his finicky demands, coupled with France's unwritten rules for neat appearance, had forced her to abandon her conviction that ironing was a pointless and old fashioned exercise. Even her student peers in Paris spent hours steaming creases into their jeans and some even ironed socks and underwear. But this morning she felt glad of a long and involved task to occupy her. She would look on it as therapy.

She folded up another pair of Ben's pyjamas and realised that in that short space of time she had ironed as many clothes as it would normally take her to iron in a week. How strange not to be interrupted! She did the dishes, made the beds and cleared away Ben's toys. His absence pulled on her heart like a tensed elastic band primed to snap.

She wandered, hands in pockets, down to the vegetable patch. Her pumpkins were coming on nicely, she counted twelve. They'd never be able to eat all of those. Even one would last the three of them about a month, unless they were to eat pumpkin every day. It's all very well growing vegetables to save money, but doesn't it defeat the object if you have to waste most of them? She could give them away to the neighbours, she supposed. But she didn't know one single neighbour who didn't have a vegetable patch themselves. The tomato plants sagged with the weight of their fruit. She half-heartedly began to gather in the ripe ones. With so little water, a good number of them

186

had formed too late to take advantage of the summer sun to ripen. She piled them into the wheelbarrow; they nearly filled it. She wheeled it up onto the back terrace. She laid the green ones out on the windowsills in the garage and took the rest into the kitchen.

A cup of tea steaming in front of her, she leafed through an ancient cookery book that had belonged to her grandmother. She'd always regarded this book with suspicion with its quarts and gills and bizarre ingredients. It was all rather 'eye of newt'. She scanned the endless list of suggested recipes for tomatoes, she came across a recipe for something called *pissaladière*. It was a sort of tomato and onion tart. She scanned the list of ingredients: bread dough, olive oil, onions, garlic, anchovies, tomatoes, black olives and seasoning. The anchovies would be a problem and she'd run out of onions. According to the recipe the anchovies should be arranged on the surface in a lattice pattern. She could probably get away with missing those out. But she couldn't do without the onions. Marie-Pierre had mentioned that the farm on the other side of the village grew them. Maybe they would sell her some.

She put on her boots and dug out Léo's lead and set off for the farm. At the greenhouse she turned up a gravel drive and knocked on the front door of the farmhouse. She didn't have to wait long. An old lady opened it. She smiled amiably at Diana. She didn't look her up and down critically, the way Diana was beginning to get used to.

'*Bonjour Madame*, my name is Diana Lescure, I live at the *Champ de Foire*'

'Aah!' she exclaimed beaming. 'I am *Madame* Camaret. How lovely to meet you! Please come in.'

'I don't want to disturb you. I just wondered if I might buy some onions from you.'

'Of course! Of course! But first you must drink some coffee with me.' *Madame* Camaret led her into a large kitchen with a huge wooden table in the centre and a range on one side. 'My sons are all out working in the fields.' Her arms flew up, her palms open, facing inwards landed on her powder puffed cheeks as if this was a terrible thing. 'What a shame! They would have liked to meet you.' She picked up an old blackened pot from the top of the range and poured thick black coffee into two tiny earthenware cups. 'Neither of them are married you know. In the old days a farmer was a good catch. These days women aren't prepared to put up with the long hours. They all want their husbands at home every evening,' she sighed. 'I think your husband does long hours, does he not?'

The village grapevine was evidently highly efficient. 'He *is* away a lot, but I'm getting used to it.'

'That's the way. In my day we were landed in a life or situation and we just got on with it, there was no question of abandoning or complaining. We had no choice.' She looked out of the window onto the road. 'I've lived in this village all my life. Not much has changed to look at, but oh how things were livelier then! We used to have dances in the village hall and people would come from miles around in their Sunday best; hoping to meet the love of their lives.' She smiled nostalgically. 'That's where I met my Georges. He'd walked all the way from Briou for that dance. Nowadays everyone has cars. They're always rushing around, chasing the clock. There aren't any dances in Saint Gabriel now. People aren't prepared to give up their free time to organise anything.' She picked up an old sepia photograph from the sideboard; it was a little ragged from much handling. 'That was my Georges.' She held out the photograph for Diana to look more closely.

A young man with strong dark features stared soberly out at her. A leather bullet belt hung around his waist and by his side was a rifle leaning against his light coloured breeches. A Springer spaniel sat at his feet as solemnly as his owner.

'That's what he looked like when I first met him. Such a good man!' she sighed. 'He's gone now. They're all gone now.' She paused and took a deep breath. She stood up abruptly. 'That's enough of an old woman's lamenting, that's not what you came for.'

Diana remonstrated politely.

*Madame* Camaret smoothed down her apron. 'Now let me see. Onions – yes, that's what you wanted. Follow me.' She disappeared down a stone corridor, leading off the kitchen. At the end of it was a stable-type door at the back of the property, the top half was open despite the murky fog outside. She opened the bottom half and led Diana into a cobbled yard hung with huge baskets of scarlet trailing geraniums; the last flowers of the season were hanging on despite their ambered leaves. At one side was a stone outhouse decked with wooden shelves. Each shelf held a different vegetable, apples, cabbages, cauliflowers, all neatly lined up for winter storage. She took a string of onions down from a hook in the ceiling and handed it to Diana.

'How much are they?'

'Oh no, these are a present. Welcome to Saint Gabriel!'

# TWENTY-NINE

## Edward

'Clothilde! Are you quite well? I was worried, it has been so long.'

'They are coming to me more and more. I am struggling to get my work done. Firmin looks so tired he is working all hours. We must pay the tithe to the *seigneuriale* soon and he has no one to help him.'

'Tell me, who is coming to you? Sit down a while and catch your breath.'

'The villagers and people from beyond with their ailments and sickness. Nothing very serious but I have been using the ointment you made for your head and it is like a miracle cure. With all the cuts and splinters they are getting through the harvest, they are bringing them all to me.'

'Then you must ask them for payment to your household if they are to take up your time; some bread or some oats.'

'I was so worried you had gone to Pontigny.'

'I will wait for the fair. I will not leave without your knowledge.' He held up his hand towards her face and then checked himself and rested it once again in his lap. 'What news of the girl?'

'The girl is on her way to recovery but I have run out of ointment.'

'I shall make some more today. Collect it after sundown.'

Clothilde caught his arm. 'Edward you were right about my mother and you were right about the girl. We cannot do without you.' Her eyes were pleading.

Edward revelled in her gaze. He squeezed her arm and said gently, 'I am glad to have been useful here and I will teach you as much as I can before I go. There are some weeks ahead of us before the fair, there is time.'

When she had left Edward busied himself with the concoction. He made it in a larger quantity this time, and once the jars were filled he settled back down with his parchment and quill to await her return.

The weeks passed and Clothilde's mother went from strength to strength. He'd eased the little girl's sunburn and the demands from neighbours and people from further afield continued. He'd been lucky that so far there had only been minor ailments such as fistulas, similar to Clothilde's and an assortment of injuries and abrasions sustained during the busy growing season. Almost every day Edward was preparing concoctions for Clothilde to collect. Her reading was progressing at a rapid speed and she was even able to take a little dictation. Clothilde had visited him almost every evening after dark, to collect the next instructions and remedies and to bring him food. With the neighbours paying her in bread and honey there was plenty to eat and Edward was glad to be earning his keep. Edward finished his prayers and sat looking at the piles of scrolls that had accumulated in the cavern. He'd built up a collection of jars and pots each containing dried herbs and wild plants that he had gathered through the abundant spring. It was indeed a fertile place, the warmth and the richness of the forest earth brought such a wide ranging selection of species.

It had been a few days since Clothilde's last visit and Edward turned his mind to the fair and his imminent departure. With Clothilde's help he'd sewn a bag from some rough cloth, for he had arrived with nothing but the clothes he stood up in. He was loathe to leave behind the carefully prepared parchment inscribed with the records of all that grew in the forest, but he could not relinquish the carefully stowed samples of the unidentified plants. He was in the process of comparing them with the species he was familiar with and noting down their differences and similarities. He would carry them with him on his long journey to Pontigny, in the hope that the monks there would teach him their uses; if he was not punished and banished back to his home land. Back to Eldric and the priory. His heart leapt as he thought of Eldric's imposing figure; such a serious man but so generous and kind. Edward sighed and turned back to his scrolls.

Beyond the forest he could hear more dogs barking than usual. The visitors had started to arrive. The fair would begin in the morning and the *Champ de Foire* would be teeming with flocks of sheep, cloth merchants and artisans. Clothilde said that last year there had even been a visiting theatre. Edward was rather excited at seeing so many people in one place, it promised to be quite an event. He was glad of the excitement to dull the pain of leaving Clothilde, and the fear of once again travelling alone to his unknown fate.

Edward slept well that night and woke in good spirits. He said his prayers and carefully began to stow away the scrolls of parchment, sorting them from the copies he had made to leave for Clothilde. It wasn't long before he began to hear voices from the village. He would wait until he could be sure that the crowds had gathered and he would be able to walk amongst them unremarked.

At last Edward clambered out of the cavern and walked through the trees towards the *Champ de Foire*. His stomach fluttered and he could feel he was shaking. He had been alone in the cavern for many months with only Clothilde visiting him. Other than his short sojourns to the edge of the trees to spy the villagers going about their daily business he had had no contact with the outside world. He was trembling as he reached the tree line. The huts and hovels of the village lay silent to one side, but beyond he could hear the commotion of the fair. He walked between the empty houses, careful to check around each corner, he did not want to be spied out in the open alone. The dogs had been released from their tethers outside the houses and were no doubt roaming the fair field for scraps. He crouched down by the mud wall of one of the dwellings and pulled his hood up over his head. He peeped round the corner and the sight he saw made his head swim. He laid back hard against the wall for there were what seemed to be hundreds of people. He took some deep breaths and stood up and blindly stepped forwards and into the crowd.

There were makeshift pens of sheep with their shepherds calling out for prospective buyers, there were stalls of bread of all different shapes and sizes, colours and textures. There were cobblers beclothed from head to foot in leather, around them were baskets of purses and belts, harnesses and a larger selection of shoes, Edward had never seen. He kept his head bent only lifting it enough to spy the contents of the stalls. Further on was a blacksmith, a weaver and on the far side of the field was a great display of the most sumptuous cloth. Great bales of the finest silks shone in the sunlight. A large number of women were huddled round them admiringly, though few looked as if they had the means to purchase any. Vegetable sellers advertised their wares calling out to the crowd, holding up early cabbages and shiny magenta aubergines that shone like knights' buckles. There were baskets of hops and flagons of beer. Feeling oppressed by the jostling crowds Edward sought a little space and weaved between the people to the edge of the field. There was a large cart with a wooden platform pulled flat from its side. A man dressed in an emerald tunic and scarlet hose sat aloft the platform cradling a lute in his lap. On his head was a broad brimmed hat to shield off the sun and his hair hung long around his shoulders. In front of him a crowd was gathering, children and peasants were sitting cross-legged expectantly. Edward started as he saw the dark habits of two monks approach the platform. He stepped back and pulled his hood lower, just peeping from the corner. They said a few words to the man and settled themselves on the grass with the others. Edward moved a little distance away but positioned himself directly behind them to make sure that for them to see him they would have to crane their necks.

The man began to play, plucking the individual strings of his instrument in quick succession and sang a few notes as if warming up. Then there was a great commotion and the audience all turned to see a procession arrive at the cart. At the head of it was a short squat nobleman dressed in garish finery, at his side his Lady. Her hair was golden and she was smiling. Her gown was of violet silk, as rich in colour as the aubergines he had seen the sellers displaying. The man on the platform stood up and bowed as the entourage arrived. The crowd scattered to make way for them. The Lady turned to her escort and curtseyed. The small round man nodded and departed leaving her to install herself on a seat, set beside her maid. Edward watched as she arranged the skirts of her gown, he found himself mesmerised by such rare beauty. He shuffled and positioned himself where he could watch both her and the platform, yet stay out of sight of the monks. She raised her arm to smooth her hair beneath her head-dress, on her wrist was an amulet of turquoise and gold. It caught the light and flashed a glint of its gold across the crowd. There was something familiar about the vision but Edward could not identify it. He dismissed the feeling and continued to feast his eyes on this true representation of noble beauty.

The man on the stage stood up again and theatrically introduced himself to the crowd. 'I am Thorin, the troubadour. I come to you from lands faraway to tell you the stories of the knights and their ladies, of love so noble and so true. Love that goes beyond the accomplishments of land, of position and kingdoms, love that can satisfy the soul for evermore.' He again bowed very low and swept the platform with his hat.

The ladies in the crowd swooned audibly in delight and a murmur of amusement crossed the men's lips. The troubadour began to sing to the magical notes of his lute.

'In a land far away lived two knights…'

Edward was transported into a world of love and jealousies, of bravery and sadness until at last the crowd was applauding with gusto.

The audience threw flowers and coins onto the platform and the troubadour was bowing low as he gathered his reward into his hat.

Edward rubbed his eyes as if waking from a long sleep. He could see the monks clambering to their feet. He quickly jumped up and stepped back into the thronging crowd.

# THIRTY

## Diana

The mixture was bubbling away on the stove and the smell of rich warm tomatoes filled the house. The dough was rising nicely on the side from the heat of the cooker. Ben had fallen asleep in the middle of his lunch making Diana feel smugly right that a full day at school would have been too much for him. He slept solidly all afternoon and was now sitting at the table eating a *goûter* of chocolate and baguette.

'Mmm! That's lovely.' Jeanette was licking a finger she'd dipped in the cooling saucepans on the cooker. 'What is it?'

'It's therapy. It's called something to do on the first day my little boy goes out into the big wide world.'

'How did he get on?'

'He loved it. In a way, that makes it worse.'

'Oh come on, they have to fly the nest at some stage – anyway it's good for them to get out and play with other children.'

'Yes, thank you, you are not the first person to say that.' Diana rolled her eyes. 'It's just, for the last three years my life has revolved around him. It has been my reason for living. First the pregnancy, then he was born and every minute of my day was taken up with his every whim.'

Jeanette eyed her frowning.

'Don't worry I'll sort myself out. I just need to find something else to channel my energies into.'

'You need a job.'

'I need something. But there isn't a job I could do around here. There's even a waiting list to be a cashier at *Leclerc*.'

Jeanette had now graduated to a tablespoon and was about to scoop it into the tomato mixture.

'Oi! Stop that! There won't be any left if you carry on like that.'

'Do you know this stuff is really nice, what are you making?'

'*Pissaladière*. Have you heard of it?'

'Mmm,' she murmured through a mouthful of tomato. 'It's an onion dish from the Midi. But I didn't think it had tomatoes in.'

'This must be an English version then, I got it out of my grandmother's recipe book.'

'How many are you making? There's enough to feed an army here.'

'I know, I just didn't know what to do with so many tomatoes, so I thought at least If I cooked them all it would stop them going mouldy. It should make about ten I think.'

'You could freeze them I suppose.' Jeanette thought for a bit. A gleam came into her eye 'Or,' she began eagerly, 'You could sell them in my shop?'

'Don't be daft; they won't be good enough for that!' Diana was laughing.

'That mixture tastes absolutely delicious and I would even go so far as to say they taste even better than the plain onion ones I remember from Marseilles.'

'You're not serious? They'd never sell.'

'I'm deadly serious. You've got nothing to lose. If they don't sell you can put them in your freezer.'

'How much should I sell them for?'

'Leave that to me. You bring them over to the shop in the morning and anything that isn't sold at the end of the day you can have back for your freezer.'

Diana was doubtful. 'This is very kind of you but what's in it for you?'

'If it makes you feel better I'll take twenty-five percent of any sales.'

Diana hesitated.

'Come on! What have you got to lose? You said it yourself. You need something to take your mind off Ben at school.'

Diana relented and waved Jeanette off up the front path. She stayed up into the small hours fashioning the dough into pizza sized shapes, brushing them with olive oil and topping each one with tomato mixture and olives. Now she wished she'd gone out and bought the anchovies. Never mind this would have to do. No one will want them anyway.

Rain lashed at the window waking Diana. She hauled herself out of bed regretting her late night. Ben was already up. He was sitting on the kitchen floor plunging a spoon into a box of cereal which seemed to be leaking milk all over his trousers.

'Ben ready,' he said proudly. 'Ben go to school.'

It was all Diana could do not to laugh. He'd dressed himself but had neglected to remove his pyjamas before doing so. His clothes were covered in milk and cereal. He had obviously dispensed with a bowl and taken the more direct approach of pouring the milk straight into the cereal box. It took a great deal of persuasion to coax him into some clean dry clothes and convince him that underwear really *was* necessary.

It was still raining hard and the front terrace was submerged in about six inches of water. At least she had parked the car undercover in the garage. Ben stopped at the top of the steps into the garage and clung onto the metal banister.

'Ben, go on bus.'

'Come on love, let's get in the car.'

'No!' he shouted and stamped a foot. 'Bus! Ben go on bus!'

What was it with that school? Did they brainwash the children from day one? 'No Ben, it's raining. Let's go in the car.'

He slumped down to the floor and pushed out his bottom lip to display that he had absolutely no intention of moving until he got his way.

Reluctantly Diana unhooked the pushchair from the rack by the back door and snapped it open. 'Come on then, we'll walk to the bus stop.'

Ben shook his head. 'Ben big. Ben go to school. Ben walk.'

Diana's heart lurched. Just one day at school had made him grow up so much. He loved the rain and she knew he would be in every puddle he could find on the short walk to the village green and would end up soaked to the skin. Diana sighed. She pulled out his waterproof all-in-one. 'You can walk to the bus if you wear this and your wellies.'

He pulled them on triumphantly. Diana stowed his shoes in his backpack and pulled on her own boots and raincoat.

The other mothers were already at the bus stop, they were sheltering from the rain under the schoolhouse awning. Marie-Pierre was there with her childminding charges. She was standing away from the other mothers. The women eyed Diana suspiciously and then fixed their gaze on Ben. He was at that moment taking a hefty run up to a huge puddle. His face was contorted into an expression of determination as he sprung from the ground and landed neatly into the middle of the pool sending the water sheeting outwards in a perfect circle.

One of the women shook her head disapprovingly. The other children stared out enviously from their regimented lines under the awning. At last the bus arrived and Ben clambered up the steps, the weight of his backpack pulling him backwards, it was almost bigger than him. He only just remembered to wave goodbye to Diana as he took the *surveillant's* hand and was led to the back of the bus to sit with his new friends.

Tears dogged Diana once again and she wondered when this agonising feeling of separation would leave her. She took a deep breath and strode swiftly back to the house through the downpour.

The rain wasn't showing any sign of letting up so she stacked the *pissaladières* in a cardboard box with a layer of greaseproof paper between each one and covered the box with a bin liner to protect it from the rain. There was still a long queue of customers at *La Petite Folie*.

Jeanette gestured to an empty shelf and Diana laid out her tarts aware of the curious stares on her back. Between serving customers Jeanette gave her her baguettes.

'Come back at four o'clock,' she whispered.

The kitchen was coated in an even film of flour and tomato sauce; she hadn't realised quite how much mess she'd made. Serge was due back at three. Strange, he hadn't called. She shrugged, amazed at her lack of anxiety over this fact. Maybe it was having something to do that just changed everything. She threw herself into clearing up the tomato bombed kitchen.

She picked Ben up from school at midday, much to his annoyance though by the time she had pulled into the drive he was already fast asleep. She lifted him carefully from his car seat and gently laid him in bed. He would have to eat his lunch later when he woke.

'*Salut chérie!*' Serge bounced into the kitchen so happily it quite took Diana aback. He kissed her warmly and fell into an armchair. 'Any chance of a coffee?'

Diana looked at her watch. Four o'clock. 'I'm sorry darling, I have to go and see Jeanette about something. Could you stay and keep an ear out for Ben?'

'I've been at work. I'm tired. I just want a coffee.' He was almost whining.

'I'll make you a coffee when I get back. I won't be long.' She trudged up the lane. Had she really just witnessed her husband refusing to make himself a coffee on the grounds that he'd been to work? Even her own father, from his antiquated generation served by domestic staff, would go into the kitchen and make himself a cup of tea.

Jeanette was beaming. 'Come and see.' She flung open the connecting door between the café and the *épicerie*. The shelves where Diana had laid out the *pissaladières* were bare.

'You didn't sell them *all*. Did you?'

'They went like *petits pains*. In fact I don't think I've had such a good day since Bastille Day.' She opened the till with a ding and took out a hundred and fifty francs.

'This is for you.'

'As much as that? How much did you sell them for?'

'I think twenty francs each is a reasonable price and what's more some of my customers asked if this was going to be a regular thing. I could do with ten more for tomorrow.'

It was ten past four and she wasn't sure she had enough olives left to make another batch. It would mean staying up late again. If she'd have known earlier she could have got them started. Still this was her freedom in question. A hundred and fifty francs was not to be sneezed at, perhaps if she made more this time. She still had two buckets of ripe tomatoes left.

'Have you got any olives? I'm not sure I've got enough.'

Jeanette reached up for a big tin of black pitted olives from the top shelf. 'Here have this. But don't pay me for it; my prices won't make it economical. Just replace it with a tin from the supermarket next time you go.'

'Jeanette, thank you so much. I'd better go, Serge is home. I'll see you tomorrow.'

Diana had an overwhelming feeling of not wanting to tell Serge about the money, but quickly saw that she would not be able to explain making so many tomato tarts in one night without doing so. There was nothing for it she would have to come clean.

Serge had moved from the armchair where she had left him sulking and was now sitting at his place at the dining table. He'd laid out a bowl of baby gherkins and one of grey shrimps. His good spirits appeared to have returned.

'Blackberry or blackcurrant *kir chérie*?'

'Serge it's not even five o'clock yet!'

'Never mind, we can still have a drink – there's no law against it you know.'

'Is Ben awake?'

'I haven't heard a peep. Come on what will it be?'

'Oh alright I'll have a small blackberry *kir* please. I'd better wake Ben up or he won't sleep tonight.' She disappeared into Ben's room leaving Serge to serve the aperitifs with the usual tender precision he employed when dealing with alcohol.

Ben woke smiling and leaned into his mother burying his face in her woollen jumper. He sat on her lap, quietly coming to, as she sipped her drink. Serge was about to pour her a second when Diana put up her hand in remonstration.

'No, one's enough for me. I have work to do.'

'Yes, you do. Your work is to entertain me,' he said with a cheeky grin.

'No, Serge. I have to make some *pissaladières* for the café.'

'What do you mean for the café?'

She told him how she had cooked up the huge quantities of tomatoes from the vegetable patch and of Jeanette's idea which seemed to have turned into a roaring success.

'First, no coffee and now no *apèritif*.' But he was smiling.

'*You* can have one. Jeanette needs these for the morning.'

'Ah hah, so your culinary prowess is stretching to the entire district, I shall be the envy of every man around.' And he poured himself another pastis.

'I think I'll make twenty this time, I've got so many tomatoes left.' She was talking more to herself.

'What? You're going to make twenty *pissaladières* now? That's going to take hours!' He looked aghast. The iron gate creaked in the yew hedge. They looked round to see Pierrot walking up the front path. His face was alight with excitement.

'Aah Pierrot, a little pastis?'

'If you insist.' He coughed theatrically as if clearing his throat. 'Have you heard?'

'Heard what?'

'The banns are up in Briou'

'The banns? Who's getting married?'

'Jeanette!'

'Jeanette? No, that can't be right. Not Jeanette from the café?'

'It is! It is!' Pierrot was almost hopping from one foot to the other in delight.

'Well, good for her! It can't be easy running that place on her own.' Serge poured water onto the pastis.

'But I only saw her today and she didn't say anything!' Diana couldn't believe what she was hearing.

'She's a dark horse that one.' Pierrot was tapping his nose smugly.

'Who is she marrying?'

'François Guémard, from over Jaunay way.'

'I don't even know who he is!' How could Jeanette be marrying someone, yet Diana had never even heard his name? Come to think of it she had looked more cheerful than usual when she'd popped in earlier, she'd assumed it was because of the success of the *pissaladières*. She decided she would not be sucked in by gossip and wait until she could quiz Jeanette in the morning. 'Gentlemen, I'm afraid I have work to do in the kitchen.'

Serge knocked back his drink. 'In that case I'm going out. Thought I'd go and see Claude Villard about the *vendanges*.' He turned to Pierrot. 'You coming?'

# THIRTY-ONE

## Hélène

By the time she got back on to her bicycle the darkness had set in. The streets were deserted and Hélène did not want to be found breaching the curfew. She looked up and down the road and crossed over into the lane that led to the school. She would take the path that Miriam had shown her that day, until she was level with the village square and then quickly cross the road to the Doctor's house.

As she reached the school house she stopped, just a little way further up the track was the woodshed where Rémy had died. She crossed herself. She was about to turn on to the path when she heard the whirring of an engine. She froze. It seemed to be coming from the back of the school. They'd closed it as a mark of respect for Rémy. But who would be at the school at this time? She jumped off her bicycle and pushed it into the ditch by the hedge; no one would spot it in the darkness. She leant flat against the school house wall and sidled carefully towards the engine noise. At the back of the building was a partially covered playground. The engine stopped and now she could hear voices.

At the far end of the roof canopy she could make out the bulk of a large vehicle. She crossed into the shadows and skirted the walls until she was just a metre from it. In the gloom she could see it was a large farm truck spattered with mud. The initials DAS were painted on the cab door just below the handle. She could hear raised male voices, though they were too far away to make out the words. She took a risk and peered round the corner of the building. Behind the truck was a German army jeep. A short round man of about fifty wearing a suede jacket edged in an ostentatious lapel of dark brown fur was arguing with what looked like a *Wehrmacht* Officer. Behind them a younger man dressed in blue work overalls was bent double pushing something. As Hélène's eyes acclimatized to the darkness she could see that he was rolling a barrel towards the back of the truck. There was a plank set as a ramp into it, and when the barrel reached it the short man signaled for him to stop.

The *Wehrmacht* officer lit a cigarette and the light of the flame flashed off a ring on the fat man's hand. Hélène tried to recall the uniforms of the Germans that they had learnt in training. It was curious that a civilian would meet an officer of the *Wehrmacht* after dark. Even then there would be no need for secrecy, surely the Germans could do what they wanted? They shook hands and the short man handed over a wad of notes to the German. The younger one rolled the barrel up into the truck.

The officer and the short man stood to one side as the young man unloaded the jeep of ten more barrels and rolled them up into the truck. The older men seemed to be chatting more amiably now, their disagreement clearly resolved. Hélène could even hear them chortling together. It made her sick to the stomach. The short man took a cigar from his pocket and the officer lit it for him. In the light of the flame, the face of Philippe Cottereau flashed in the darkness. Hélène pushed herself against the wall under the canopy and tried to calm her breathing. The engine of the jeep started up, they would be following the track around the back of the playground and she would be seen. She quickly ran round to the front of the school and crouched down low in the porch. It wasn't long before the truck lollopped clumsily over the potholes. It turned left and headed out on the road to Saint Gabriel. As soon as they were gone she returned to the covered playground and the spot where the vehicles had been standing. On the ground was a German issue cigarette butt and a pool of liquid. She dipped a finger in it and smelt it. Diesel. Barrels of Diesel.

When she returned to the surgery, *Madame* Clément was clearing up from supper.

'Aah, *Mademoiselle.* We were worried about you, you must be careful if you are found out after dark you will have serious problems.'

'I went to see Floriane Legrand.'

'That poor woman! You are good and kind but the *Docteur* will have words with you in the morning. He was not very pleased and sick with worry. At least you are safe and sound.'

'Is the Doctor here?'

'No, he had to go out.'

'At this hour?'

'He was called away. I heard the telephone ring earlier and he rushed his supper and left. Here, yours has been warming in the oven.' She took a plate from the range, piled high with vegetables. 'I'm afraid we have again run out of potatoes, but swede is very good for you and I have brought some bread from home.'

'*Madame* Clément you must not use your rations on us again.'

'It does not matter, the *Docteur* allows me to eat here very often. It is a fair exchange.'

She sat down at the table in the kitchen and ate her meal while *Madame* Clément pottered around her, washing up and tidying away. At last the housekeeper took off her apron and hung it on the back of the kitchen door and pulled on her coat.

'You often leave after dark, will you not get into trouble?'

'My house is just three doors up opposite the church I have never had a problem. Anyway the centre of the town seems to have the least police, as if it would be too obvious.'

As soon as *Madame* Clément had gone Hélène went upstairs to change. She undid the floorboard in the cupboard and from around her radio she unwrapped a pair of dark green canvas trousers she had pinched from Antoine's wardrobe. They were of course way too big so she hiked them up at the waist with a piece of rope. On her top half she wore a thick black jumper. From the coat cupboard in the hall she pulled some brown shoe polish and smeared it over as much of her face as she could without getting it in her mouth or eyes. While she was there she cut a lump of polish from the tin and wrapped it carefully in a handkerchief. She stowed it with her radio in the base of the cupboard in her bedroom. She quickly scrawled a note and left it in the hall in the kitchen for the Doctor.

SORRY I WAS LATE, I WAS VISITING MME LEGRAND I HAVE GONE TO BED HELENE

She hoped that if he returned before she did, he would not check that she was in her bedroom. She glanced out of the stair window. Nothing stirred on the square, everyone's blackout was well installed and not a glimmer of light came from any of the windows. She slipped out of the back door. Her nerves were rising, she knew that if she was stopped in this outfit she would be arrested. She shook herself. There was no way she could shin the walls and fences at the back of the surgery in a thin cotton print dress so she would have to make sure that she was not seen. She checked the back windows of the neighbouring houses and all were blacked out and shuttered.

Out over the gardens, through the vegetable plots and into a field she went. She had to follow the edge of the first field as it was freshly ploughed, at least the mulch had been ploughed in, but she could not risk leaving tracks. The next one had been left fallow and there she could cut straight across it. Although the moon was rising fast, her dark clothing against the field would not be spotted.

She approached the edge of Saint Gabriel and passed the back of the Meffret Farm. Agnès had said that the old monastery at Lusigny, Cottereau's place, was out to the east of Saint Gabriel, the first property on the right on approaching the hamlet. She skirted the back of the village and headed east keeping to the boundaries between the back gardens and courtyards, and the fields. There was a low wall on the right hand side that seemed to run a great distance along the edge of the field. Behind it a yew hedge grew tall and impenetrable. She checked the whole perimeter away from the road and could find no gaps from which to spy. She doubled back on herself and crouched low at the corner of the wall, just feet from the road and listened. All was quiet. She looked both ways and walked along the front of the property. Here, the wall was taller, it curved up to an arched gateway. An iron door hung open, just wide enough for her to slip through without risking the hinges creaking. As she stepped through her feet crunched on gravel, she cursed herself and froze to the spot.

Two cars and a truck were parked in front of a high wall which ran along the courtyard to a large barn with arrow slits and a low wooden door. No one had heard her. She took off her jumper and laid it out on the gravel in front of her with the sleeves forming a runner. She tiptoed along it, the wool sunk into the gravel and muffled out the abrasion of the stones. When she reached the end of the furthest sleeve she picked up the other end of the jumper and swung it round to repeat the process. As she got closer she recognised *Docteur* Legris' car. At last she reached the edge of the wall and stood in the flowerbed at its base. The truck was to her right, on the door she could see the initials D A S clearly painted. So Philippe Cottereau had brought the diesel here, to his home. She leant up against the low wooden door in the side of the barn and listened. Inside she could hear voices. Not conversation; the sounds were more rhythmic. She listened harder. It was more like chanting. A stone staircase hugged the furthest outer wall of the barn. She carefully sidled along the wall taking care to step on the beaten earth at the base and avoiding the gravel. The staircase led to a wooden hatch at the top but the hinges looked as if they were rusted fast. She could not break directly into the room where the voices were coming from, that would be suicide. She went round the back of the building. At the other end of the barn wall she could see a seam in the stonework, and to the right of it, another low door. The hinges on this looked as if they had been recently oiled. The door must open into an adjoining room. She carefully twisted the iron ring handle and it moved easily. She pulled the door to very gently, lest the hinges should creak, but they moved soundlessly. The voices were more muffled from here. Satisfied that she was not about to walk straight into the room, for all to see, she stepped inside and carefully shut the door behind her.

She was in a sort of vestibule. To the right of her was a glazed door, there was a glimmer of light coming from a room in a distant corridor but the immediate area was unlit. There was a coat stand laden with hats and scarves and coats. A large door on the left led to the interior of the barn. Strangely there was no light coming from beneath it. The chanting was getting louder. She lay on the flagstones and peered underneath the gap. There was in fact an amber glow not powerful enough to radiate into the hall. It must be candle light. The chanting stopped suddenly and there was complete silence. Hélène held her breath. Then it started again quietly. She could clearly hear men's voices speaking in unison.

'Heal Saint Thomas, Heal Montgommery' with each word the chanting got a little louder. 'Heal Saint Gabriel' and then they reached crescendo 'Heal France!' The final syllable was pronounced in a staccato fashion and then all fell silent.

Hélène heard shuffling inside and it was coming closer to the door. She rolled back towards the little door and crouched in the corner behind the coat stand. The iron handle of the barn door turned and the door opened. From her hiding place she saw a figure in a dark cloak with a hood come into the vestibule. He was wearing a monk's habit and was carrying a candle. He put it down on a table by the glazed door and lowered his hood. It was Philippe Cottereau. Then another cloaked figure appeared and removed his habit; it was Julien Legris. The doctor turned towards the coat stand and Hélène didn't move a muscle. His arm came within just a few inches of her head to take his greatcoat from the stand. He hung the habit in its place, thankfully shrouding Hélène more effectively. He stepped towards the door that led to the courtyard and the parked cars. Cottereau kissed him on both cheeks and put a wad of notes in his hand.

Then came a younger man who looked familiar, but Hélène couldn't place him immediately. He removed his habit as the doctor had done and took a shooting jacket from the stand. As he put it on he recognized him from his photograph in Agnès Camaret's kitchen. It was Georges Camaret. Again he kissed Cottereau on both cheeks was handed some notes and departed. Another three men followed suit, but Hélène had never seen them before. The last one to appear was of slimmer build and when he removed his habit he revealed blue overalls, it was the younger man she had seen earlier, rolling barrels into the truck. He didn't kiss Cottereau and nor did he receive any money. He stepped out after the others and Cottereau shut the door and pulled a bolt across it. Then Cottereau crossed the hall and bolted the door by which Hélène had just entered. He blew out the candle on the table and went through the glazed internal door to the rest of his house. Hélène let out a long breath and waited until she heard no more crunching on the gravel outside and that all was quiet in the Cottereau household. The light in the distant corridor was at last extinguished and Hélène carefully unbolted the door by which she had come and stepped back into the safety of the darkness.

# THIRTY-TWO

## Diana

At nine o'clock the dough had risen and the tomato mixture was cooling. It would take another two hours to roll out and fold the dough and top With tomato mixture. There was a knock at the door. Claude Villard's mountainous outline loomed in the dark.

'What's happened?'

Claude shrugged his shoulders looking confused.

'Is Serge alright?'

'Serge?' he frowned. 'I was coming to see him. He *is* home isn't he? I saw his car pulling off the motorway this afternoon. Isn't he back?'

'Yes, he is back. He said he was coming round to see *you* this evening… about the *vendanges*.'

'That's what I wanted to talk to *him* about. I've been out all evening. I wasn't sure if I should pop round, what with you having visitors.' He was peering over Diana's shoulder into the sitting room.

'Visitors? We don't have any visitors.'

'Oh. It's just,' he hesitated.

'Yes?'

'It's nothing.' He turned away as if to leave.

'Claude.'

He stopped and turned.

'Why did you think we had visitors?'

'There was a lady in Serge's car.'

'A lady?'

'Yes, a blonde lady. I, I must have been mistaken.'

Diana managed to claw back some composure, 'I shall tell him you called'. She hadn't meant to sound curt. It wasn't Claude's fault. He must have made a mistake. He was getting on a bit, his eyesight was probably failing a little. Maybe Serge had given someone a lift and had forgotten to mention it. And why had he been driving on the motorway? There was no need if he was catching the train back from Paris. Serge and Pierrot must have gone to the café for a drink. There was surely a perfectly reasonable explanation for all of this. She ran herself a hot steamy bath with lavender oil to get rid of the pungent smell of tomatoes and garlic that seemed to have imbibed her skin and

207

hair. Having managed to partially empty her mind in the warm luxurious water she went to bed setting her alarm for five am to give her plenty of time to prepare the *pissaladières.*

The alarm woke her in darkness; the autumn days were getting shorter. Diana fumbled around not wishing to turn the light on and disturb Serge. As she came to, the events of the evening before came washing over her again and she felt the bed next to her. Feeling only sheets she turned the light on. He had not come home.

She didn't bother with a shower as she knew that she'd smell of tomatoes again before breakfast. She didn't check the garage to see if Serge's car was there. Nor did she rush out the front to see if he was asleep in front of the church. She shut out his absence and concentrated on the job ahead. She began to cut, roll and fold the huge squashy balloon of dough into the *pissaladière* bases. She managed to fill each one with sauce and decorate with Jeanette's olives by half-past seven. She put the first batch in the oven and cursed the inadequate size of it. If this was to be a regular thing she would have to think about modernising her equipment. She laughed at herself. One minute she had been lamenting her baby's embarkation on the big wide world, and a second later she was laying the foundation block of her, so far, successful career. She brought herself back down to earth. Making a few *pissaladières* for the local café was hardly big business.

She woke Ben to get him ready for school and sat him at the table to eat his breakfast. It wasn't until she sat down next to him that she realised how tired she felt. Her shoulders felt weighted down as if someone was sitting on them. As she poured the hot tea into a mug she thought of *Madame* Camaret. '*We just got on with it,*' she had said. Diana knew this was good advice. You had to get on with things. She let out a deep breath, stood up, symbolically dusted herself down and went to swap the batches of *pissaladières* around in the oven.

An hour later she had delivered Ben to the bus and was laying out her creations on the shelves in the *épicerie* of *La Petite Folie,* while Jeanette served the queue of customers with their bread. At last the baguette racks were almost bare and the queue had melted.

'Do you know, this village is incredible,' said Diana.

'Incredible is not the word I would choose personally!' Jeanette laughed.

'I heard the most ridiculous rumour yesterday.'

Jeanette stopped and stared at Diana.

'What's the matter?'

Jeanette didn't answer.

'It's not true is it?'

Jeanette turned and reddened a little. She managed to eke out a weak smile.

'You *are* getting married?'

She nodded.

'I am so surprised.'

'So am I!' She was laughing. 'It's not every day one gets a proposal.'

'Have you known him long?'

'Since we moved here; he is my drinks supplier.'

'Well, then congratulations are in order.' Diana kissed her on both cheeks.

'*Merci!*'

'When is the happy day?'

'In a month, but it will be just a small do. At my age you don't want to make a lot of fuss.'

'I'm not sure you'll be able to escape that in this village. I'd better get off we must catch up later. I don't suppose you saw Serge last night?'

'He popped in not long after you came and had a drink with Pierrot.'

'Did he stay long?'

'No, he only had one and then he went.'

'Did he say where he was going?'

'No. Diana is everything alright?'

'Oh, it's fine don't worry.'

She wanted to clean up the kitchen before Serge returned, whenever that was likely to be. This wasn't the first time he'd gone off but what was curious was that he hadn't really been in a temper. Slightly miffed; yes, but not furious. What if there was something in what Claude had said? She'd always imagined married life to be warm, cosy and safe. Not analysing your every move and chanting 'Just get on with it' like a mantra every time things got difficult.

She got to the front gate and stopped. What sort of prison was she living in? She could hear a car coming up the *rue de l'Abreuvoir*. It was a diesel engine. It sounded like Serge's. She ducked into the church entrance and hid in the porch. What on earth was she doing? She felt nauseous. She watched as the man that she loved with all her might parked in front of the church and got out. His hair was

209

uncombed. It was unusual for Serge to be anything but immaculately turned out. He was crossing over the lane to the gate. She should come out of the church and show herself. One, two three…now! Now! But she was paralysed. Her stomach was churning, and goose pimples spiked her skin. Revulsion engulfed her. It was as if an invisible force was gluing her to the spot. Try as she might she could not step forward to follow her husband into the house. He would be walking into the kitchen by now. He'd be looking at the tomato mess all over the surfaces. Her feet moved forwards towards the gate and then stopped. She couldn't cross the lane, as if it had become a magnetic force field that wouldn't let her through. Instead, her legs took her up towards Marcel and Pierrot's. She walked past *La Petite Folie* and up the road towards the onion farm. She felt cold walking into the wind. She wasn't wearing a coat as she'd been late for the bus and had rushed out of the house in her sleeves.

She stopped at *Madame* Camaret's door and knocked. She could pretend she needed some more onions. The bag she'd lugged back the day before was nearly empty. She would pay for them this time. She searched in the pocket of her jeans for the hundred and fifty francs and remembered she had hidden them in the soup tureen on display in the sitting room. It couldn't be helped she couldn't go back for them now.

'Aah! *Madame* Lescure! Come in, come in,' she sang. 'I think congratulations are in order. I tasted one of your *pissaladières* over at old Claude's place yesterday. I didn't realise there was such gastronomic talent in Great Britain.'

Diana reddened with the compliment. 'Actually I was wondering if I could buy a sack of onions this time, I've nearly finished the bag you gave me.'

'Of course you can.'

'It's just I've rather stupidly forgotten my purse.'

'Oh don't you worry about that I'll get Marc to drop them round tonight you can pay him then.'

*Madame* Camaret's gentle features, framed by her soft white curls, made Diana feel safe.

'Now you sit down there while I pour you a coffee,' she paused, 'You look pale my dear. Are you feeling unwell?'

It had been such a long time since anyone had enquired how she really was, that Diana had to concentrate to keep her composure.

*Madame* Camaret put her hand on Diana's shoulder. '*Ma chérie*, I think there is something more serious?'

The tears exploded from the corner of Diana's eyes and streamed down her face.

Without speaking the old lady opened a drawer and pulled out a box of tissues. 'Plenty of sugar I think for your coffee.' She waited until Diana had wiped away her tears and found a semblance of calm. 'Now, tell me what has happened.'

Diana told her of Serge not coming home the night before. She poured out how lonely she felt and how she was trying to make the best of things but that everything just seemed to get harder.

*Madame* Camaret listened patiently until she had finished and her sobbing had subsided. 'Why did you move to Saint Gabriel?'

'I wanted to live in the country. I couldn't bear to be enclosed in a small space for hours on end, alone. I wanted a garden and things to do.'

'Mmm, I couldn't live in the city I would feel trapped too. So I assume Serge wasn't keen to move?'

'No, he was worried about leaving his friends and his social life.'

'Claude Villard thinks quite highly of him, he tells me he is often in the café. He seems to have made a new social life down here.'

'Yes, though, I haven't. Apart from Jeanette at *La Petite Folie* and Marie-Pierre you are the only person in the village I have met to talk to properly. I fear I will go mad with boredom and loneliness.'

'That's why you thought you'd try your hand at cooking for the café?'

Diana nodded. 'It was Jeanette's idea. I thought it was the ideal opportunity.'

'And so it is, my dear.' She looked into her coffee cup as if searching for something. 'People are like animals. When they are frightened they become dangerous. Your husband is frightened. He has moved to the countryside to make you happy. That alone shows that he loves you. He is changing, adapting to this new lifestyle, but what he hadn't bargained for is that you must also adapt. He is scared of losing control. French men are very proud. They are the masters of their households and are often self-indulgent. As a French woman that can be difficult to bear, but as a foreigner I think it is far harder.

'I knew a girl once, a long time ago. She was English like you, though I didn't know that until later, much later. You reminded me of her when you came round yesterday. She lived in Jaunay during the war.'

The old lady leant back in her chair and sighed. 'She was a good friend to me. The most generous person I think I've ever met. She would do anything for anybody if it was in her power. She was greatly respected, until one day they found out something about her and the villagers had to adapt to thinking of her in a different light. Coming from a foreign country she'd seen things and done things that no one here could understand and that frightened them. She went from being a pillar of society to almost an outcast. People are very cruel. Time would have mended it, but she did not give it time.' Sadness swept the old lady's face. She took Diana's hand in hers. 'She was impatient and clever, like you. The people round here don't have your optimism. They are fearful people, they suspect even their neighbours. Newcomers frighten them. People here aren't welcoming and are quick to criticise. But they will accept you in time, and Serge, he needs time too.'

'But Serge is a stranger to Saint Gabriel and he has made friends easily.'

'Your husband is French and he grew up in the countryside. There is less of a mystery about him for the locals. Serge may be doubting his choices, but you must stand strong, both the village and he will come through this. Believe in yourself and don't let them beat you.'

'What happened to your English friend?'

'Tomorrow, bring your little boy here for his *goûter,* I will tell you then. I don't have any grandchildren so I must rely on other people's!' When *Madame* Camaret laughed her whole face shone. 'Now, go home to your husband and remember everything I have said. For Ben's sake you must be strong. I will ask Marc to drop off the onions tonight.' She patted her hand and stood up to see her off.

Serge's car was gone from the front of the church. She went through the farm gate and down the side of the house to check if he'd moved it into the garage. It was empty; there was no sign of him. She went into the house and took down the tureen from the shelf in the dining room. It was also empty. He had taken it. How could he? How would she pay Marc Camaret for the onions? She would be alright if the *pissaladières* sold. She looked at her watch. Half past eleven. She could nip in to the café on the way from picking Ben up. Maybe the lunch rush would clear them out.

She was once again greeted by empty shelves and a beaming Jeanette. 'There's only one left so that makes two hundred and ninety-nine twenty-five. Let's call it three hundred.' She handed three crisp one hundred franc notes to Diana.

'Thanks. I've run out of ripe tomatoes so I can't make any more until the next ones are ready.'

'I think we've saturated the local market in *pissaladières* for this week perhaps you could make something else?'

'I'll have a think and let you know.'

She put Ben down for his afternoon sleep and went into the garden to check the vegetable patch. The pumpkins were already a handsome size though it was too early to cut them. There was a good six weeks to go before Halloween. She would cut some into lanterns for Ben. When they were ready she could use the rest to make pumpkin pies and soup for Jeanette's shop. She counted fifteen huge orange balls glowing in the grass. Along the opposite side of the garden, apples had begun to fall to the ground. She went over to inspect them, not knowing if they were cookers or eaters she picked one up and wiped the mud from its skin and took a bite. She instantly spat out the sharp flesh. Definitely cookers! Apple Crumble would be the thing.

The phone trilled through the kitchen window. She ran up the garden and pounced on it before it woke Ben.

'*Allo,*' she said, out of breath. There was some crackling but no one answered. '*Allo,*' she repeated more loudly.

'Diana?' She heard a woman's muffled voice speaking in English.

'Yes, Diana speaking.'

'It's Liesel.'

'Hi. What's wrong? You sound funny.'

Liesel coughed. 'Err, I wasn't expecting...'

'Wasn't expecting what?'

'Just... How are you?'

'I'm fine,' replied Diana tentatively, feeling confused. Another pause ensued. 'Liesel, what exactly did you want?'

'I, I was wondering… do you fancy a coffee in Beaugency? I, err, haven't seen you for ages.'

'Actually Serge is home at the moment but perhaps next week.'

'I'll be away next week at a conference. Never mind, I'll call you when I get back.' Her voice was sounding steadier now.

'Righto. Talk to you then.' Poor Liesel, something was wrong. She sat down on the sofa with a huge pile of cookery books to search for a crumble recipe. She dropped off to sleep and was woken by the clang of the iron gate. It was Serge. He looked tired and harassed.

'Get your cooking done?' he asked dejectedly.

'Yes, all done. I shan't be doing any more today. You don't look well.'

'I had a bit of a night of it.'

'Where did you sleep?' She tried not to sound like she was interrogating him.

'Over at Claude's.'

'But he came round looking for you last night.'

'I know I caught up with him later on. They're doing the *vendanges* over at his place tomorrow, apparently the forecast is good.'

Claude Villard had a small vineyard in one of his fields and the picking of his grapes had become quite an event in the village over the years. His great grandfather had planted the original vines and many generations of St Gabrielois had helped out with the *vendanges,* for the sole reason of being paid in kind with the vintage of previous years. It seemed to be the only time the women officially granted their men permission to over indulge in alcohol, or maybe they didn't really have a choice.

'Liesel phoned this morning.' Diana said brightly. 'She didn't sound too good though.'

'Oh?' He looked up abruptly. 'What was wrong?'

'I don't know she wouldn't say.'

He shrugged. 'I need to lie down.' He went into the bedroom and shut the door behind him.

A figure appeared at the French doors. Her heart sank. It was Jérôme Couteau, grinning. Behind him at the entrance to the courtyard was Bébert's truck. Did these two go everywhere together?

'Diana.'

Had they been on first name terms? She couldn't remember. She scolded herself, she was becoming as formal as the French. '*Monsieur,*' she replied sternly. She had always scoffed at the French formality but now its usefulness was becoming clear.

'You look lovely today.' He employed the familiar '*tu*'. This was really going too far.

'Serge is asleep,' she said in a school maamish manner.

He was smiling as if titillated by her effrontery.

214

'Listen,' she continued. 'Is there something you want? I'm really very busy.'

'A pretty thing like you? Now what could *you* be busy doing?' He pushed the door and stepped into the sitting room.

Diana took a step away from him.

A glint of gold tooth flashed from the recesses of his widening smile. 'I had no idea there were such beautiful women in England.' His hand was stretching out to her hair.

Diana ducked out the way. 'Serge!' she called softly lest she actually wake him.

'There's no need to disturb him. I expect he's exhausted after his night out. He's a popular man, your husband, especially with the ladies.'

'What on earth do you mean?'

'I've heard the English believe in equality and freedom between men and women. What is it they call it? Open Marriages? That sounds like just my cup of coffee.' He took a step closer to her.

Diana backed away. 'I have no interest in what you might have heard *Monsieur* Couteau. My marriage is no affair of yours, now kindly leave before I wake my husband.'

His expression changed to a venomous snarl. He opened his mouth to say something, but Bébert appeared at the door behind him.

'*Bonjour Madame*!' he called out gaily. 'Jérôme, I've been waiting for you. What are you doing?'

'Just having a chat with *Madame* Lescure here.'

'Well come on I need that electric. *Madame*, is it alright if we plug our electric cable into the garage? I need to saw up the last of the metal frame.'

'Yes, yes, of course. And now I must get on, I have plenty to do.'

She closed the French doors and when she was certain that the men had returned through the side gate to the courtyard she went round and locked all the exterior doors. What on earth was he playing at? He was supposedly Serge's friend. She cast her mind back to the café. Had she encouraged him? She'd been friendly but she was certain that she hadn't sent out any other signals. She could tell Serge, but how could she explain it? Jérôme Couteau had only made insinuations, unpleasant insinuations nevertheless.

# THIRTY-THREE

### Edward

He scanned the crowd around him for a sign of Clothilde, but there were too many people. There seemed to be more and more arriving. This was only the eve of the main day of the fair. Edward suddenly felt tired and wanted to sit down. The monks were nowhere to be seen. There was a well at the edge of the field so he went over and sunk down in the grass and leaned his aching back against its stone wall.

'Edward… Psst…Edward!' Clothilde gave him a push. 'Wake up!'

Edward stirred.

'Edward, wake up!'

Edward opened his eyes with a start. The *Champ de Foire* was quiet save for the stall holders that had set up camp around their wares. A couple of them were laughing and pointing at Edward.

'They say that you have had too much ale. Come on we must go.'

Edward hurriedly clambered to his feet and went as fast as dignity would allow to the edge of the woods. Clothilde went after him. As soon as they were behind the leafy screen Clothilde took his arm.

'I must speak with you. You are planning to go to Pontigny tomorrow?'

Edward had forgotten with all the excitement of the fair and the troubadour. He hung his head. 'Yes, I must go tomorrow.'

'Did you see Montgommery today?'

'Yes, with his Lady?'

'That's right. Well, I think we may be in trouble for news of your healings has reached the *seigneuriale.*'

He sat up with a start. 'The *seigneuriale*?'

'Today two of Montgommery's men were waiting for me at our house and demanded that I visit *le Seigneur* at once. He has an affliction and wants me to cure him.'

'To cure him of what?'

'Well, that's just it I don't know what is wrong with him. I don't have your knowledge. Mother says he has been weak since his birth. That's why it is his brother who has gone to the east, to the holy land,

216

to fight for the Lord. He has stayed to oversee the *seigneurie*.' She was gabbling, her face ashen.

'Slow down. Tell me, what are his symptoms?'

'Well he is pale and he is very round. You saw him.'

Edward nodded.

'Though noblemen all seem to be pale and wan to me, and their Ladies even more so. He says he tires easily and feels the cold.'

'The cold? But this is the height of summer. Did you ask him his diet?'

Clothilde looked confused.

'I mean what he eats.'

'No, I hardly dared to speak. You see he is not a kind man. He is always angry and sad, all at once. Everyone in the village is scared of him. Once, one of the children was caught in his orchard stealing apples and he had him flogged until he bled. Those people have so much when we have so little, it is unjust that they should punish us whilst we simply try to survive.'

'Yes, it is only now that I realise how hard it is to live outside the priory. I used to think that all the wretched souls who journeyed to our hospital brought their ailings on themselves, and that curing them served to purify our own souls. But now I see that there is much to be done for the ordinary man. So there are no other symptoms?'

'He said that some mornings he cannot put his feet on the ground for the pain. He took off his shoes.' She screwed up her face. 'I have never seen such white puny limbs attached to such a rotund torso. His feet were swollen, red and purple. Such a thing I have never seen. Not in my family, nor the villagers.'

'Hmm,' said Edward. 'That doesn't surprise me. It would appear that the *Seigneur* is suffering from too much fine living. Leave me to ponder the problem.'

'I must return to him tomorrow.' She frowned.

'Speak, Clothilde. What worries you?'

'I am afraid. The *Seigneur* is prone to rages. His fuse is short and I am afeared as to what he will do. What if I were to get it wrong?'

'This is not a disease that can be fixed quickly. It would take a change in diet and long weeks taking remedies, for it to calm itself completely.'

'Oh Edward! I cannot tell the *Seigneur* what he must eat! He may cast me out.'

Edward wasn't listening. 'Wood Betony. We have a little time. I must search the woods for what I need before the sun sinks. I shall prepare a remedy tonight. You will take it to him, if all fails do not worry Clothilde, I shall present myself to him. He will surely take the word of a cleric.'

'But then your existence would be revealed and we will lose you!'

'I would rather I was lost than you. I shall say I was on my way to Pontigny with a message from Canterbury and that I had passed you on the road and you had told me of the *Seigneur*'s problem, and that I could not pass by without helping.'

'So be it. You are good and honourable. But you will miss your chance to go to Pontigny. For in two days the fair will be over and the visitors will have left.'

'I cannot leave you in such trouble. This is my doing and I feel badly for having put you in this situation.'

'You saved my mother.'

'It was nothing.' He paused. 'Now go, and be sure to return by sun up, I will have the medicine waiting for you.'

Edward was sitting on the edge of the opening dangling his legs into the cavern. He was carving a stick to a point with his knife, listening to the hustle and bustle of the fair field in the distance, when Clothilde appeared.

'Edward, I have been followed, get down in the den.'

Edward scanned the trees and bushes and gathered up his stick and knife and slid beneath the forest floor.

Clothilde followed pulling a nearby fallen branch to obscure the opening as she went.

'By whom?'

'I believe it was one of Montgommery's men. There were twigs cracking at a distance behind me and when I turned to see, I saw a flash of a leather scabbard behind a trunk. They do not trust me. The *Seigneur* must have given orders to watch me. I think I lost him. I ran out of sight and climbed a tree. He followed but he did not raise his eyes and when the tracks disappeared he turned back.'

'You must not come here for a while.'

'But how will I get your instructions?'

'We must find a hiding place and drop off messages to each other. It is the only way. Your reading has much improved, it will work.'

'Let me think.' She paused. 'The well, where I found you napping yesterday on the *Champ de Foire;* in the summer months it is often dry; we use the spring in this season. On the inside of the well there is a crevice just a little way down. I can reach it if I lean in. It is big enough to hide a pouch. We tether the goats there when the fair is gone, when I go to milk them I can collect it without arousing suspicion. But you must only visit it at the dead of night, it is in open ground and by day you would be easily spotted.'

Edward nodded. 'Now, here take this remedy to Montgommery and tell him he must avoid butter and meat and eat plenty of vegetables.'

'He will surely flog me.' Her face was drawn and terribly afraid.

'Clothilde you must, he has consulted you and you must obey. Then you must wrap his feet in the wood betony doused in water and tell him to keep them raised for at least a day and a night. It should bring down some of the swelling almost immediately.'

## THIRTY-FOUR

**Diana**

Ben's face lit up when Agnès Camaret set a plate of *réligieuses* in the middle of the table. Two choux pastry buns set on top of each other really did look like nuns; the topping of chocolate icing resembling wimples. Next to them was a myrtle tart.

'You are a big boy!' she said stroking his head. She piled a chair with cushions so that Ben, balancing precariously on their summit, could reach.

'*Chocolat*!' exclaimed Ben pointing at the cakes.

'Are you hungry?'

Ben nodded solemnly. He watched the old lady intently as she picked up the biggest one and put it on a small plate in front of him. He didn't say a word, seemingly overcome by the thought of sinking his teeth into this masterpiece. At last he picked it up and bit the entire top off it, smearing his face with the delicious chocolate cream oozing from its centre.

'I assume that Serge is back?' She poured the coffee into the two little cups and cut two slices of the myrtle tart.

'Yes, he came back yesterday. He says he stayed at Claude Villard's.' She decided she wasn't going to tell her about Claude's visit.

'Aah, yes Claude,' she said witheringly. 'I have known Claude Villard all my life. His family farmed in Jaunay for more than a hundred years. He's one of the originals. He used to be a great man, Claude Villard. He was leader of the communist movement in this area you know.'

'I did hear him preaching rather in the café.'

She shook her head laughing. 'Claude's political days are over, I think he misses them. You mustn't take too much notice; his tongue loosens after a bit to drink. Claude wouldn't hurt a fly; he is someone to count on. The only thing wrong with Claude is not enough work and too many parties, particularly since his wife passed away. Miriam was a strong woman and Claude respected her. Whatever she said Claude did.'

'Serge is over at his place this afternoon for the *vendanges*.'

She rolled her eyes but she was smiling. 'Is it that time of year again already? There will be some sore heads in the village tomorrow. I remember when Georges used to go. Every year he swore he wouldn't touch a drop of Claude's wine, but every year he would come back as drunk as a *seigneur*.'

'Didn't you get very cross with him?'

'I did at first, but I soon realised that there was no point. There wasn't a man in the village who didn't look forward to the *Vendanges de St Gabriel*. It is important to let them have their fun. We don't let them know they are being 'allowed' to have it, we just ignore it. We turn a blind eye. If they realised they were permitted it would spoil it for them. Men like subterfuge, it's in their make-up.' She waved a finger warningly. 'But not too much subterfuge mind!'

'You said you would tell me about your friend; the English woman.'

'Aah! Yes.' She drew in a breath and her eyes fluttered from side to side as she collected her thoughts. 'A lovely girl, she was. She was a nurse at the doctor's in Jaunay. Georges and I had not been married long, about three years I think. Yes, we already had three boys! Antoine was engaged to be married. He was Georges' best friend. His father ran *Ferme* Meffret the farm next to this one. You know, the one where the horses are now?'

Diana nodded.

'Where was I? Yes, Georges and Antoine were great friends. They were the most eligible bachelors in the village; both farmers' sons and the eldest at that. Well Georges and his twin brothers, they were the eldest but sadly they died, in a concentration camp. In those days it was the eldest who took the farm over. It's not like that anymore. Now inheritance is divided up equally between the siblings. It's fairer I suppose, but it always leads to the farms having to be sold off to give everyone their share. Such a shame! Our farm is the only one in the area which has stayed in the family.' She poured another coffee.

'Yes. Georges and Antoine were best friends. Antoine's fiancée was a girl from Jaunay. Well-to-do she was; a banker's daughter. Antoine was a good catch as a local landowner; she wasn't the only one who vied for his attentions. It all started when his father suddenly fell ill with tuberculosis. His mother had died of influenza in the 1919 epidemic when Antoine was just a lad, about eight years old I think. Poor Antoine, he was busy from dawn 'til dusk running that farm on his own. In fact Georges and I were surprised when he had got engaged so suddenly. We were sure he was doing it to have someone to look after the house. That was how marriage worked back then. Only the lucky ones married for love.

'*Bon*, Céline, the banker's daughter wanted only the best. She wanted the full frills of a dress from Paris and a ten-course meal followed by a *Pièce Montée*, but it was wartime and rationing made it very difficult to get hold of these things even on the black market. Although, she seemed to get everything she wanted, that one.' *Madame* Camaret let out a long sigh.

'With the war their engagement became a long drawn out affair and in the meantime Antoine had no help at home. The doctor sent Hélène to look after Antoine's father. She was new to the area. It was so strange really. There were a lot of new people, and people missing, particularly in the early part of the war. When the Germans arrived there was quite an exodus from Paris to the countryside and she certainly wasn't the only stranger. But a girl on her own she was and that was enough to set the tongues wagging. Aah, she was a good friend!'

There was a clunk and Ben's head had fallen onto the table; he was fast asleep.

'You better get this little lad home, I seem to have worn him out! We shall finish my story another day.'

As she opened the back door she could hear the telephone ringing in the kitchen.

'*Madame* Lescure?' A man's clipped voice boomed over the receiver. '*Capitaine* Lemenier here. I need to speak to Serge Lescure.'

'I'm sorry he's out, at the moment.'

'I need him to come to the barracks for nine o'clock tomorrow morning.'

'But he's not due into work until Monday.'

'Half the men have gone down with gastroenteritis; we need him to cover tomorrow. Can you get hold of him?'

'Yes, yes of course I shall try.'

'Please ask him to call me as soon as possible.'

Ben was still dead to the world in the pushchair outside the back door. She would have to go to Claude's and find Serge, just in case he wasn't coming back until late. She'd never been there before, but Serge had pointed it out to her once or twice. Without taking her coat off, she locked the back door again and pushed the sleeping Ben back

222

down the *rue de l'Abreuvoir*, past *La Petite Folie* and along the road towards Lusigny.

About a hundred yards along she came to the broken down farmhouse. There was no gate on the entrance and chickens were scratching in the earth and straying over the road. She looked over to the vineyard but could see no one picking grapes. She went to the house and knocked. There was no reply. She heard voices coming from a barn a little further up the lane. It didn't look like the same property, but as she reached a small gravelled courtyard she saw Serge's Mini parked in it. She knocked on a low door but there was no answer, though she heard voices coming from somewhere behind the barn. She tried the handle and it opened. Opposite was a glazed door and through it she could see a figure in a dark cloak with a hood. It looked like a monk. Diana stepped back into the courtyard closing the door behind her. This must be the old monastery; the mayor's house. Surely there were not still monks here. She hesitated. This can't be the right place, but Serge's Mini *was* outside; she had to find him. She stepped up to the door and knocked loudly. She heard scuffling and footsteps and the door opened. It was the man she had seen at Jeannette's that morning when they were going to have a coffee.

'*Madame*?'

'I'm sorry to disturb you. I was looking for my husband, Serge Lescure. His car is outside.'

He nodded and gestured for her to follow him. She left Ben sleeping in his pushchair. He led her through a vestibule and through the glazed door on the other side. A group of men were sitting on stools round a giant wooden spool empty of cable that had been laid on its side to make a table. Serge was patting Claude on the back and laughing. Edouard Moreau, the mayor, was pouring water into glasses of pastis. His wife was sipping at what looked like a small *kir*, she was staring at Diana as if she had a bad smell under her nose. Pierrot and Marcel weren't there. When Serge saw Diana, his expression changed to fury.

'What are you doing here?' He was nearly bellowing.

'I'm sorry.'

'Can't a man even have an afternoon to himself?'

The other men were staring at the ground, like little boys.

'*Capitaine* Lemenier called.' She was shaking.

Serge stopped, his expression became worried. 'Well spit it out!'

'They need you at work at nine o'clock tomorrow, they're short-staffed.'

Serge swore.

Diana waited.

'Off you go!' he patronised. The men were still concentrating on the floor beneath their feet.

'He wants you to call him urgently.' Diana turned and headed back through the vestibule, grabbed the pushchair and marched across the courtyard and onto the lane. Her heart was beating fast. How could he humiliate her like that? She hadn't wanted to interrupt his fun. Surely he could see that?

She awoke alone. Had he phoned *Capitaine* Lemenier? She assumed he had, given the fact that his boss had not called back. If he wasn't at work he would lose his job. Surely he wouldn't risk that? Would he? She sat down at the table. Her head was thumping as if flu was descending on her.

'Just get on with it,' she said to herself out loud. She looked out the window at the garden. Leaves were falling fast from the Virginia creeper that adorned the front walls of the house. She took her tea and sat in the chair flooded with sunlight streaming through the windows. She would have to wake Ben to catch the bus.

What had happened to them? Should they have stayed in Paris where Serge was so happy? She shuddered at the thought of the interminable housework and the lonely abandonment of the capital. There had been no *Madame* Camaret or Jeanette there. But then there had been no Jérôme Couteau either. Had Jérôme been at Claude Villard's the day before? She couldn't remember. She thought about the man wearing the monk's habit. What on earth were they up to? He clearly wasn't a monk and she was certain Lusigny was no longer a monastery. She would go and see Jeanette later. She always knew what was going on in the village.

Diana stood under the apple trees inspecting them for ripeness when she heard a tractor chugging its way slowly along the Briou road. She could see Michaud at the wheel. He turned the corner into the village. She expected him to carry on through the village towards his farm, but he turned down the little lane that ran alongside the privet hedge bordering the *Champ de Foire*. She began to gather windfalls feigning ignorance of his approach. The tractor came alongside the hedge and stopped. The engine juddered to silence.

She looked up in staged surprise, and immediately realised how ridiculous this was, unless she was profoundly deaf.

Michaud swung his feet out from the cab and jumped to the ground. 'Picking apples?'

'Windfalls. It would be a shame to waste them.'

'I was wondering, since the weather is so good today...' He paused and looked at his feet.

Diana waited patiently.

'I've got two horses to exercise *and* a field of hay to cut and I'm rather pushed for time to get all of them done. Would you do me that favour you promised and exercise one of them for me?'

'On my own?' she asked doubtfully.

'No, I'll come too.'

Diana thought for a moment. Jeanette would be appalled, not to mention Marie-Pierre, the mayor, Serge and the rest of the village. At that moment Bébert's truck rounded the bend in front of the church and drew up in front of the courtyard gates. The threat of Jérôme's possible presence clinched it for her.

'I'd love to. What time?'

'I've just got to get this tractor home and change, say about ...' He looked at the sun. 'Half an hour?'

Ten minutes later Diana had located the cardboard box in which her jodhpurs had lain banished to inactivity since her schooldays. She pulled them on, thanking the Lord for Lycra's forgiveness and covered over the more unpleasant lumps and bumps with a long jumper. She decided to take her car and then if she was pushed for time after her ride she could zoom straight to Talcy to pick up Ben. The apples would have to wait.

She felt strangely liberated at the thought of going for a ride with a handsome man, and the thought that at last she really would be doing something worthy of wagging tongues. She creaked her car into action and drove out of the garage waving casually to Bébert who was perched high on the frame of the hangar, and headed for Michaud's farm.

The track was bumpy and pitted and shook the suspension violently; no wonder she'd lost a wheel off the pushchair. As she approached the wide, low stone farmhouse, chickens scurried over the straw strewn concrete in all directions. Two hens flew up suddenly in fright and bashed into her windscreen. Diana slammed on the brakes. One of the chickens flapped to the ground but the other thudded to the concrete motionless. She jumped down from the car, alarmed but the hen came to and reassuringly got to its feet and strutted, Egyptian-dance-style across the yard toward the rest of the flock, clucking indignantly as it went.

Michaud was standing in the doorway. Diana hardly recognized him. His dirty blue overalls were replaced with gleaming white breeches, a shirt and a tweed jacket. Now it was her turn to feel scruffy. He must have had a shower as his hair was wet. A few untamed curls flopped over his brow. She wasn't sure how long he'd been there.

'Sorry about the chickens,' she said guiltily.

'No, *I'm* sorry about the chickens. They're such stupid creatures; they're always in the way.'

'I thought I'd killed that one.'

'I think they have two minute memories, by now they should be used to cars!' he replied laughing. 'Come on, we'd better get going, I suppose you need to be back before lunch to pick the little one up from school. Sorry, I'm forgetting my manners would you like a coffee?'

'No, I've just had one at home,' she lied. She would feel more comfortable with him out in the open.

'Let's get going then. You're riding Nuit Calico.' He led her away from the house and through a high arch to a row of stables.

A beautiful bay mare was tethered to an iron ring set in the stone wall of the stable block. Beneath her tack, her coat gleamed. She blew out loudly through her nostrils as they approached. Michaud stroked her nose and she whinnied affectionately. Her hind legs were in perfect proportion to her forelegs. A far cry from the fat native British ponies of Diana's childhood. Panic set in. This horse was evidently very valuable and no riding school plod.

As if reading her mind he said, 'She's very gentle, you have nothing to worry about. I'm riding Sarrasin.' He disappeared into a stable and reappeared leading a huge creature. He must have been at least seventeen hands. His black coat reflected the sky like a mirror.

'I had no idea you had such beautiful animals.'

'You were right I don't. These two don't belong to me I just keep them in livery for their owners. They are extremely valuable. Luckily the villagers don't know the first thing about horses and couldn't tell one end of them from the other. I wouldn't want news to get around; if I lost them it would put me out of business.'

The animal skipped playfully as he led it out of the stable. Diana's stomach did a flip. She'd been a keen rider in her childhood and teens but she hadn't had the opportunity to get on a horse since she'd met Serge. Now a feeling of self-preservation swept over her. Who would look after Ben if something happened to her?

Michaud took her hand and guided it to Nuit Calico's muzzle. The mare whinnied again as she stroked the suede surface of its nose. Her jitters were as much to blame on the closeness of this powerful animal as her awkwardness at Michaud's touch.

'You mount and I'll adjust your stirrups.'

Diana swallowed hard trying to banish her fear. He obviously trusted her to ride a valuable horse in his care. She hoped his trust was not unfounded.

Michaud cradled his hands around her knee and she put her other foot in the stirrup and swung her leg over. She was on. Nuit Calico skipped a little sending Diana's butterflies dancing once again. She found the other stirrup and by chance they needed no adjustment.

Michaud vaulted lithely on to Sarrasin and kicked him on down the drive to the road. The horses ambled steadily past *La Petite Folie*. What would Jeanette say if she saw her? There was no one in the street, although she was certain net curtains must be twitching. The horses' shoes clattered on the tarmac proclaiming their passing like a clarion of bells from the church on a Sunday morning.

She must have been holding her breath, because when they had cleared the green and the *Mairie*, she gasped. She began to relax as the horses walked between the sunflower fields. Her body loosened and rocked with the rhythmic motion of the animal beneath her.

'Let's trot to the edge of the forest,' said Michaud turning round towards her.

Diana instinctively adjusted her reins and kicked Calico into a trot. The creature responded immediately and Diana was rising in time with the mare's steps as if she had done it yesterday. She was smiling with satisfaction. On horseback she could see over the tops of the now drying sunflower heads, to the forest, the water tower at Briou to the left and the monastery at Lusigny in the distance to the right.

The clatter of the horses' hooves dissipated as the road surface became littered with oak leaves and pine needles. Michaud turned Sarrasin into the track she had taken with Marie-Pierre. He slowed and waited for her to come alongside. She was about to speak, but Michaud lifted a finger to his lips and pointed, but she could see nothing. Then she saw a movement and heard a crack of twigs. Not very far away from them was a fawn foraging in the undergrowth. They pulled up the horses and watched.

The fawn's coat was almost the same colour as the autumn leaves he was rummaging through. One of the horses blew out through his nostrils and the fawn lifted his head in alarm. Diana expected it to run, but it remained motionless for a few seconds and then bent its head down once more to search for food in the undergrowth. A few moments later it was joined by a large doe. The adult deer spotted them immediately and bolted off into the trees with a flick, the fawn, following its mother's example, skipped behind and with two flashes of white tail they were gone.

'That was amazing! I'd heard there were deer in these woods but I hadn't seen any.'

'There are a lot of deer around here. The best way to see them is on horseback. They're not scared of other animals, just humans. The horses cover our scent.'

The horses began to stamp impatiently, so they kicked them on up the track. They rode companionably in silence for a few minutes. The partially denuded oaks still blocked out a fair amount of light under their canopy. Diana peeled her eyes on the trunks and undergrowth in the hope of seeing some more wildlife. Over the path ahead the tips of the trees bent over until they touched, creating an arch. Sunshine poured through it like the mouth of a tunnel. They had to lean right down over the horses' necks to fit through. Beyond was a clearing of sumptuous meadow grass. A stone chapel stood behind a cherry tree. The tips of its branches submerged below the surface of a pond. As they approached a paddling of ducks flew off with much vocal remonstration.

'They call this place Saint Thomas,' said Michaud.

They both sat quietly for a moment listening to the birds in the trees and the snorting of the horses. 'Stay there, I won't be a minute.' Michaud dismounted. He went to the other side of the pond and began gathering wild flowers. She willed him not to present them to her. She looked the other way while she rehearsed suitable phrases that whilst being polite would not implicate her in any way. When she looked back he had disappeared. A few moments later he reappeared at the door of the chapel empty handed. She felt relieved but a little foolish. He climbed back on Sarrasin without a word.

'It's a strange place to have a chapel.'

'It was named in memory of an English clergyman, they say. They think he hid here during trouble in his own country. Thomas of Canterbury.'

'Thomas Beckett?' she asked excitedly.

He shrugged, 'I don't know much about it but historians take a great interest in it.'

She looked at his rough hands holding Sarrasin's reins and his brown, sun-beaten face. She'd never imagined a man like that would be interested in history.

'Surprised?'

Diana tried to rearrange her features into a neutral expression.

'I do have other interests other than horses and farming you know.'

'Of course, I just never imagined...' She stopped herself, she could feel she was only digging herself in deeper. 'I'm sorry; I guess I'm just not used to having those sorts of conversations with people around here.'

'No, me neither. Let's get going there's still a way to go before we head back. Fancy a canter?' He didn't give her time to answer but gathered up his reins and kicked Sarrasin on. Sarrasin's legs were longer than Calico's and it took a few minutes before Diana could catch up with him. They sped up a narrower path that went beyond the chapel and edged a large lake covered almost entirely with lily pads. Michaud slowed to a trot as the branches across the path became lower and harder to negotiate. At one point they had to dismount to squeeze under some overgrown ivy screening the entrance to a field. A group of labourers in overalls, caps and boots were harvesting onions. They stood up straight clutching their backs to wave. Michaud waved back.

'I usually gallop this bit. Are you up to it?'

'I sure am.'

Calico needed no signal and was off on Sarrasin's tail, her ears forward and hooves pelting the ground between the rows of onions. The two horses streaked past the pickers. The wind in Diana's ears, the air battering her face, and the sheer speed sent adrenalin coursing through her body. They slowed as they approached the back of the Camaret's farm. She was breathing heavily from the exhilaration.

'You all right?' asked Michaud.

'I've never been better,' she puffed.

Back at the stable block she dismounted and lurched as her feet came in contact with the ground. Michaud put his hands on her shoulders to steady her. For a moment they looked at each other. His dark blue eyes seemed to look deep inside her.

She pulled away abruptly, mumbling her thanks. She set about sliding the stirrup irons up the leathers and under the saddle flaps to fill the void of awkwardness. She untacked Calico, rubbed her down and led her back to her box.

'Thanks for helping me out.' Michaud was leaning against the wall of Calico's stable when she reappeared. His eyes were still twinkling.

'I am glad to be of service,' she replied politely, avoiding his gaze.

'You handled her beautifully. I knew you would. Feel free to take her out whenever you like.'

'Oh no, I wouldn't take her out on my own.'

'Does that mean you'll come again?'

Diana thought of Jeanette and Marie-Pierre and decided not to reply. She just shrugged and smiled before she climbed back in her car. She couldn't understand what they had against this extraordinary man.

# THIRTY-FIVE

## Hélène

Hélène slept badly. She slapped water on her face in an attempt to tighten the bags beneath her eyes. She pinched at her cheeks to take away the wan look of exhaustion. She had lain awake most of the night trying to make sense of what she had seen the evening before. Philippe Cottereau: banker, head of the education board, mayor of Jaunay and Antoine's future father-in-law buying what could only be black market diesel from a *Wehrmacht* officer in the curfew hours. The insignia on the truck D.A.S. and the young lad who had been driving it. Then dressing as a monk and performing some sort of ceremony at his house, the old monastery. She knew she had to find out what was going on before the drop. She needed to know if she would be putting anyone in danger. If Cottereau was in league with the Nazis he was very dangerous indeed. Then there was *Docteur* Legris, what could he have been doing at Lusigny? She was thankful that she had not revealed her identity to the *Docteur,* even so she could not be sure he didn't know who she was.

She waited until the doctor had breakfasted. As soon as she heard the door to his consulting room close, she quietly descended the stairs and went into the kitchen. *Madame* Clément was already dusting in the dining room. She poured herself a cup of chicory coffee and drank it down as fast as its temperature would allow. She grabbed an end of baguette and fetched her bicycle.

Floriane Legrand was sweeping her kitchen floor when Hélène knocked.

'*Bonjour mademoiselle.* Mimi will be cross she missed you.'

'I didn't see her playing outside.'

'No, the school has reopened.'

'Without a teacher?'

'*Monsieur* Cottereau works very fast.' She tutted. 'You know life must go on. Or, so they tell me.' She hung her head and sighed.

'Floriane, come and sit down.' Hélène took her by the hand and she allowed herself to be led to the sofa like an invalid. 'Jean was a wonderful man and the villagers speak very highly of him.'

'Did you know him?'

Hélène quickly shook her head. 'No, but people talk to me and I know he was greatly respected in the community.'

'Ha, if only you knew.'

'Floriane?'

She shook her head. 'That man, Cottereau he did not respect Jean. Not one bit. He would have him working all hours of the day and night. As soon as he had achieved one task Cottereau would set him another.'

'But the school is not so big. What work did he have to do at night?'

'I don't know exactly, but Cottereau would make him come to his house during the curfew hours. He was lucky he was never caught.'

'What did he go there for?'

'I don't know. Jean always said it was just school business. Sometimes he would go out in the middle of the night.'

'When was the last time he did it?'

'The night he died.'

'What time did he leave?'

'I don't know exactly. I woke up long before the cocks were crowing and he was gone.'

'You must have been so worried.'

She shrugged. 'I know now that I should have been, but it happened often. Sometimes it was just because he couldn't sleep and he would do some marking in the sitting room so as not to disturb me. He was such a considerate man.' Tears began to roll down her face.

Hélène squeezed her hand and tentatively put an arm around her shoulder. Floriane leant into her and the tears began to fall fast. Hélène gently rubbed her back while she sobbed uncontrollably, until there were no more tears to come.

'I am so sorry.'

'You must not be sorry. You must grieve, and that is what I am here for.'

'I have been holding out so well. Apart from the funeral, Miriam has not seen me cry. I do not want to frighten her.'

'Miriam is an intelligent child, Floriane. Your tears will not frighten her. She may not yet truly understand the impact of her father's death; she is so very young. But she understands the sadness that both she and you must deal with.'

'I talk to him you know.' She blew her nose into a handkerchief. 'I talk to him, I tell him about the news, and I imagine him snorting in disapproval at the censorship.'

'Have the police visited you?'

'Gaston came round the day he died. You know, to tell me.'

'But he has not been back?'

'Just to tell me that they think it was an accident and that there would be no investigation.'

'I know this is painful and I am sorry, but I am sure it will help you to talk about it just a little. Who found him?'

'Cottereau. He was supposed to meet him early at the school and when he did not turn up he went to the woodshed to fetch some logs for the burner.' Floriane was calmer now. She dried her tears and straightened her hair. '*Mademoiselle,* you have been very kind. I hadn't realised how much I needed to do that. I must not keep you.'

'Please call me Hélène.' She stood up to leave. 'Tell me what is D.A.S.?'

'D.A.S.? That is *Distribution Agricole Solognote*, it is where the farmers go to send their produce to Paris.'

'Where is it?'

'Out on the Lusigny road from Saint Gabriel, it belongs to Philippe Cottereau. Why?'

'Just curious, I saw a truck on the road the other day that's all.'

As Hélène cycled out of Jaunay towards Saint Gabriel and the Meffret farm her mind was whirring with Philippe Cottereau. At least she knew there would be no investigation into Rémy's death, it would make her own investigation safer, without having to dodge the police at the same time.

Antoine was tinkering with a tractor in the courtyard as she arrived. She wished she could quiz him about Cottereau but she knew he wouldn't take kindly to being interrogated about his future father-in-law again. Instead she simply waved at him as she glided past. She leant her bicycle up against the barn and went into the farmhouse to see old *Monsieur* Meffret.

Mid-morning she made some chicory coffee on the range and poured a cup for Antoine and took it out to him in the courtyard. He had laid a collection of tractor parts out on the cobbles and scratching his head.

'Problem?'

'Aah, I don't know what is wrong. I have so much ploughing to do but there is something not right with this engine, it is spluttering its way round the field and seems to be using much more fuel than it needs.'

'I have brought you a coffee, well chicory I'm afraid. It must be difficult running tractors with the fuel shortages.'

'Aah, yes. It is the same for everyone, but I have converted this to run on firewood.' He tapped a round cylinder at the front of the engine.

'Perhaps it is that that has gone wrong?'

'Do you know about engines?'

She shook her head. 'Do you not get hold of any diesel for your farm?'

'I get my rationed amount and sometimes my father-in-law gives up some of his for me.'

Philippe Cottereau giving up his fuel ration to his future son-in-law? Hélène could not help but smell a rat. 'Do you buy it from D.A.S.?'

'That's where everybody gets it from, for the farms and businesses at least.'

'And I heard that D.A.S. belongs to Cottereau?'

'That's right. Philippe is a man of many talents. What else have you heard *Mademoiselle?*' He was teasing her.

'Well,' she said playfully. 'I have heard that the school has reopened.'

'They have a new teacher?'

'Apparently. I popped in to see how Floriane Legrand was this morning and Miriam had gone to school.'

'Have you met him?'

'What makes you think it is a man?'

'Trust me, it will be a man. Where Philippe Cottereau is concerned it will always be a man.'

The postman swung up the drive on a bicycle and screeched to a halt by the tractor. 'Post!' he yelled. He handed Antoine a letter, 'It is from Tours,' and then settled himself on his handlebars expectantly.

'Thank you, Pierre.' Antoine put the letter into the pocket of his overall. '*Bonne journée* Pierre.'

Pierre looked mightily disappointed and turned his bicycle around, doffing his hat to Hélène, '*Ma'm'selle.*'

As soon as he was gone Antoine took the envelope from his pocket and opened it. As he read the letter he took a deep breath. 'It is from the hospice in Tours they need an immediate response to take up the place.' He leant against the tractor and looked up to the heavens as if hoping for guidance.

'Only you can know what is right, Antoine.'

'It does not seem right that the man who has provided everything for me should be sent away to die amongst strangers; but how can I continue here running the farm and looking after him? Now it is winter but when the good weather comes the farm will be busier than ever and he is likely to be much worse by then.'

'I am here to look after him for the moment.'

'For the moment?' He looked stricken. 'Are you planning on going away?'

She took his hand and rubbed it. 'No, Antoine but this is wartime and we, none of us, know what will happen. Look at the situation we are in now, we would never have imagined this.'

'Hélène, I do not want to send my father to Tours. I want him to stay in his home with the people who love him, with what he knows.'

'Then there is your decision. You must write and tell them immediately and I will take the letter to the post office in Jaunay when I leave. Now come inside you will not have the head to find out what is wrong with the tractor until it is done.'

Antoine turned to her and took the cup she was holding and carefully balanced it between the cobbles of the courtyard. He put his arms around her and kissed her. She returned his warmth and lost herself in his embrace. His great strong arms enveloping her slight frame made her feel safe, as if she had come home. As if she had known him all her life.

'I don't know what I would do if you were to go.'

'But what about …?'

He touched his fingers to her lips. 'You have saved me from more than you know.'

# THIRTY-SIX

## Diana

After his morning at school Ben fell asleep as soon as his head hit the pillow. There was still no message from Serge. Determined not to be drawn by the anxiety that was spawning an invasion of her subconscious, she went out to the garden to finish gathering up the windfalls. As she filled the wheelbarrow with the least blemished fruits, she marvelled at her new found strength. It had been a perfect morning. She couldn't remember a time when she'd done something just for her. The feeling of power that had swept her senses as she had flown across the onion field on Nuit Calico seemed to have cleansed her soul.

She thought of Michaud and his easy manner. It was funny how Michaud knew what time Ben needed picking up from school. He didn't have any children. Serge didn't even know what time Ben went to bed. He'd always just trundled through life as if he had no one relying on him. He went out when he pleased and stayed in bed when he pleased. She had just accepted it. She chided herself for comparing them. They were incomparable. She was married to Serge, the father of her child. Michaud was a mere acquaintance who needed a hand with his horses.

She trundled the wheelbarrow up to the back terrace and took an armful of apples into the kitchen. Apple crumble always went down well with her French friends, they had all been smitten by its comforting sweetness and texture. If she was to make it for the *épicerie* she would have to go to the supermarket and pick up disposable dishes to cook it in and some flour, butter and sugar. She looked at her watch. Two o'clock. Ben wouldn't wake until at least half past three. She would go then. At least she could peel enough apples to make ten crumbles and leave them in water and lemon juice until she got back.

It was half past six by the time she returned from Beaugency. She drove past the Camaret's farm and Michaud's and past the café, up the *rue de l'Abreuvoir* past Mémère Claudette's cottage and felt almost as if she belonged. She swung the car in front of the church and her senses leapt. Serge's car was parked outside.

'*Papa, Papa!*' yelled Ben gaily.

Her spirits fell. She opened the gate and drove into the garage. She got out and lifted Ben down from his seat. She drew herself up as tall as she could, put her shoulders back and breathed deeply. He must only have been called in for one day. She climbed the back steps to the hall in trepidation.

He was in the kitchen boiling some water for his coffee. He didn't look up when she entered the room with the shopping.

'Hi.' She managed a weak smile. There was no response. 'How was work?'

'Fine,' he grunted.

'I didn't know when you were coming home.'

Again he ignored her.

'When do you have to go in again?'

He looked up at her his eyes flaring with anger.

'Why the interrogation? Why do you always have to know what I'm doing? Why can't a man have some privacy?' His voice quavered as he shouted. 'It's always the same.' He slammed his cup onto the work surface. 'I'm going out.'

Diana was left standing stunned in the kitchen. She felt empty; there was no urge to cry, or to shout; just a powerful yearning to be alone with her baby. Not alone with the threat of his unannounced imminent arrival but alone, once and for all. She fed Ben and put him to bed. She cooked up the apples and made the crumble mixture. Every time she heard a noise outside she flinched like a wild deer and ran out to see if Serge had returned. The smell of the crumble reminded her of the days when her parents were still together at Watcombe House. It would twist its way up the back stairs from the kitchen and fill the hall giving anyone who may be lingering in the vicinity hunger pangs. She poured the piping hot apple mixture into the foil dishes and then sprinkled them with the crumble topping. At half past nine all the crumbles were complete and cooling on the side in the kitchen. She would take them over to the café in the morning. Then it dawned on her that the *pissaladières* may only have sold so easily because people knew what they were. The majority of the French nation had never heard of apple crumble, which would be enough suspicion to leave them untested on the shelf. She would have to label them with the ingredients and cooking instructions. She rummaged in the stationery drawer and found some sticky labels. She had just finished writing out the last one when she heard the iron gate in the yew hedge clang.

She ducked into the kitchen, not wishing to face Serge again. She heard him trudging round the side of the house to the back terrace. The back door opened and shut again. The floorboards in their bedroom creaked and then all was quiet. He'd gone straight to bed. She waited a good five minutes until the silence was assured and then crept to the bedroom door which was ajar. She peeped through the gap and smelt the familiar odour of cigarettes and beer. He was stone drunk.

The next morning Diana was up early, so that he wouldn't notice she'd slept in the spare room. She just couldn't stomach sharing a bed with the stench of a drunkard ever again. Both Serge and Ben were still sleeping, so she loaded the buggy with the cooled, labelled crumbles and took them to the café. Jeanette would be just opening up her doors. It was Saturday morning and too early for the villagers to have commenced the day's bustling. The *épicerie* was deserted.

'You're early.'

'I've brought some apple crumbles for you.'

'Ooh. They look nice. What is apple crumble?'

'I've written out some labels explaining. Look I can't stop long everyone is still asleep at home.'

Jeanette caught her arm and lowered her volume. 'Diana, Serge was in here last night.'

'Yes, I thought he must have been. I could pick up my baguette while I'm here.' She deflected the subject.

'Diana, listen. It's serious. He was shouting his mouth off about how attractive he is to women. He was with that Jérôme Couteau again.'

Diana raised her eyes to the ceiling and sighed.

'He was teasing the others that they didn't have *his* sexual charisma. Old Claude snapped in the end and said "So attractive that your wife goes riding horses with another man." Serge was furious. Pierrot and Marcel had to hold him back to stop him from punching Claude.'

'Oh Jeanette. I'm so sorry.'

'I warn you there is no good to come of all this.' She waved a finger at her. 'You must keep away from Michaud.'

'But there is nothing wrong with him. I just went for a ride. That's all I did. I didn't do it secretively, there were plenty of witnesses and not one person could swear that we had done anything else.'

'Folk round here won't see it like that. And another thing, he was boasting that he had a woman chasing him.'

Diana's face drained of colour. 'What woman?'

'I don't know but Claude said he'd seen her.'

Diana's mind raced back to the evening that Claude had called round looking for Serge. He said he had seen a blonde woman in Serge's car. Diana's blood went cold. The only blonde she could think of was Liesel. She suddenly felt a need to be alone.

'Jeanette, I must get back before Ben wakes Serge.' She picked up her baguette and left the shop. She didn't want to know anymore. As she walked back up the lane to the *Champ de Foire* she thought of Liesel's phone call. That's why she'd hesitated when Diana picked up the phone; she had expected Serge to answer. Surely she must have realised there was a fifty percent chance that *she* would answer, unless Serge had given her reason to believe that she would be out. Whatever that reason was it meant that Serge must have seen her before that phone call. There was no doubt in her mind, the blonde lady in the car could have been no one other than Liesel, and the fact that Serge hadn't mentioned it only compounded her suspicions. But suspicions were all they were, she must keep a handle on reality. Until she had proof she could do nothing.

She opened the door from the back terrace, the house was still silent. Ben hadn't stirred. She sat down in the armchair in front of the burnt out fire in the grate. She was angry and shocked. She felt she ought to be sad, she was bubbling with so much emotion that there was no room for sadness. What if Jeanette was mistaken? She thought of *Madame* Camaret 'we just got on with it,' she had said. Surely that didn't stretch to putting up with adultery? What would another woman do? They'd probably go round and see Liesel and scratch her eyes out. What would that achieve? She could go and kick Serge out of bed and scream and shout at him, letting him know that he was found out. No, she had to be smarter than that. She would have to wait until he was back at work, then she would have time to think in peace. She suddenly had an overwhelming urge to be held by a caring human being. She opened the door to the garage and let Léo in. She slumped down to the floor and buried her face in his fur.

By the time Serge emerged, Diana and Ben were weeding the vegetable patch. He came striding across the lawn towards her. He was carrying a creamy coloured bundle. As he got closer Diana could see they were her jodhpurs, he must have searched for evidence of

Claude's statement and found them in the laundry basket. She swallowed hard.

'You went riding, I see,' he announced, almost triumphantly throwing the jodhpurs onto the brown, freshly dug earth.

'Yes, I went with Michaud'

'I see. Michaud...' He stood legs apart his hands on his hips. His angry stare frightened her.

'Yes, you and Liesel,' she paused playfully.

His eyes got wider and his mouth closed.

'Both you and Liesel said I needed some time to myself.'

His features relaxed again, but his face was reddening. 'Time for yourself? Did I say with another man? And it's not what Liesel thinks that's important. Why are you dragging her into this?'

Diana shrunk from the temptation of implicating her. 'I'm not. I just went for a ride, he said he needed a hand exercising one of his horses and I said I would.'

'Keep away from him.'

'Why should I do that? You told me I was breathing down your neck. You told me I needed to find myself something else to do.'

'He's a bad man Diana.' He was shouting now.

'Keep your voice down.'

'Keep my voice down? You're worried people will find out about you and him? Worried about your blessed reputation?'

Diana was aghast, how could he stand there throwing unfounded accusations at her whilst he was playing Casanova with Liesel. She was only just realising Serge's capacity for deceit.

'Your reputation is already in tatters. Do you know what they're saying? The little English tart and the murderer!'

She looked up at him in alarm. 'What did you say?' She stared at him in disbelief.

'You heard me. He's a murderer Diana, everyone knows that.'

'What *are* you talking about?'

'How do you think he got that farm? He conned the old farmer out of it, that's how. Claude told me all about it. He turned up here three years ago out of the blue. He was just a farm hand. Just a few weeks later the old farmer died mysteriously and he, the farm hand, inherited everything. Everyone knows.'

'If everyone knows, why isn't he in prison?'

'That one, he's clever. There was no proof. But why should a man leave all his belongings to a complete stranger?'

Diana stared at him astonished. All thoughts of Liesel had vanished.

'I bet he's after our house now. I'm back at work on Monday and if I hear that he has come anywhere near you by the time I come back I'll knock him to kingdom come. I promise you that.' He turned and stormed back to the house.

Ben was sobbing now. Diana picked him up and held him tight, as much to console him as to steady her own nerves.

Michaud a murderer? She couldn't believe it. Anyway, how could she believe the words of a liar? Just two days and she would be alone again, alone and peaceful. Liesel would be away then too. She'd said she was going to a conference. Diana gasped. Surely not? They weren't that blatant were they? She went back to the house. Serge was nowhere to be seen. She hoped he'd gone out. She grabbed the telephone book and ruffled through the pages until she found P for *psychologues.* Liesel had never mentioned her boss's name but there was only one in Mer. It must be that one. She dialled the number.

A woman's voice answered. It wasn't Liesel's.

*'Bonjour, Madame.* 'I believe one of your employees *Mademoiselle* O'Ryan will be attending our conference next week?'

There was a short pause. 'Oh, that must be the Cognitive Behavioural Therapy conference in Maisons-Alfort?'

Diana thought quickly. *'Yes,* that's right. Please would you pass a message on to *Mademoiselle* O'Ryan and ask her to pick up her parking pass at the front reception desk.'

'Wait a minute, *Mademoiselle* O'Ryan has just arrived. One moment please.'

Diana hung up. She stared at the phone for a few seconds trembling. She hadn't wanted to be right. Liesel's conference was in Paris on Monday and Serge was due back at work in Paris on the same day. Although she could guess what they were up to this wasn't enough of a coincidence to be evidence. There was nothing strange in Serge going to Paris – that was where he worked; and the capital was not an unlikely place to host a psychology conference. The only other clues she had could be talked away as hearsay. She needed real proof. The village must have known about their liaison long before her. But if the village had known surely Jeanette would have been the first to know. But if she was planning to keep it from her she wouldn't have said anything to her this morning. Diana resolved to get to the bottom of it; she would have to follow them.

'I won't be beaten,' she whispered to herself.

# THIRTY-SEVEN

**Edward**

The fair was over and the buzz and hum of the newcomers had gone from the air of Saint Gabriel. All was once again as it was. Edward had not left and for that he was thankful. He wondered where he would be by now had Clothilde not needed him. At the abbey at Pontigny? With those monks perhaps that he had seen listening to the troubadour? Or mugged and murdered in a desolate country ditch by the side of the road, never to be found? The summer was indeed beautiful in these exotic woods and he felt blessed to have such a friend as Clothilde. The *Seigneur* would soon be well and Clothilde would then be safe from his fickle wrath.

Edward watched carefully from the edge of the field but the village was quiet. He could see the dark shadows of the goats tethered in the furthest corner from him. They would be unlikely to be startled by him at such a distance. He could see the well on the opposite side of the fair field. It was perilously close to the huts, but the village was quiet and the dogs safely curled up inside the doorways. He sidled along the edge of the trees towards the well. When he was certain there was no one to spy him he ran awkwardly across the tussocks, bent low. He crouched down behind the well while he caught his breath. Then heaved himself up and felt around the inside of the walls and felt nothing but rough stone. He leant in a little further and as Clothilde had said he came across a crevice and in it was a leather pouch. It was large and heavy. He opened it and took out a scrap of parchment carefully rolled up, and a large earthenware pot with a wooden stopper.

RETURNING TO THE CHATEAU IN THREE DAYS WILL NEED MORE WOOD BETONY

The letters were formed carefully though childishly. He removed the stopper of the pot and sniffed at it. Clothilde had left him some broth. He secreted the message and the pot of broth beneath his habit and stowed his own pot of goutwort together with the instructions to make a restorative poultice for the *Seigneur's* feet. He perched the pouch carefully in the crevice and slipped back across the field to the safety of the trees.

He returned to the den and set the broth to warm over the fire. Just one day and night had passed since Clothilde's last visit and already he missed her. Though until the *Seigneur* was on his way to improving there was nothing to be done.

The honey in the broth brought him a sense of comfort and wellbeing. To think that this homely nectar had been prepared by the hands of this beautiful child. He thought of her long locks which she flicked through nerves or worry, or tossed backwards in triumph, or shrouded her face in sadness; like a splendid weather vane of her emotions.

After he had drank every last drop of broth he went back out into the woods to gather more wood betony and prepare the remedy. He was packing it neatly into a jar when he heard a crack of twigs from above. Alarmed, Edward dived into the furthest corner of the cavern from the opening and lay on the floor in a ball. At least if someone looked into the cavern they would mistake him for a pile of clothing.

'Edward! Do not fear! It is me, Clothilde.'

'Clothilde! You should not be here.'

'I was careful; I lost the men at the entrance to the village.'

'What news of the *Seigneur?* '

'He was not happy but I wrapped his feet in the wood betony and I told him he should avoid butter and red meat and eat vegetables, as you told me.'

'How did he take it?'

'He was quieter but he is a miserable man. *Dame* Héloïse was at his side this time. She is a fine lady and she appears to calm him a little. She told him that if he had called me as his counsel he must follow my instructions. I told him it would take a few days before he saw any improvement. Edward, will it only take a few days?'

'If he follows the instructions he will indeed feel better just for his diet!' Edward couldn't resist smiling. 'You have done well, Clothilde.'

'The *Dame*, she was very beautiful and dressed so finely.' Her look became wistful.

'Yes, I saw her at the *foire*. She wears beautiful clothes.'

Clothilde was gazing in the distance a little melancholic.

'What is it?'

244

'It was strange. As I was leaving, she stopped me. She took my hand and squeezed it very hard. So hard it hurt.' Clothilde rubbed the back of her hand as she remembered. 'There was a tear in her eye. She told me I was beautiful! Can you believe that? A Lady talking to the daughter of a mere servant like that!'

Edward laughed. 'Indeed I can. *Dame* Héloïse is a discerning woman. You are very beautiful.'

Clothilde blushed and looked away. 'But I was thinking that about her at the very same instant. She told me she had lost a child many years ago in childbirth. Every day since, she said she had imagined what that child would have looked like had she lived. She said she would have been very proud if her child was in my likeness. I didn't know what to say, so I just curtseyed and said thank you and departed.'

'When must you return?'

'In three days.'

'I have prepared some more wood betony, here take it now. I have left you some goutwort and instructions in the well. You must alternate the wood betony and the goutwort and the *Seigneur* will soon be recovered. Now go before they miss you.'

She disappeared soundlessly through the woods as the rising sun cast a rose glow across the trunks of the trees.

# THIRTY-EIGHT

## Diana

Diana managed to avoid Serge for the rest of the weekend using dog walks and weeding as pretexts to be out of the house. Her crumbles had sold well and Jeanette had got away with charging fifty francs for each one and handed Diana three hundred and seventy-five francs. Together with the three hundred from the *pissaladières* she had enough for her trip to Paris. She longed to quiz Jeanette about Michaud and the old farmer but the café was busier than usual, Jeanette was also distracted by the arrangements for her wedding. It would have to wait.

That night Diana's sleep was a whirl of Liesel, Serge, Michaud, Claude and the old farmer. Could so many people be wrong? The old adage 'there's no smoke without fire' haunted her. She had to find out, but one thing at a time.

On Sunday evening Serge was already preparing to go back to barracks. Diana couldn't help noticing the care with which he was packing his things. Normally he would just throw some stuff in a bag. He said he had to work for five days this time.

She needed to see Jeanette but she would have to time it right. Winter was approaching and it was getting dark earlier. The hunters would be heading for the café at sundown to show off their trophies. She would have to go before then if she didn't want an audience.

At about four o'clock she announced she was taking Léo for a walk. As she had hoped the café was empty, the Sunday lunch crowd had hit the road and Jeanette was just clearing up the digestive glasses before the next onslaught.

'Jeanette, I have heard things about Michaud.'

Jeanette looked at her warningly and carried on wiping the tables in silence.

Diana grabbed her arm, she hadn't meant to but her urgency got the better of her. 'Serge says he's a murderer.'

Jeanette's finger flew to her lips to shush her. 'Come in the kitchen.'

Diana followed and Jeanette shut the door behind them.

'Look, perhaps I should have told you before. But, I will tell you now. It was three years ago. Michaud turned up in the village working for old Antoine. Antoine owned the farm Michaud lives in now. Anyway, Antoine employed him as a farm hand. That wasn't really surprising, everyone had always wondered how Antoine had coped with the farm all those years alone, and he was getting on a bit. Just a few weeks later, Antoine fell ill with flu. It went to his chest and then it turned into pneumonia. It was autumn, about this time of year. I remember the doctor was in and out of there nearly every day for about three weeks. The doctor wanted him in hospital but he refused to go. Michaud offered to look after him and moved into the farmhouse, to be there for him day and night. When he got really bad the doctor insisted he should go into hospital. The old man still refused to leave, but they say he was losing his marbles by then. Michaud had a row with the doctor and refused to allow Antoine to be taken out of the house. Without Antoine's consent the poor doctor's hands were tied.

'Instead the doctor brought in an oxygen bottle and checked on him every day. Poor Antoine didn't last long. He died in the night with Michaud at his bedside. Michaud seemed really stricken by grief. That surprised everyone; he'd only been working for him a short while and the village began to talk. Some thought he was overacting. It wasn't until the will was read that the gossip escalated. Old Antoine had left the farm, his land and money to Michaud. The lot! Can you imagine? He'd left his entire estate to a complete stranger! No one could understand it.'

'Surely, the will was contested?'

'There wasn't anyone *to* contest it; Antoine had no family, he had no brothers or sisters and his wife died just after the war. The mayor launched an investigation. The police were all over that place. They went through every bit of paperwork, and did an autopsy. But everything was as it should be. Antoine had rewritten his will when he became sick leaving everything to Michaud. The solicitors said that Antoine hadn't appeared to be under any pressure to do so. Quite the opposite, he had been almost excited about it.

'Death was by respiratory failure due to the pneumonia, there was no proof of anything untoward. The case was dropped, Antoine was buried at the church and everything calmed down.'

'If the police couldn't find anything and the solicitors were unconcerned why aren't the villagers satisfied?'

'I do think it's very strange that a man no one has ever heard of turns up working on a farm, and just two months later, the farmer dies and the stranger inherits the lot. Some think Michaud smothered him with a pillow. Others think he could have been saved if Michaud had allowed him to go into hospital. Then there's the theory that Michaud quite simply conned him into changing his will. No, there is definitely something wrong. Nobody trusts him and nor should you.'

'I couldn't imagine such a gentle man doing anything so callous.'

'Don't be a fool Diana. You keep away from him.' The bell went on the café door. 'I'll have to go.'

'Before I forget, could you do me a favour and pick Ben up from the bus for me tomorrow? I'm going shopping in Blois and I'm just a bit worried that I'll get held up in traffic.'

'Yes, of course.'

'It gets in at quarter to five.'

'I'll be there. Don't worry about a thing.'


Serge had left before the sun had risen to be at the barracks for nine. Standing at the bus stop she had felt self-conscious in her city clothes. Marie-Pierre had already asked her if she was doing anything nice, to which she'd replied as light-heartedly as she could muster, 'Just shopping!'

She drove to the station as soon as the school bus had turned the corner towards Briou. She caught the 9.08 from Beaugency to Paris - Austerlitz. The train was full of students going back to their colleges and universities after a weekend at home. Some were listening to headphones, the noise blaring so loudly that Diana could make out the words. Winging her way back to Paris felt like a return home, to the last place that Diana Hunter had existed, where her life had once been positive and fun. She sharply reminded herself of the nosy, bad-tempered concierges, the pushy aggressive Parisians and the lack of sky.

The train sped through the Beauce; the flat grey landscape that stretched to the horizon. There were deer grazing in groups on the edges of woodland and foxes fled across the fields from the rumbling train, only the rabbits carried on their business of munching through the grass undisturbed by the metal monster tearing through their territory.

As the train approached the metropolis, the landscape became shrouded in electric cables and thickets of publicity boards advertising DIY chains, supermarkets and discount electrical stores. The Eiffel tower came into view soaring above the rambling city. She remembered the first time she had come to Paris as a foreign exchange student and had fallen in love with its unfathomable air of bohemia. She'd never felt the same way about London. Paris was cleaner, more elegant and held a kind of magic that you couldn't quite put your finger on. The locomotive slowed as it trundled through the high-rise graffiti spattered towers and suburban stations. The passengers were beginning to pack away their things and put their coats on. Diana realised that she had never taken hers off. The journey seemed to have flown in a flash.

Now she was here, she felt foolish. What on earth did she think she was doing? She could hardly go knocking on the barracks doors to find out if Serge was really there. Nor did she know exactly where the conference in Maisons-Alfort was being held. She'd been so concerned that neither Serge nor Liesel should see her that she had overlooked the fact that her real problem would actually be *finding* them, let alone finding them together.

The passengers poured out of the train doors and automatically changed into city mode walking at high speed as if they were late for something. Diana found herself doing the same without knowing where she was going. At the entrance to the *Métro* station she stopped and studied the giant map fixed to the wall. The only starting point for her search could be Serge's barracks in Les Halles. She would need to change at Bastille. She thought of the evening she had met Serge at *La Place de la Bastille*. She didn't want to go anywhere near the site of that fateful night. Instead she chose the alternative route changing at Odéon. The train stopped at Jussieu and Diana could feel the years falling away from her. Jussieu was her world before she met Serge. It was here she had studied and met friends after lectures at Finnegan's Wake, a dingy but cosy Irish bar, just up a steep lane opposite the *fac*.

Just as the doors were about to close a group of four students got on carrying files and laughing. They only had eyes for each other, immersed in their student world; everything else around them was invisible. Diana was envious. At last she arrived at Odéon and found the platform for line four - destination *Porte de Clignancourt*. Just four stops and she disembarked at *Les Halles*. She spotted some Americans head high above the rest of the travellers, their polo necks and white teeth shining over the sea of dark grey and blue clothing that Parisians were so fond of. The passengers getting off the train were obliged to push their way through those getting on. It was only their designer suits and briefcases that differentiated these people from schoolchildren jostling in the corridors to go to assembly.

Standing in the biting cold on *rue Rambuteau* she caught her first glimpse of the city for a long time. The hairs on the back of her neck rose. After the empty rolling fields of the Beauce she was overwhelmed by the number of people teeming up and down the pavements, scurrying like mice. She wandered down the road slowly, looking in shop windows. Pedestrians huffed and puffed when they found themselves slowing down behind her. She began to enjoy the anonimity. No one would be twitching their curtains here.

To her left she could see the church of Saint Eustache marking the entrance to *rue du Jour* and the way to the barracks. She swallowed and purposefully strode towards the gleaming flying buttresses. As she reached the corner, she could hear a siren. In panic she quickly crossed the road and hid behind the pots of box topiary outside the *Pied de Cochon* restaurant in *rue Coquillière*. She turned her back to the fire engine and pretended to examine the ornamental bushes. Once it had sped off towards *rue Montmartre* Diana stood up again. It hadn't dawned on her that it wasn't just Serge she must conceal herself from, but the rest of his crew as well. If any of them spotted her they would be sure to mention it to him. This was going to be trickier than she'd imagined.

She looked to see if the restaurant still kept a piglet chained up in a kennel outside. Poor thing, he lay languidly looking at the passers-by. She wondered if he would end up in the pot when he got too big for the kennel. She was thankful that they'd never had enough money to afford a meal there.

She peeped round the corner of the street in front of *Agnès b.*; Serge's favourite clothes shop. Having reassured herself that the coast was clear she began to walk down the left hand side keeping close to the shop fronts ready to dart into a doorway. There were two cafés in the street; one right opposite the barracks, the *Brasserie de l'Eglise* and another a little further up the street. She headed for the furthest one. From there she could watch the barracks entrance without being spotted too readily. She bought a newspaper from the kiosk on the corner as cover and put her head down and walked briskly towards the café.

She sat in the back with a clear view of the front window. There were few customers so her vista was unobscured. She spread the newspaper out in front of her ready to take cover should the need arise.

Even if someone she knew appeared on the pavement outside it was unlikely that they would identify her from such a distance. She ordered a large cream coffee from the waiter.

She kept her eyes peeled on the window. Just as the waiter brought her coffee and interrupted her concentration, a small red fire van came swinging out of the barracks, its light flashing blue. She glanced at the cab but she didn't recognise its occupants. Her heart was racing; she had to resist the temptation to dive under her newspaper right in front of the waiter. He set down the coffee and put a plastic green saucer with the bill next to it. When he retreated she took a large mouthful of the warm milky liquid. She must calm herself. She turned the page of the newspaper and surreptitiously looked round at the other customers. She wasn't the only woman alone. She sipped her coffee slowly trying to make it last, not wanting to dip into her earnings more than was necessary; she'd already seriously depleted them with the train ticket.

The street was busy and Diana was worried that she'd miss Serge if she took her eyes off the window for a second. Passers-by were wrapped up in coats and scarves making it difficult to see their faces. More than once she thought she recognised a couple of Serge's colleagues and sunk down behind her paper.

A tap on her shoulder startled her. She swung round. She hadn't chosen her table well; she had failed to notice the door to the Gents just behind her.

'Christian!' she shrieked too loudly for normality.

He was frowning. 'Are you meeting Serge?'

'No, no,' she stammered. 'I mean yes.' She could feel herself flushing. She forced herself to smile but was conscious of appearing phoney.

'He's just gone out on a call. I don't know how long he'll be. Are you sure you got the time right?'

'Oh, silly me,' she laughed. 'That's right! He did say to meet him at twelve. I've got a head like a sieve.'

Christian narrowed his eyes. He had known Diana since the day she and Serge had met and the one thing she didn't have was a head like a sieve. 'Are you alright?'

'Yes, yes. I'm fine. How are you?'

'Fine.' He was still frowning. 'Well, I'd better get back I'm still on duty. When he comes back I'll let him know you're here.'

'No!' Diana panicked. 'No, don't do that, I'll just go for a wander and come back in an hour, it'll only annoy him.'

'Diana, what is going on?' He looked long and hard at her.

Diana looked down at the newspaper to gather her wits.

'You're not meeting him are you?'

Diana stared at the newspaper trying to think of a sensible reply.

'He doesn't know you're here, does he?'

'Christian, please don't tell him,' she pleaded.

'Diana, he's my friend, don't ask me to keep secrets from him.'

He was right, this wasn't fair of her. She thought quickly, she wasn't prepared to have her cover blown so early on in her mission. 'It's just…' Her mind whirred 'It's a surprise!' She said brightly. 'I thought I'd take him out to lunch.' She held her breath, aware of the feebleness of her explanation.

Christian's features relaxed. It had worked.

Diana let out an internal sigh of relief. 'So please don't tell him and spoil my surprise.'

'Thank the Lord, I thought for a minute you were following him. How stupid of me!' He laughed embarrassed at his mistake.

Diana laughed with him. 'Oh, no! Nothing like that.'

He grinned conspiratorially, 'My lips are sealed. I'd better get back. Delphine and I must come down and see you again. I'll fix it up with Serge.'

'That would be lovely!'

He turned to leave but hesitated and turned back. 'I've just remembered. I think Serge was planning to go out to Maisons-Alfort this afternoon. He was asking me directions this morning. He said he was meeting up with an old mate from the *Gendarmerie Mobile* down there.'

'Perhaps I could surprise him there?' she said quickly. 'Do you know where exactly?'

'Well, he wanted to know where *Le Scalpel* was. It's a café just down from the vet school.'

At last Christian left. She'd walked past *Le Scalpel* a couple of times when she'd met Delphine from college. Good, kind Christian. He'd had no idea how he'd implicated his friend. It was obvious he knew nothing of Serge's affair. At least she could rule out conspiracy. If Serge hadn't confided in Christian perhaps this thing with Liesel wasn't that important. Perhaps they could patch this up. Her spirits lifted momentarily. There was no going back; she would have to find out for herself.

She drained her coffee and walked back past Saint Eustache buttoning her coat against the penetrating wind. The warmth of the *Métro* station only compounded the smell of ammonia seeping up from the floor. Diana shuddered in disgust. She studied the huge map on the wall. *Ecole Vétérinaire de Maisons-Alfort* was quite a way out in the suburbs. It would take about three quarters of an hour to get there. If what Christian had said was true and Serge had gone out on a call he wouldn't be able to get there until at least one o'clock. She had two hours to burn. She decided she'd use the time to reconnoitre the area should an escape be necessary. She walked to *Châtelet-les-Halles* and caught a train to *République*. The last part of the journey from *République* to *Ecole Vétérinaire* was above ground so she could gaze out of the window at the narrow grid like streets.

As the little train edged further and further out of the city the streets became wider, and the trees changed from plane trees to poplars planted in sterile rows. She got off the train and headed out onto the *Boulevard Géneral de Gaulle*. The huge archway of the *Ecole Vétérinaire* loomed majestically up above its ornate iron gates. Now which way? She looked about her. *Maisons-Alfort* was nothing but a huge concrete jungle. She felt saddened by the hardened, blank faces of its inhabitants. She realised she could never swap her remote life in the green rolling fields of the Beauce for this soulless uniformity.

She wandered slowly; the pavements were deserted; only cars hared up and down the main boulevard. Up ahead a group of youths with woollen black hats appeared with skateboards under their arms. They were speaking with the deep abrupt accent of the suburbs. She speeded up and kept her head down as she passed them. They ignored her. She turned up a street where she could see a blue and green cross flashing above a chemist, there were a few more people around here. She felt a little safer. She slowed down again aware of the long wait ahead of her. She looked in the shop windows aimlessly and revelled in the freedom of being childless. There was no manoeuvring of cumbersome pushchairs or thwarting Ben's attempts to free himself from the shackles of his harness.

She caught sight of *Le Scalpel*. She looked at her watch Serge would be knocking off about now. She peered through the window. It wasn't the sort of place she would imagine Liesel frequenting. The terracotta tiled floor was strewn with cigarette ends. The tables were

Formica topped and a collection of elderly gentlemen stood around the bar cradling glasses of red wine. This was a man's drinking hole. Maybe he really was meeting a friend from the *Gendarmerie*, it was hardly the venue for a clandestine amorous rendezvous. Maybe Christian had got it wrong, maybe this wasn't the right place. Or had he deliberately put her off the scent?

She continued up the road, looking for somewhere to watch the café from. Further up on the opposite side of the road she came to another café, this looked more like it. A large silver and black sign spelt out *Project Café,* the tables and chairs were in bright chrome and the walls were covered in murals of bold abstract art. There was a spiral staircase also in chrome. This was by far a more fitting location. What was she going to do? They could be coming to either of these places. If she was wrong and Serge really was meeting a pal he would be furious if she was discovered. Even if she was right, she was certain she must remain concealed. Deciding it was too much of a gamble, she realised she would have to find the conference centre. She had three quarters of an hour. She couldn't risk missing them. There was an estate agent's next door.

'*Madame*, could you direct me to the conference centre?'

'Next to the *Ecole Vétérinaire*,' barked a young girl absentmindedly.

Diana double-backed along the street and headed up past *Le Scalpel*. The youths were still milling about on the main boulevard pavement. She crossed onto the other side of the road and headed for an expanse of shiny white building just past the archway. The street was busier now, with the lunchtime throng of office workers. She would have to hurry. *Le Centre Conferencier de l'Ecole Vétérinaire* was emblazoned on a signpost. She walked into the main entrance, flicked her hair back and held her head high and marched purposefully up to the reception desk. A middle-aged woman complete with regional snarl, her hair swept back into a fastidiously tight bun was intently tapping away at a keyboard.

'*Bonjour Madame*, I'm looking for the psychology conference.'

'Psychology Conference? You mean the conference on Cognitive Behavioural Therapy?' She sneered as if Diana was educationally subnormal. She raised one eyebrow. 'The morning session will be finished in five minutes do you have an invitation?' The woman looked her up and down.

'No, no, I'm meeting someone. Thank you, I'll wait.'

The doors to the conference room opened and people started pouring out. Diana rushed outside and hid behind a pillar. She examined each person as they left the building. She didn't have to wait long. Liesel's blonde head contrasted boldly against the black fur coat in which she was enveloped. She paused outside the gates and took out what looked like an A to Z of Paris. Diana's heart was thumping. She studied the map for a minute, slung her Gucci handbag over her shoulder and headed for the street Diana had just come from.

It wasn't easy keeping up with her but at least she could melt into the conference centre crowd who were all heading in the same direction. Her fellow crowd members were gathering speed and jostled to be ahead of the others, creating a rather bizarre impression of being involved in a variety race at a school sports day with overcoats and briefcases replacing the eggs and spoons. Though Diana wasn't very tall Liesel was, and her blonde head served as a beacon. She turned down the street towards *Le Scalpel*. A big man in a dark overcoat pushed in front of Diana. Liesel was only obscured from view for a second, but once the man had raced ahead, Liesel was nowhere to be seen. She looked up and down the street to no avail.

She hung back in the recess of a garage entrance wondering what to do. Just a few doors up there was a florist's shop. The door opened and Liesel reappeared clutching a single red rose. Diana felt sick, how very 'this century' of her to offer a man flowers. She bolstered herself up with the thought that this would be totally lost on Serge who was a firm traditionalist and would think it effeminate.

Liesel continued up the street. She walked right past *Le Scalpel*. Diana was right, the café was far too down market for this prima donna. She hung back a little and waited for her to go into the *Project Café*. But to her consternation Liesel walked straight past its entrance and headed away from the shops to the quieter end of the street. Where on earth was she going? There were less people at that end; it would be more difficult for Diana to keep out of sight. If Liesel turned round now she would have nobody to duck behind. Instead she stood staring into a hairdresser's shop front with one eye glancing sideways towards Liesel's departing back.

Liesel veered left and disappeared into a doorway. Diana waited a few moments to check she wasn't going to come out again and then followed. Black lettering on the smoked glass doors read *L'Hôtel de Gaulle*.

It was worse than she thought. Surely Liesel was staying with her parents in *Maison Lafitte*? Diana's head began to spin with the sordidness. Serge could be along at any moment. She scurried quickly back down the street and ducked into the *Project Café*. If Serge was innocent he would be meeting his friend in *Le Scalpel*. If he was guilty she would see him walk past the *Project Café* and into the hotel. She ordered a brandy and knocked it back in one gulp and almost choked on the unfamiliar firewater.

She'd recognise that gait anywhere. Serge was ambling along the opposite pavement. Diana's heart lurched just as it used to when they were first dating. He'd put gel in his hair and was carrying a bouquet of gerbera and grasses. Her subconscious urged her to rush out into the street to him, but reality stopped her. His attentions weren't meant for *her*. Her stomach swung as if she was falling from a great height and it was all she could do to prevent herself from crying out in agony. She forced herself masochistically to watch him as he stepped through the smoked glass doors of the hotel in Liesel's wake.

She remained mesmerized, staring at the space he had left behind. Those broad shoulders, the gelled hair, which had once been hers.

'*Mademoiselle,* are you alright?' The waiter stood over her looking worried.

She realised tears were streaming down her cheeks. She rubbed them away and thrust a banknote into his hand and fled.

Diana only came to once settled back on the train. She couldn't remember any part of the journey back to Austerlitz. It wasn't until the train left the capital behind that she could begin to think straight again. Her mission was accomplished; she'd seen it with her own eyes. She would never be able to trust him again, that had changed forever. Her fervent love for him had been turned to inexplicable pain.

# THIRTY-NINE

## Hélène

Hélène did not notice the cold as she cycled up the gently sloping lane to Jaunay. She did not notice the ache in her legs as the gradient increased. All thoughts of Cottereau and the drop were pushed out of her mind. Antoine Meffret was hers. She hardly dared believe it. She thought of London, if they were to get wind of it they might pull her out. She could not bear the thought of leaving Antoine, of leaving his father with no one to look after them. As she stepped through the front door of the surgery she could hear voices coming from the dining room.

The doctor opened the door and called to her, 'Hélène, come in, come in. I would like you to meet our new school teacher. You have met *Monsieur* Cottereau.'

Philippe Cottereau bowed low and shook her hand. '*Mam'selle* Godard. We meet again.'

'This is Edouard Moreau. He has taken over as school master.'

Edouard Moreau was a tall, wiry man. He was wearing an expensive looking suit; curious for the meagre wages of a schoolmaster. The young man shook Hélène's hand. '*Mademoiselle.*'

'*Mademoiselle* Godard is our nurse. We have been so lucky to have her, with so few available to help. Welcome to Jaunay and if I can be of service please don't hesitate to ask.'

As soon as she could Hélène politely extracted herself from the guests and went up to her room. She needed to think. She must find out about the diesel. She needed to know whose side Cottereau was on. Was he responsible for the disappearance of the containers? Bringing down such a powerful man would be dangerous indeed but if she must, she must.

## Diana

Pulling into the village along the same route she had taken five months before, Diana was a different woman. The poppy field was now bare like her heart. All those months before she had been a respectable young wife and mother, now she felt like a discarded dishcloth. Dusk was drawing in. A tractor was ploughing a field with its headlights

257

illuminated. She thought of *Madame* Camaret in her kitchen, no doubt warming a *pot au feu* stew or a *cassoulet* in one of her huge cauldrons that sat on the range. She would be looking forward to her strapping boys coming in from the fields, tired and hungry. She would share their conversation on the day's events. She could just make out a light in Michaud's window at the end of the lane and smoke coming out of the chimney. She continued past, trying not to think of her fireplace bereft of warmth and her lonely bedroom in which love and security were nothing but a distant memory.

*La Petite Folie* was busy. Claude and Marcel were sipping their glasses of pastis. Frédeau, Jeanette's son was manning the bar.

'Aah, Diana! Ben is eating his supper in the kitchen with *Maman.*' He gestured for her to go through.

Concerned by her possibly blotchy appearance from her tears, she scuttled past mumbling, '*Bonsoir*'.

'*Maman*!' shrieked Ben, standing up on his chair delighted.

Diana only just managed to sweep him up into her arms before he toppled off sideways.

'What did you buy?' asked Jeanette eagerly.

'Buy?' That morning had seemed such a long time ago her fictitious shopping trip had escaped her memory. 'Err, not much,' she replied lamely.

'Diana, your face!'

'It's the cold I think. Thank you for looking after Ben,' she said to divert her. 'Well I'd better get him home and bathed.'

'I'm coming to help you.'

'I don't need any help. Anyway you've got customers.'

'Frédeau will deal with them. I'm coming with you,' she repeated firmly.

Diana was glad of some friendly company but she knew that Jeanette was on to her and she didn't feel like digging it all up just yet, she'd had enough for one day. Too weary to argue she let Jeanette load the pushchair into the back of her car and pulled up the dark lane to the *Champ de Foire*.

With Ben bathed and tucked up in bed Jeanette produced a small bottle of brandy from her bag with a gleam in her eye. 'Come on, you're always going on about how we French don't do the girls' night out thing; well this is a girls' night in.'

'Jeanette, I'm really tired.' Apart from anything she didn't think she could ever drink brandy again.

'Yes, I can see that. But there's something else isn't there?'

Diana opened her eyes as wide as she could in order to look as if she had no idea what Jeanette was talking about.

'I saw your car at the station. You didn't go to Blois did you?'

Diana took a deep breath, she couldn't hold up the façade any longer. The tears came cascading down her face once more, like a fountain. She wondered whether it was possible to become dehydrated from crying.

Jeanette sat sipping her brandy and listened patiently until Diana had finished. 'What are you going to do?'

'I really don't know! What can I do?'

'Well, you need to think about it quickly. If you're going to leave him you need to think where you will go, there's Ben to think about too.'

'All I know, is I can't stay with him, but if I were to actually leave I could only go back to England.' Diana thought of her mother in her cottage in Little Watcombe and her father in Watcombe House. She thought of how she would have to choose between them if she returned. Was this what she was doing to Ben? Would he have to choose between them? If she was to return to England Ben wouldn't even have that choice. 'I couldn't go back to England. This is my home. I'm not leaving.'

'When is he due back?'

'Friday.'

'Right, that gives you four days to work out what to do. You get to bed and I'll be round in the morning.'

'Jeanette, honestly I'll be fine.'

Alone at last Diana went into the bedroom. It smelled of Serge's cologne. His wardrobe door was swung open revealing an assortment of designer jackets and trousers. It felt like a mausoleum; worse - a mausoleum for someone who wasn't dead. She pulled the sheets off the bed and put them in the washing machine and switched it on. She found some clean ones in the airing cupboard and remade the bed. She emptied Serge's wardrobe into bin liners and stacked his unbelievable number of pairs of shoes in boxes and dragged the whole lot out to the garage. She went to shut the wardrobe door but decided against it, with it open she could be sure that not a remnant of his possessions remained in her vicinity. She at last felt able to sink beneath the clean, fresh smelling sheets and slept surprisingly well.

The cold light of day only brought the reality of a miserable situation crashing back with more certainty than ever. She heard Ben stirring in his bedroom forcing her out of bed and into action. Ben had to go to school. She would only have to show a brave face until he was on the bus.

She was just walking past *La Petite Folie* when Jeanette came bounding out of the *épicerie*.

'Diana, come in for a moment, there's someone I'd like you to meet.'

Diana stepped into the little shop. A rather smart lady stood next to the counter smiling.

'Diana this is *Madame* Ségur, from the *Château de Montgommery.*'

'How do you do?' said Diana politely holding out a hand, not feeling in the slightest bit gracious.

'I am told that you are the lady who made those delicious *pissaladières* and those, how do you say, crumbles?'

Diana blushed. 'I'm glad you liked them.'

'I was wondering if you make anything else?'

Diana hesitated, Jeanette was standing behind the lady mouthing 'yes' at her and nodding her head vigorously.

'Yes,' she said obediently and racked her brains for something to add.

'My grandson is going to be baptised shortly and we're holding an informal late summer party to celebrate.'

Diana looked at the woman's elegant clothing and decided there was nothing informal about this lady.

'I can't get a caterer at such short notice, you see the baptism is in two weeks.' She pulled out a small diary from her Hermès bag. 'Yes, Sunday 25th September. My son lives abroad and has rather left everything to the last moment.'

Diana looked at the woman, wondering what on earth she wanted with her.

'I gather you are English?'

Diana nodded, blushing a little. That had not as yet been advantage in these parts.

'We're all terribly keen on English food and we were hoping you might be able to supply a hot buffet for the guests, English-style?'

'I don't think ...'

'Yes, I'm sure she could,' Jeanette interrupted vehemently.

Diana looked at her in horror.

Jeanette avoided her gaze. 'How many guests would there be?'

'My son doesn't like big affairs so it will just be close family. Say around thirty?'

Diana knew she would never be able to cater for thirty people on her own from her little kitchen, and with Ben to look after on top it would be a nightmare.

'I would pay you well, provided the food was up to the standard of the *pissaladières* of course.'

The money was enticing but she had never done anything on that scale before. She thought quickly. She didn't want to turn the lady down, nor did she want to give her a definite yes without working things out a little.

'I would need to check my diary.' Diana paused. 'Perhaps, if you gave me your telephone number?'

The lady broke into a smile. 'Excellent. Here's my card. I look forward to hearing from you.' She thrust a thick embossed card with gilt edges into her hand and swept out of the door with a flourish.

The minute she'd disappeared, Diana turned on Jeanette. 'Jeanette, what *are* you up to? How on earth am I going to pull that one off? I don't have a big enough oven, nor a big enough car to transport it all to the chateau.'

'Come on Diana, this is exactly what you need. You'll work it out, it'll be fine.'

Diana was left stunned. How had all that happened? She'd allowed herself to be bullied into it. She would go and see *Madame* Camaret and the minute she got back she'd phone *Madame* Ségur and tell her she was sorry but she couldn't possibly do it. As she walked up the road towards the Camaret farm she realised she hadn't thought about Serge for a whole hour. The moment she did, the feeling of desolation engulfed her spirit once more.

*Madame* Camaret's face lit up when she saw her. '*Ma Bichette!*' she exclaimed excitedly. 'Come in, come in. Surely you haven't run out of onions already?'

'Oh no!' She managed a smile. 'Are you busy?'

'Not at all, a nice warm coffee? My boys saw you out riding the other day, they were quite impressed.'

'I used to ride a lot when I was growing up.'

'Aah, Hélène used to ride too. Of course back then the only horses in the village were old nags, the ones the Germans didn't steal. She rode them anyway.'

'Hélène, was your best friend wasn't she?'

'Yes, I suppose she was. She nursed me through an infected leg and that was how we met. Hélène Charles. It's funny I had not thought about her for so many years. She called her little boy Charles. Aah, he was so like his mother, thick dark hair and beautiful blue eyes, quite unusual.'

'I used to be Diana Hunter.'

'And I, Agnès Joly. We are still who we are Diana. Our circumstances change and we change with them, but deep down we are who we were. I married very young, but I married a good man. If you married for love you were one of the lucky ones for there was no way out if you didn't. Things were different then. It was the war and nobody really had any control over their destiny. Life is different now. Women can make their own choices. When France was occupied by the Nazis we were too scared to get close to people. If you fell out with somebody they could find an excuse to tell the Germans about something you were doing, which could get you into very serious trouble and even have you shot. There was no trust between people. But you, you've got your whole life in front of you. If you want to change something in it, you must do it, whatever it is. Hélène fought for her country and for France. She fought for Antoine and for the villagers. The villagers didn't thank her for it of course. But she never fought for herself. If she had, she would still be here now.'

'Serge ....' Diana faltered 'is having an affair.'

*Madame* Camaret gasped. 'Are you sure?'

'Yes, I followed him yesterday, in Paris.'

'That was a brave thing to do. Have you asked him about it?'

'No, he doesn't know I know. He's still there with *her*... in a hotel.' Her stomach flipped in abhorrence. 'He's not due back until Friday.'

'Do you still love him?'

'I, I don't know.'

'If you are both strong you can get through this.'

'That's just the problem. He isn't strong. He is weak. And as you said the other day; if you are unlucky enough to marry a weak man you must find the strength to pull you both through. I simply don't have that strength.'

'Oh Diana! Don't pay any attention to me, I am only a silly old woman who sits in her kitchen all day mooning about her dead husband, and waiting for her beautiful sons to come in from the fields.'

'No, no, you were right, but the thing is not only do I not possess the strength to pull us both through, nor do I wish to find it. What you said about Hélène; if she had only fought for herself she would still be here today. I feel that I should put up with it for Ben's sake but …' She hid her face in her hands.

'Do you want to?' she said gently.

'No,' she whispered choking back the tears.

'Well, then, you must end it with him. If you stay with him, Ben will suffer. A child living in the care of an unhappy person will make him unhappy too. But remember you will have to take the consequences, a decision like that cannot be undone.'

'No.' Diana took a deep breath and let out a long sigh. '*Madame* Camaret? What happened to Hélène?'

The old lady shook her head. 'Not now, *ma bichette.* It is a sad story and you have sadness enough at the moment.'

## Edward

Three days had passed and Edward had been waiting for a sign from Clothilde that the *Seigneur* was feeling better. But there had been silence. He waited for the day to give up its heat and for the sun to set deep below the earth before he ventured out of the forest and to the pasture. He knew his way through the woods so well by now that he no longer needed to mark the tree trunks or check the position of the moon.

He got to the field and glanced furtively towards the village. There was a little smoke rising from the odd chimney but not a soul stirred. He quickly ambled over to the well and leaned inside. Sure enough, the pouch was settled in the crevice. He opened it eagerly to read Clothilde's message. But the message was his own, the one he had left just before her last visit to him. She cannot have picked it up on her way back to the village. He lifted out the jar and felt carefully around the inside of the bag, but there was nothing from Clothilde. Then he leant into the well again and ran his hand over the rough surface of the crevice lest he had missed something. There was nothing. Maybe he had made a mistake with the time. Perhaps she was returning to the chateau the day after tomorrow, she was still mastering writing. He would leave it another day – that must be it. He returned to the den trying not to give in to his heavy heart.

# FORTY

## Diana

Diana had picked another barrowful of apples and was struggling to push it up the grassy slope to the back terrace. The ground was wet and the wheel was sinking in. This would be her third batch of Apple Crumble. It seemed the villagers couldn't get enough of them. She could hear the phone ringing through the kitchen window. She abandoned her task gladly and rushed off to answer it before the answering machine took over.

'*Madame* Lescure?' A man's voice echoed over the wires.

'Yes, speaking.'

'I am calling from *L'Hôtel de Gaulle* in Maisons-Alfort.'

She held her breath.

'You left your scarf in the hotel when you checked out this morning.'

'I think you're mistaken,' she stopped abruptly as realisation dawned on her. How could she? How could he?

'*Madame*, are you there?'

'Sorry, would you send it on to me?' She gave the man her address and put the phone down. She sat down next to the phone stunned. Jealousy was an unknown concept for Diana. Was this what she was feeling? Or was it humiliation? Jealousy - the feeling of wanting something that someone else has got. But she certainly didn't want anything Liesel had; not even Serge. He would never be hers not after what she'd seen. Before they'd moved to the country she had thought he was, but now that she thought back to Ben's birth, Serge had always been off doing something more 'worthwhile' than spending time with his son or his wife.

Everyone had a wife. Why shouldn't he? He had a foreign one at that. Full marks on the exotica levels. She pulled herself up. Come off it. He *had* loved her and she had loved him. She marvelled at her use of the pluperfect. Just a few days ago she'd loved him in the present. She remembered watching that burly man looking back at her as she walked up the aisle. Every eye in the congregation was on her. She could feel his adoring gaze searing through her as she approached the altar. She was sure her mother had been in tears, she was almost in tears herself with the sheer emotion of it all. But now she couldn't have been more certain that that love was gone. *Madame* Camaret was right, she had the choice to free herself now. She didn't even care that Serge and Liesel had booked into the hotel using her name, because it wasn't her name. She wasn't Diana Lescure, she wasn't Diana Hunter either. It had been a long journey. She was just Diana.

Serge was due back in twenty-four hours. She felt no emotion, just a dull numbing of the senses. There was no fear or hatred. Ben would be safe out of harm's way at school. She prayed the scarf would arrive before Serge returned then there would be no need for him to know that she had followed him. Of course there was a chance that he would bump into Christian, who may possibly ask how his surprise lunch went. The scarf would be her evidence. It would be her lever to get him to leave. She was not going to upheave Ben from his life in the village. *She* had chosen this house, *she* had dug the garden and cleared the brambles and painted the walls herself. This was her home.

For all Serge's bravery at a disaster scene, when faced with the trivia of family life he crumbled. It was almost as if he needed the thrill of danger all the time. He needed adrenalin to survive. She looked out of the window through the thinning foliage of the weeping willow and down to the poplars and the forest beyond. Here was peace and serenity. No adrenalin, no excitement just a calm and cosy existence. He would most likely move back to Paris and take up his frenzied partying again, and meet another girl, in another bar. Somehow she felt she could cope with that idea, but the thought of him establishing a lasting relationship with Liesel made her blood boil. Betrayal was an altogether different thing.

The phone rang again, she hesitated to answer it for fear it would be Serge. It could also be the school, something could have happened to Ben. She reluctantly picked up the receiver.

'*Bonjour Madame.*' Came the shrill voice of *Madame* Ségur.

Damn! She thought. She'd meant to ring her and turn her down. If she was to split with Serge she would need as much money as she could get. What was the worst that could happen? The meal could be revolting, her reputation as a cook could plummet and all that in front of an assembly of local high society.

'*Madame*? Are you there?'

'Er, yes. Sorry. Yes. *Madame* Ségur I was just about to call you. I've checked my calendar and Sunday the 25th will be fine.'

'*Superbe!*'

'Let me work out some menus and I shall call you to discuss them.'

'Tonight will be convenient. Come up to the chateau about six o'clock.'

'Right. Erm. Yes six o'clock it is then.' Why was it that people with money always knew how to get what they wanted out of people? And on the double! Or maybe it was for that reason that they *were* rich. She would have to ask Jeanette to have Ben again. Well, it *was her* idea after all.

She looked at the barrowful of apples on the back terrace, she wouldn't have time to peel and slice them now. Sighing she made herself a sandwich from the rest of the breakfast baguette and took it to the dining table where her cookery books had now taken up permanent residence.

This time she consulted *Constance Spry.* That had been Cook's bible at Watcombe House, she'd given it to Diana as a keepsake when her parents had divorced and been obliged to dismiss her.

She turned to the chapter entitled '*Some Special Parties'.* The first suggested menus threatened possibilities such as *Galette aux Fraises* or White Coffee Ice, *Fritto Misto* and *Pommes de Terre Siciliennes.* Diana shivered and began to wish she had paid more attention at that expensive cookery course her mother had insisted she attend after leaving school. What was she getting herself into? She didn't fancy attempting to make such complicated dishes as *Cornets de Jambon Lucullus* or *Consommé aux Paillettes d'Or.* Besides she had been asked for English-style food. She sighed and turned the page. There she found a menu that looked to be more in keeping with her knowledge and ability. Granted *millefeuille* was French but *Madame Ségur* wasn't to know they didn't have it in England!

*Mulligatawny Soup*
*Sliced Scottish salmon garnished with asparagus tips*
*Chicken Millefeuille (a mousse of chicken in layers of crisp pastry)*
*Baked Ham with Cumberland Sauce*
*Stuffed Eggs*
*Celery stuffed with cheese*
*Rose Petal Ice*
*Strawberries in Muscat Syrup*

The Rose petal ice put her slightly on edge, but she knew that this was the sort of menu *Madame* Ségur would expect. There were no ingredients that might prove difficult to get hold of at this time of year, except for the rose petal jam of course which could possibly be difficult to get hold of at any time of year. Never mind, if she had to change at the last minute she would. She set about translating the dishes into French and set them out on a piece of velvety bond paper for the *Châtelaine's* perusal. When she had finished she sat back pleased with her work. The menu was a perfect mix of English dishes rounded off with French panache and all in keeping with the 'late summer party' *Madame* Ségur had requested.

Jeanette was delighted to take charge of Ben once more and Diana, armed with her menu, drove off to the chateau. She couldn't quite bring herself to drive her rusty car up the long sweeping gravelled drive of *Château de Montgommery*. Apart from the shame of arriving at such a magnificent edifice in an inappropriately shabby vehicle, she needed a little time to organise her opening line and speech without her ineffectual suspension heralding her arrival well before time. Not daring to step on to the pristine lawn, she crunched over the gravel as discreetly as she could towards the smooth stone archway. On the other side of it, was what looked like a mini quadrangle. It was edged with a path of small rectangular paving stones and in the centre a neat square of grass bearing a stone well. Beyond was a low stone wall enclosing a sumptuous rose garden. The late summer blooms glowed in almost every colour. There was a large wooden double door set with an ornate knocker of a staff intertwined with a serpent. She lifted it and winced as it fell back against the wood sending an echo through the passages within.

*Madame* Ségur opened the door. Diana smiled and held out her hand. She ignored it and blankly ushered her into what looked like a drawing room furnished in ornate gold and white Louis XIV furniture. Her manner was no longer as gracious as it had been when they'd met at the shop. She seemed distracted as if Diana's visit was not as important as she had purported at their first meeting.

'Please, come through to the kitchen.' She swept off down a corridor and into a huge kitchen which could have been quite happily portrayed in a Jane Austen novel, bar the shiny stainless steel industrial sized cooker. She sat down at a large slab oak table covered with dents and cuts.

Diana managed to tear herself away from the gothic elegance of the property to find *Madame* Ségur sitting stock still and staring at her expectantly. Diana jolted into action and produced her menu. *Madame* Ségur slipped her glasses, which were hanging round her neck from a gold chain, onto the end of her nose. Diana watched her face intently, one eye went up in what appeared to be disapproval and Diana began to prepare herself for a quick exit. When she got to the end, *Madame* Ségur removed her glasses and smiled.

'I think that will be perfect. I think we said thirty people didn't we?'

'Err, yes. I must say though, I have never done this before.'

'Oh, I don't think that is entirely true.'

It was Diana's turn to raise her eyebrows.

'Only the other day *Père* Auguste was telling me what a splendid spread you provided for your guests at your own son's baptism.'

Now Diana really was surprised, she would never have imagined that *Père* Auguste would have harboured even an ounce of approval for her.

'The ceremony will finish at around noon. So I imagine the guests will be returning here by about half past. When they arrive I would like you to serve them an *apéritif*.'

'I didn't think I would have to provide drinks,' Diana exclaimed as calmly as she could.

'Oh no! My husband will choose the wines and have them delivered the week before, but I would like you to manage the service and the chambering of the wines.'

Diana's heart picked up a pace. How stupid could she be? Of course she would have to serve the buffet as well. She could feel the blood draining from her face. She really had made a fool of herself. In times like this the best thing was to own up.

'*Madame* Ségur, as I said I have never done this before and I don't have staff. I certainly wouldn't be able to manage on my own.'

*Madame* Ségur's smile disappeared. She cast an irritable eye on her as if she was bothering her with an unnecessary triviality.

Diana gave into the intimidation and added, 'But of course I'm sure I could find some help. I'm afraid it's been rather short notice to work out a price as yet.' Diana thought she was going to argue and knew that her nerves would not allow her to stand up to this powerful, elegant lady and she would cave in instantly. Instead she plumped for a long pause in the hope that it would be more effective. She tried to arrange her features into a hardened business woman's stare.

'My husband will discuss that with you.'

Diana realised that this lady was far too eloquent to talk about the filth of money, and suspected that she was rather like the queen and didn't even carry it on her person.

She walked back down the drive. She felt she ought to have been feeling triumphant, but she realised that she had now been saddled with a new problem. Not only did she have no idea how she was to cook all this food in her ill-equipped kitchen, which was by no means small but was certainly not adequately sized for the banquet she had promised to supply. Nor did she know how she was to transport it all to the chateau in her rickety old car, whose suspension would only toss the food all over the place before she even got there, but now she had to provide waitresses as well.

Back at *La Petite Folie*, Marcel was jiggling Ben on his lap.

'How did it go?' Jeanette was pouring a *demi* of beer for Marcel.

Diana pulled a face. 'She liked my menu, but now she wants waitress service. I don't know why I agreed to it, the whole thing seems to have got completely out of hand.'

'We'll think of someone, you've still got two weeks. How are those apple crumbles coming on? I've sold out again.'

'Oh no! I completely forgot they're still at home.'

'I had a thought. Could you make some *compôte*? You know sort of country style. That's a good way of using up your cookers.'

'Yes, I could I suppose. I'd have to get some jars though.'

'Don't worry about that, I've got a load of clip top jars out the back in the shed. You'd need to get new seals of course. You've got the car outside?'

Diana nodded.

'Right, Marcel you'll help us won't you? We'll load it up now. You go with Diana and help her unload. Ben's perfectly happy here with me. When you're done you can come back for him.'

The last thing Diana wanted to do now was to wade through the cobwebs of Jeanette's shed, but Marcel was already on his feet so she followed him obediently into the kitchen to the back door.

It took a good half hour to load the car and drive to the *Champ de Foire*. She managed to fight off Marcel's insistence to help her unload them. She was at the end of her physical tether and really didn't have any energy left to find a place for them where Léo wouldn't knock them over.

She left the car in the courtyard and walked back to the café for Ben. He was tired and fractious and had decided to be difficult. He walked as slowly as was physically possible without actually standing still. He stopped to examine just about anything he could find on the ground; litter, a bit of stone, even a cigarette end. Diana managed to quash her irritation knowing that if she were to chide him he would only get worse and bedtime would end up being a long drawn out stressful affair. They were just walking past Mémère Claudette's front door when they heard a shout from the direction of the café, she turned to see who it was. It was difficult to see in the twilight but the shadow resembled Michaud. Michaud! Michaud, the murderer! She pulled Ben's hand. She would carry on as if she hadn't seen him.

Ben stamped his feet and shouted, '*Non!*'

In desperation she picked him up and walked fast towards the house. She could hear footsteps. Michaud must have crossed the road and was coming after her. Had he already heard that her marriage was over? Perhaps he was coming to claim her and her property for himself. Perhaps she was to be the object of his new plan. She walked faster, managing to resist the temptation to break into a full-scale sprint. She was nearly there, nearly at the gate. Surely he would give up if she could only manage to get through it, into the safety of her own garden. He had speeded up too, he was gaining on her. Her pulse was thumping. What did he want? He was almost upon her, she put her hand on the handle of the gate. A hand touched the back of her jacket, she swung round violently ready to shake him off.

'Didn't you hear me? What's the matter?'

She was about to run inside the gate and shut it back in his face, when he waved Ben's bag in the air.

'You dropped this!'

'Oh, Ben's bag.' Diana's face burned with her own foolishness. Even if he *had* ripped the old man off, or even suffocated him on his sick bed it didn't mean he would chase her in the dark and attack her. 'It was dark. I didn't know it was you.'

He simply nodded, his face betraying feelings of sadness. He turned and trudged back towards the café his shoulders hunched.

# FORTY-ONE

## Hélène

As she cycled into the courtyard at *Ferme* Meffret Antoine stepped out of the barn smiling.

'Shouldn't you be out in the fields?'

'I knew you would be arriving about now.' He looked around and when he was sure there was no one in view he pulled her into the barn and kissed her hungrily.

She sank into the warmth of his embrace. She fought with her conscience as she thought of Céline Cottereau. At last she came to her senses and pushed him away.

'Antoine, you are engaged to be married.'

He sat down on a bale taking her hands in his. 'Hélène I have loved you since the first day you stepped into this farm. I thought I could marry Céline. I thought it was the right thing to do to keep Cottereau at bay.' He looked at her pleadingly. His voice faltered. 'To keep the farm.'

'To keep the farm?'

'We ran into difficulty after the Germans arrived and Cottereau offered us a way out that I could not refuse.'

'He offered you money to marry his daughter?'

'No, not in so many words, but he made it clear that there were strings attached and he encouraged me to court her. There are not very many attractive women in this area and I am not getting any younger. Céline is a pretty girl but I do not love her. I have not loved her. I hoped that perhaps one day I would learn to love her.'

'But surely if you break off with her you will put the farm in danger again?'

'It is the farm or my life, and Hélène I would like you to be my life.'

She touched her fingers to his lips. 'Not yet, Antoine. Wait till it is right and proper.'

'It will be, in just a few days.'

'I need to talk to you about Philippe Cottereau. I saw him the other night.' She told him about the encounter with the *Wehrmacht* officer at the back of the school.

'He is buying the diesel from the Germans?' His face was white. 'I knew he must not be getting it from an honourable source, and he charged way over the market price for it. Without the black market a lot of us could not run our farms or businesses so we just don't ask questions.'

'If Cottereau is running a racket with the Nazis he could well be informing them too, which means that we are all in danger.'

'Then I am glad I will no longer be joining his family.'

'Do you think he could be responsible for the containers disappearing?'

'He is dishonest, and it would not be unbelievable. But how would he know about the drops? Surely he would have to have been on the reception committee.'

Hélène thought back to the day she had landed in the woods. She had only seen two men. There was the man who had tried to grab her chute and Rémy. It was dark, she remembered that the first man was rather round and that his face was obscured by a scarf. Could that have been Philippe Cottereau? Had Philippe Cottereau known all along who she was? Did the doctor know too? Hélène felt uneasy. If they knew, why hadn't they made it known to her?

'Antoine, we must be very careful. I think Philippe Cottereau murdered Rémy, and that he has been stealing the containers to sell on the black market. We cannot trust him.'

Antoine gasped. 'I have done something very stupid. Philippe agreed to help with the next drop. We could all be in great danger.'

Hélène thought carefully. 'We will only be in danger if Cottereau stands to gain nothing. If he will be feeding his own greed, the drop will be safe from the Nazis. He would not inform on it if it meant him losing out. We must turn his greed to our advantage and catch him in the act. You must not break off your engagement with Céline until afterwards. We cannot risk upsetting him until we have him where we want him.'

'And what will we do with him?'

Hélène looked at him gravely and pursed her lips. 'Leave that to me.'

Antoine had fear in his eyes, but he nodded and held her tight.

## Diana

The first frost of autumn had hit the Loire Valley. The fields were clothed in a thin white veil. The chimneys in the village were puffing

273

great clouds into the sky sending an earthy smell of wood smoke across the village.

When Diana returned from the bus stop, a package was lying behind a pot of frosted, shrivelled geraniums outside the front door. She ignored it and walked round to the back door. She had at least four hours before Serge was due home. Normally he would have phoned each day he'd been away. Diana recognised the freedom of not caring or wondering why he hadn't. From now on she was the mistress of her own destiny and would no longer be beholden to anyone but herself and her beautiful little boy. Only four hours left of Diana Lescure. She was determined to savour each moment of the calm before the storm and left the package, as if non-existent, where the postman had tucked it.

She lined up Jeanette's jars on the back terrace and hosed them carefully to rid them of the majority of cobwebs and dead bugs before bringing them into the kitchen and washing them thoroughly in warm soapy water. She peeled and cored the rest of the barrow of apples, wincing as the water seeped into her cracked skin. She would have to go round and see Mémère later to ask if she could borrow her steriliser. If business was going to carry on like this she would have to invest in her own. She looked at her watch, just an hour and a half left. She filled her preserving pan once again, added the sugar and lit the stove.

Only then did she turn her mind to the biggest thing she had ever done in her life. She retrieved the parcel from the geranium pot, now a little damp round the edges and opened one end. The smell of Liesel's perfume wafted out of the brown paper like a war cry. She closed it quickly; she couldn't bear to look at it, not until she had to. This was betrayal in its physical form, a scarf doused in another woman's perfume. She stuffed the package into the top drawer of the dresser where it would be easily retrievable without leaving the room.

Serge would most probably drive through the gate into the courtyard and round into the garage. She pictured him walking up the back steps to the kitchen. She had to concentrate on keeping level-headed and denying the revulsion that her emotions were forcing on her. She must separate herself from the situation; she must not show any anguish that may be misconstrued as vulnerability.

He would call out, 'Salut!' in that high-pitched tralala that they had adopted since early on in their relationship. Her stomach did a somersault. She thought hard. Where must she be when he found her?

Should she be in the garden digging, so that he would have to search for her? No, it would be too easy for her to carry on working as if nothing had happened. She must confront him and go through with it. She must be sitting at the table ready for him. She looked around the house searching out any mess that would need urgently clearing before he arrived. Irritated at her conditioning she wondered at the tidiness. Normally there would be toys strewn in corners, Ben's bottle of hot chocolate left abandoned on the sofa, a pile of dirty laundry in front of the washing machine. But today, ironically, the house was ordered and spotless just the way Serge liked it. That's just what she must do, have everything the way he liked it; a tidy, elegant wife with a house to match. She would hold everything he had always wanted dangling in front of his nose like a carrot, and then take it all away in a split second. She began to feel a little stronger, humiliation was beginning to leave her and the sweet smell of revenge was setting in.

She looked at her apple splattered cuffs. She dug out her tightest jeans which would show off her figure, now not quite so dumpy with all the gardening. She pulled a belt through the loops and brushed her hair. As she reached for her make-up bag she caught the twinkle of her engagement ring flashing in the mirror. With tears in her eyes she wrenched it off, together with her wedding ring. There. Just some make-up to cover up any redness on her eyes and she was prepared for battle.

What if he was late? There could be heavy traffic from Paris on a Friday. She heard a car coming up the *rue de l'Abreuvoir* past Marcel's place. She dashed to the window, but couldn't see any movement through the bars of the iron gate. She waited. No car pulled up outside the church, or paused at the gate. It must have gone straight on.

Léo was scratching at the back door to come in. As she turned to take up her place in the window once more, she heard a car crunch on the gravel outside the church. This time it was unmistakeable, she recognised the sound of the engine. The crunching ceased and the engine fell silent. He'd parked in front of the church. He only did that if he was planning to go out again. That would make things easier. She heard the car door slam.

She leapt to the top drawer of the dresser and pulled the silk scarf from its brown paper sarcophagus. She held her breath to fend off the fumes of the heady perfume and wrapped it about her neck. Praying that she wouldn't pass out with the smell of treachery, she sat at the table facing the French windows onto the front terrace. That way he wouldn't be able to miss her. She took a deep breath and forced herself to stare straight ahead at the opening iron gate.

Serge's foot came first, and then his trousered leg, finally his suede jacket with the collar turned up, rock-star fashion. And then, the unthinkable happened; close behind him appeared a blonde head, hair tightly scraped back into a pony tail. Red lipstick flashed in contrast with the yew hedge and the fake fur jacket floated with the stealth of a vixen stalking its prey.

The sun was at its highest in the sky and must have been reflecting off the windows, as it was obvious that neither of them could see her sitting waiting solemnly. Diana wanted to run, she had counted on him being alone. She mustn't let them get the better of her. She must remain seated, stalwart in her mission.

Serge opened the door. Liesel, who had arranged her face into a smile, gasped and laid her hand flat on her throat as she realised her scarf was missing.

Diana stood up. 'How nice to see you both,' she said with a steely smile. 'Did you come to pay your old friend a visit, Liesel?'

Neither of them replied or moved as they took the scene in.

'I really wasn't expecting the pleasure of both of you. But hey ho! The more the merrier,' Diana jeered.

'Diana,' murmured Serge.

'Oh, Liesel, I think you must have lost your scarf.' Diana pulled it from her neck. Liesel stepped forward and tried to take it from her, but Diana tossed it out of her reach. 'Oh, no, now I think this must be Exhibit A for the divorce court, it would be very careless of me if I let it fall into the wrong hands.'

'Diana, we can talk about this.' Serge was holding up his hands as if in surrender.

'But Serge, I think we already are.' Diana was beginning to enjoy herself.

'Where did you get it?' Liesel snapped.

'Apparently, *Madame* Lescure left it at her hotel room in Maisons-Alfort. How clever of you to choose a hotel with such caring staff. They made every effort to return it.'

'Liesel, go and get in the car.' Serge's voice was wavering now.

'What a shame! And we hadn't seen each other for such a long time!' Diana had had no idea that she could do sarcasm so professionally.

Liesel turned and stomped back along the path to the gate, her stilettos clip clopping on the uneven paving stones. Diana willed her to catch a heel in the gaps, and trip.

'What the hell are you playing at?' growled Serge as soon as they were alone.

'Come on Serge. Even you must realise that the game is up.'

'There was no game. I was going to tell you this weekend.'

'How gracious of you!' Diana sat down, without an audience to play to she didn't feel she could keep the hard act up. She stared down at the grain in the tabletop to obscure her face from his view.

'Liesel and I,' he paused searching for his words, 'We're in love.'

She stared at him in disbelief. A fling, an affair, a mistake – yes, she could cope with that. But love? Now that was underhand.

'She's asked me to move in with her.'

She was supposed to be kicking *him* out. She was supposed to be the top dog in this parting of the ways. He'd stolen her thunder. Wasn't she already losing enough? Not once had it dawned on her that Serge may have been planning to leave already. She couldn't look at him now. She wanted him to go. She needed him to go. She stared hard at the little knife marks on the table which Serge had accidentally made when trimming down a candle for their first Christmas lunch together.

'I'm sorry,' he began.

'Just go!' she whispered not trusting her voice on any higher volume.

'Diana.'

'Go, go, go!' Her eyes shut tight, her voice reaching crescendo. When she reopened them he was gone. All that remained was Liesel's scarf. She couldn't bear the smell of it any longer and stuffed it back into the package and sealed the stench of adultery into its interior, and stowed it back in the top drawer of the dresser. She sat back down and stared at the iron gate from whence the banshees who had turned her life upside down had come. What had seemed like a few seconds must have turned into a good hour. She shook herself from her trance. She must pick herself up and soldier on, just get on with it. She filled the jars with *compôte* and delivered them to the café as if in a dream.

**Edward**

'*Frère!*' The whisper sounded like a man's voice.

277

Edward sat very still. Who was this calling him?

'*Frère*, it is I, Firmin.'

Firmin? What was he doing here? Edward gathered himself up and raised his head through the hole between the roots of the great oak. 'Firmin. What are you doing here at this late hour? Is it your mother? Is she unwell?'

'No, no. It is very bad news. They have taken Clothilde.'

'Who has taken her?'

'Montgommery's men.'

'Come down by the fire, here. Sit with me and tell me what has happened.'

'They came to our home. There were three of them on horses with the sheriff and they arrested her.'

'On what charge?'

'They say she is trying to murder the *Seigneur*. After taking the remedy he fell very ill with terrible pains in his chest. He says she has poisoned him.'

'That is ridiculous. That remedy was only made up with wood betony and goutwort. It is only his cosseted lifestyle that has made him ill.'

'What are we to do?'

'Where have they taken her?'

'To the dungeons at the chateau.'

'Let me think.' He stared at Firmin for a moment as if hoping for divine intervention then he spoke. 'I shall have to step into her place, there is no other option. I must stand by my promise.'

'I will come with you.'

'No, I must think first. I must be certain that Clothilde will be released. Now, leave me Firmin. Go and look after your mother and your brothers and sisters. Clothilde will be returned amongst you, I promise you that.'

Edward paced up and down outside the den in the moonlight. What am I to do? I find myself dogged by cowardice and self interest once more. This time I must avail myself of my sins. I must put this right or I shall burn in hell for eternity. They will either charge her with being a witch and she will be burned or with murder and she will hang. How can I be sure that they will take me in her place and spare her. Oh Lord, guide me in this difficult time and tell me what I must do.

Edward slept fitfully and visions of Clothilde came to him, her face once more covered in weeping sores from a long sojourn in the dank, rat ridden dungeons of the castle. Her feet in chains and her hair dull with the damp of her prison. Her cheeks were no longer pink and healthy but pale and grey in pallor. Surely this is not how it will be?

Then another image; this time *Dame* Héloïse wandering through the chateau garden, picking roses and laying them in a straw basket hung over her velvet sleeved arm. She is humming to herself as she bats off the bees that try and settle on her gathered roses. Every now and then she stops and looks wistfully into the distance though her gaze does not settle, as if she is thinking of something that preys on her through her waking hours. She looks almost expectant, as if a long dreamed of image will materialize in front of her eyes. Then she sighs and returns to her task. Her hair is even more golden than on the day of the fair, the sunlight catching it and making it glow. On her wrist is the amulet of turquoise and gold, the one he saw her wearing that day at the fair.

Edward awoke with a start. The amulet! It came to him; it was almost the same as the amulet he had seen Clothilde fidgeting with over her mother's sick bed that night.

'Is my mind playing tricks on me? Am I mixing the images of my one true love with my troubled imaginations? Or is this the Lord's guiding sign for me to follow?'

# FORTY-TWO

## Diana

There was no time to sit around moping. She must work out the price for the catering but first she needed to find some serving staff. There was Marie-Pierre; she had said work was difficult to come by in the region. Presentation might be a problem there; she would have to specify a uniform of some sort. Jeanette was her immediate thought but loathed asking her when she had the café to run and had already done her so many favours. Of course she would pay her, this would not be a favour, it would be business. There were a few other women in the village who she knew by name but she certainly wasn't on terms any more intimate than saying 'Good Morning'. In fact they didn't even stand with her as they waited for the bus to come back from Talcy.

Then there was the problem of transporting the food; her car was not nearly big enough to carry everything at once and the suspension would entirely destroy any carefully arranged dishes. She shut it from her mind; she would find a way around everything. Her cooker would have to suffice, perhaps she could warm everything that was required in *Madame* Ségur's industrial oven.

She stood up with purpose and put on her coat and headed for Marie-Pierre's. She found her sitting at the table reading a photo story magazine. Diana was relieved to find that Mémère was out visiting.

'I've never done any waitressing before.'

'Don't worry I will show you what to do and when to do it,' she said authoritatively but simultaneously thinking that no, nor had she. 'It will be easy. All you need to do is to wear a black skirt and a white shirt, I'll supply the apron. I'll be serving with you so there's really nothing to worry about.'

Marie-Pierre went quiet obviously thinking carefully about the proposition.

'Of course I'll pay you. Unfortunately I can only afford the minimum wage.'

'I'll do it.'

Diana heaved a sigh of relief, with Marie-Pierre reserved, even if she couldn't find anyone else she could pull it off.

'I saw Serge going into town earlier on, giving that friend of yours a lift.'

Diana took a deep breath giving her time to formulate a reply. There was no point pretending everything was OK. The village would find out sooner or later, she may as well take the plunge. 'Serge wasn't giving her a lift. He's gone to live with her.'

Marie-Pierre's jaw fell open. 'You mean … he's left?' Her eyes were as wide as windows.

'Yes. He has left and has gone to live with Liesel, his new lady friend in Beaugency.'

Marie-Pierre blushed to the roots of her hair.

'Don't be embarrassed, please. I promise you it is for the best.'

Marie-Pierre searched Diana's face for signs of emotional discomfort but could find none. They walked together in silence to the bus stop. She was not as animated as usual. Diana could sense her excitement as what she had told her sank in. By the time the bus arrived she could feel Marie-Pierre willing her to take Ben home quickly so she could spill the beans to the village. At least she had the decency to wait until she had left, unlike some members of the community who were so impatient to discuss the affairs of their fellow villagers they didn't care who was listening. Diana didn't hold it against her. The village would gossip for a couple of days but at least it would have come directly from Diana and that way things stood less of a chance of being twisted. She would now be the woman spurned in their midst and they would be right. She would hold her head up high. At least the weekend was upon them and she could stay in the shrouded safety of her own home for a couple of days.

The weather turned colder and the house became draughty. The log basket on the hearth was empty. Serge always stocked it up before he went back to Paris. She would have to do it herself from now on. She pulled on a jumper and her old thick walking anorak, dressed Ben in his all-in-one and wheeled the wheelbarrow down to the barn. It was heavy work loading them up. Most of them needed splitting but for the moment she would have to make do. She'd never used an axe before and she didn't fancy trying it with Ben in the wings. She worked up a sweat manoeuvring the great lumps of oak and stopped to catch her breath. She found the exercise invigorating, out in the early autumn air.

She managed to get the fire roaring in the sitting room and Diana and Ben ate their supper at the coffee table in front of the television, a luxury that had only been permitted in Serge's absence. If he could have seen her he would have no doubt labelled her an unfit mother for showing mealtimes such little reverence. Of course it was absolutely fine to shack up with an old acquaintance when the whim took you, but to eat supper on the sofa was an aberration. Anger began to surge up inside her, swamping her momentary smugness. She mentally checked it and to comfort herself she decided to do the 'unthinkable'. She would put Ben to sleep in her own bed. No more sleeping alone. Even when Ben was a newborn Serge would never allow him to sleep with them, forcing the already exhausted Diana to have to get up two or three times a night to feed him in the next room.

She awoke late to the sound of the phone ringing in the kitchen. She lay back into the pillows waiting for the answering machine to kick in. Jeanette's voice came wafting across the house with tones of urgency. She must have heard the gossip in the café last night and was no doubt a little miffed not to have got the information first hand. Daylight was filtering through a chink in the curtains. Ben was still breathing deeply next to her. She carefully sneaked from the bed so as not to wake him. She pulled on a dressing gown and a pair of espadrilles. Stepping into the sitting room she looked about her. Everything was neat and tidy, she didn't have to rush about clearing up or put her mind to intricate preparations for lunch. The day was her own, as the next would be and the next. She opened the shutters. The lawn was again frosted. The starlings had arrived for the winter and were rummaging in the fallen leaves. She shivered; it wouldn't be long before she would have to light the boiler. She wasn't even sure it worked properly.

She sat at the dining table and wrote out a shopping list. If she bought the ham directly from the pig farm in Beaugency she could cook it herself and save some money. She only had a hundred francs left of her last earnings and that wouldn't be enough. She would go and see Jeanette to see if her *compôtes* had sold. She heard a clunk and her eyes flew in the direction of the iron gate, it was only Jeanette.

'Are you alright? Marcel told me that Serge left yesterday.'

Diana made Jeanette some coffee and told her all about the events of the day before.

'You should have called me, I would have come round.'

'Honestly, I was fine. I just needed to be alone to take it all in.'

Jeanette looked a little hurt. 'But there must be something I can do.'

'You can help me with the buffet at the chateau?'

'It's next Sunday isn't it?'

'Oh Jeanette, I'm sorry I hadn't realised that's the busiest day of your week!'

'Don't worry about that, Frédeau will cover the bar and I'll ask Séverine to back him up for the coffees in the kitchen. He enjoyed it last time. Anyway I've never been inside the *Château de Montgommery*.' She grinned playfully.

'I don't suppose the *compôtes* sold did they? It's just I'm running a little short of cash.'

'Oh, I almost forgot.' And from her pocket she produced a small wodge of notes.

'This can't be right. I thought they were only selling for twenty-five francs a jar?'

'Aah, yes,' she exclaimed mischievously 'When I saw how popular they were I took the liberty, as your financial advisor, of upping the price a bit.'

## Hélène

STAND BY MOON TONIGHT STOP

Twilight was already upon them, the weather was clear though it was too early for stars. She looked above the steeple of the church but the moon was still too low in the sky. She needed to get word to Antoine quickly but she could hear *Madame* Clément clattering in the kitchen, a *pot au feu* was bubbling on the range. Supper would be served at seven. She had two hours.

'*Madame* Clément, what a lovely smell! With you in the kitchen it does not seem like wartime.'

'Oh, you flatter me.' She glowed with pride over her oversized apron.

'I just need to nip out.'

'But *Mademoiselle*, it's dark.'

'I forgot something in my bicycle basket. I won't be long.'

It took just five minutes to cycle to Saint Gabriel. The lights were lit in the kitchen of the farmhouse. She could see them from the road, they should have put the blackout up. She knocked on the kitchen door. Inside, she heard a rumbling of voices and a door deep in the farmhouse closed with a clunk.

'Hélène! What are you doing here at this time?'

'Tonight. It's tonight.'

Antoine looked out into the sky and nodded.

'Midnight at the chapel.' She got back on her bike and cycled back to Jaunay as fast as she could.

After supper she waited until the doctor was settled by the fire with a medical journal. *Madame* Clément had returned home just after serving. Hélène said goodnight to the doctor and went up to her room. She pulled on Antoine's trousers and drank in the smell of him. She took the lump of polish from its wrapping and daubed it over her face.

'Revolver – check, torch – check, compass – check.' She crept past the drawing room and slipped out of the back window of the kitchen, sliding the sash down as quietly as she could, only donning her boots once she was safely in the back garden. She checked that the blackout was pulled down over the neighbours' windows. Out over the gardens, through the vegetable plots and into a field. She took the same route as for the old monastery at Lusigny. Then she cut down the side of Saint Gabriel and headed for the forest through a field of sunflowers that had already been harvested. The spiky stalks caught her shins, even through her thick trousers. At least the ground beneath them was compacted and would leave no tracks. Not a sound came from the village.

As she reached the woods she took out her compass. Alone in the darkness amongst the trees, she could feel herself losing orientation. She stopped, took a breath and looked back to the village. Beyond St. Gabriel, directly due south was Jaunay, then Beaugency. The clearing was directly north so with her back to the village she tracked a straight line.

The woods were bigger than she remembered. She stepped amongst the damp trunks. She heard a twig crack not too far away. She stopped immediately holding her breath and flattened herself against a large oak. The moon was spilling through the bare branches of the trees, casting eerie shadows. In the distance she could see two tiny lights. It could only be about ten o'clock. The team should not assemble until eleven. The drop could happen anytime between one and four, after that the Lizzie would have to be back in British airspace. The lights didn't move, they shone at about shoulder height as if suspended in mid air. They weren't big enough to be torch lights.

Then they approached her slowly bobbing up and down. She hugged the trunk willing herself to become part of it and disappear. The lights were coming straight for her, it was no good she would have to confront them. She grabbed her torch and flashed it in the direction of the lights, her heart racing. As soon as she switched it on the lights disappeared and she caught the flash of a white tail dashing away into the woods. A deer! She leant back against the tree to catch her breath.

She set off again and quickly fell upon the edge of the clearing. Other than the dark shapes of rabbits grazing it was empty. She located the chapel and slipped through the front door. Shrouding her torch light she scrabbled at the earth by the altar and retrieved the blackout material. She hung it over every crevice of the window frame before switching her torch back on.

Once she could see properly she began to dig a little deeper in the bottom of the cavern. It was hot work but the earth was dry in the chapel and she had excavated a further foot into the ground. She then replaced the board and covered it in earth. Right she was ready. She switched off her torch light to save the battery and sat on the earthen floor and leant against the wall and closed her eyes. It would be a long exhausting night and she must appear fresh and rested for her day's work in the morning.

She woke to a strange feeling that she was not alone. She listened in the darkness, there was no sound other than the screech of an owl and the rustle of branches.

Then there was a whisper. 'How dark it is!' Came Antoine's gentle tones.

'For such a night,' she completed the password.

He slipped through the door and embraced her warmly. 'The others are on their way. They will come from different ends of the forest.'

'And the transport?'

'Hidden and camouflaged by the exit tracks. All is in place.'

One by one dark shapes slipped through the door of the chapel until all were present. Only then did Hélène flick on her light. In front of her, huddled low on the ground, were five men. Antoine sat crossed legged and next to him was a thin wiry chap. He could be no more than about eighteen, his eyes flashed left and right, he was clearly very frightened. Another, about the same age as her, leant on Antoine's shoulder companionably. There were two men who looked disturbingly similar, their clothing matched as did their moustaches, they were dressed in French army uniforms that had seen better days. Behind them stood Philippe Cottereau.

'*La nana!*' he exclaimed. 'Antoine, you didn't say it was a woman, the little nurse from Jaunay!'

'I am Francine and you will do well to remember that *Monsieur*,' she said firmly, shaking each of their hands.

'The vehicles are in place?'

The men nodded. The bank manager took out a packet of cigarettes and offered them round. Each took one and lit it drawing the smoke into their lungs as if their lives depended on it.

Philippe began to speak, 'Right. Gaston you come with me, the Camarets together and Francine and Antoine. Gilbert you go with the Camarets.'

'We need someone here in the chapel.' Hélène did not want such a frightened individual on her first exercise.

The bank manager looked at her, incredulous that she should be so bold. 'Do we now?'

'Philippe, please, she's right.' Antoine was standing up now.

'Huh. If the whole French army couldn't fight off the Germans it sure as hell won't be a woman who could do it.'

'*Monsieur* Cottereau,' she began, in a school maamish tone, 'I can understand your reluctance to take orders from a woman so I shall not give any. I shall merely make suggestions and when those suggestions are adopted I shall exchange the necessary information to complete this drop. Now, stay in position until the plane has dropped its load. Antoine and I will retrieve the first container and *Monsieur* Cottereau and Gaston the second. Bring them as quickly as possible to the chapel where we will empty them, and the Camarets will take the containers to the transport to be taken away for disposal.'

He stared at her indignantly for a moment, then his demeanour changed again to one of control and confidence. 'It is better that Gilbert stays here as lookout.'

'And you, *Monsieur* Cottereau, who will you be with?'

'Don't you worry about that my little lady, I can look after myself.'

She eyed him and decided to let it go as long as she and Antoine could get to the container first it didn't really matter.

'Formation letter 'L'. *Monsieur* Gaston at the head, the Camarets and *Monsieur* Cottereau in the middle. I will be on the point and Antoine at the end. I will make three owl screeches in quick succession. As soon as you hear them switch on your torches and hold them upwards towards the sky until the plane has dropped two containers then switch off. If you get into difficulty make one long warning screech. If you hear a warning screech immediately switch off your torch and lie flat against the ground. Don't move until you have heard two short screeches as the all clear or until circumstances oblige.'

All the men nodded except Cottereau. He just stared vacantly at her.

'You have your torches?'

They held them up.

'Torches off. One by one. Gaston first. *Allez – vite!*'

Hélène stood in the damp, cold clearing waiting for the familiar sound of the Lysander's engine. As soon as she heard its distant hum she let out three short screeches. She glanced around the clearing and all were in position and had lit their torches including Cottereau. As the plane approached she kept her eyes trained on the hatch. The first container was released and its chute once opened jolted it upwards then it floated gently towards the ground, veering towards the edge of the clearing. It landed with a soft thud in the grass. She headed off across the clearing as fast as she could. She could hear Antoine loping over the tussocks a little distance behind her. She tripped a couple of times in the darkness. When she finally got there, Cottereau was already upon it. The container was open and he was stuffing something into his jacket.

'Leave it!' she whispered.

'It is easier to carry the contents without the container.'

'Leave it!' She pulled out her revolver and stuck it into his back. 'Leave it!'

He straightened slowly and raised his arms in the air.

She let out one long owl screech and waited.

Antoine arrived close behind. 'What are you doing?' He looked genuinely shocked.

'Antoine, close up the container and with Cottereau here, carry it back to the chapel.'

Antoine nodded frowning.

Keeping the barrel of her pistol trained on Cottereau she walked behind them wondering what on earth she was going to do when they got there. Surely she wouldn't have to kill him? If she did she would have to disappear, she would have to leave this place. He was definitely the link. There was no question. They reached the chapel and the men took the container inside. At least the others would be lying flat waiting for the all clear and would not appear.

'Antoine, please empty the container and then search out the other one.' She kept her gun trained on Cottereau until all the packages were lying on the chapel floor. She looked at Antoine, now go to the others.

'You will wait for me here?'

She nodded. Antoine glanced at Philippe Cottereau whose arms were shaking above his head, sweat was dripping down his neck.

'*Allez!*'

And Antoine was gone.

'*Mademoiselle* Godard, you are a nurse. You will not hurt me, you have made promises to become a nurse and respect human life.'

'Turn around!' she bellowed. 'Philippe Cottereau you are charged with collaborating with the enemy against your country for your own personal gain and for the murder of Jean Legrand. I am Ellen Charles of the Secret Operations Executive, London and my mission is almost complete.' She held the revolver level and looked him straight in the eye and pulled the trigger.

He fell like a stone to the floor, his skull bounced as it hit the earth. She would have to move fast or Antoine and the others may come back to the chapel before time. She grabbed Cottereau's body by the shoulders and dragged him out of the chapel and around the back and laid him against the back wall in the darkness of the trees. She had to stop a couple of times to catch her breath, he was so heavy. She let out two short screeches before stepping back inside. She quickly swept the packages into the cavern and covered it over with the board. The men didn't take long to appear with the other container. They quickly emptied it and took both the empty containers to the vehicles. She was left standing with Antoine.

'Where is Cottereau?'

'He has gone.'

'Gone?'

'He ran off and we must find another hiding place for these supplies, or he may return to plunder them.'

'My hayloft will do temporarily.'

'Can you get them there now?'

'If we can get them to the transport we can drop them off tonight.'

The men returned and they loaded each of them up with the packages. Antoine picked up the last of them.

'You will go back to the surgery now?'

'I will stop by at the farm on the way.'

He kissed her and stepped into the darkness after the men. As soon as they were gone Ellen dragged the body back to the chapel and with the packages gone, he fitted perfectly in the cavern. She pushed the board over and covered it with earth.

She set back off across the fields until she reached Antoine's farm. All was quiet in the courtyard. They must already have unloaded. She pushed the front door to quietly, not wanting to knock and wake old *Monsieur* Meffret. Antoine was sitting by the range waiting for her. He stood up and kissed her warmly.

'I will break my engagement with Céline today.'

'Before you do, I must tell you that I am in great danger and I must disappear. As long as I am here I am putting you in danger too. I have written a message to my contact. He will be in touch to distribute the supplies. Check the laying boxes everyday for a reply. He knows who you are. Antoine, I love you and I will be back. I am sorry that I cannot tell you everything now but your ignorance will protect you.' She kissed him warmly and with tears in her eyes she stepped back into the night and was gone.

# FORTY-THREE

## Diana

The landscape was grey and unappetising. The sunflower fields had been pillaged of their seed heads and were nothing but dead brown stalks sticking up haphazardly at all angles. Only some of the fields had been turned over ready for the winter wheat.

With Ben strapped into the back seat Diana was returning from the supermarket. She had managed to pick up the ham from the pig farm in Beaugency. She slowed the car to turn right towards Saint Gabriel. As she approached the Camaret's farm, there was a huge bang under the car. The back of the car seemed to have collapsed onto the road. It skidded and scraped along the ground until it swerved into the ditch.

Ben was screaming. She sat in shock for a moment. She was certain she hadn't hit anything. The rear wheels seemed to have buckled under the chassis. Her car door was jammed against the side of the ditch so she climbed through the car into the back and unclipped Ben from his harness to comfort him. She stroked his hair and made soothing noises until his sobbing subsided. She hadn't brought his buggy with her. She would have to carry him to the village for help. She heard a car approaching from the Jaunay road, but it went straight on, a puff of black smoke rising in its wake. Diana swore. The number plate had a 75 on it, a Parisian. Then she picked out the sound of a tractor engine in the distance. It chugged onto the Saint Gabriel road and Diana's heart sank when she recognised Michaud at the wheel. It was as if he could smell when she was in trouble. The one person that everyone had warned her off seemed to be the only one who was around when she needed a hand.

He stopped behind her and got out. He ran towards the car anxiously. 'Diana, Diana!' he called frantically.

Witnessing his concern, the full realisation of what could have happened hit her. Tears began to race uncontrollably down her cheeks and she started to shake. She tried to pull herself together but delayed shock had seized her. Ben, feeling his mother's body convulsing, began to howl again.

Michaud pulled open the passenger door and Diana let him take Ben from her lap. As soon as Ben was in Michaud's arms he stopped howling and just gazed up at the big man in wonder. He sat him in the passenger seat of the tractor and came back for Diana. He took her hand, the warmth of his palm was comforting. He helped her to clamber onto the road and led her still shaking to the tractor.

Ben already seemed to have recovered and was chanting, 'Tractor, tractor!'

Without a word Michaud climbed into the driver's seat and started up the engine. He negotiated the cumbersome vehicle around Diana's car and rumbled into the village. He pulled up outside the church and with the same gentleness he lifted Ben down and opened the garden gate. She fumbled for her keys, and he waited patiently while she unlocked the back door. Just as she opened it she remembered the shopping.

'The food! It's all still in the car.'

'Leave it to me. You go in, I'll sort it out.'

She nodded obediently and watched him swagger back up the path and through the door. Her body seemed to give up. Fatigue swept down through her bones like a tidal wave. She dragged her energy up to make some sandwiches for Ben, and put him to bed for his afternoon sleep. She settled herself on the sofa and was asleep in no time at all.

When she awoke rain was lashing at the windows and the sky was very dark. She had no idea what time it was. No sound came from Ben's room. There was a tap on the door to the back terrace. She opened it. In the gloom was a large figure clothed in bright orange waterproofs. Michaud was standing in a sea of carrier bags; in his arms he was brandishing the ham.

'Are you feeding the five thousand?'

'Thank you so much,' she said laughing.

'I'm sorry it took so long. We had to get a breakdown truck from Jaunay to take your car away. It couldn't be towed.'

'I'm sorry I went to pieces earlier on.'

'I'm not surprised you did. You were very lucky. The back axle snapped. I don't know how it didn't come up through the floor and hit Ben.'

She carried the shopping into the kitchen. Michaud remained politely on the doorstep. She knew she should invite him in. The rain was dripping off him in rivulets. She wondered if he knew that Serge had left her. The whole village must know by now. Or was he just being neighbourly?

'I expect you have plenty to catch up on now that I've taken up your afternoon,' she said in the hope of dismissing him.

He didn't move.

She tried her new found long pause treatment she'd used on *Madame* Ségur, but that would require looking deep into his eyes and she knew that was best avoided.

'Yes, I mean, no.' He looked down at his muddy boots. 'I'd better get on,' he stammered, obviously disappointed. He turned to go up the path, but hesitated and turned back. 'If you need anything…'

'I shan't need anything,' she interrupted. He did know about Serge, she was certain now.

The phone rang. '*Madame* Lescure? This is *Bonnet & Fils.*'

'*Oui.*'

'The garage in Jaunay. Your car.'

'Yes, of course. Thank you for picking it up.'

'You were very lucky *Madame.* The little boy he is lucky to be alive. I have worked out an estimate for you. I am afraid it will be a lot of money. We think around eight thousand francs. This is a big job. The damage to the car was extensive.'

Eight thousand francs was nearly a thousand pounds. How was she going to pay that?

'Shall we go ahead and order the parts?'

'Err, no. Could you give me a day or two? I'll give you a call.'

'Of course, that is no problem at all. But I must warn you that such a large part would need to come from Paris and that may take a few days, not to mention the time it will take to mend it.'

She wondered if the car was even worth eight thousand, she was sure it wasn't. But she needed a car. With the baptism in just seven days she couldn't do without it. At least she already had the bulk of the shopping, except the rose petal jam. She cursed Serge for buying her such a clapped out vehicle while he jaunted about in his state-of-the-art Mini. She had a feeling that a week would not be long enough to find the money and get the car fixed. She'd blown all the apple money on food for the chateau and wouldn't be paid until Sunday. She had no choice; she would have to ask Serge for it.

She braced herself and dialled Liesel's number. There was a clicking sound and Liesel's tones came syruping through the receiver.

'Liesel and Serge are unavailable to take your call. Please leave a message after the tone.'

Liesel and Serge! Liesel and Serge! Liesel and Serge! The message repeated itself in her brain like some sadistic mantra. Nausea swept her. Liesel had wasted no time setting up her happy home with someone else's husband. The bleep sounded and Diana composed herself.

'Serge, this is Diana. Ring me urgently.' And she put the phone down trembling. So much for running her life herself she thought. She was still relying on men to survive; Serge's money, Michaud's kindness. She had no money and now, no car.

On the table was a yellow envelope from the *Crédit Solognot* that had arrived that morning. She reached for it and tore it open. There were four sheets of statement. The figure at the bottom read 3000F whether that was positive or negative was unclear. She would ring the bank on Monday morning. Either way it wasn't enough to pay for the car. She would have to dig out the chequebook. Serge had refused to pay the charge for a second card on the account and instead had given her a weekly amount of cash. She would have to raise the money somehow.

She wandered round the house looking for things to sell but their furniture was made up of antique hand-me-downs. Although it had all been worth something once, it was scratched or split or discoloured by sunlight. She went out to the garage. Serge's ride-on lawnmower sparkled in the gloom like gold bullion. It would have to go. Deciding that long grass was better than no transport, she rang *Monsieur* Plessis. It had cost nine thousand just a few months ago, she could probably get eight for it now. She was greeted by another answering machine. Even rural France was turning to robots to run their lives. She left a message and crossed her fingers that she could pull this one off.

A couple of hours later there was still no phone call from Serge. He must have gone out for the evening. Either that or he was ignoring her. She tried to ring again. She rang Liesel's number once more but slammed the receiver down when she heard the click of the answering machine. She couldn't sit through Liesel's cosiness again.

Diana walked Ben to the bus stop. The other mothers stopped talking as she arrived and stared. She felt she could read their minds. Diana Lescure – single mother, jilted by her husband for another. Marie-Pierre came and stood by her as if offering silent support in the face of the village. The bus came and went; carrying Ben away to a day of painting and play. Diana returned to her empty house and headed for the study and the bank paperwork. The phone rang, somehow louder than usual.

'*Allô oui.*'

'*Monsieur* Lescure, *s'il vous plaît.*'

'I am sorry, he is not,' she hesitated, 'Here at the moment.'

'When will he be back?'

'Who's calling please?'

'*Monsieur* Gérard from *Le Crédit Solognot.*'

'This is *Madame* Lescure, can I help you?'

'I'm sorry *Madame* this matter is confidential I can only speak with your husband. When will he be available?'

'I, I don't know,' she stammered.

'This is a matter of utmost importance.'

'He doesn't live here anymore,' she said it quickly as if it would take the edge off it.

There was a long pause on the other end of the line. 'Do you have a forwarding address?'

'I don't I'm afraid.' Diana was choking back the tears of humiliation. 'But *Monsieur* Gérard, our account is a joint account; surely I have the right to know what is going on?'

'Well, in fact I suppose this matter does affect both accounts.'

'Both accounts? But we only had one.'

'No. *Monsieur* Lescure also holds a personal account from which he transfers a monthly amount of money into the joint account to cover household bills and the property loan payments. The transfer has been blocked due to insufficient funds in his personal account. As a result the payment of the property loan will not be covered. He must make the payment soon or you could risk losing the property.'

'But I received a statement on Saturday morning, it said there were 3000 francs in the account.' Diana could hear him tapping at a keyboard.

'Yes, here it is. That statement was dated a few days ago but a substantial amount of money was withdrawn from the account on Saturday. I shall be obliged to block all direct debits until the shortfall is filled. Do you have any way of getting hold of him?'

'Yes, well I don't know. Could you tell me what direct debits are set up on the account?'

'Just one moment please.' Diana could hear more tapping over the line. 'Are here we are, yes. *Eléctricité de France, Pétroleum Solognot, and L'Association des Eaux.*'

'My electricity, heating oil and water.' Diana's voice trailed off aghast.

'*Madame*? Are you alright?'

'*Monsieur* Gérard, thank you for informing me of the situation, but how much time do you think I have to rectify this situation.'

'Perhaps a couple of weeks, but anymore than that and procedures will be set in motion.'

She went straight outside to the old cellar where the boiler stood silent. She checked the gauge on the oil tank in the courtyard; it was half full. At least that was one blessing. She would have to conserve any energy she had for emergencies. She would heat the house with the firewood saving the central heating for when the weather really took a turn for the worse. If the electricity was cut off she would have to rely on candles and live in rhythm with the sun. If need be she could cook on the fire too. She would move Ben's bed into her room and use hot water bottles. The cooker would warm the kitchen and the fire the sitting room. But she couldn't do without water.

She wondered how many disasters one person could encounter in such a short time. Until Serge contacted her there was little she could do about the bank, she realised she needed to seek legal advice but even that she could not afford to pay for. What was he playing at and where was he? The money from the chateau would cover her food for a while and the car would be solved by the sale of the lawnmower. She must ring *Monsieur* Plessis.

'Aah! *Madame* Lescure. Yes, I got your message late last night we have been away for the weekend. How can I help you? I hope there is no problem with the mower.'

'No, no. It's nothing like that, it's just I would like to sell it and I was wondering if you would be interested.'

'I would be glad to take the lawnmower off your hands, it is almost new, but alas I would not be prepared to do so until spring.'

'I really need to sell it now,' she said quietly through pursed lips.

'I will gladly give you seven thousand for it in March.'

'I shall bear that in mind,' she replied tersely. She'd been counting on that money. Seven thousand was almost an insult. She was sure it was worth more. She would have to put an advert in the local paper but that would take time. She sighed, overwhelmed with dread and misery. Where the hell was he? She decided to call the barracks.

The young fireman who answered the phone mumbled, 'One moment please.' It was *Capitaine* Lemenier's voice that told her that

Serge had requested a week's leave. She left a message that she required Serge to call her as soon as he returned. Her next phone call was to the *République du Centre* placing an advert which would come out on Thursday, for the moment she would have to somehow make do.

She spent the rest of the morning drawing up a timetable for the preparation of the food, and made a list of the final items she would need to buy in Beaugency. She would ask Jeanette if she could drop her at the supermarket when she went to the wholesaler. She priced up the meal for the baptism adding on the wages she must pay Jeannette and Marie-Pierre. If she was to make enough money to cover her and Ben's expenses for a month she would need to charge three thousand francs which worked out to a hundred a head. She shook her head, closed her eyes and took a deep breath. Business was business and as *Madame* Ségur had pointed out this was a short notice booking and she wouldn't get anyone else now. She set out her bill on the bond paper and sealed it in an envelope.

## Edward

The sun would be up any moment. There was no time to lose. He heaved himself from the den still in darkness and headed for the village. Not a sound came from the houses where all were sleeping soundly. Just a misguided cockerel had begun to cough his half-hearted crowing. He was careful to keep out of sight of the dogs that were still deep in slumber in the doorways. Through the village and past the church, it was strange to be walking so openly in the centre of civilization even though it was still night. He could see the turret of the chateau in the distance. He reached the gates and hung back. Two sentries were dozing lazily. He edged behind the chateau wall and followed it a little way down. There was a rowan leaning against the outside wall. He inexpertly climbed up it, catching his habit on its spiky branches as he went. At last he reached the top of the wall. The sun was just appearing in the east over the treetops of the forest. He slid himself to the ground and landed awkwardly. He had to stifle a wince as his ankle resisted the landing. He sat for a moment leaning against the wall. There was the dungeon window and within would be his dear, dear Clothilde.

He ran, bent low, and flattened himself against the wall. He peeped through the side of the window and on the floor huddled in a tight ball was Clothilde. Her rough wool shawl was wrapped tightly

296

around her and her face obscured from view. His heart lurched to see his beloved so uncomfortable and so desperate. He pulled away not wanting her to call out and alert the sentries in her surprise.

Not far from the dungeon was a thicket. He ran towards it and cowered amongst the spindly trunks of a hazel from where he had a view of a low walled garden. As the sun rose the stone took on an amber glow. Through an iron gate he could see rose heads illuminated against the sombre greenery in the morning half light. There it was, and just as he had dreamt. There was the garden. He must wait to see if the good lady would appear. It would be a few hours before the chateau's occupants would be going about their business.

At last *Dame Héloïse* was approaching the garden. Her hair was glowing in the morning light just like in his vision. Over her arm, she carried a basket and in her hand a small knife to cut flowers. She was humming to herself. Now she was here, Edward found himself frozen to the spot. What was he supposed to do? Should he speak to her? The sunlight fell on her and a flash glinted off her arm, off the amulet Clothilde had spoken of. He must get closer. He looked about him but the grounds were quiet, the sentries must be at the gates and the workers in their fields. He pulled his hood over his head and ambled low across the grass to the garden wall. What if she had a handmaiden with her? She would surely discover him.

*Dame* Héloïse turned to attend to the roses, she was almost facing Edward. He stifled a gasp. This lady was simply an older, more mature version of Clothilde. It could not be. The amulet. The lost child. Clothilde's colouring. Could Clothilde be a Montgommery?

Edward cowered low and scrambled back towards the thicket. Suddenly there was a great deal of shouting. The lady dropped her roses and ran to the house. There was a rattle of chains and the door of the dungeon clunked open.

Edward sunk back against the wall.

'The *Seigneur* is dead!' someone yelled from the window of the chateau. Great uproar took over the castle. People came running from all quarters to hear the news.

With the *Seigneur* dead Clothilde will surely hang! An innocent life taken when it was he that should be put in her place. Edward kept his eyes fixed on the chateau. A man appeared in a dark robe, not unlike his own habit, a large cross hung about his neck. This must be *Père* Barthélemy. A thought crossed his mind. If he were to surrender there and then how would he clear her name? Though if he did not

Clothilde would lose her life. Sweat poured beneath his habit in the hot morning sun. He must go to Clothilde's mother. She is the only one who can help.

# FORTY-FOUR

## Diana

She was woken by the telephone. She could see through the gap at the top of the curtains that it was still dark outside; it must only be about six. She dragged herself to the kitchen before the phone woke Ben.

'I'm ringing about the lawnmower in the *République du Centre*. Can I come and have a look at it?'

An hour later she was counting out eight thousand francs in two hundred franc notes. It made a nice wodge all rolled up together. It was too early to call the garage; the sun was barely high enough in the sky to see outside. She carefully stowed the cash under her mattress, so that if Serge dropped by he would find the housekeeping tureen empty.

She took Ben to the bus with a spring in her step and as soon as she returned she would call the garage. The bus was running late and it was nine o'clock before the children had climbed on and it had trundled off on the Briou road towards Talcy. When she returned home the answering machine was flashing.

'*Bonnet & Fils* here. Your car will be ready for collection tomorrow morning.'

What on earth was he talking about? He probably meant to ring someone else and got the numbers mixed up.

'No there is no mistake *Madame*. The axle is replaced, we have completed the body work and we have just resprayed it. It will be dry by morning.'

'But I have only just got hold of the money to pay your bill.'

'But you have paid your bill already!' he replied incredulously.

'I most certainly did not. I told you before, I couldn't afford it. You must have mixed up your accounts.'

He was indignant now, 'Listen *Madame*, I received your envelope marked with your registration and the sum of eight thousand francs in cash inside. It was on the mat on Monday morning. We were lucky to get the parts so quickly. We went as fast as we could. Now that you're alone and everything...' His voice tailed off, as if he was biting his tongue.

Did everyone really know so much of everyone else's business round here? Or was it just her existence that was deemed to be public property? Diana tired of arguing with him and conceded. 'Thank you. I'll be over in the morning.'

Someone had obviously paid the repairs. Diana felt uncomfortable. It couldn't be Serge; he hadn't even called her back. He wouldn't have any idea that her car was broken. It must have been Jeanette. She thought of Jeanette's phone call with her supplier, there was no way she could afford to pay other people's bills on a whim. But she couldn't think of anyone else. She had better go over there right away and thank her.

'Jeanette, you shouldn't have done it. I can't afford to pay you back!'

'It's only a coffee. There's no need to feel indebted.' She looked at her in surprise.

'Not the coffee, I mean the car.'

'I wish you would stop fussing about me driving you to the chateau on Sunday, it really isn't a big deal. What are friends for?' She smiled at Diana and picked up a tray of glasses and carried it down to the other end of the bar to the washer.

Diana followed her. 'I meant for my car repairs.'

'You really aren't making any sense now.'

'You didn't pay for it, did you?'

'Didn't pay for what?' She was becoming impatient.

Diana didn't sleep a wink that night. Jeanette hadn't managed to come up with any likely candidates for paying her garage bill and was as intrigued as she. She tossed and turned but she couldn't shake off the uncomfortable feeling that someone had their eye on her, like some kind of ominous fairy godmother. What worried her most was what that person may be expecting in return. As soon as she found out who it was she would pay them the money and be done with it.

The next morning Jeanette dropped her at the garage and waited, just to check it really was her car that had been repaired. Diana took the keys from *Monsieur* Bonnet who was leering at her. But then she reminded herself that she was on the 'up for grabs' list now that her husband had walked out on her. That must have been what Jérôme Couteau had thought. She groaned internally, the last thing she needed now was a queue of amorous locals flashing their pearly whites at her or in some cases not so pearly. At least Jérôme Couteau was nowhere to be seen; he was probably already propping up a bar somewhere.

'*Monsieur* Bonnet, do you still have the envelope you received the money in?'

'Aah you're a very lucky lady *Madame* Lescure.' He parted his lips in what Diana supposed was a smile. 'You must have a rich admirer.' Cackling, he rummaged amongst the papers that littered his desk and handed her a crumpled manila envelope. On it, in black ink was printed Diana's number plate and the sum of 8000F. Underneath in a beautiful curly script was her name. It wasn't Jeanette's handwriting but then she already knew that.

She took the envelope from him, muttered a thank you for his quick work and drove back to the house. The car was running better than it had ever done. She no longer noticed every dip and bump on the road surface. She was pleased to have it back, but the pleasure was wholly tarnished by the mystery surrounding her secret benefactor. She would have to put the whole incident to the back of her mind. With just two full days left before the do she must get on.

She set the ham simmering in the preserving pan, throwing in peppercorns and a couple of bay leaves. She took the chickens out of the freezer to defrost,t ready to roast the following day. She turned her attentions reluctantly to the rose petal ice, she would have to go into Beaugency to the delicatessen in the hope that they may have a jar of rose petal jam lurking somewhere on their shelves.

Diana returned home armed with both Muscat Syrup and the jam. The phone rang.

'*Madame* Lescure, it's *Madame* Ségur. I was just ringing to let you know that we have received your estimate and it looks fine. How are the preparations going?'

'Everything is in hand. Don't worry about a thing. I need to be at the chateau at nine o'clock to get set up, will that be alright?'

'Of course!' Her voice went softer. 'One of the reasons I was phoning was that I heard you may have some transport problems. If you require it, I could send Charles over to ferry the food.'

'No, no. Everything is fine. I shall be there at nine on Sunday.' Diana put the phone down. How on earth did she know she had had transport problems? *Madame* Ségur certainly didn't frequent the café, although she could have overheard it in the *épicerie*. She found it rather surprising that a lady of her standing would listen to gossip. She looked at her watch; Ben's bus would arrive at any moment. She quickly hooked Léo up to his lead and set off for the village green. All she needed to do now was ask Mémère Claudette to babysit on Sunday and pick up the aprons Jeanette had offered to lend her.

Sunday dawned on a drizzly foggy landscape. The trees seemed to droop, in keeping with the gloomy backdrop. She had left Ben happily ensconced with Mémère Claudette early. As she loaded the car up with her carefully prepared food she realised she would have to make more than one trip to get it all over to the chateau, especially since the front seat would be taken up by Marie-Pierre. This time she had no choice but to drive up the main chateau drive. Since the repairs the engine seemed to be quieter too. She drove it round to the back of the stable block where a few horses lolled their well-bred heads over their stalls to watch what was going on. She parked as close to the kitchen door as she could.

Jeanette followed her closely behind. They were both looking very smart. Diana smiled to herself, this was the first time she'd seen Marie-Pierre in anything but fluorescent acrylic knitted jumpers and saggy, black leggings. She really scrubbed up very well – there was clearly nothing a razor couldn't sort out.

Diana turned the handle on the back door to the kitchen, but it was locked. She would have to go round to the main entrance, she hoped there wouldn't be any guests milling around. She left Marie-Pierre and Jeanette waiting by the car and wandered round to the front. The French doors were open and Diana stepped inside. The great hall was set with tables and chairs and a long trestle table covered in a crisp white tablecloth. Just inside the doorway to the hall was an old fashioned easel that reminded her of her school days. On it was a large board holding a seating plan. So much for 'informal' Diana thought. She glanced around the room at tables bedecked with name cards and centrepieces of dried thistles and teasel. She glanced back quickly at the seating plan. The names of the guests were neatly set out in a curly script. Her hand shot to her coat pocket. The crumpled manila envelope was still there, where she had left it. She pulled it out and smoothed it in her palm. She held it up to the board. The handwriting was a perfect match. There was no doubt about it. The capital 'L' of Lescure on the envelope was exactly the same as that of a *Monsieur* Langage on the plan. Surely *Madame* Ségur hadn't paid the bill. She can't have done, otherwise she wouldn't have asked if she had transport problems. She would have known that her car had been repaired. It must be one of her household though. A shiver went down Diana's spine. The chances were that she would be serving lunch either for, or at least in full view of her mysterious benefactor and not know who it was. She was about to scan the guest list for familiar names when she heard frantic knocking coming from the direction of the kitchen. She had completely forgotten Marie-Pierre and Jeanette were still waiting outside the back door.

'It's cold out here!' Jeanette was fussing, as Diana unbolted the door. They unloaded the car and put the potatoes in the oven to roast. She heaved the ham onto the table and unwrapped its foil protection.

'Ooh!' exclaimed Marie Pierre. 'That looks fit for a *dauphin*!'

Diana felt reassured; deep down she was very nervous that the English Fayre *Madame* Ségur had requested would not be quite what was expected. At least she had had the aforethought to include some French dishes, and she would of course keep the Cumberland Sauce separate aware of the terror some French felt at the thought of mixing sweet and savoury. She pulled the coverings off the dishes ready to transpose their contents from Diana's own tatty crockery onto *Madame* Ségur's elegant Limoges porcelain.

Diana unlocked the door that led directly from the kitchen to the great hall. Marie-Pierre and Jeanette lined up behind her like excited children on a school trip.

'I've always wanted to see the inside of this place,' said Jeanette, almost pushing Diana out of the way in her eagerness to snoop.

'I see, and *I* thought you were doing this from the kindness of your heart.'

'Oh no!' said Marie-Pierre. 'Just to see how the other half live and for the money,' she added grinning.

The two women stood in the middle of the great hall letting out sighs of admiration at the high ceilings adorned with intricate plaster mouldings edged in gilt paint. On the walls were paintings of hunting scenes and wan looking ladies stroking lap dogs. An immense sideboard stretching across one end bore a card with the word '*Cadeaux*' written in the same hand as the seating plan. Diana was becoming increasingly worried that *Madame* Ségur had misunderstood what an informal buffet denoted. The bouquets of autumnal plants, which looked as though they had been put together by a professional designer, would have been at home in Buckingham Palace. The five round tables had been spread out across the room, presumably to detract from the vastness of the space. She looked despondently at the sheer size of the table which would no doubt dwarf her meagre offerings.

As if reading her mind Jeanette said, 'Diana, you are a wonderful cook. *Madame* Ségur knows that too and that's why she asked you to cook for her. Once we start laying it out you will see, this table will be filled.'

Diana stood staring at the empty tables as if entranced by her nerves.

'You still have to get back and get the last load,' continued Jeanette. 'We'll start arranging the food and we'll see you back here in twenty minutes. Come on, Marie-Pierre, we've got work to do.'

When she returned Marie-Pierre and Jeanette had cut the ham into sumptuous slices and arranged them dominoes style on a silver salver. Jeanette had chopped parsley into fine sprinkles which she was dusting onto the Chicken *Millefeuille.*

Diana cut the spring onions, fraying the ends until they curled artistically and strew them between the stuffed eggs. Marie-Pierre sliced the strawberries lengthways and doused them with the Muscat Syrup. With the napkins folded into lilies and the food carefully arranged and garnished, they had managed to transform an informal buffet into a stylish display of European cuisine. Just as Diana had finished filling the last silver goblet with the rose petal ice a Bentley swooped past the window. She quickly stacked the goblets in the freezer to stop them melting before time.

'They're here!' called Diana. She grabbed a pile of serving spoons and began polishing them nervously. *Madame* Ségur floated in, wearing what looked like a *Cacharel* outfit. Diana stiffened waiting for the verdict on the presentation.

'*Formidable! Absolument formidable!*' Her smile glowed through her *Chanel* lipstick. 'It all looks wonderful. I knew you could do it. The guests will drink their aperitifs in the vestibule, but Charles thinks he can manage on his own with the drinks. We shall direct them in to eat in say, half an hour?'

Jeanette winked at Diana as *Madame* Ségur's elegant person turned and floated back out of the room to greet her guests.

'You did it!'

'It's not over yet,' Diana warned ominously. She smoothed her apron over her black skirt and rubbed her court shoes quickly with a stray bit of kitchen towel. She checked her make-up in the stainless steel door of the oven and nodded to Marie-Pierre and Jeanette to take up their posts behind the tables, armed with serving spoons. As they stood and waited, they glimpsed guests as they flashed past the doorway to the vestibule. Diana could only see the odd flick of a skirt or a jacket.

Her mind was buzzing. She would have to find out who had written the seating plan. It could have been *Monsieur* Ségur, or their son. She hadn't met either of them. Either, there were two people in the community who had identical handwriting or somebody here was the author of both the envelope and the seating plan.

Someone was tapping a spoon on a glass and requesting the party to move into the dining hall for lunch. Marie-Pierre and Jeanette were standing to attention, serving spoons and forks poised for action. The first person to step over the threshold was *Monsieur* the Mayor. Well, he certainly wouldn't have paid it.

'*Madame* Lescure – you are a woman of hidden talents!'

Behind him a blonde woman was scuttling proprietorially in his wake sporting a skirt too short to befit her years, as she approached Diana recognised Edouard Moreau's wife, Céline.

'I don't think you've met my wife. *Chérie*, this is our gracious chef today.'

Diana forced her features into a welcoming smile.

'How enterprising of you! I suppose it's what one must do when one's husband has abandoned one,' she sneered gleefully. Although no taller than Diana, this woman appeared to be the size of the Statue of Liberty glaring down menacingly like Cruella de Ville. '*Chéri*, I wonder if Diana has been to see you about registering. We all know what the penalty is for trading with no licence.'

Diana went scarlet. How stupid of her not to think of the paperwork she may have to do. 'Oh dear! I didn't think.'

'Well, there's a surprise. But I am sure my husband can sort something out for you. Can't you dear?' she snarled.

'Oh yes, I am sure we can do something. I shall catch up with you a little later. No harm done.' And he moved off to talk to another guest. Michaud stood like a mountain where the mayor had been.

'What are you doing here?'

'It's lovely to see you too!'

'Have you been invited?'

'Well, I'm certainly not gate crashing if that's what you're implying.'

Diana blushed. 'No, I'm sorry. I didn't mean…'

'It was a joke. Not all sectors of local society have rejected me you know.' Seeing that Diana's embarrassment only heightened with this last remark he added, 'I look after the chateau stables, if you're wondering how I have managed to ingratiate myself with the rich and powerful.'

Diana blushed again, this time to the roots of her hair. How did she manage it? She'd put her foot in it again.

'I do brush up quite well, for a farm lad though. Don't you think?' He gave a little bow.

Diana realised he was making fun of her and salvaged her sense of humour. 'Yes, you do… for a farm lad!'

As he strode off to join his table, she couldn't help but notice just how well he did brush up. His trousers and jacket were of a stylishly cut brown tweed, a black Kashmir polo neck jumper, the exact same colour as his hair, only accentuated the azure of his eyes. There was no denying it, he was an incredibly handsome man. If the Ségur's trusted him then perhaps she should too. After all she felt she was more inclined to trust the judgement of successful landowners than the petty sniping of bored villagers, scrabbling for something to occupy their minds.

The guests were drifting over to the table and in no time at all dishes had been emptied and every guest was provided with an overflowing plate. She had received numerous compliments and some women had even asked her for recipes; the highest accolade indeed. She smiled to herself, perhaps she was recovering quicker than she expected. Only a few weeks ago she was an invisible being who just cooked, washed and cleaned for a resident drunkard. Now, she was a local businesswoman – albeit on the bottom rung, rubbing shoulders with the local *crème*. The guests lingered over their food obviously enjoying each mouthful, the cheese and desserts were devoured with a similar gourmet expertise. How satisfying to cook for people who appreciated good food! It wasn't until three o'clock that the last guest had departed to the drawing room for coffee and the women were at last alone in the great hall.

Time was getting on and there was a lot of clearing up to do. Diana was a little anxious about leaving Ben at Mémère's too long on his first visit alone. She would have to hurry Marie-Pierre and Jeanette along to get the dishes cleared and washed up. Jeanette was in the kitchen at the sink and Marie-Pierre was drying.

Diana picked up the remains of the strawberries from the hall to carry back to the kitchen. In her haste she hadn't noticed a dollop of cream that had been dropped on the floor. The heel of her court shoe landed square in the middle of the unctuous mess and skidded spectacularly. She fell over backwards. The bowl she was carrying spun through the air spraying Muscat syrup in all directions, it then proceeded to land on the main trestle table sending a cheeseboard clattering to the ground. The noise was shattering as it echoed round the acoustics of the ancient hall. It must have been audible from the drawing room as Michaud was the first to reach her. He took her hand and pulled her to her feet gently.

How stupid could she be? Her face was flushed with embarrassment. Her ankle pulsed with pain, she flexed it still leaning on Michaud's arm. She tried to stand independently but he resisted. She looked up at him questioningly.

His gaze held hers with such strength that she found she could not look away. His face leant towards hers and she reciprocated, she found she couldn't stop herself. It was as if there was a magnet hovering between them, pulling them together. His lips were on hers kissing her firmly but gently. He pulled away, a hint of a smile on his motionless mouth.

Diana stood as still as she could; inside she was wobbling like jelly. She could hear footsteps outside the dining hall. Michaud must have heard them too for he took his arms from around her and whispered. 'I'll help you clear up.'

Diana watched his words float up round his head, twisting and turning in wisps like cigarette smoke.

Jeanette appeared by her side with Marie-Pierre in close pursuit. 'We'll help her clear up, thank you!' said Jeanette tersely.

Diana resurfaced with a jolt. 'Yes, of course. You're a guest,' she tried to say but although her lips were moving, no sound came out.

'You're wanted in the drawing room,' Jeanette ordered Michaud in her headmistress tone.

He was still gazing at Diana, oblivious to Jeanette's frustration. 'I'll come and find you before you go,' he whispered again. As he let go and turned his back, Diana felt the warmth seeping from her body with every step he took away from her.

Jeanette was red-faced and staring at her. Marie-Pierre was shaking her head and tutting. Diana shook herself back to reality and busied herself wiping up the cream.

'What came over you?' Jeanette began her lecture as she washed the dishes. She didn't give Diana a chance to reply. 'Think of your reputation. That man is trouble. We've all told you, he's up to no good. You've only been on your own five minutes. That is no way to carry on. What will people say?' She let Jeanette witter on as much to keep the peace as to soak up every delicious moment of her embrace with Michaud.

Five years before she had believed that Serge was the one for her, but she had never had a moment of such powerful intensity as that. Not even at the beginning. She could see that she had in fact, been on her own for years.

'Drunk, I bet!' snorted Jeanette. I saw him knocking back the aperitifs earlier. You saw him didn't you Marie-Pierre.'

Marie-Pierre nodded vehemently.

Diana sighed. 'I expect you're right Jeanette. Just forget it ever happened. I have.'

The two women stood staring at her a moment longer as if waiting for further proof of this. When they saw that this was Diana's final word on the matter they returned to wiping and clearing the kitchen in silence.

*Madame* Ségur wafted in through the door just as the kitchen had been returned to its former pristine sparkle. Her face was positively twinkling, either from pleasure or wine. 'That was a fabulous meal. I'm very pleased.' She handed her a fat envelope. 'Your bill.'

'*Madame* Ségur. I wanted to compliment you on your calligraphy.' Diana said carefully.

'My calligraphy?'

'The seating plan.'

'Oh, no that wasn't me! Charles did that. I'm afraid I don't have the patience or the time to do such a thing.'

'Charles?' Diana frowned.

'Yes, you know him. I saw you chatting to him earlier. Charles Michaud. He is a very gifted man, not just a good horseman.'

Diana nodded in slow motion.

'Well, thank you again and please take any leftovers with you. With just my husband and I here they will just end up in the bin,' and she swept out of the kitchen.

## Edward

The news had not yet reached the village. Clothilde's mother was tending to the goats in her absence. He could not risk walking into the field in daylight, not yet. He must somehow get her to come to the trees at the edge. Edward had an idea. He let out an owl's screech just as Clothilde had taught him to do. Clothilde's mother looked up startled. She looked around her and when she could see nothing she went back to her task. Edward screeched again.

'Clothilde?' she whispered as loud as she dare.

Edward screeched again in response.

She dropped her buckets and ran to the trees. 'Where are you my child?'

'Don't be afraid. It is not Clothilde, it is I, Edward.'

She started backwards ready to turn on her heels and run.

'I am a friend of Clothilde's I must speak with you.'

She paused and took a step nearer. 'Show yourself.'

Edward stepped from behind the oak trunk.

'The monk! It was you who cured me.' But her face was awash with fear as if she had seen an apparition.

'Yes, but I am no ghost as you were led to believe. They lied to you to protect me. Your daughter's life is in peril and we must save her together. Follow me somewhere we can talk, away from prying eyes.'

She nodded.

'Collect up your buckets for if someone were to notice them they would arouse suspicion.'

He led her to the den.

'So this is where she goes. I knew of it though I have never been here.'

'The *Seigneur* is dead and they believe that he died at Clothilde's hand; poisoned.'

The woman's hands flew to her face in horror.

'But it cannot be so. The remedy had no poison in it, but I need your help to prove it.'

'You are a good man, *Frère*.'

Edward shook his head. 'I wish that were true but I have a lot to put right before I go to the gallows.'

'This was not Clothilde's remedy but mine. I must reveal myself and take her place without delay.'

'What can I do, *Frère*?'

'You must be frank and open with me. I need to know something.'

Her eyes widened and looked at him with intent.

'Tell me. Clothilde - she is fair.'

The woman pursed her lips.

'You and Firmin and the little ones, they are dark in colouring.'

She closed her eyes and took in a deep breath.

'Clothilde, tell me. She is not your child?'

A tear was rolling down the woman's cheek. She shook her head, her eyes closed with the grief that was sweeping her.

'How did you come to take her into your home?'

'I cannot tell you this *Frère*. I have been sworn to secrecy.'

'But her life is in danger, do you not want to save her?'

The woman thought for a moment. 'She was abandoned,' she blurted, casting her eyes down to the ground as if she were expecting to be swallowed up and sent to eternal damnation.

'Abandoned? Where?'

'It was *Père* Barthélemy who found her. Just a few hours old she was. He brought her to me late at night. She needed milk and I was still feeding Firmin. But a mite he was too, my Firmin.'

'But where? Where did *Père* Barthélemy find her?'

'He told me not to ask. He just said that I would be blessed in heaven were I to take her in.'

'But your husband, did he ask no questions?'

'He was already gone, to the crusades with *Seigneur* Montgommery, the elder, the true *Seigneur* of Saint Gabriel. He is a good man, he left his sickly brother here to oversee the *seigneuriale* and to protect his goods and chattels until he returns, I hope one day. It has been thirteen long years since he and my husband departed. I pray that they will be returned to us safely.' She crossed herself.

'Tell me about the amulet I have seen Clothilde wearing. It is turquoise and gold.'

'When *Père* Barthélemy brought her to me as a tiny baby she was wrapped in a soft shawl fastened with the amulet. I have kept it for her all these years, but now that she is older I allow her to wear it now and then.'

'*Dame* Héloïse wears the very same amulet.'

'Do you think …?' Her face became pale.

'I believe that Clothilde is a Montgommery, I do not understand how she has come to live amongst you but the only person who knows is *Père* Barthélemy. You must go to him and persuade him to tell the truth so that Clothilde may be released and her life spared. She must be restored to her true position; that into which she was born. Then you must tell him of me and the role I have played in treating the *Seigneur*.'

'But, *Frère* they will come for you!'

'Then so be it. My sole mission is to free Clothilde. I shall wait here in my den until they come for me. Now go!'

She gathered up her buckets and clambered up to the forest floor and was gone.

Alone again, he gathered up the rolls of parchment so carefully inscribed with the many remedies of Eldric's teachings, and wrapped them in a rabbit skin that had been curing by the fire. He dug a little way down amongst the roots of the oak tree until he had created a cavern deep enough to stow the bundle within and then covered it over with the earth from around. He did not want Clothilde being accused of witchery; such a charge would not save even the *Châtelaine*. And it was still by no means certain that she would be welcomed into the Montgommery clan. Then he clambered above ground and lay on his front his arms spread asunder in the shape of the cross and waited for Montgommery's men. This is why God had sent him here, he was sure. To reunite Clothilde with her natural mother and put her in her rightful place at the head of the Montgommery household, until the return of her natural father, *le Seigneur de Saint Gabriel*.

He hoped it would not be long before Montgommery's men came with their horses to drag him to the dungeon. Here, on this day, Edward of Canterbury would be arrested for the murder of a French Lord. This would be the justice that should have come to him the day he directed those knights to his Grace in the chancel. But now he understood that the Lord had one last mission to absolve him of this error. 'I, who had no mother, was sent to reunite another with theirs. For that I am honoured and now, I may have secured a place in heaven with Sire Thomas and my own mother.' The thought comforted him as he awaited the delegation from the *seigneurie* and the chastisement that would follow.

# FORTY-FIVE

## Diana

Diana's emotions were flung into turmoil once again. Michaud's first name was Charles. She'd never thought to ask. Everyone just called him Michaud. If he had written out the seating plan, then it was he who had paid her garage bill. The awful realisation hit her. He had paid her bill and was now taking his payment in kind. He felt he had some kind of right over her. Not only had she been duped by her husband but she was becoming a sitting duck for every man in the vicinity. She thought of Jérôme Couteau and the sordid advances he had made on her own doorstep, with her husband sleeping just feet away, the leering grin of *Monsieur* Bonnet at the garage and now Michaud who thought he could buy her attentions. She felt dirty, sullied. She had broken the social rules in the village by frequenting the café and speaking to men as her equal and now the village was punishing her. She thought of Hélène, was that what she had gone through?

'Diana, you've gone quite pale. Sit down. You look faint.'

'I'm fine, let's get out of here.'

'What about the food?' said Marie-Pierre dumbfounded at Diana's brisk actions.

'You take it home, for your brothers.' She pulled out the envelope *Madame* Ségur had given her and pulled out two crisp two hundred franc notes and handed one each to Marie-Pierre and Jeanette.

'This is too much.' Jeanette remonstrated but Diana had picked up a pile of empty dishes and carried them outside to the car. As she went to open the boot, *Monsieur* Moreau appeared at her elbow.

'*Madame* Lescure. About the arrangement I mentioned earlier,'

'Yes, I am so sorry I really didn't think about what I must do for the authorities to be allowed to trade like this.'

'No problem. I think *Madame* Ségur has just paid you?'

Diana didn't answer.

'If you just give that to me and we can call that forgotten, for now at least.'

'What do you mean?'

'The penalties for operating without a licence are considerable, in certain cases there can be a custodial sentence.' Then he broke into a smile. 'But, I am a reasonable man and as you can see I only want to help, so you pass that to me and we can consider that a down payment.'

'*Monsieur* Moreau, I have no intention of doing any such thing until I know my rights.'

'That is a dangerous decision *ma petite dame.*' He was leaning on the side of the open boot of her car.

Diana looked at him straight in his elfin eyes which were becoming more troll-like by the second. She grabbed the lid of the boot. 'Not half as dangerous as where you are standing, *Monsieur,*' and she slammed the lid down hard. The mayor only just ducked his head out of the way in time.

'You will regret this!' He stormed back into the house.

Diana jumped into the car and roared across the gravel and out on the road back to Saint Gabriel.

'You look terrible.' *Madame* Camaret's kitchen glowed with the evening sun reflecting off the yellow walls. 'Come and sit down.' She pulled out a chair and Diana sat on it droopily, like a rag doll.

'I can only think that it did not go well.' The old lady reached for the black iron coffee pot warming on the hob.

'No, I think it was a success. I had a few compliments and *Madame* Ségur was thrilled.'

'So why the long face?'

'*Madame* Camaret,' she began.

'Please call me Agnès, I think we know each other well enough now.' The old lady smiled at her kindly.

'It's this village!'

'What's happened now?'

Diana thought for a moment and decided against sharing the mayor's threats; she no longer knew who was in league with whom in this village. Instead she asked, 'What happened to Hélène and her baby?'

'Well, I told you that she was looking after old Albert Meffret, Antoine's father. She and Antoine became close, it was obvious to me and I think obvious to others too. But as you know Antoine was engaged to be married to Céline Cottereau, the bank manager's daughter. Then a terrible thing happened. Philippe Cottereau disappeared. He vanished off the face of the earth. It was 1942, I remember it as if it was yesterday. Céline and her mother were beside themselves, terrible it was. Antoine and Céline's engagement was called off and Hélène disappeared too. She just got on her bicycle one afternoon and didn't come back. The rumours that flew around Saint Gabriel were awful. Some said she had murdered the bank manager and had fled. Others said the bank manager was having an affair with her and they had gone off somewhere together. Some believed she had been murdered. It was a couple of years before we found out the truth, well some of it anyway.

'When the war was finally over people began to drift back to their homes to carry on as before. Of course for so many this was not possible, people were changed, some had lost everything and everyone. Well, Hélène, she returned to Saint Gabriel too. The villagers did not greet her kindly, they were upset that the nurse had abandoned them in their hour of need and some still believed she had murdered the bank manager. I knew Hélène and I knew she was not capable of that. She returned to the village and married Antoine very quickly, they were the happiest couple I think I have ever seen; except for Georges and I of course! When they married, Hélène had to produce official documents and that was when we found out she was English. She told us that she had been dropped in by parachute by the British government to help the resistance. She wanted to help France fight the Germans. People are stupid, they felt deceived and didn't want her to care for them after that so she could no longer work. Some people even crossed the road to avoid her. They taunted her with comments about Churchill bombing French civilians and called her a traitor.'

'Hélène was a spy!'

Agnès nodded. 'She and Antoine had a baby boy and they called him Charles Albert Meffret. A beautiful little man he was. Antoine worked long hours on the farm and Hélène did her best to stay cheerful despite the village. Then one day she could take it no more and they found her in the chapel in the woods.'

'The one in the clearing?'

'That's right, she'd taken her own life with a revolver.'

'And left Antoine and her baby alone?'

'It was a terrible thing. It cast an awful shadow over the village. I have never known a better or fairer person in my life. She loved Antoine more than anyone is capable of loving. She would rather have lost her own life than sadden him. She could never have betrayed him.'

'But that's exactly what she did, betray him I mean. By ending her life she left him alone.'

'Yes. She hurt him more than she will ever know. Such a beautiful woman! She had long shiny black hair. As straight as straight, it was. She used to pile it on top of her head.' A tear escaped down her cheek. 'Such strange colouring. Hair as black as night, but her eyes were so blue,' she sighed.

Diana caught a tear and wiped it from her face.

'So you see. Your situation is not as bad as that. You've been through a terrible trauma with Serge leaving but you must just take life one day at a time. Everything will work itself out in the end. You'll see.'

'But what happened to her baby?'

'It was the hardest thing Antoine ever had to do. He couldn't cope with the farm and a baby on his own. He didn't want to marry again, he was heartbroken. He had poor little Charles adopted. Such a sweet child!'

Diana finished her coffee, her mind racing a hundred to the dozen. She may not be in the same situation as Hélène but she was certainly being held to ransom by Michaud. That was nearly blackmail. 'I'm sorry I need to go. There's something I must do.'

'Of course!'

As she got back into her car she could see Agnès peering anxiously through her front window. She screeched the clutch and pulled away.

## Ellen

EVACUATION STOP INSTRUCTIONS NEEDED STOP

Ellen trembled as she transmitted. The house was so quiet she worried her creaking around would wake the doctor. Her whole body ached from the digging. She had scraped her hands to clean off the mud until they almost bled. She sat back and waited in the hope that London would answer immediately. It didn't take long.

CONTACT FOUCAUD STOP

It was stupid of her to imagine that they would risk another Lysander in the same place so soon after tonight's. Of course she would have to go somewhere they could land. There was no choice she would have to go back and leave a message for Foucaud to get her out and hide out somewhere. The cockerels were crowing all over the village and it wouldn't be long before the household would be awake. She took the radio and wrapped it in a bundle of clothes. She crept downstairs and out to her bicycle. She fixed the bundle on the back of her bike and obscured it with kindling, from the log store, and set off for the woods.

# FORTY-SIX

## Diana

She swung the car round the corner and pulled up outside the church. She dashed into the *Champ de Foire* and took the wodge of notes from under her mattress. Back in the car she accelerated up the *rue de l'Abreuvoir* and onto the Jaunay road once more. She jerked the car into the track to Michaud's farm and lurched it over the rough ground to the courtyard. The chickens scattered in alarm. She slammed on the breaks and leapt out. Within seconds she was beating on Michaud's door.

He opened it.

Diana thrust the wodge of notes into his hand. 'That should cover it!'

'Diana what are you doing?'

'I am reimbursing you for the repairs on my car. Now I've paid you back. I don't owe you anything.'

'Of course you don't owe me anything,' he was shouting now. 'I just wanted to help.'

'Oh yeah? Like you wanted to help old Antoine? Don't you know that there's no point trying to con me out of *my* house. I don't even own it!' she cried triumphantly. 'I am not the poor little woman on my own that you all seem to think I am.' She turned and began to stomp back to her car.

'Diana! What are you talking about?'

She ignored him. She went to open the car door. He was behind her now, he grabbed her shoulders. She tried to shake him off and pulled open the door, but he threw his weight against it and it wouldn't budge.

'What do you mean, help old Antoine?'

She kicked him.

He winced in pain but he didn't loosen his grip.

'Don't try to deny it. Everybody in the village knows what you did.'

'Well then you'd better tell *me* what I did.'

'You wheedled your way in here, bullied the old man into changing his will and then smothered him on his sick bed.'

'That is not true,' he shouted the words angrily.

317

'Well you would say that wouldn't you?'

'I can prove it.'

Diana wasn't listening. She tried to pull away from him but he was too strong.

'I said, I can prove it.'

'How?' she spat. Her eyes were round with fury.

'I will show you. Just come inside and I will show you.'

'You'll have to show me out here.'

'You must promise to wait.'

Diana was not about to promise any such thing. She remained rooted to the spot, ready to bolt as soon as his back was turned.

Sensing her doubt he breathed in sharply and his voice became desperate, 'I won't hurt you.' His tone was plaintive. 'I *couldn't* hurt you. Trust me Diana.'

Diana gave in and nodded.

Michaud retreated into the farmhouse.

'He's a bad man.' 'He's up to no good.' 'Keep away from him.' Jeanette, Marie-Pierre and Serge's voices were chanting in her head. The voices were getting louder and louder. She should run, but her feet wouldn't move.

The farmhouse door reopened and Michaud came out waving a piece of paper. The voices in her head fell silent. He held it out to her. She took it from him checking his distance from her, but he wasn't coming any closer. She looked down at the piece of paper. It was a birth certificate.

*The twelfth March one thousand nine-hundred and forty-eight at ten o'clock was born at Meffret Farm, St Gabriel, Loir et Cher : Charles Albert of male sex to Antoine Albert François MEFFRET farmer born in St Gabriel the thirteenth of May one thousand nine hundred and eleven and to Ellen Sarah Charles his wife, nurse, born in Eastbourne, Great Britain the twenty-first May one thousand nine hundred and twenty-two.*

Diana read the piece of paper three times as if the words were a lie. She looked up at him. Ellen Sarah Charles. Not Hélène but Ellen. Of course the French would pronounce the two names the same way. But this was the birth certificate of Charles Meffret not Charles Michaud. This could have been in the paperwork after the old man died.

'But your name? Michaud?'

'I was adopted. I took my adoptive family's name.'

'Hélène was your mother?'

It was his turn to be confused. 'You know about Hélène?'

'Agnès Camaret told me about her.'

'And Antoine Meffret was my father. That is why he left me the farm, I was his legal descendant.' He put his hand in his pocket and pulled out the wodge of notes. 'I'm sorry about the garage bill, I didn't want to interfere. I only wanted to help. I heard that your husband had left and I couldn't bear the thought of you holed up in this village alone like a prisoner. I can see how it must have looked.' He cast his eyes down at the concrete, crestfallen.

Diana studied this burly man with his dark blue eyes and hair, black as night like his mother's. 'You should have asked me first.'

'You wouldn't have accepted.'

'No,' she murmured. 'I wouldn't.' They stood awkwardly for a moment like a couple of schoolchildren who had forgotten their lines in a school play.

It was Michaud who interrupted the silence. He took a step towards her, tentatively as if she might try to run off again. 'Diana, I love you.' He was staring straight at her. I have loved you from the first moment I saw you.'

Diana didn't move and just stared back.

He took another step and put his hands on her shoulders.

She didn't resist. He bent down and kissed her with the same strength and passion as he had done in the middle of the Great Hall at the *Château de Montgommery.* Diana's senses swung and looped through every hue of ecstasy. She had paid him back and owed him nothing, he was not a murderer and to boot he loved her.

Suddenly she pulled away. 'Ben!' she cried. 'I have to go; he's at Mémère's.'

'I'm coming with you!'

'But what about…'

'The village? They'll have to know sooner or later, there's no time like the present.' He grinned, slipping his hand around her waist and whispered, 'I never want to be parted from you again.'

They arrived at Claudette and Marie-Pierre's cottage. Mémère came to the door her eyes like saucers. Marie-Pierre stood speechless behind her.

'Thank you for having Ben. I've come to pick him up.' Neither woman replied, they just stared at Michaud. Ben came running from the kitchen.

'*Maman, Maman!*' When he saw Michaud he just pointed and made clippy cloppy sounds.

Diana scooped him up, thanked the still mesmerised mother and daughter and whisked Ben off to the car. When they were all settled and strapped in, Diana turned to Michaud.

'There's someone who needs to meet you,' and she pulled away and headed for the Camaret farm.

Agnès came to the door smiling. Before she could open her mouth Diana spoke.

'Agnès. Let me introduce you to Charles…' She hesitated and looked up at Michaud. '… Meffret.'

Agnès Camaret furrowed her brow. 'Meffret?'

'Yes. This is Antoine's boy.'

She gasped. 'Antoine Meffret's boy? Hélène's baby?' Tears filled her eyes and she threw her arms around him. 'Why didn't you say? You've been next door all this time. What a fine man you have become!'

Diana and Michaud drove back to the *Champ de Foire*. As Diana's car approached the house they noticed the iron gate into the garden was flapping open and banging in the wind.

'That's strange. I bolted that from the inside when I left.'

'Let me have a look.'

Diana stopped the car and Michaud got out. He pushed the gate wide to reveal the French doors at the front of the house had been smashed.

'You've been burgled.'

Diana leapt out of the car and scooped Ben from the back seat. The sitting room was a mess. The sofa and armchairs were tipped up. Books were strewn across the floor and plant pots smashed spilling their earth over the rugs.

'What on earth? I'm calling the police. Where's your phone?'

'Hang on. I think I have an idea. And I don't want the police involved until I know what my legal position is.'

'You better tell me what is going on.'

Diana righted one of the armchairs and told Michaud about the mayor and his threats.

'That's it! I have had enough of that family holding this village to ransom.'

'What do you mean?'

'They sent some heavies to lean on me when I first set up my livery business. But I am no defenceless woman on my own, and I sent them on their way with fear in their eyes. I bet you had a visit from the white van. I've seen it at the café once or twice. I wanted to help Jeanette but as you know she wouldn't have anything to do with me. Did you write anything down that would prove you received money for the food you sold at the café?'

'No, but I sent a bill to *Madame* Ségur for the party.'

'Don't worry about *Madame* Ségur I can talk to her.' He picked up the phone and dialled. The police arrived within half an hour.

Two rounded *gendarmes* stood in the middle of the sitting room stroking their chins and shaking their heads. 'Is there anything missing?'

'I looked but I can't see anything.' Diana cast her eye around the room frantically. Just underneath one of the upturned armchairs she could see a small square of paper. She picked it up. On it was a wax seal with the imprint of a crest in the centre. It was a staff with a serpent entwined around it. 'What's this?'

Michaud had a look at it. 'I know who has done this. *Monsieur le Maire* and his wife Céline Moreau. That's the crest on the doorway of the chateau and over the door of the old monastery at Lusigny, the Moreau family home.'

'*Monsieur* if nothing is missing it is hardly a burglary.'

'But it is criminal damage.'

'*Monsieur,* I can understand that you are upset but without proof there is nothing we can do. We would need to catch them in the act.'

'Then that is what you must do. Every second Tuesday of the month, a white van pulls up outside *La Petite Folie.* As soon as the *épicerie* is closed and the last customer has left the café, about noon, two men get out and go into the café to extort money from the landlady. I am certain they are the authors of this mess. They will be there next Tuesday. You be there at eleven am to wait for them and I can promise you the biggest arrest of the area this decade.'

The men looked at each other thoughtfully. 'The allegations you are making are serious. *Monsieur* and *Madame* Moreau are well respected members of local society. Our *chef* would strip us of our rank without enough evidence.'

'Well respected, my eye. They prey on defenceless people who are too scared to do anything about it. Just think of the promotion you could get for bringing down such a ring!'

The *gendarmes* shuffled on their feet and nodded at each other. 'We'll be there on Tuesday but we will only intervene if there is enough evidence. Is that understood?'

## Edward

The beating of hooves rumbled through the forest against a cacophony of barking dogs.

'They are come,' he said out loud. He could hear the faint echoes of a large crowd gathering in the distance.

As the crowd approached he could hear them chanting, 'Murderer! Murderer! Murderer!' in rhythm with his beating heart. He did not flinch as the horses approached his supine body. The crowd fell to an eerie silence as two of Montgommery's men grabbed a shoulder each and dragged him to standing.

They bound his wrists together with chains and fixed an end to the saddle of one of their fine horses. He was jerked violently sideways as the horses moved off toward the chateau pulling Edward stumbling and tripping over the roots of the forest floor. It was all he could do not to be pulled to the ground and dragged.

The villagers had all come out to watch the spectacle. Some jeered and shouted 'Hang him!' whilst others cheered their triumph at his capture.

He spotted Firmin in the crowd, his face was ashen and he stared at the ground.

## FORTY-SEVEN

### Diana

'Jeanette will never agree to it. I went round there and found her sobbing, her microwave smashed on the floor. She pretended she'd dropped it. Now that she's getting married maybe it will stop.'

'Jeanette is getting married? Who on earth to?'

'I've only seen him once, his name is François Guémard.'

'What does he look like?'

'Well, he's big, like a rugby player. He has brown hair. Oh and a tattoo, I remember now.'

'Was it a tattoo that looked rather like this?' He held up the square of paper with the seal on it.

'That's exactly it.'

'That's one of the white van men; Edouard Moreau's lackeys. We better get over to the café.'

Claudette and Marie-Pierre had been no less efficient than usual as the news had evidently reached *La Petite Folie* for there was quite a crowd at the bar for a Sunday evening. Frédeau was still holding the fort. He gestured them through to the kitchen where Jeanette was resting her feet after the day at the chateau.

'It is out of the question.'

'Jeanette, it is our only chance to free Saint Gabriel from these crooks. They smashed up my sitting room and are threatening to do worse. I saw your microwave for myself.'

'You don't know what you're getting into.'

'Then tell us.'

Jeanette looked from Diana to Michaud. She glanced behind them to check the café was still empty. 'The mayor caught me selling alcohol out the back door to one of the villagers. I could have lost my licence and my livelihood if he'd reported me. That wife of his owns the brewery that supplies my drinks and I owed them money. They kept increasing the amount I owed and the more I paid, the more I seemed to owe. The only way I could wipe the slate was to agree to marry François Guémard. He said he would sort Edouard Moreau for me.'

'Jeanette, without proof the police can do nothing. You cannot marry a man you do not love let alone like. Free yourself and the village from his grip.'

'What if they get let off? They are not nice people; I dread to think what they would do to me.'

'She's right Charles. What if they get off? We could both be in danger.'

'They won't get off. The mayor will be stripped of his office and his job at the school, and he and his wife will be sent to prison for a long while. The media will put paid to them ever returning to Saint Gabriel. They will be made an example of. And as for those thugs they don't have a gram of imagination between them and without the backhanders they're receiving from the Moreaus they won't come near the village again. I promise you both, if they do I will personally stay by your sides all day and all night.'

Jeanette stared at both of them earnestly. 'What do I need to do?'

'You need to break off your engagement but not until I have spoken to the *gendarmerie*.'

## Edward

Edward lay awake in the dark dungeon only thankful for the coolness of its position. The day had been unbearably hot. There was still no news from Clothilde's mother, nor from *Père* Barthélemy. He was alone in the dungeon so at least he knew that Clothilde was no longer imprisoned. He must wait; his future was in their hands.

He fell in and out of sleep as he intermittently watched the looming shadows of the rats on the dungeon wall as they scampered to and fro, small at first and then as huge as oxen. If the rats wanted him then they could have him. There was a rattling of chains. Edward started and braced himself for the news. Would he be hanged there and then with no trial? Or had *Père* Barthélemy told them his story. He bent low to awkwardly cross himself with his wrists still chained. He only prayed that Clothilde was safe.

'Edward.' It was Clothilde. 'Edward, it is I, Clothilde.'

'Clothilde! You are safe.'

In just those few hours she was changed. Her clothing was fine, on her feet she wore delicate slippers threaded with gold. Even the way she held herself had altered, her features framed by the finery of such a noble family. From serf to *Seigneur* in just a few hours. This was Clothilde Montgommery of Saint Gabriel, no longer the poor waif who had cared for him and fed him back to health.

'Are you hurt?'

'No, do not worry for me.'

'I cannot yet release you. We must first prove that your remedy did not poison the *Seigneur*. *Père* Barthélemy has sent a rider to the Abbey at Pontigny to bring back an apothecary to check your remedy, and to see the *Seigneur's* corpse. It will be a while longer. I am sorry.' She cast her eyes down towards her silken shoes.

'It is no matter my child. To see that you are released and are restored to your true family is the greatest gift I have ever received.'

She took his chained arms and rubbed them tenderly. 'And I, in turn, will have you released.'

'Have you learned of how you came to be reared with Firmin and his family?'

'*Dame* Héloïse was told by the *Seigneur's* brother that I had died shortly after my birth, though she could not understand it as the baby that she had given birth to had fine lungs and a pink complexion. *Père* Barthélemy has told of how one of Montgommery's men brought me to him having been ordered to kill me. The man could not bring himself to do such a thing and entrusted me to him. I was taken to the village and to my mother and there I stayed until you landed in our forest.'

'But why do such a thing?'

'He wanted to be sure that his brother had no descendants. He was certain that he would not return from the east and that the chateau would become his.'

## Diana

Later on that evening, with Ben tucked up in bed. Diana and Michaud lounged together on the sofa. Michaud had built up a roaring fire and brought in a handsome load of oak logs which he had stacked neatly against the fireplace.

'What would I give to be a fly on the wall when they find out!' Diana was laughing.

'I can think of much better things to be doing!' He pulled her towards him and kissed her neck, and shoulders. They retired to the spare room. Diana had shuddered at the thought of taking this beautiful, good man to Serge's bed. As their bodies entwined, Diana felt as if she had at last come home. This was where she belonged.

'Now you must tell me the full story of coming to Saint Gabriel.'

'Must I? Right now?'

'Yes, you must. I don't want to risk any more misunderstandings in our relationship or for that matter in the village.'

'Very well, my parents, my adoptive parents, died not long ago. At the reading of the will, it came to light that my name had not been mentioned anywhere in it. They had left their entire estate to my brothers. We were all shocked. My brothers wanted to contest it. But then the second bombshell came. The solicitor dug out some old adoption papers with my name on. I didn't believe it at first. Apparently the papers hadn't been properly completed. There had been a mix up with the end of the war. My parents had never signed the final papers. So legally, I had no right to my parents' estate. My brothers wanted to sign a third of it over to me. But I refused. If my adoptive parents had wanted that, they would have written it into their wills. They must have known that the paperwork wasn't complete; it was almost like an unwritten message. I knew I must leave and find my natural parents.

'My brothers were, of course, very upset. They didn't oust me, but they were ashamed that our parents had kept my origins such a secret. I had always known that I was somehow different from them; I'd developed a passion for horses which the rest of my family couldn't understand. Farming in Brittany is mainly potatoes and dairy and that's all they were interested in. Horses were expensive things to have and they didn't pay their way. Eventually I persuaded Father to give up a field to a paddock and I got two horses. Now I know that I inherited my love for them from my mother.

'When I arrived in Saint Gabriel, Antoine welcomed me with open arms. I didn't need to prove to him who I was. He broke down and wept. He said I was every bit my mother.'

'But why didn't you tell anyone you were his son?'

'Antoine was worried for me. When he met my mother he was already engaged to be married to a girl over at Lusigny.'

'The banker's daughter, Agnès told me.'

'Well that 'girl' over at Lusigny still lives there, in the old monastery.'

'But that's the mayor's house.'

Michaud nodded. 'And she has a viper's tongue.'

'Not ...'

'I think you've met her on several occasions.' He was grinning teasingly.

'His wife?'

'That's right. Céline Moreau used to be Céline Cottereau and she was engaged to be married to my father until Ellen Charles was parachuted into the woods to fight for France.'

# FORTY-EIGHT

**Edward**

Edward awoke to the rumble of footsteps deep within the chateau. They were coming for him. He pulled himself to sitting. His arms were red and raw from the tight chains around them. The rats scattered as the noise approached.

Clothilde stood before him. 'Edward, it is done. The monks from Pontigny have been and they have looked at the remedy and say it is only Wood Betony. The *Seigneur* died a natural death in the eyes of God. The monks have said that it is his deceit that killed him. There will be no trial. You are to be freed Edward!'

Settled at a table with a bowl of steaming broth and a hunk of bread, Edward turned to Clothilde, 'Now is the time for me to be moving on.'

'Why? There is no need, you are a hero Edward. Look at the gates?' There beyond the gates a crowd had gathered just like the occasion when he was being dragged in chains by Montgommery's horses but this time they were cheering and smiling.

'Why are these people here?'

'These are the people who have heard of the cures that have been administered in this parish and they are pleased to have at last identified the author of such good works. Do you not see? Edward you are to stay here amongst us. *Dame* Héloïse is agreed. She would like you to install yourself here in the chateau to heal the sick and keep disease from our doors.'

Edward stared at her wide-eyed while he took it all in. He looked around at his sumptuous surroundings. The great hall with its long wooden table, the walls hung with an array of woven hangings and grand candles that burned light into the darkness.

'No, not the chateau. Although I have not yet taken my vows I do not wish to be surrounded by such riches. I do not deserve it.'

'Edward, can you not see, that whatever may have passed before, the Lord has forgiven you.'

'If I am so blessed to have been forgiven, I must continue on the path I began and I shall continue to renounce all worldly goods and live simply.'

She sighed and stared downcast at the table. Then she brightened. 'Then I shall build you a chapel in the woods.'

## Diana

Charles was sitting by the fire reading out the headline of the *République du Centre*. 'HEADMASTER AND MAYOR JAILED FOR TEN YEARS', when there was a knock on the French doors.

'*Madame* Lescure, I am Raymond Chenet. Marcel gave me the pot you found in your well.'

'I'd completely forgotten about that! Come in, please.'

'The parchment was well preserved but the ink was almost gone. They have managed to discern part of a recipe for a herbal remedy. It's really terribly exciting. The curator has found a record of a monk, Edward of Canterbury who was an apothecary under the auspices of the Montgommery family at the *Chateau de Montgommery*. They believe he worked out of the *Chapelle Saint Thomas* in the Marchenoir Forest.'

'The little chapel in the clearing?'

'That's right.'

'I thought that was named after Thomas Beckett.'

'There have been rumours to that effect but in actual fact it is simply too long ago to know for sure who it was named after. Apparently the Montgommery family and this Edward formed a foundation to ensure that there was always a provision for the community to have access to medical help. Later the foundation was moved to the monastery at Lusigny when it was built in the sixteenth century. What is curious about it is that the monastery was never affiliated with any particular order. It would appear that it operated solely under the authority of the chateau; most unusual. I have brought this copy of an entry in the parish register. There is an insignia here.'

Diana and Michaud looked. There was a rough shield with a staff entwined with a serpent.

'I shall translate it as the language is not easy to understand. *The foundation of Saint Thomas resideth here in the monastery at Lusigny. Its purpose will be to care for the community of Saint Gabriel and Fontenay and any travellers who may apply for succour within this parish.* Have you seen the front page of the *Republique du Centre* yet?'

'I have it here.' Michaud picked it up.

'You will see that when *Monsieur* and *Madame* Moreau were arrested their house was searched. There have been a pile of documents recovered that show records of the Foundation continuing for centuries. They have found lists of goods being sold to local residents through the Second World War, which can only mean that the Foundation had turned to less honourable occupations. It was a hub for the local black market. The curator is studying the documents as they will be invaluable in piecing together a little more of the history of this village.'

'When I went to Lusigny to find Serge to tell him he must go to work. That man, François Guémard, the one Jeanette was going to marry, was wearing a monk's habit. I'd almost forgotten about it.'

'I think you'd better tell the police. They found a pile of habits in the old barn. It would seem that the Foundation of Saint Thomas has been operating for very many years possibly centuries in illegal activities. It wasn't only *La Petite Folie* that suffered but the *épicerie* in Jaunay and a number of farmers as well as a few businesses a little further afield. They are still going through the documents to uncover any members who may still be living.'

'But why was the pot in my well?'

'We will never know the answer to that, but we do know that this property is called the *Champ de Foire* because it was built on the site of the fair field of the middle ages, your well was most likely the communal water source for the villagers as far back as then.'

# EPILOGUE

The plane trees in front of the *Mairie* were festooned with streamers. Outside the little iron gate of the *Champ de Foire* a sign swung in the breeze. It read *Champ de Foire Restaurant Familial.* Strings of lights hung across the terraces which now bore tables of wild flower arrangements.

Inside, Jeanette was clearing away the debris of the previous day's festivities. She was grateful to Diana for having offered her the position of manageress after the receivers had called in their debts on *La Petite Folie.* Her back was aching but it had been worth it to see Diana so happy, as Charles Meffret, the youngest mayor the village had ever elected, was sworn into office.

The whole of Saint Gabriel had been there, except *Monsieur* and *Madame* Moreau who were unavoidably detained. Marcel and Pierrot had worn their Sunday best and Mémère sported a brand new wig for the occasion. Marie-Pierre had surprised everyone and appeared with Bébert on her arm. Agnès Camaret had been invited to unveil the restored memorial with the newly carved name at the bottom of the list of those who died for France. 'Ellen Charles-Meffret, SOE'.

Lightning Source UK Ltd.
Milton Keynes UK
UKOW02f0339021016

284262UK00001B/54/P